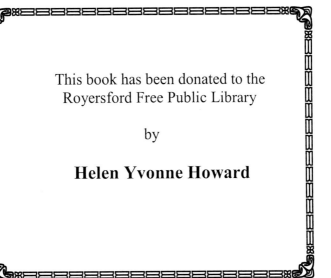

This book has been donated to the
Royersford Free Public Library

by

Helen Yvonne Howard

Above All

Laine's Beech Mountain Story – Book 2

A novel by

Peggy Poe Stern

Moody Valley
Boone, North Carolina

Published by
Moody Valley
475 Church Hollow Road
Boone, NC 28607
moodyvalley@skybest.com

Cover painting by: Peggy Poe Stern
Cover design by: David Kenneth Stern

Library of Congress Control Number
ISBN: 1-59513-047-0

Printed by Moody Valley

475 Church Hollow Road

Boone, NC 28607

November 28, 2007

Dedicated to:

Those who love the land

Chapter 1

He came walking toward me looking bigger than life itself. His handsomeness caught me, the broadness of his shoulders, the strength in those powerful hands of his, the green of his eyes. It was those eyes that held me transfixed in my chair on the kitchen porch. There was neither gentleness nor love in them as he looked at me. They were filled with accusation, rage, and the smoldering need that I recognized so well.

"Rafe . . ." my lips said, but no sound came from me. It couldn't for I was paralyzed with fear. Rafe Johnson could not be alive. I had put him in his grave, planted flowers for him, and visited that spot often.

"Laine," he said my name, and I heard the struggle of his words, the need to get them spoken before it was too late. "You - - - I - - - loved."

I wanted to get up from my chair, run to him, hold his tormented body in my arms; after all, he was my husband, my baby's father.

I would have done it if it hadn't of been for Junie. She was running across the yard stark naked.

"That's nothing. She's nothing." Rafe said as though his words could wipe her from my vision. "You're the only wife I want, the only one I've ever wanted."

Suddenly the mean boar hog was there, grunting as it looked for something to eat, something to vent its anger on.

I wanted to scream, would have, but Abe was holding me down, protecting me from the boar hog. "Stay still," Abe was saying. "Don't make a sound."

I wanted to tell Rafe to run, but all sound was mashed inside me as Rafe shouted at me, at Junie, at his own self.

And then I saw that attack! The ripping of flesh, the warmth of the blood, the rising of steam in the air, the smell - the awful smell of death.

My eyes opened. Thank the good Lord my eyes opened and I saw the chickens scratching in the yard, the birds flitting through the bushes, heard their sweet singing. I breathed deep and hard as I looked toward the hill where the oak tree shaded the graves. I got up and walked toward them.

I stopped to pick a bunch of field daisies. I saw one lonely pink bloom on a wild rose bush. I picked it and continued on to the graves.

I placed a few daisies on Mr. Holloway's grave, a few more on Boise's and her baby's. The most daisies and the delicate pink wild rose, I placed on Rafe's grave. I thought it fitting, that wild rose with petals that could not survive for long, be given to Rafe. Regardless of all Rafe's physical strength, he was as fragile as a pinch of elder down, as fragile as this beautiful rose.

"I never wanted you to die like that," I told him. "I wanted you to be a good husband, a good father."

Only the wind sounded in the oak leaves and the wild flowers trembled in the breeze. I said a prayer for the Holloways, for Rafe and for me and my baby.

Life continued even after a death. It always had and it always would. I raised up and went back to the house.

It was probably the baby kicking in my belly that made me think of Rafe so often. Mine and Rafe's baby was moving about as restless and discontent as its daddy had been during the time we were married. It kept me awake at night kicking like a mule that wanted to knock down the barn door, much like Rafe had done. I wanted to miss my dead husband as a wife ought, but I didn't.

I didn't want to admit it, but it gives me relief to know Rafe is under the big Oak tree where the wind blows softly over his grave. He won't be tormented any longer by his ways and I won't be either. I have come to think of Rafe as a sad person. One who was searching for something he could never find. I try to understand Rafe, even yet, but I'm not sure that I do or ever will.

As for me, I have never been as happy in my life as I am here on this mountain – happy without Rafe, without Momma and Susie. I don't even miss Dad as much as I could because he seems to be with me at times. I hear him talking to me, but I know it's all in my head for the dead don't come back and talk. Alive is alive and dead is dead, but I'm glad I can hear him. It takes away a little of my loneliness. And loneliness does creep upon me even when I am happy.

Rafe and Dad aren't the only dead people that seem to talk to me, but again I know it's only my imagination, and perhaps my being here alone so much. Even the animals and the blowing winds seem to talk after you've been by yourself for a long while. Animals can say a lot with their sad-eyed look, their movements. The wind can keep up a moaning conversation all night through, along with spirits of the dead that have refused to pass on and leave the living at peace. But it's not only during the night that I hear Dad's voice or Boise's. Sometimes in broad daylight I know one or the other is trying to talk to me. I listen the best I can.

There is one thing that troubles me more than I let on. I am too happy. I know such a good thing as happiness can not last forever. I've always heard that if you let yourself get carried away by the good life, fate will slap you down - hard. A person wasn't put here on this earth to be happy.

They were put here for toil and strife, or so I have heard, and I guess I do believe it, to a certain extent anyhow.

I'm not all happiness. I do have some worries. I won't admit it to Jonas, but I become obsessed with fear at times. I'm afraid my baby will die like Boise's did and join its daddy under the big Oak where the wildflowers grow. If it lives, I'm afraid that it will be a boy just like Rafe or a girl just like Momma. Why can't babies come with a guarantee of health and sanity? Why can't all adults be sane and productive? Why do people have to settle for what life shovels out to them?

Then there is the mountain lion that left its claw marks on my body. It put something inside me that I don't like to think about. It put a different kind of fear, one that goes bone-marrow deep to lie there waiting and threatening to appear like a bad taste. I pushed that from my mind like always because it was done and over with and I wouldn't allow myself to think about it.

I got a cold jug of water from the spring house, took it along with a plate full of food out to the field where Abe Farrow was cultivating a patch of field corn. He still wore his overalls without a shirt underneath, but his skin was not as red as his hair any longer. He was as brown as a buckeye, and I could see him growing into a man instead of a skinny boy during the time he had been working for me.

I went over to a large Maple tree, sat the jug on the ground, put two fingers against my tongue and whistled. The horse pricked its ears and Abe glanced toward the tree. They both knew the signal for a noon break.

Abe unhitched the horse from the cultivator and led him to the creek behind the barn to drink before he came to me. He dropped the horse's reins underneath the shade of the big Maple and let him nibble at a few sprigs of grass.

"It's uncommonly hot today," Abe said. "I think it might come up a thunder storm directly." He looked at the sky before he looked at me.

"Won't surprise me," I told him, feeling uncomfortable because of the unusual heat for June, especially on Beech Mountain.

The sky above us was a pure blue without a cloud in sight. It was the kind of blue that goes on forever in the clean, sweet mountain air, the color of blue found in the delicate petals of blue-eyed grass. The hot sun shimmered off everything it touched; the barn roof, the creek, the cultivated ground, even the tree I stood under tingled with heat waves.

"You feeling okay?" he asked as he sat and picked up the jug off the ground. He drank deep and long, his Adam's apple bobbing up and down like a cork in his throat. I lowered my lumbering body down near him and leaned my back against the tree trunk.

"Of course," was my answer. The question and answer had become so common place neither one of us paid any attention to it. It was like saying good morning or good night.

"Saw Jonas last night," he told me as he took the dishtowel off the plate of food.

I squirmed a little at the mention of Jonas. Longing, guilt, and a strange kind of need ran through me every time I thought about him, which was all too often.

I have to admit that I'm aggravated at Jonas for wanting me to leave the top of Beech Mountain and stay somewhere in Banners Elk until my baby is born. He should have enough sense not to ask me to leave my home. He knows I won't do it. This place is my lucky charm. It represents everything that's good in my life and I don't intend to leave it, ever. I know if I leave my mountain my happiness will crumble around me like a stale piece of cornbread I feed to the chickens.

"He worries about you," Abe gave me a sidelong glance as though he wanted to study my reaction to his words.

"No need for him to do that when you're here. He knows you'll watch after me."

Abe grinned. My words had pleased him greatly. He ate several bites of food before he spoke again. "Yeah, there is reason to worry. I know it and so do you."

"Women have babies all the time."

"Little women like you that have grown as big as a barn?"

I almost laughed at that. "I'm not so big."

"You cast a bigger shadow than a yearling steer."

I looked him in the face. "You've been around a lot of expecting women to know how big one is supposed to be?"

He squirmed and his face turned red. "No, but Jonas has. He knows a lot about women," he said between bites of food.

"And Jonas says I'm as big as a barn and cast a shadow the size of a yearling steer?"

"He says you're as hard headed as a mule, too."

This wasn't part of our daily conversation and I found that I wasn't enjoying it.

"Jonas said to tell you he'll come by tonight after he does his rounds at the hospital. Folks sure do keep him busy down there in Banners Elk. He don't have time for much else."

I watched Abe wipe at his empty plate with a piece of a biscuit, sopping up the juices, put it in his mouth, chew and swallow. His Adam's apple moved up and down in his skinny neck and his jaw muscles contracted. I thought it interesting watching him so obviously growing from a boy into a man. It seemed to be a difficult transition for him.

"I won't be spending the night here, tonight." He downed his head and squirmed a little. "It's Saturday. Thought I'd quit a little early and go to church being Jonas is coming and all. Don't reckon you'll be needing me around with him coming."

"Sounds good," I told him. For the last couple of weeks, Jonas had insisted that Abe stay on the farm at night as well as work during the day. Jonas claimed my baby was surely to come during the night. He said I never did anything the least complicated way.

I could tell Abe didn't like staying on the mountain. Sometimes when evening came I would catch him staring off into the valley as though he wanted to go home, but he never left me alone. He slept in Mr. Holloway's bedroom where he could hear me if I hollered.

At times, I liked Abe being there. A big house can get lonely when there is only the sound of your own feet walking on the floor, but it's a good kind of sound, too. It's the sound of freedom, and freedom comes with a price. For me it was the price of occasional loneliness, but that wouldn't last long. My house would be full of laughter after my baby got here.

"Maw said she could come help you out if you need her."

"I don't need her," I told him quickly. I certainly didn't want another woman in my house. Being raised with Momma and Susie had me convinced of that.

"There hain't nobody like my maw. She's worth her weight in gold," he said proudly.

"I'm doing fine. Where are you going to church at?" I asked Abe to get him off the subject of his mother. I'd never heard a boy brag on a mother like he did. He surprised me when his face reddened, and he became real interested in the snorting of the horse.

"First one and then another," he mumbled, obviously not wanting to tell me.

I was tempted to ask him more questions just to see him squirm. I figured he was taking a girl to church. Abe was older than me and ripe for a little courting, but I wasn't mean enough today to tease him. It was just too hot for laughing or playing.

"That was good," he said. "Almost as good as Maw's cookin."

"Thanks."

He got up and stretched his lanky body. "Best get back at it if I get done before the storm hits. I bet I'll get wet going back home being a storm is coming and it's such a long ways."

He picked up the reins and led the horse to the field where he hooked up the cultivator. I almost envied the girl he was courting. Abe was lithe and strong, eager to be hard working and pleasant. He would do everything in his power to make somebody a good husband. He certainly worked hard enough at trying to please me, and I was thankful to have him on my mountain.

I thought of a man and a woman together, not as Momma and Dad were together, or as Rafe and I had been. I thought of them the way they should be. Holding hands as they pulled the same load. Going to bed each night together knowing when they woke up the other would still be there. Having someone to count on. Yeah, that was it. That was what marriage was all about, having someone to count on.

I wondered about my baby, too. A child needed two live parents, a dad as well as a mother, but right now, while my baby was unborn, and a few years while it was little, all it needed was me. I had plenty of time to marry Jonas if the need ever arose.

I was in the kitchen when the storm hit. The sky turned nearly as black as night, lightning flashed and struck somewhere on the Pinnacle. The sound of the strike ripped the air like a shotgun blast right before a clap of thunder came with enough force to shake the earth and tremble the house beneath my feet.

Through the kitchen window, I saw Abe making a run for the barn leading the horse. He'd taken time to unhook the horse from the cultivator. A good move, for lightning tended to strike metal, especially this high on the mountain. Lightning favored animals, too. Old man Andy Harmon had his favorite cow struck down just last week. She was standing near a barbwire fence under the shelter of a black birch tree. I overheard him telling Abe about it when he came by to go hunting with him. Both of them were plum crazy about hunting and bragging on their dogs. Both of them liked to tell big whoppers about their adventures.

Andy Harmon owned a large tract of land adjoining me, and was a carpenter by trade. He said he helped Mr. Holloway build this fancy house I live in. He now builds coffins, said he was doing a right swift business because folks weren't as tough as they once were.

"Dropping like blowing flies," he'd say. "Don't know what'll happen when the old folks are all gone. This nation is bound go to the dogs for younguns are born soft nowadays."

I hoped mine would literally be born soft and easy. I couldn't see how something as big as the baby in my belly could get out of a place so little. I did cast a shadow about as big as a yearling steer, and that was a fact.

Everything lit up in super brightness and the earth itself rumbled and twitched worse than it had before. There was a strange sulfur smell in the air followed by the odor of smoke. The lightning has struck something other than the rocks on the Pinnacle this time. I rushed onto the porch and saw Abe running from the barn toward the house. He saw me and stopped. "Go back inside," he hollered at me as relief came to his face.

"What happened?"

"Lightning struck something. At first, I thought it was the house. You go back inside and I'll check it out, see what it did hit." He ran toward the woods and the sulfur smell.

It started raining, huge drops, as though the lightning strike had ripped the heavens open. I turned and went back inside, but not to stay. I was finding a coat and hat to keep some of the rain off. If there was a fire near by, I wanted to know about it.

By the time I got back outside, Abe was no where to be seen, but there was a blue tail of smoke rising above the trees. It was coming from the direction of the old house where Nate and Junie Patrick used to live.

They weren't there any longer. I hadn't asked them to leave, although I didn't want either of them anywhere near me or living on my property. It wasn't that I blamed Junie for Rafe's death. I blamed her for greed. She had wanted what Bosie had, which included the house and Rafe. She hated me for getting it instead of her.

Still yet, I hadn't asked them to leave. It was their home long before it was mine.

It was Nate that decided they should leave Beech Mountain. He never really told anybody why he wanted to go, but I think I know. It does something to a man's pride when everybody knows his daughter wasn't fathered by him. It further strips a man of his dignity when folks are talking and sniggering about his wife. All of Avery County knew how I had found her with Rafe; and how she was stark naked as I chased her out of the house where she let the mean boar hog out of the barn lot.

Folks didn't blame her for the boar hog killing Rafe. She didn't know that would happen. They blamed her for being the way she was, and that was what Nate couldn't take. When a man can't hide his humiliation, he hides himself.

I was thinking of all that as I hurried down the hill through the rain. The ground was getting slippery and my feet flew out from under me. I sat down in the mud and slid a few feet, got up and went on.

When I caught up with Abe, he was standing in the rain watching the little house burn. There was nothing else he could do. The flames were reddish orange with their tips outlined in black smoke and they were reaching skyward as though trying to find something higher up to feed the inferno.

Abe caught my movement from the corner of his eye and turned to face me.

"What are you doing here? Goodness gracious, just look at you. Jonas will give me a tongue lashing for letting you out in this storm in your condition."

"It's gone. It's already burned to the ground," I said.

"You're covered in mud. Did you fall and hurt yourself?"

I was too dumfounded from looking at the fire to answer his question. "That little house had been there for years, and suddenly it's gone in minutes." I said for I couldn't believe the quickness, the finality of a strike of lightning. Things could be gone just as fast as life could be gone. I shivered.

"I've got to get you in the dry and warmed up."

"Will it catch the woods on fire?"

"It's pouring down the rain, so maybe not. I thought the barn would catch, but it hasn't yet."

"If it does?"

"Then it's a goner."

"It's the tin roof. Lightning is always attracted to metal," I said.

"Happens, but more likely, it's the luck of the strike."

Andy Harmon came out of the woods, broad in body and stooped in the shoulders, and walked up beside us.

"She got a direct hit," he said. "Not a loss but a blessin. Empty house always brings on trouble. Houses aren't meant to be empty"

"It can," agreed Abe. "But it's a shame it's gone. A lot of folks don't have that good a place to live in."

Andy glanced at me. "Get her in the barn where it's dry. Ought not to be out here in her condition," Andy said as though I was some kind of invalid.

"Didn't want to take a chance on the barn. Thought it might catch fire," Abe said as though he was explaining why he hadn't already sought shelter in the barn.

"Naw, not now. Sparks aren't flying high any longer."

"I'm all right," I told them. "It feels good to cool off a little."

"Get her in the barn," Andy repeated. "Let the rain slack off before you take her back home. Bad omen for a woman in her condition to watch a house burn. It's like seeing the fires of hell."

Abe took hold of my arm with gentle fingers and led me away from the heat of the fire to the barn. Andy took off his wet coat and spread it around my wet coat. I didn't object as I knew he wanted to look after me. However, wet on wet was nothing but heavy.

"Sit down in the hay. Don't watch that fire," Andy advised. "Ought not to of brought the little gal out in this, Abe."

"I told her to stay in the house. She followed me." Abe sounded defensive.

Andy looked at me and grinned as though he wasn't surprised. "She's too feisty for her own good."

I saw the twinkle in his eyes when he said that and knew he liked feisty – as long as it didn't belong to him.

Jonas had told me that Andy Harmon and his wife had been married fifteen years when she died. Jonas didn't know why she died. Doctor Smith had told him she just dried up like a starved bird. Didn't weigh sixty pounds when she finally gave up the ghost and crossed on over.

They never had children and Andy never took another wife. "One good woman was all I ever wanted," folks told of Andy saying time and again.

I wondered if she really was a good woman. Once you've had good, you tend to want good, but when you've had bad, you never want to take a chance on getting bad again. That's the way I felt about Rafe. Once burned, twice shy.

"That storm sure did set down right on top of us, didn't it?" Abe said.

"Does that right often. Reckon it's because this mountain is above all else. I've known lightning to hit the Pinnacle three, four times during a summer. Don't usually hit down lower like this. It hain't a bad thing, though. You've not suffered a loss." He glanced at me. "You warmed up any, little Missy? Use that hay to swipe all that mud off yourself. Did you fall down and roll? Didn't hurt yourself none, did you?"

"I'm fine. I didn't fall, just sat down and slid a little."

"Don't need no jarring in your delicate condition. With Abe here to help you, you ought to lay about aplenty. Good Lord knows you won't have time for laying about once that baby gets here."

"She won't listen," Abe said. "She's taken on a streak of stubbornness here lately."

"A sight of em do. What about you, Abe? Heard you was sparkin heavy. Your maw say it was time for you to get married and settle down?"

Abe's face turned bright red and he went to the door and looked out. "Rain's letting up and the fire's almost out."

Andy chuckled at Abe's refusal to talk about courting and said, "Good thing it rained hard or it might of caught the woods on fire. This place was burned over once before my time."

"Pap told me about that time," Abe said.

"He couldn't have been old enough to remember it."

"His pap told him."

"Would of had to." Andy turned to me. "You're being foolish," he said.

I didn't know what he was talking about, and I certainly didn't want to ask. Jonas said Andy Harmon was known for speaking his mind. He was also known for keeping to himself, except for time spent on the gossip porch of the store, and building coffins. I didn't know he existed until a few weeks ago when he and Abe started hitting the woods with guns and dogs.

"I had to know what was on fire," I finally said. "I couldn't just sit home and wonder."

"I know that, but it's not what I'm talking about. Your foolishness comes from not marrying Jonas Jones."

Abe's head snapped up and he looked hard at Andy, as though Andy was heading in a direction he didn't belong in.

I didn't know what to say. "Rafe . . ." I began, but Andy interrupted me.

"Wasn't much as far as husbands go. Everybody knows that. Like a good wife, a good husband is a treasure, and you deserve a treasure after what you had. Of course, Jonas might make you behave a little, calm your nerves down if you know what I mean. Now, I'm telling you, Jonas is what a gal like you needs."

I didn't know if he expected me to say something, but I couldn't. Why were folks always thinking a woman needed a man?

Andy took off his rain-drooped hat and hit it against his overall legs as though dislodging the water and then put it back on his gray shock of hair. I knew he was feeling uncomfortable at what he was telling me, but he just had to get it said. He looked out the door.

"It's stopped raining," he said to Abe. "I'll stay here a while and make sure the woods doesn't catch fire. You take her on back and see that she dries off plenty good. Summer colds are the worst kind."

"I'll do it." Abe motioned for me to get out of the hay.

I gladly took off Andy's heavy coat and handed it back to him. "I appreciated it."

He nodded. "Take her the long way through the woods. It'll be slick going up that steep, rocky hill."

Abe went through the woods with me following behind him. He was going slow, as though I was feeble and couldn't walk as fast as normal, which had a small grain of truth to it, but I wasn't sickly or incapable of doing what I'd always done.

We had walked a long ways in silence when Abe said: "He's right."

I wasn't going to ask about what, but my silence didn't stop Abe.

"It's time you married again. You do need a good husband but Andy could of spoke it wrong. I'm not sure it should be Jonas."

That did surprise me a little coming from Abe. Jonas had looked after Abe almost like a father would.

"Why?" I asked as much to put him on a spot as from me wanting to know. "Just why should I marry and why not Jonas? He's a doctor and he's well thought of around here."

"You should marry because of your baby, and it should not be Jonas because you need a farmer that can manage all this land," Abe glanced over his shoulder at me as if to see my reaction

"A doctor can afford to hire farm help. He don't have to spend his time plowing."

"The kind of man you need can't be hired, besides, there's her."

"Her?"

"Never mind," he mumbled and acted as though he had changed his mind about talking to me.

"Her who?" I insisted.

"Uh," he hesitated for a moment or two like he was considering what to say next. "That Francis Dewhitte."

I'd never heard of such a person. "Who is she?"

"Folks know she's wanted Jonas ever since he came here. She's picked up some speed here lately. She's laying herself on him right thick and heavy. Doesn't want to let him out of her sight. Reckon a woman that bound and determined to have Jonas will get her way."

"Is Jonas laying it back on her thick and heavy?"

"She works for him. Besides, you never know what might happen when a woman goes after a man. She can . . . well, you know."

I knew I simply didn't want to get married again. Why couldn't folks leave a widowed woman alone? "Rafe has only been dead a short time. I'm still in mourning."

Abe chuckled. "I've known folks to marry two days after a funeral."

"It's not respectful."

"Respect goes out the window when necessity comes in the door."

"There's no necessity."

"Depends on how you look at it. You need a man around here, and I've been that man for a long while. Have you ever thought what would happen to this farm if I wasn't here?"

He hesitated, but I said nothing so he continued.

"As far as respectful goes, it hain't respectful for a man like me to be sleeping in your house, and it hain't respectful for Jonas to stay here over night like he sometimes does."

"He's a doctor, and you're young," I pointed out. It made perfect sense to me for either of them to stay in my house.

His back went rigid as a hoe handle. "I'm a full grown man, Laine Johnson. Folks know it and they're beginning to gossip about you. You ought to consider having Maw here instead of Jonas. She'd be the right chaperone for me and you."

"I don't care about gossip."

"Maw says the young can't see far ahead. She says you'll care with time," Abe said with sincerity. "What a girl does comes back to haunt the woman."

"What makes you so smart?"

"Maw," he answered with pride. "I've heard her telling my sister things, and I believe she is right in her advice. Actually, she's never been wrong."

"Your maw says I ought to marry?" The very thought irritated me. It was my business who I married, not Abe's mother's, or Andy Harmon's, or anyone else.

"She says a mother ought to consider her baby more than you're doing. If that baby is born with Rafford Johnson as its daddy, it will always have Rafford Johnson as a daddy, and believe me, that's a bad mark against it. Folks around here never did think highly of him and you know why only too good."

"Rafe *is* its daddy." His remark about Rafe irritated me. Rafe *was* my husband and he wasn't all bad. I could think of good things if I tried.

"Not if you marry before it's born."

"What?"

"It's the law. If you are married when the baby is born, the law says your husband is the baby's legal daddy. You can write his name down on the birth certificate and in years to come, folks will forget that he isn't the real daddy." Abe hesitated and spat out the side of his mouth. "If it was me, I'd appreciate my maw not making me belong to a man like Rafford Johnson."

Chapter 2

What Abe said hit me hard. I couldn't stop thinking about it. I thought about it as the rain-water dripped off the trees onto my coat while we walked through the woods. I thought about it as Abe told me he was going to do up the work early so he could go home and clean up before church. I thought about it as I dipped warm water out of the stove reservoir to wash the mud off me. I thought about it as I stood on the porch and looked up the hill at Rafe's grave.

Rafe hadn't wanted his and Boise's baby. He hadn't cared that it died along with Boise, and he sure didn't want to admit Junie's baby girl was fathered by him. If I was honest with myself, I didn't think he would care a thing about this baby either, much less want it. Someday he might have had some pride in telling folks he had a son, if it was a son, but as far as wanting a child, I didn't think Rafe had ever wanted to have a baby of his own. I tried to stop thinking about Junie and her green-eyed baby girl, but I knew I never would.

Still, for me to deny a dead man his rightful child didn't seem right. On the other hand, what would I be denying my living baby?

Abe had changed clothes and the evening sun had come out bright and warm by the time he was ready to leave.

"Are you sure you're all right?" he asked as he came down stairs and onto the porch where I was. He had a bashful way of looking me over fast, determining how I was feeling, what I was thinking or hiding.

"I feel wonderful," but he knew I was lying.

"Tired, aren't you? Do you hurt anywhere, like your back or belly?"

"Your maw tell you to ask me that?"

He grinned. "Maw said if you complained about your back or belly hurting, for me to go get Jonas fast. She said if your water broke suddenly for me not to leave you for any reason. She said for me to stay by you and deliver your baby just like I would do it if you were a cow."

I didn't much like what he just said. It aggravated me for some reason. Probably because I wasn't a cow or a yearling steer, and me having my baby wasn't for Abe's eyes to see.

He grinned bigger causing the peach-fuzz on his jaws to lump up. "Maw said cows and women are just alike. I told Maw I wasn't sure if I could make you eat the afterbirth like a cow does."

"That's not funny," I said irritably.

"Maw thought it was. Are you sure you'll be all right if I leave?"

"I think I would know if I was going to have a baby. I've heard it's a very long and painful process."

"You're going to have it, but we don't know exactly when." He was still grinning no doubt from his mother's humor as well as his own.

"Get yourself away from here before I find a big stick and chase you off this mountain. You don't have to watch over me twenty-four hours a day."

"Jonas will be here about dark," he said gently and strode off. "Feisty's right," he mumbled.

I watched him stride across the yard to the barn, saddle one of Jonas's saddle horses and ride away. Jonas insisted he keep a good horse handy for when it was my time.

Thoughts of Jonas made me walk off the porch and up the hill to the little graveyard. I stood there looking at the graves wanting to know all the right answers. The Johnny-jump-ups of spring were gone and in their place were the weeds of June. I knelt down and pulled weeds from the mound of dirt over Rafe.

Abe was right. No one would take pride in having a man like Rafe Johnson for a father, but what about my land? What about my freedom? Was I willing to give up my freedom just so my baby would have Jonas' last name? No, I answered that in a hurry for a name didn't mean much to me, but a good father meant a lot. I knew what Dad had been to me.

I wished Abe hadn't done up the work. I needed to be outside doing things familiar so I could think. I put my hands on my stomach and felt my baby kick as though it wanted my hand gone. Love fill me so full that tears came to my eyes. There was nothing I wouldn't sacrifice for this little being inside me.

It was almost dark and Jonas hadn't come. I had supper pushed on the back of the stove to keep warm and I was pacing the floor. I had thought long and hard all evening and worried myself into a frenzy. I heard the sound of the horse's hooves and rushed out to meet him before he could dismount.

His hat was pulled low over his black hair and his shirt sleeves were rolled up almost to his elbows. His hands appeared strong and in control as he held the reins of his high stepping horse. He looked a little thinner than he used to be and a lot more tired.

"What's wrong?" he asked me fast.

"You've got to go back to Banners Elk," I told him, forgetting about supper.

His eyes widened with concern. "Should you ride? I can deliver the baby here."

"It's not the baby, it's the preacher. You've got to bring him back here."

"The preacher?"

"I want us to get married right now."

Jonas was completely silent for a full two minutes. His blue eyes were looking at my face as though there were written words for him to read.

"All right," he finally said as though he had made a difficult decision. "I can do that, but it would be faster if I put you in front of me and we went to the preacher's house together."

I reached my hand for him to help me climb onto the horse. He lifted me up. His muscled arms hugged me close to his warm body as he settled me across his lap.

"Are you comfortable?" he asked.

"I'm comfortable, being I'm finally where I belong," I admitted in hopes it would please him.

"You are," he agreed. "You finally are where you belong."

I leaned against Jonas and listened to the sound of his beating heart. I remembered riding in Rafe's wagon with Dad on the way to the preacher the night Dad had given me to Rafe. I didn't know Rafe, hadn't wanted to marry him, but I had no alternative because Momma didn't want me any longer. I didn't understand why Dad was getting rid of me back then and I was hurt beyond belief. Now, I realize that he was simply doing what he thought best – as I am doing now. Like Dad, I wanted my baby to have the best chance at life it could have, and Jonas was it.

I expected Jonas to ask me questions as to why I had suddenly changed my mind about marrying him, but he didn't. Instead he asked: "Have you had any labor pains?"

"No, I don't think so."

"You don't think so?"

"I was kind of tired and uncomfortable after the fire."

"Fire?"

"Abe didn't tell you when he dropped your horse off?"

"I didn't see Abe. What happened?"

"Lightning struck the old Patrick place earlier this evening. Burned it to the ground."

"Lightning struck it? Was it during the storm?"

"Yeah, but it didn't burn the barn."

"At least nobody was hurt. It's good it happened now and not last summer when they lived there."

"Where are they?" I thought Jonas might have heard something about the Patricks being he came in contact with a lot of gossip.

"The Patricks? Last I heard they went to Tennessee where her parents live."

"I'm glad they're gone."

"I know," he let his chin rest against my head as his hand rubbed along my stomach. His fingers were probably feeling for secrets only doctors knew. "Your body is ready for that baby to be born any time."

"You told me that a few days ago."

"You're more ready now."

I smiled. "My baby has been restless today."

"I can feel that it's in position, head down low in the pelvic region, but babies usually quiet down once labor starts, so I assume you're not in labor. Pre-labor perhaps. It has been said women start nesting a day or two before labor."

"Nesting?"

"Arranging a place for the baby, house cleaning, marrying, things like that."

Sounded like what I did every day to me, so I got back to the fire. "Andy Harmon got there right after Abe and I did. He heard the lightning hit and saw the smoke. Jonas, why did he never marry again? I mean the real reason?"

"He didn't want to marry again and there wasn't a real reason why he should. He was perfectly capable of caring for himself."

"I bet he got lonely."

"I'm sure he did."

"Do you ever get lonely?"

"Every moment I'm not with you." I knew he was smiling although I didn't look up to see. I also knew he was picking at me, trying to ease my nervousness. I was afraid I was making a mistake in marrying him, and this time, I had a choice. I also suspect he knew I was doing it for my baby.

"I won't stay at your place," I told him. "Not tonight or any other time."

"I know you won't."

"I just thought I ought to tell you now, before we reach Banners Elk."

"It's all right," he said gently. "I'm not going to ask you to leave your mountain or even spend your wedding night away for it."

"I want to keep Abe on after we're married."

"That's a good idea."

"Who's he courting?"

"I don't know."

"Andy said he was sparking heavy. I thought you'd know who it was."

"I don't."

"Who's Francis Dewhitte?"

"Who told you about her?"

"Abe. Who is she?"

"She's just a woman."

"Do you like her?"

"Like as in desire, then the answer is no. Like as in another human being, then the answer is not much."

For some reason that relieved me, but I was certainly getting tired riding in Jonas' arms while the horse ambled along. There was no place where my stomach could find a place to rest, and the bouncing from the horse made my back ache.

"How much further?" I asked.

"Not too far. Would you like to get down and stretch?"

"No." I wanted to get this over with. I was already questioning my wisdom in getting married. Suddenly, I didn't think it mattered who my baby's father was. All that mattered was what kind of person my baby would be. And I was the one that would make sure my child would be well brought up and grow into something a mother would be proud of.

"There were twins born at the hospital today," Jonas said. "Big babies, nearly seven pounds each. The mother was as slender as a fence post. She probably never got to sit down a minute during her pregnancy. She has eight other children."

"Boy or girl twins?"

"Girls. It was a lucky thing she had previously delivered eight or I might not have saved mother and babies."

"What happened?"

"They were back to back and blocking each other. I pushed one backward and had the nurse hold it in place from the outside while I turned the other one in the correct position and then pulled it with forceps."

I shuddered all over at the image forceps brought to my mind. I knew Jonas would have to pull my baby, too. He had compared me to a steer, and I remembered seeing Dad pull a calf once.

"Suppose I am having twins?"

"You're not."

"How do you know?"

"I examined you very carefully."

I remembered and felt myself blush. "Didn't you examine the other woman?" I asked quickly to take the memory of Jonas touching me from my mind as much as possible.

"I only examined her after she was brought to the hospital. Most folks don't go to a doctor until there is trouble in progress."

"I'm scared, a little." I admitted out loud for the first time ever.

"That's normal, but you are going to be fine."

"How do you know?"

"I'm your doctor. Besides, you're as tough as a pine knot. You'll pop that baby out like a dog having a puppy."

I didn't tell him I wasn't tough at all. I was weak and afraid I couldn't do the things that had to be done. Yet, I was ashamed to admit my weaknesses.

We rode in silence for a good while. I was lost in my thoughts and I guess Jonas was lost in his. Jonas turned the horse into a little path of a road and a small, white house suddenly appeared there in the trees.

"We're here." Jonas eased me forward and lifted me down before he dismounted. I noticed that he limped with his first few steps. It hadn't occurred to me that his legs would go to sleep from my weight. He tied the horse to a tree limb, took me by the arm, guiding me to the door and then knocked.

A big man with wavy black hair and a broad face opened the door.

"Carl," Jonas said in greeting.

"Jonas, come on inside."

"This is Laine Johnson, Carl, and Laine this is Carl Stout."

I mumbled hello in response to his greeting and put my hand into his big paw to shake. I shuddered like a wind-blown leaf standing there before another preacher.

There was just something about preachers.

Oh, how I was regretting my hasty decision. I wanted to get out of this house and not marry Jonas now or ever. I wanted to spend the rest of my life taking care of my baby and myself. I didn't want a life catering to a man and having to do the things he liked, even if the man was Jonas.

"What can I do for you, Jonas?"

"We came to get married if you have time to oblige us."

"I'd make time for that. I've been praying that very thing would happen and God has answered my prayers." He looked me in the eyes. "You won't regret this, little lady."

I said a prayer myself, one in which he was right, but somehow I doubted it.

"You're exhausted," Jonas helped me get on the horse again. "Are you sure you don't want to stay at my house tonight?"

"No," I told him firmly. "I told you I was going back home - afterwards."

"Okay," he soothed. "Perhaps it would be easier on you to ride alone in a saddle. What do you think?"

I thought about it and he was right. It would be easier on me and him both. "Probably so."

"We'll ride over to my place and I'll saddle up the horse Abe rides."

Jonas didn't live a quarter mile away, but it was pitch dark by now. His house was small and the barn even smaller. I was surprised because I always thought doctors made all kinds of money. It was a neat little place, though.

Jonas had taken well care of it from what I could tell in the pale light from the moon.

"Do you want something to drink or eat?" He asked.

"No," I told him, but I did need to relieve myself awfully bad. "I'll just step behind the barn while you saddle up."

"Want me to get you a light?"

"No." All I needed was a couple minutes of privacy.

I hadn't realized how badly I needed to go until I squatted there in the dark. I hung my head and closed my eyes feeling as though I couldn't move another muscle. Every inch of me ached, but I wasn't going to give in and spend the night here. I was going back home even if I fell off the horse and had to crawl.

"You ok?" Jonas asked when I finally came back.

"I'm fine. I just want to be at home where I can rest." I knew I sounded like a spoiled child, but at the moment, I couldn't stop myself. It was taking all my determination not to burst out in a crying fit.

"You can ride my horse back. He's tired and won't be inclined toward friskiness. I'll ride the one Abe usually rides."

"He didn't take it courting?"

"It is up to him to provide his own transport for such events." He hesitated and then continued. "When you ask a man to do a job, you provide him with the tools necessary to accomplish the job, but that is where it should end. My tools are not for accomplishing his whims or taking him courting."

I thought it a little mean of Jonas not to allow Abe a nice horse to show out to his girl friend. It seemed to me that Abe did Jonas' bidding uncomplainingly. He hadn't even complained when Jonas had him quit helping him at his doctor's office and start helping me on the farm.

"Are you certain you're up to this ride? It is almost eleven o'clock."

"You don't have to come with me," I said a bit peevishly. "I'd like to borrow your horse though, since it is a long ways to walk."

In a voice exceptionally calm and gentle Jonas said, "My wife is more exhausted than I thought." He put his arm around my shoulders and his hand on the back of my head and held my face against his chest. "Would you object to me giving my bride a kiss? Carl is the only preacher I know that doesn't believe in letting the groom kiss his new bride. He believes all affection should only be done in the privacy of one's own home."

I didn't answer, but Jonas lowered his head anyway and covered my lips with his. His kiss was warm and gentle, but it scared me a little. I couldn't help remembering Rafe stopping the wagon in the dark and making me get off and then what he did to me on the cold hard ground.

It seemed to take a long time before his lips left mine, but it might not have been long for I was tired and impatient.

"I'll help you on the horse before you fall flat on your face," he said gently. "I think my wife has enjoyed all of this day she can stand."

It was after midnight when we finally made it up the mountain. The summer night had been balmy in Banners Elk, but it got nippy on higher ground. Beech Mountain rose up over a mile high and stood a head and shoulders above some of the other mountains. Only Grandfather Mountain held its own with the Beech.

It was the height of mountains and the coldness in the air that I was thinking about when Jonas helped me down from the horse. I didn't want to think about how much I ached, or the way exhaustion was spinning around me like a twirling top.

"I'll stable the horses if you can make it inside without me."

"I certainly can," I mumbled as I looked at the long distance between the barn and house. Surely my legs would carry me that far. I put one foot in front of the other until I came to the porch, opened the kitchen door, and didn't bother to find a light. I held onto the stair banister and gratefully made my way to my bed.

I awoke with morning's light to find I had slept in my clothes. Jonas was sleeping beside me with his arm around me and his hand cupping my stomach.

"Good morning, my sweet wife," he whispered in my hair.

It wasn't a dream. I really had married Jonas Jones, even after months of claiming I wouldn't. I had grown weak, couldn't stick to my own determination. But, I knew it was because of what Abe's maw had said, and she was right. I had to do everything I could to assure my baby the best life I could give it, even if it meant I was the one that would lose.

"Good morning and I'm sorry," I told him.

"About what?"

"Falling asleep like I did before you came inside."

"I was thankful you didn't fall off your horse. I took your shoes off, but was afraid you'd wake up if I undressed you."

I could feel that Jonas was undressed. I wondered if he was going to do what Rafe had done to me. I hoped it wouldn't hurt my baby.

He patted my stomach.

"The baby is moving vigorously this morning. It's as tough as its mother. I didn't feel any contractions during the night or now. So, I don't think the baby will arrive today. I hate to leave my new bride, but it's late and I need to be at the hospital to check on patients and the mother I told you about. She isn't young and the delivery was difficult. "

Of course, he would leave. I shouldn't expect him to stay here today just because we were married last night. I couldn't help remembering the times Rafe took off without telling me he was leaving, and he would be gone for weeks.

"I'll get through as quick as I can. I want to spend some special time with my bride. Besides, Abe will be wondering where the horse is. He won't want to hoof it all the way up this mountain if he decides to come back today."

Tools, I thought, Jonas was providing tools for Abe, just like he was providing tools for my baby. His name and a good standing in the community were tools.

"You lie here and rest as long as you can stand it, go back to sleep. Extra rest will be good for you and the baby. I'll work though lunch and try to get back early. Being I feel no contractions, I think you will be okay alone for a couple of hours until Abe gets here.

"I don't like being watched like a boiling pot," I told him. "Go do what you have to do."

He leaned over me and kissed my cheek for one long tender moment before he got up and dressed.

The house felt empty after he had gone, and I was suddenly disappointed without knowing why. I put my hand on my belly to feel my baby. "I did it for you," I whispered out loud. "You'd better appreciate it."

I was just too miserable to lie in bed. When I got up I found I was just as miserable being up. My entire body ached from the unusual amount of riding I did yesterday. My legs, my back, my arms ached and I could find no position to relieve the pain. I thought of going out and finding a willow tree and making myself a tea out of the bark but I was just too miserable to do all that work for a drink of bitter tea.

I did go to the toilet a lot and dreaded every trip I made. Thoughts of the chamber pot came to my mind, but I'd put that pot in the barn after Rafe's death. I had wanted it out of my sight, probably because it made me remember Rafe and Junie and me wanting to kill them both with it. Finding Junie naked and astraddle of Rafe would make any wife go a little crazy.

It still made me mad to think back on it.

I wished I'd cracked Junie's head a good one, wished I'd left a knot bigger than a goose egg. I was glad lightning took care of where they had lived. I wanted all traces of her and Nate gone. I certainly didn't want her child growing up anywhere near mine.

You've fathered two live children, Rafe Johnson, and none will ever carry your name. I almost laughed at that thought, almost.

Suddenly, it occurred to me that Abe wasn't here. The animals hadn't been fed or milked. The realization made me happy. I would get to milk my own cow, feed the hogs and chickens. I could even hoe my garden without Abe telling me I wasn't in condition to do it.

A different feeling swept over me. Oh, did it ever feel good to be on my own, able to do what I wanted when I wanted. I wasn't going to give up this good feeling again – ever again. I wasn't Momma or Susie. I wasn't weak. I was Elaine Elder Johnson Jones. I was now a doctor's wife and I could do jolly well what I pleased – and things were going to stay that way.

I got the milk bucket and headed to the barn. The cow was waiting for me. I measured chop, which was ground up corn cobs, corn, shucks and all, in her wooden trough, and watched her calf lick at it before I turned her in for the calf to suck. I milked one teat while the calf was sucking the other three. I figured that was fair enough. The calf didn't need all that milk to grow; besides too much milk gave it the scours.

When I had finished milking, I found it hard to straighten back up, and being squatted down made my belly uncomfortable, but I was okay once I had stretched the kinks out of my back.

I let the cow out, strained my milk and sat it in the spring trough, fed everything, and happily headed for my garden with the hoe. It wasn't much past seven o'clock and the morning was still fresh and sweet, but the ground was too wet after yesterday's storm to hoe. I picked a few late peas from the vines and ate them raw. I had always thought cooking hurt the taste of peas and corn. They were perfect eaten right in the garden.

"You're out and about early," said Andy Harmon.

I jumped at hearing a voice when I hadn't expected it. "It's not early. Morning is half gone already."

"For some folks. Came by to tell you the old house is ashes but nothing else was touched by the fire."

"I'm glad the woods didn't catch on fire."

"Could of been worse. Not much lost."

"You're right about that."

"Where's Abe?"

"Not got back yet."

Andy chuckled. "Happens to a young man. His wants wear him out. Has to rest up after a long heavy night of sparkin."

"I suppose." I looked at him standing there with his arms resting on the garden fence. He looked drawn and exhausted. His face was wrinkled and cracked like old shoe leather that had been through too many years of ammonia and waste. His still broad shoulders were now bent with age along with an unseen load he had obviously carried for years, so I thought. He had to be eighty years old or nearing it, which was an extreme age when I wasn't yet seventeen.

I figured a man his age had only his memories left to rest up from.

I wondered if he thought about dying and what he was leaving behind. I'd heard Abe say Andy owned twice as much land as I did and didn't have a single living relative to pass it on too. Abe said he'd give his eye teeth if Andy would let him work out a deal to buy it.

"It's too wet to work your garden, Missy," he said.

"I discovered that. That's why I'm just standing here eating peas. Want some?"

He opened the gate and came to me, picked a pea, shelled it and ate the peas.

"I'd almost forgotten how good a raw pea tastes."

"It's raw peas, tender corn, early mornings, and the freshness after a rain that makes life good," I told him whole heartedly.

"That it is, but I never figured a slip of a gal living in a fancy place like this would think that. Don't you want shiny gold trinkets and folks to wait on you hand and foot?"

I was insulted by that and I guess I showed it.

"I might be wrong," he added.

"You are," I said. "I do love my home and land, though. I love every rock and clot of dirt on this mountain."

"Most women would sell it for an easy town life."

"I'm not most women."

He grinned. "You know the real reason I came by here this morning?"

"Not just to be neighborly," I quipped.

He shook his head and scratched under his flopped hat. "Nope. I'm ashamed to admit it hain't. I came to ask if you'd sell me this land."

I bristled. "I will not," I told him firmly. "And it makes me mad when somebody tries to get it away from me."

His bright eyes looked me over. "That's what I hoped you'd say. Don't have much respect for a person that'd give up their land for money."

"Then why did you ask me to sell?"

"I've heard a lot of gossip about you, and I wanted to see just what kind of woman you really are."

He was being honest, but that didn't mean I liked it any better.

"I dare say I'm every bit as good a woman as you are a good man," I told him and felt the tension in my back tighten. I picked another pea near the ground just to be moving. It wasn't easy straightening back up.

"Feisty," he said. "That you are."

"Like I said, Abe's not here, yet. You can wait on him or go back home."

He held his knotted, callused hand out toward me. "Glad i got to know you a little better, and I'm mighty proud we're neighbors."

I looked at his outstretched hand, at his wrinkled face and twinkling eyes. I put my hand in his and felt the remainder of strength that had once been tremendous as his fingers closed over mine.

"Wish I'd a met you thirty years ago. I'd a married you," he said as he held onto my hand. "I'd gladly give all I own if it'd somehow make what you're carrying in your belly mine. I always wanted to be a father."

That made me a little uncomfortable. I pulled my hand away and took a step backward.

"Don't mean any harm by my words. I'm just speakin the truth. Seems I've spent too many years making coffins to bury the dead in not to have an appreciation of new life. I wanted younguns, but to tell you the truth, I never thought I was good enough stock to pass on my seed. God must of thought that way right along with me, cause I never did."

I wanted to be left alone. I wanted to sit down in the garden and rest because a sudden weakness came over me. Heat went from my toes out the top of my head. I needed a cold glass of water, needed to cool off. I clutched a post that the peas were twined to. The garden twirled and I feared I was going to fall. I felt a stronger heat wave flood me again and felt something tickle my legs. I looked down and could have cried with my embarrassment. I was standing there peeing in my bloomers.

"Good Lord in heaven," Andy said. "Your water just broke. You've got to get back to the house and I don't know if I'm strong enough to carry you."

"I can walk." But, I wasn't sure if I could for my body felt as though it had tied itself in a hard knot that wasn't going to loosen up.

He reached for me. "Put your arm around my waist and lean all your weight on me. I'll hold you up if you can walk. One step at a time and we'll get you in bed. Where the hell is Abe and Jonas when they're needed?"

"Women have babies every day," I managed to say.

"Not when I'm around, by gosh. Don't want to start at my age, either."

"I want Jonas," I whimpered like a scared child.

"Hell if I don't too, and in the worst sort of way."

Fear was overwhelming me. It was about to paralyzed me and I new I had to calm myself for my baby's sake. Desperately, I said, "You'll have to eat the after birth?"

"What the hell?"

"Abe's mother said having a baby was just like a cow having a calf," I managed to get the words from between my gritted teeth. "But I won't eat the after birth, you'll have to do that."

"Shit! You're making jokes at a time like this."

"Beats crying."

"Well, Missy, we'll both be squalling our heads off any minute now, and there's no joking about it."

I thought Andy was going to turn loose of me, run to Abe and grab and kiss him when he came riding into the yard.

"You take her in the house and I'll go for Jonas," Andy yelled at Abe. "Her water just broke."

Abe gave me a blank stare before the situation registered. "Get her to bed. I can ride faster than you."

"No you can't," Andy yelled back, but it was too late. Abe was already hitting the woods, taking the shortcut straight down the mountain to Banners Elk. At least he was going down hill and might not break the horse's wind for the horse was going full speed and kicking up clots of dirt with all four feet.

"Keep them legs clamped together mighty tight," Andy blurted out. "I hain't going to be delivering no baby at my age."

He was right. I delivered the baby by pushing so hard I thought my body was ripping apart, but it was his big callused hands my baby slid into.

"I'm going to use the sheet to clean its little face," he said to me, his voice shaking with emotion, tears sliding down his rough cheeks. "You'll have to wash the bed things as it is."

"Is my baby all right?" I asked because I didn't hear crying.

"It wiggled and I think it's a boy. Yeah, it is if my eyes hain't fooled. Where the hell is Jonas?"

His words seemed to bring Jonas bursting through the door. "My God, Laine," he blurted out. "Couldn't you wait on me?"

"Here, take it," Andy said. "It's not breathing."

Jonas did and Andy disappeared through the door, running, his big boots pounding the stairs.

"It's all right, darling. Everything's all right. I'm here now. I wouldn't have left you if I had realized." The calmness in his voice scared me worse than my baby's silence.

"My baby?" I pleaded, seeing Jonas hold the little blue body up by its feet. I was sure it was dead and I couldn't live with that. He gave the baby a rough shake and thumped it on its butt, hard.

The most beautiful sound I ever heard was the cry coming from my son.

Once he was squalling like a caught pig, Jonas took a string from a jar in his bag and tied the cord in two places. He took a pair of scissors out of another jar and cut between the tied places.

"Do you know that Leonardo Da Vinci invented the scissors?" he said to me.

"Who's he?" I asked and saw him smile.

"A painter. Are you doing ok?"

"Is my baby ok?"

"He's a big healthy boy."

Then I was okay. Jonas got a towel from the dresser and wrapped it around the baby and brought him to me.

"Hold him close to your body while I take care of you. Babies become stressed when they are taken from their mothers."

I held him close and took in that beautiful little face. He was so perfect, his squinted eyes, his little rounded mouth, his perfect nose, and dark brown hair on his pointed head. For a moment, I saw Rafe as plain as day in my baby's face, and expected his eyes to fly open for me to see green eyes. When his eyes blinked open they were dark in color like mine. Relief flooded me and I refused to see anything of its dead father ever again in my baby – my baby.

Jonas pressed on my belly and pulled on the cord. It hurt.

"What are you doing?" I asked without taking my eyes off my baby.

"Expelling the after birth."

"It hurts."

"Not much."

"Enough."

"It's not as painful as having the baby."

"Nothing was ever that painful." But it was worth it just to hold my baby. To know he was mine, all mine to love and care for.

"So I've been told."

I glanced at Jonas. He was all doctor, doing what he was supposed to do with a patient; being meticulous in his movements, a blank expression on his face.

"I wanted you here desperately," I told him.

"It will take a month for my two horses to be normal again." He glanced at me and smiled. "Abe and I both tried to make them fly instead of run. How long were you in labor?"

"I don't know."

"How long were you uncomfortable?"

"I wasn't feeling too good around seven o'clock. It was a little after that when my water broke."

"Andy Harmon was with you?"

"He'll never be the same again. He moaned louder than I did." I rubbed my finger over my baby's face. He wasn't crying anymore and his face was just as pink as could be. "When my pains got bad, Andy paced the floor and beat on the walls with his fists."

"I should have been with you."

Yes, I thought so too, but I wasn't going to say it. If he was as good a doctor as he should have been, he'd have known I was going into labor.

"I never felt any contractions during the night," he said as though he knew what I was thinking. "A woman is usually in labor ten to fifteen hours with the first baby, maybe longer. I wasn't gone from here four hours when Abe came flying in."

I was just glad it was over and my baby was all right.

"You don't weigh over a hundred and five pounds and you're solid muscle. The baby didn't have any fat to get through and your muscles could push with force. Still, he's a big baby for a little mother and big babies take longer to get out."

"How much does he weigh?"

"Eight, nine pounds or better."

"I'm sleepy," I said, and Jonas started rubbing harder on my stomach.

"That hurts."

"I have to make your uterus contract and stop bleeding. Loss of blood can make you sleepy"

My baby wiggled his hand free from the towel and bobbed it at his mouth.

"Does my baby need to suck?"

"Whenever you feel like it, but he'll be fine for a few hours."

"He's gnawing at his fists."

"Good. That means he is healthy."

"Jonas?"

"Humm?"

"Do you see anything wrong with him? Does he show any problems from the panther attacking me or . . . anything?"

"Not a one," Jonas said.

Chapter 3

I was napping when I heard a sound. Andy Harmon was tiptoeing from my bed across the floor toward Jonas who was standing at the open bedroom door watching me.

"What a fine boy," Andy whispered none to low, although he was trying not to wake me. "He's a keeper, and that little Missy, well, what can I say except I was proud of her."

"So am I," said Jonas.

"She never screamed once." There was bragging in his voice. "I tell you it wasn't an easy thing either. Not like a cow having a calf, I'm here to tell you. It's worse, more, well, more strainful."

"Birth is more difficult in humans than in animals."

"What did she name the boy?"

"Weston Andrew Jones."

"Andrew? Jones? My name is Andrew." There were a few moments of silence as they crossed the hall.

"She's going to call him Drew." I heard Jonas say. "In honor of you."

"Drew not Andy. Well, that's a fine name. Appears congratulations are in order twice. It's not every day a man gets a wife and a son in a matter of hours. Abe said she married you last night."

"Yes, she did."

"You're a lucky man. Take good care of her and that boy. The three of us went through a lot."

He said that fast and I heard his boots going down the stairs in a hurry, like he was embarrassed being inside the house near me and wanted to escape.

Jonas was smiling as he came in the bedroom and to my bedside. "Sorry to wake you. Andy had to make sure you and the baby were ok with his own eyes."

"He stayed right with me, even though he didn't want to."

"Andy is a good man. The kind the world needs more of."

"It was a good thing I was wearing a skirt instead of britches or he might not have caught my baby."

"Why's that?"

"He didn't want to embarrass me or himself by looking at my privates, yet he did what he had to do." I admitted, feeling embarrassed that a man, even one as old as Andy, knew what I looked like in that area.

Jonas seemed to understand. "Better Andy than Abe." He bent over me and stroked the hair from my face. "I'm fixing supper,"

"I'm not much hungry."

"Eating gets your strength back and helps you give milk for the baby."

Jonas knew the magic words to get me to do what he wanted. I'd eat if it would be good for my baby.

"What time is it?"

"Almost six o'clock."

"I've slept that long?"

"Time flies when you're having fun." He smiled at me and kissed my forehead.

"I don't want any more of that kind of fun."

"At least for a while," Jonas touched the towel with his finger exposing the baby's face more and smiled. "I'll find him some clothes and a diaper while supper cooks."

I had almost forgotten that I was Jonas' wife and he would expect certain things from me that would produce more babies. That was the trouble with being married, but I had a few weeks time before I had to do my wifely duties.

🕊

"How are the woman and the twins?" I asked Jonas as he took baby Drew from me, allowing me to sit up in bed. He had sat a plate containing a bowl of vegetable soup cn the night stand and I carefully picked it up.

"Fair. She went home although I tried to keep her a day longer in the hospital. A woman needs to rest for at least nine days, and then take things easy."

"Nine days? Why not a week or ten days?"

"Nine is the magic number. Nine months to have a baby and nine days of rest, or so old wife tales go.."

"How long before I'm totally well?"

"Six weeks."

"Not nine weeks?"

"No, not nine this time, unless I'm wrong." He grinned as though he was picking at me.

Little Drew woke up and cried as Jonas dressed my baby with the clothes I had made him. I thought of my brother Joey the day he was born. His little face had been all scrunched up and red, but I had thought him beautiful. My baby was much more beautiful. He really was, and I would never let him out of my sight. He would never get near honeybees.

"He needs his mother to feed him. As soon as you finish eating and drinking your glass of milk, you should work on getting him to suck."

"Work on it?"

"Sometimes it doesn't come natural for a baby or a new mother."

I hadn't known that, but I need not have worried even for a moment. Drew went at it like he was starved and determined to get what he wanted.

"Oh, he's a vigorous little man. He's a tough one just like his mother."

I looked up at Jonas just then and caught a look of sadness on his face before he controlled it. I understood why. His wife was nursing a baby that he hadn't fathered. That had to hurt a man. I almost told him my next one would be his just to make him feel better, but I didn't want another baby, and I didn't want to go through what it took to make one.

As soon as Drew was full and sleeping, I had to pee and sat up in bed. I remembered the chamber pot was in the barn. Going down the stairs or even behind the house seemed more than I could manage. I heard a noise and Jonas was there with the chamber pot washed and in his hands.

"Thought you might be needing this. Abe brought it in before he left."

"Abe left?" I was hurt because he hadn't come in to see my baby.

"I told him to go on home early. He'll be back in the morning."

Jonas sat the pot beside the bed and held out his hand toward me. I hesitated.

"I'm not only your doctor, I'm your husband now."

"I know," I mumbled, still feeling self conscious.

"I can't have you fall or pass out."

I remembered a few months before when the panther had clawed me. Jonas had cared for me and got the pot even though I wasn't his wife. I reached out and touched his face. He seemed surprised.

"How lucky can I get?" I whispered and meant it. Jonas Jones was a good man.

Drew woke me up several times during the night to be fed. He wouldn't suck long before he would fall back to sleep.

"Wake him up by diapering him," Jonas told me. "Then feed him again."

I did and Drew and I both slept late. I heard a woman's voice down stairs and for a moment it was like Junie was back. I looked at baby Drew and made myself remember all that had happened.

Rafe was dead, Junie was gone, I had a baby, and Jonas was my husband now. I felt like crying and I didn't know why.

I heard steps coming up the stairs and it wasn't Jonas'. A strange woman came into the room.

"Good morning, Elaine. I'm Hazel, Abe's maw. Jonas hired me to look after you until you're back on your feet."

I didn't know why she was using my given name, but I ignored it, remembering that Eula at the store and Doc Robinson had always used my given name. I simply thought they didn't hold with nick-names.

Hazel Farrow wasn't nearly as old as I had imagined, and she was rather pretty in an Abe Farrow sort of way. She had the same red hair pulled back in a severe bun, and sparkling little eyes that missed nothing. Her grin was constant and filled with a strange sort of humor. Her chin was set square and jutted out stubborn and unyielding. She was as skinny as a rail in a raw boned yet muscled sort of way. Oddly, I got an image of a snake, lean and powerful and ready to strike.

"I don't need looking after." I told her as I eased into a sitting position without waking Drew.

"Abe told me you'd say that and I shouldn't listen."

"He did?"

"Oh, yes. He quotes you right often. That boy thinks the world of you."

"Not as much as he quotes you, I bet."

"Oh dear," Hazel said. "If you won't believe what he tells about me, I won't believe what he tells about you."

"Deal."

"I fixed your breakfast and I'll bring it up. Jonas says you are to eat if I have to sit here and spoon feed you."

"Where is he?"

"Oh, honey, he left a long time ago. Sick people are waiting in line for him down in Banners Elk. Goodness knows how that poor man does all he does. Folks have a lot of admiration for that good doctor. They know he'll bust his gut to be there when they need him."

I should have known he'd be gone before daylight. He could hire a nursemaid for me but he could never replace himself. Her words made me feel selfish because I wanted him here.

"I can manage on my own," I told her.

"I'd say you probably can. Women do it all the time, even when they have a houseful of kids and a demanding husband, but having me here will ease Jonas' mind and keep Abe from running in here every thirty minutes to check on you."

"You have raised a fine son," I told her with confidence. "I hope I do as good a job with mine."

"Abe is a fine boy, but I tell you something. Some children are just born good. It doesn't take no special raisin. Just like some children are born bad with seemingly no one to blame. But I'll tell you one thing, young lady, the way a child turns out does have a lot to do with its mother."

I looked down at Drew. He was going to be perfect. I just knew it for I was going to be the perfect mother.

"You have a fine baby and you had him without a lick of trouble. You're a lucky one for certain, and perhaps as tough as Abe claims you are."

"I'm not tough," I admitted. "I never knew there could be such pain, I..."

"Wanted to sleep by yourself for the rest of your life while you were hurting so. Every woman thinks such thoughts during her pain, but a good woman forgets about the pain in return for what she has been blessed with." She laughed after she said that.

I grinned, too, for I was glad to know I'd never have to go through such pain again. I'd eat roots and herbs in order to stop it, use a gallon of vinegar to wash out after Jonas finished his manly thing.

"Would you like for me to take him for a while, give you a break?"

"No," I told her quickly and saw that she approved.

"Listen, talking as a woman that's had children, you can get up and move about when you feel like it. Doctors say you have to lay in bed for nine days, but you don't. After a couple of days, light work is good for you, but you don't have to tell men that. Let them wait on you all they will. Lord only knows women don't get waited on enough. It's women that does all the waiting on other. So you just take it easy for a while and enjoy your baby."

I watched her go out of the room, but I had an idea she'd never been waited on much in her life. If nothing else, her red, raw hands gave that away. I wondered if she resented being here taking care of me.

Abe came upstairs right before the noon meal was ready. He peered at me with a shy grin on his tanned face. I thought of asking him about his date for church, but I just didn't have enough energy to tease him.

"Sorry about leaving you with Andy, but I knew he would take all day getting Jonas."

"It's ok. All turned out good. What do you think of my little Drew?" I asked him, knowing that an old man that had once been married was a better choice to stay with me than a boy that knew nothing about women or their parts.

He tiptoed over to the bed as though he was afraid to make any noise. "He's so little."

"Jonas says he's a big baby. He weighed nine pounds and three ounces according to the scales."

Abe looked at him and then his face became solemn as though his thoughts were deep and not altogether pleasing. "I see you done listened to me for once. He's too fine a baby to start life with a mark against him."

"You're talking about me marrying Jonas?"

"Yeah, reckon I am. I'd better get back down stairs or Maw will be up here seeing why I'm taking so long. I just - well, congratulations."

I watched him walk away with his back ram-rod straight and his head hung in a disappointed way. That girl he was sparking was a lucky one. He'd make a good husband come time.

Chapter 4

Three days later Jonas didn't come upstairs when he first got home. I left Drew sleeping and went down the stairs knowing something wasn't right. Jonas looked as worn and hurt as a whipped dog.

His face paled as he saw me standing there and hurried to pick me up in his arms. "You shouldn't get out of bed, not this soon."

"Really, I feel fine."

"I don't care if you do feel fine. I'm not taking any chances with you."

"Oh, Jonas . . ."

"Don't argue, Laine. For goodness sake, listen to what I'm telling you. I don't know why people won't listen to a doctor's advice."

There was too much hurt sounding in his voice. I knew something had gone wrong. Someone had died or been badly hurt, so I didn't argue as he carried me up the stairs and put me down on the bed.

"What happened?"

"Busy day," he said, not wanting to tell me. Suddenly I knew what it was. Something had happened to the mother or her twins.

"Is it the twins? Did they die?"

He took in a deep breath and shook his head. "The mother did."

I thought of those two little babies without their mother, and the other eight children without her. And then I thought about the mother's sorrow at having to leave them behind.

"What will happen to them?" I wondered if I could take the babies. If I had enough milk, I might raise them along with Drew, but the father would never allow that. He would bring in a wet nurse to care for those babies or put them on bottles. Maybe the oldest child was big enough to help care for the rest of the children.

"Their father gave them away, all ten of them. He dug his wife's grave just hours after she died, buried her, let anyone that wanted the children take them, and he got on his horse and rode away."

"He'll come back," I said hopefully. "He can't walk out on his children."

"He did, and the hell of it is those ten children are probable better off for it."

"No."

"Life can be cruel, Laine. Just damned cruel for the young and the helpless."

"He'll come back," I said again. "Just as soon as his hurting eases up."

Jonas shook his head and sat down on the bed beside me and looked at little Drew.

"Ben Alfred isn't the coming back kind. He'll find a place where nobody knows him and start all over again. He'll have another wife and another gang of children he can't take care of."

"What can be done about it?"

"Castration," Jonas said and I thought he was going to cry by the sorrow on his face. "Some men need it."

I put my arms around him and held him close for as long as he would allow it.

"I never intended on telling you about the Alfreds. It's something you don't need to know."

"I'm glad you did."

"Why?"

I didn't know exactly how to answer that. "Because," I finally said. "I want to share your life – the good and the bad."

He bent his head and kissed me on the lips.

I was surprised to find that I was kissing him back, needing to be held and to hold.

He eased me away from him, but I saw in his eyes that he didn't want to let me go. His needs were deep and urgent as he looked away.

"It's a damned shame. Poverty propagates itself. All a poor man can do for pleasure is make love to his wife, or drink liquor. Love makes children and more children, and liquor makes for worse poverty."

"A large family is a blessing to a farmer," I repeated what Dad always said. "It doesn't take long until he has a lot of help for himself and his wife."

"It doesn't always work that way," he told me as his hand reached out and stroked my back. "A poor man gets stuck with a barrier of poor ways and he just can't work himself over the barrier. He and his family can scrap and save for years and it can all be gone with one sickness, one bad crop, or a bad winter, one mother dying, one father leaving. We need something in these mountains that brings in cash money besides farming. Often these rugged hills only grow enough crops to keep the body and soul together."

"What?" I asked as I thought of the sawmilling Dad had done. I didn't see that as an alternative. It had killed Dad as sure as a bullet in the heart.

"I don't know, but there has to be something. It's these mountains, Laine, these wonderful, beautiful, horrible mountains. They can keep people out and lock people in just as solid as a jail cell."

"Folks need to work harder and longer. They can get ahead if they do." I told Jonas with confidence. Dad always said if a man worked long and hard enough, he would get ahead.

"It's not that simple. Life is not simple."

Jonas left me alone and went down stairs to do up the work being Abe and Hazel had only worked half a day. I opened the bedroom window to let some fresh air in. I heard hammering at Andy Harmon's place and wondered if he had built that poor mother a coffin before her husband put her in the ground.

Chapter 5

I heard Hazel come into the kitchen, and exasperation flooded me. I didn't want another woman in my house doing my work. I was still tired and sore but I wasn't sick or incapable. I wanted my life to be normal again, and I wanted worse for Hazel to be gone. I suspected she wanted to be gone too. She had started looking at the fine things in the house and lifting her square chin at them. I had caught looks of contempt in her eyes along with the shaking of her head. She was making me feel as though I were to blame for the nice house and its contents, like I had done something wrong to obtain them.

This morning she brought my breakfast to my room with her jaws set in a hard line. "It's time to rise and shine."

"I ate with Jonas," I said as I looked at the biscuits and gravy.

"Well," I saw irritation in her face that she couldn't hide. "I'll have Abe feed this good food to the hogs."

"I might eat a little," I said guiltily. "I've been in bed too long. I need to work to have an appetite."

"You should be grateful you're able to lay about. Not many folks have things as easy as you do." Her voice was accusing, her eyes hard as glass.

I resented that. She didn't know my life. She only saw Boise's fine things that she obviously didn't have and resented me because I did.

"Some people have nothing," she stated.

That comment brought the scattered Alfred family to my thoughts. I told Hazel about the family, but there was no need. She knew more than I did.

"It happens," she said simply. "We should all say a prayer of thanks that it didn't happen to us."

"He was wrong to give his children away." I felt raw emotion rising in my chest at the thought of those poor children without their mother or father. I expected Hazel to feel similar.

"You don't know what you're talking about," she told me harshly. "You've always been spoiled and pampered. Men cater to the likes of you. How many women marry a man that left them with this? How many women marry rich doctors that hire help for them when they have a baby, and that's just one baby, not ten."

I wanted to yell, kick, and scream at that. She must have known it for she reached out her hand and placed it on my arm. "As for the Alfreds, it's the law of survival. The strongest and the fittest survive. Haven't you watched animals? We can't change the law of nature. It's God's way. You have to put your trust in God."

I didn't believe it was any more God's way than Heaven having streets paved in gold was God's way.

When I came down stairs to eat the noon meal, Hazel looked at me with the most gentle and understanding expression on her face, just like I was her child and she was bound to guide me in the right direction.

"Laine," she said. "You need to get off this mountain and start going to church with me - to the Church of Jesus."

I didn't know what to say.

"You have a baby son now, and you've got to start learning how to raise him right. You have a responsibility as a mother and as a doctor's wife to become a Christian influence. You don't have to spend every minute of your time putting food on the table like most women do. You have a responsibility to God for allowing you to enjoy all this --- this triviality."

Still, I was speechless.

"As for Ben Alfred, his dead wife and scattered children, God never meant for life to be easy on people, especially women. You have heard about Eve, the snake, and the apple, haven't you?"

I think I nodded.

"Good. It's time you learned more about religion and started practicing it and spreading God's word. You are a sinful person if you don't, and sinful people receive God's wrath."

I was glad that Drew cried for me. I was able to get up and walk away from Hazel Farrow.

That night Jonas lay down in bed beside me as tired as he usually was.

"I don't want Hazel to come back," I told him.

"What? Why not?" He sounded irritated with me.

"I'm fine now, Jonas. There's nothing she does that I can't do for myself."

"It's not been nine days."

"Depends on how you count them. I count them as nine days tomorrow."

"You count strange."

"I don't want her back," I said more firmly. "When you go to work in the morning, go by their place and tell her I can take care of myself."

"Tell me why, the real reason?"

"She's starting to tell me how I should live my life. She even told me I have to go to her church in Banners Elk and start spreading God's word because He has granted me more than other women have."

"She's very religious. People should respect her for that, even you should."

"Jonas. . ." I must have sounded as irritated as I was feeling for he interrupted me.

"I won't argue with you, Laine, not tonight. If you don't want a fine woman like Hazel Farrow helping you, then you can manage on your own. Goodness knows a woman as head strong as you are will always get her own way."

I turned my back to him and pretended to be asleep, but he knew I wasn't sleeping, and I wasn't going to say anything else to him. If he brought Hazel back, I'd ask her to leave myself.

It was pure heaven having my own home back. I could cook what I wanted and eat when I wanted. Why, having Hazel here was almost as bad as having Momma around. No, that wasn't true. Nothing was that bad.

Abe let me know he'd brought his dinner from home when he brought the milk in. "It's time for you to sell that calf," he said.

"Why?"

"She's prime fat right now. You need to sell her. I'll tie a rope around her neck and take her with me this evening. I can sell her for you at the going price."

I saw something in him. The way he acted wasn't exactly right. I figured he was mad because I had not wanted his mother back.

"I'm keeping the heifer." After all, it was the only calf I would ever own from walking the woods of home, taking Pet to Jonas' father's bull. The calf gave me a special kind of connection to dad.

I saw disappointment in his face, and perhaps a touch of anger.

"You don't need her."

"Yes I do. I'll need two cows because one has to be turned dry when she calves and I'll need milk for Drew."

"You're being too greedy." He turned his back on me and went out the door.

This wasn't like Abe at all. He had never acted this way. All I could credit it to was his mother.

Puzzlement made me watch Abe during the day. He didn't work like he usually did. He just piddled around the place accomplishing nothing. I saw him looking at the team of horses, the hogs, chickens, barns, equipment, and the house.

At noon, he headed through the woods toward Andy Harmon's place. He didn't come back to cut the meadow of hay like I had wanted. I thought a few days of dry weather was coming and the grass was producing seed heads and needed cutting now.

That night I mentioned Abe's behavior to Jonas.

"What did you expect?" Jonas said in a tired voice. "You sent his mother away when she was making cash money from me."

"She knew it was only temporary when you hired her."

"It doesn't take long for people to like having a little cash in their pockets, especially women."

I remembered Momma and her greed for every red copper she could get. I knew Jonas was right, but I didn't see that as justification for the way Abe was acting. I thought there was something else.

"She was starting to resent me, resent the house and the things in it." I tried to explain to Jonas, but he didn't seem to really listen.

"That's just a woman's nature."

I didn't know about that, the nature part. It seemed more to me like spitefulness and jealousy.

The next day, Abe sent word to Jonas that he was sick and wouldn't be showing up to work for a while.

"Is he really sick?" I wanted to know.

"There's been something going around. It's been mighty rough on the old and the young."

I instantly thought of Drew and feared Jonas might bring something home to him. "Is it catching?"

"It seems so."

"Then I'm glad Abe won't be around. What can I do to protect Drew?"

"Scrub your hands often and wear clean clothes."

I started using lye soap like there was no end to it. My hands cracked and Jonas gave me some salve for them.

"Jonas," I questioned as I rubbed salve into my hands. "Are you mad at me? You seem irritable."

"No," he told me. "I've been working hard lately."

A warm rain came the first day of July and the pasture grass came to seed head. A week had passed and Abe wasn't back. I began worrying about getting the hay cut. I knew I could hook up the horse to the mower and cut it myself, but I didn't want to be away from Drew and he was too little to take to the field with me. I might be able to run to the field and mow one swipe at a time while Drew napped, but I still didn't like not being close to him every minute.

Before Drew was born, I hadn't realized how confining a baby could be. It took away almost all outside work from a mother, but if there was a will, there had to be a way. Of course Drew wasn't six weeks old yet, but that didn't stop the hay from needing cut, and I knew Jonas couldn't help. He was pushed beyond his limit by sick folks.

I had Drew in my arms and was standing by the fence looking at the grass when Andy Harmon walked out of the woods.

"Mornin Missy," he said. "How's our little man?"

"Wonderful." I uncovered his face a little more and leaned him toward Andy.

"Looks just like his mommie. He sure has grown." Andy's eyes sparkled and he smiled as he looked at Drew. I thought he looked proud.

"He's a good baby, and he hardly ever cries unless he's hungry or wet."

"Abe not working?"

"No. He's not been here in a week."

Andy frowned. "Why not?"

"He sent word to Jonas that he was sick."

"Folks do get sick right often."

"Jonas said there was something going around."

"Always is." Andy agreed. "Of one sort or another. He talk to you any?"

"Jonas?"

"No, Abe."

"What would he talk to me about?" I asked.

"He came to me a few days back wanting to trade work for land. I told him no, my land wasn't for sale or barter. Besides there's no work on my land I can't do for myself. It's not like I'm trying to make a living at farming anymore. I just grow a garden, milk my remaining old cow, have some chickens for the few eggs I eat. I buy what little stuff I need by selling a coffin every now and again."

I was beginning to see things a little clearer about Abe, and I didn't like what I was seeing.

"I'm guessing," Andy said. "That he's got marrying on his mind and he wants a place of his own."

That was making sense. "That's why he wanted my heifer calf."

"He wanted your calf?"

"Yeah, I think that's what he wanted. He said he'd take her to sell, but I refused."

"Has he been after you for land in trade for work?"

"No. He knows I won't sell an inch of my land."

Andy glanced at my face like he was studying it. "I think he was struck on you." Andy said suddenly.

I shook my head. "He's the one that convinced me to marry Jonas."

"How's that?"

"He said my baby deserved a good daddy, and a good last name. He said I was being selfish where my baby was concerned by not marrying and allowing my baby to be born with Rafe Johnson's name on his birth certificate."

"Is that why you married Jonas?"

I nodded and he spat and put his foot on the lower fence rail. "Missy, I'm going to give you a bit of advice here, even if you don't want it."

He waited for me to answer but I didn't say anything.

"Never tell Jonas that. Such knowledge can hurt a man to the quick."

"I think Jonas already knows it."

"Then do something to take his hurt away."

"What?"

"By loving him like crazy."

I felt blood rush to my face and Andy seemed uncomfortable, too, as he quickly added. "I'd say Abe Farrow was playing you there. Everybody knew that Jonas had done everything in his power to get you to marry him and you wouldn't. I'll bet my boots that Abe though he could set you up to marry him instead of Jonas for your baby's sake.

"He wouldn't be that dumb." I thought of the cunning intelligence of Abe and the way he had looked after things before I married Jonas.

"Dumb can never be applied to a Farrow," Andy said with conviction.

"He has a girl friend." I reminded Andy, not wanting to talk about this any more.

Andy didn't say anything further about Abe as he looked out over the meadow. "That grass is getting over ripe."

"I was just studying on it. I think I can hook up the mower and mow a little at a time."

"That could take a while with a little one like Drew. It'd probably rain on it before you could get it up."

"I wouldn't try to do it all at once."

"You know what? I need a little hay for my cow this winter. Let's make a trade. I'll mow and stack your hay in return for what I'll use."

"Don't know if that would be a fair trade for you."

"I think it will, if you're agreeable."

There was no question about me being agreeable.

Andy took his foot off the rail and looked at the two horses. "I'll take one of those horses and get started."

"Are you sure you want to do this?"

"I'm sure. You get that little fellow inside before he gets that precious face sunburned."

I couldn't get Abe off my mind as I washed and dressed Drew. Surely someone as nice as Abe wouldn't have tried to marry me for my land. He had commented many times on what a fine place this was and how he would like to own it. I hadn't paid any attention to him because I thought it was a fine place, too, and I loved every single inch of it.

I remembered what Abe had said to me about marrying for my baby's sake and tried to remember him saying I should marry Jonas, but he hadn't. He had reminded me how he had been taking care of the place, and said I should marry not that I should marry Jonas. Did he really have himself in mind? Did he want my land that bad?

Abe wanting my land made me mad, really mad. I picked Drew up and held him to my breast. I knew Jonas hadn't married me because of the land, at least I didn't think so. But I had married Jonas because of Drew. Would that hurt Jonas just a bad as it would hurt me if he had married me for land?

I recalled a sad expression on his face sometimes when he looked at me, and wondered if Andy could be right. Was Jonas hurting? He certainly hadn't tried to do to me what husbands did. I knew it was because I had just given birth. Jonas said I needed six weeks to be back to normal, and he was waiting like a man should. If it had been Rafe, I knew he wouldn't have waited a day.

That evening I cleaned the kitchen and found one of Boise's nice table cloths to put on the table. I fixed a supper I knew Jonas would like, and put the fancy plates on the table. I even went outside and picked field daisy's and fern leaves to make a pretty flower arrangement for the center.

I made a point of keeping Drew awake longer than usual so he would be asleep when Jonas got home. I recalled how hard I had tried to be a good wife to Rafe. Why should I try less with Jonas?

My mind went back to the first time I saw Jonas. My heart had quickened because he had startled me and because I thought I was in trouble by being caught stealing breeding service from Pete Jones' bull. I remembered the way he had wiped my face with his handkerchief after the cow had dragged me down. His touch had made me tingly and itchy all over.

Oh, Jonas, I thought, I do owe you a lot.

Anxiety made me start supper early and Jonas was late getting home. I ran outside when I heard him and threw myself at him as he climbed off the horse. He caught me by the shoulders.

"What's wrong, now?" he asked in a tired voice.

"Nothing," I said as I kissed him on the soft part of his neck. "I just couldn't wait for you to get home."

His eyebrows shot up and he gave me a quizzical look. "You're certainly in a good mood. Why is that?"

"I got to thinking about you today."

"Only today?"

"Especially today. I want to be the best wife you could ever have."

He grinned, but he didn't seem overjoyed by my words. "I'm glad," he said. "I'll unsaddle the horse and turn him loose."

"I've got supper ready."

"It has been so busy today I've not even thought about eating food."

I followed him to the barn and watched him remove the saddle.

"You're working too hard."

"I just didn't realize how much time traveling back and forth every single day took. I start out behind each morning and have to work late of an evening to catch up."

"Couldn't you find another doctor to move here and help you out? Surely there's someone that'd like to move to Banners Elk."

Jonas got the horse by his halter and let him out a side door into the horse pasture. "I'll have to think about that. It might be a good thing for someone and help me out a little."

Jonas' eyebrows shot up again when he saw the fancy table, and he grinned.

"How pretty," he said. "You've been busy."

"I didn't do much, but I think I'm about well. I'm not sore any more and my energy is back."

"You can't keep the young and healthy down for long."

"You're young and healthy," I told him. "You've certainly not slowed down for a minute."

"Not as young as my little wife."

At least Jonas ate hardily even if the food was a little over cooked. When he had finished, I didn't take the plates off the table to wash. Instead, I got up and stepped behind Jonas. I put my hands on his shoulders and began to massage thoroughly.

"Oh, sweetheart," he said after a few minutes. "Do you realize what you're doing to me?"

I wasn't exactly sure, but I had an idea. After all, I had been married. I gritted my teeth for a few moments. I didn't want to do that sort of thing ever again, but it was a woman's duty to please her husband. And I wanted to please Jonas for giving my baby his last name. I didn't want him to feel hurt or cheated and it was my responsibility to see that he didn't.

He reached around for me and pulled me down in his lap. His lips took mine. He tasted like coffee and blackberry pie. I kissed him back because I thought that was what I should do.

My hands lifted to his chest, and then caressed his face, neck, and his hair. I remembered my feelings that cold night Jonas had showed up and kept the little Munson girl alive. I remembered my desperation, my need for Jonas. That same need fired in me again, and I realized this time it had every right to be inside me. I was Jonas' wife now.

I kissed him for real and he came alive. I no longer felt his tiredness. Instead, there was new energy, new strength in him. His lips never left mine as he picked me up, but he didn't take me up the stairs. He took me to the narrow spare bed off the fancy living room. I wanted to ask him why here, but I didn't. I suspected he didn't want to wake the baby.

His lips came from mine and he mumbled, but I wouldn't allow words. I didn't want to think of what we were doing. I didn't want to remember Rafe. I pressed my lips against his again and tightened my arms around his neck.

I felt him fumbling with our clothes, found we were skin to skin. His flesh was warm, strong, comforting to me. The hair on his chest was dark and curly as it moved against my breasts. I felt milk ooze, but Jonas didn't seem to notice for I clung to him tighter, urging him to hurry, but Jonas was in no hurry.

He took his lips from mine and kissed every inch of my body. "Jonas," I whispered. I was shivering by the time his lips came back to mine.

I felt his knee spread my legs apart and prepared myself for what was about to happen, prepared myself to endure.

Some time later, I lay in his arms. I was as limp as a wet rag. I didn't want to get up, didn't want to move an inch. I had never been so content in my life as I snuggled against Jonas. I wanted to say something, do something that would tell Jonas what I was feeling, but the right words would not come to my mind. Finally, I let my lips rub against the tender soft-place below his ear.

"I love you," I whispered and those unexpected words almost scared the life out of me.

"It's about time you admitted it," he said as his arms closed tighter around me.

Jonas was a little later leaving the next morning and he was smiling when he did leave. I was smiling, too, for I was seeing a future I hadn't expected. One where a man and wife could share their love and happiness as a married couple was supposed to do.

I nearly jumped out of my skin when the kitchen door opened and Hazel Farrow walked in as though she owned the place.

"What are you doing here?" I asked none too friendly.

"I left my good apron here." She walked right over to a drawer and pulled it out. "I'm certainly not going to leave it here for you to use as a rag. Besides you and I need to have a little talk."

She gave me a sweet smile that made the skin on the back of my neck prickle.

"Have you had your breakfast yet, dear? There's nothing quite so endearing to a woman as having another woman's helping hands."

"Jonas and I ate a long time ago." I was getting the same warning feeling from her I used to get from Momma and I wasn't liking it.

She took my coffee pot from the stove, pitched the left-over coffee and old grounds out the door and fixed herself a fresh pot to perk just as though she owned my kitchen.

"What do you want?"

She gave me a reprimanding look as though I was an unruly child and she the parent. "Laine, dear, you really must watch the tone of voice you speak in. It does not have a Christian ring to it."

I was going to tell her it wasn't intended to, but she didn't give me a chance.

"Now then." She sat down at the table. "We need to have a heart to heart talk."

"I happen to be busy this morning. I've not got time for heart to heart talks."

"Of course you do, my dear. Laine, do stop using that tone with me. I simply won't have it. Now, I came to talk to you about the Patrick place burning down like it did. You do know that was the hand of God. He sent it to you as a sign. A sign that the place was not intended for you. It is intended for my Abe."

"What?" I almost strangled on the word.

"You heard me correctly. Abe has been a fateful servant of God and He sent the thunder and lightning as a sign that you should give Abe that tract of land. It's what God Himself wants."

I couldn't believe my ears, nor could I believe my eyes. She was sitting there in all her righteousness telling me I should give her son my land because he wanted it.

Her face was set in a serene expression with a tolerant smile on her lips. But there was something in her eyes, something cold and calculating that she couldn't hide.

How dare her! How dare this conniving woman try pulling something like this on me! I longed for the shotgun Rafe had given me and at the same time I was glad it wasn't within my reach for I might have used it.

"Get out of my house!" I said through gritted teeth.

"Laine! I'm warning you one last time to watch that mouth of yours. God is listening."

"Good. Maybe He can repeat this for you in case you don't hear me correctly. Get your greedy ass off my land and don't you ever step foot on it again."

She jerked, insulted to the core. "I have never. . ."

"And you never will get one inch of my land or anything else that belongs to me," I added.

"You'll regret this."

"What I regret is ever letting you in my home. I knew better and I assure you it won't happen again."

She jumped up from the table, her eyes flashing, her mind working. I knew she wanted to slap me. If she did, she would fair worse than Jeb had faired when he tried to molest me. I would definitely cold-cock her with the skillet before I went for my shotgun. I would not be run over by the likes of her or anyone else.

She must have seen something of my intent in my eyes, for a portion of her bravo left her, but she didn't want to show her cowardliness.

"My son will never help the likes of you again," she added as though it was a terrible thing to threaten me with.

"You're right about that. If he or you ever set foot on my land again, I'll blow enough holes in you until you could pass as a sieve. Now, leave my home and my land before I'm forced to help you along."

"Hussy!" she yelled. "You're the devil's spawn and I'll let the entire world know just what you are!'

"Good!" I yelled back as I opened the door for her to go through. "You let the world know that Laine Jones will not be taken advantage of by a hypocrite like you!"

"You'll pay! You'll pay!" she yelled as she hurried from the kitchen, off porch, and toward the woods, her apron swinging from her hand.

Andy Harmon was coming out of the woods from the opposite side of the house. I saw him stop until she was out of sight. Then he came to the porch where I stood.

"What was all that about?"

I told him and he surprised me by laughing. "I wondered how long it would take for you to put her in her place."

"What do you mean?"

"She's a Farrow."

"Abe is a Farrow." I had once thought him a fine boy.

"A Farrow that has been brain-washed into thinking his mother eats, breathes, and speaks perfection."

I didn't know what to say or do as I stood there looking at Andy. Anger was till churning in me. I felt unjustly attacked and could find no relief.

"When Jonas gets home tonight, tell him what happened and then forget about it. Not that you can forget, but don't hire either of them back." He turned toward the horse pasture and I heard him say, "It's women like Hazel that made me not marry again."

I went back in the kitchen, took the coffee pot from the stove and dumped its contents off the side of the porch. If she hadn't taken her apron with her, I'd have burned it in the stove.

☙

Jonas didn't want to believe me when I told him what had happened. Instead, he looked at me rather strange. "You misinterpreted Hazel."

"I did not. Andy said she had brain-washed Abe into thinking she eats, breathes and speaks perfection."

"Are you sure Andy said that?"

"I know what he said. If you don't believe me, ask him for yourself."

"Don't go getting on that high horse of yours. It's not that I don't believe you. Sometimes people misunderstand what others are trying to say, and there's always more than one side to a story."

"Then get her to tell you her side."

"She doesn't need to tell me hers. You are all I care about. Besides, I'm sure to Hazel's way of thinking, she was doing the right thing."

I had a strong urge to deliberately burn Jonas' supper. I might have done it too, if it wasn't already cooked.

"I guess that puts an end to Abe's work around here," Jonas didn't sound too disappointed as he sat down at the table.

"Andy is helping some. He's the one cutting the hay."

"I've never known Andy to hire out to anybody. I doubt he needs the money."

"He didn't hire out or ask for money. He said he would cut the hay in return for what he needed this winter."

"Hummm," Jonas grunted thoughtfully. "Have you ever seen Andy's place?"

I shook my head. I hadn't visited any of the neighbors and didn't have more than an idea where Andy lived. I did know it was close enough for me to hear his hammering when the wind was just right.

"He owns a lot of land," Jonas said. "Talking about land, Steve Banner was in my office today. He had cut a gash in his leg with the ax. It took twenty-two stitches to close it up. Anyway, he has a tract of land that runs from my place up the mountain and joins your land. It's a narrow strip and too steep and rocky for farming, but it has some good timber on it. He asked me if I was interested in buying it."

"Yes," I said so fast that Jonas smiled.

"You don't even know what price he was asking."

"You should buy it," I told him firmly.

"I was thinking that Abe might be interested in it."

"Abe wants good farming land. Beside, he can't afford land. He wants to trade work for land."

"How do you know that?"

"Andy Harmon told me."

"Seems like Andy has done a lot of talking to you lately."

"I'm not complaining."

"Me either, but I would think Abe had money. I paid him cash when he was working for me."

I had paid him cash too, after Rafe died. "I'm glad you aren't complaining. I can't imagine you being jealous of an eighty year old man."

Jonas grinned. "Jealous is something I'm not. Besides, you're too mean for an ordinary man to handle. Only a fine specimen such as me can deal with the likes of you." He grabbed me when he said that and placed a kiss on my lips.

When he turned me loose, I took his hand in mine. "If you can afford that land, do buy it."

"What for?"

"Land is something they're not making any more of."

"So I've heard."

"I'm serious. I'd buy every inch of land I could. If you don't want it, tell him I'll buy it." I wondered how I could pay for it. If Rafe hadn't left enough money behind, I'd have to grow and sell produce like Dad and I did back home.

"Greedy aren't you."

The way he said that hurt my feelings. I didn't see myself as being greedy for loving the land. Somebody had to own it and I didn't see why it shouldn't be me as long as I had the money to pay for it.

"Too much of anything can be a burden, even land," Jonas added.

"There's no such thing as owning too much land. So please buy it if you can."

"Me buying it might not be a bad idea. I need to be a land baron the same as my wife." He put his arms around me and kissed me again, but this time there seemed to be something missing.

Chapter 6

Jonas ended up buying the land for one simple reason. He had saved up enough cash money to pay for it. It seemed a least a dozen people wanted Steve Banner's land, but they all wanted it on a barter system. Jonas was lucky he had the cash. People wanted to pay Jonas in things like eggs and hams. Jonas had worked out a way to sell their produce to the local store much like Dad did with Eula.

That was what I was planning to do with my farming. I had Rafe's wagon and I could haul things into Banners Elk. That's why I went to the field where Andy was stacking hay around the hay pole. He had been cutting on my hay for the past two weeks. Two days of solid rain came a few days ago and stopped his haying, but Andy was at it again.

"Brought you a cold drink of water," I said as I shifted Drew to a more comfortable position.

"Thank you Missy. I was getting a mite thirsty in this hot sun." He looked at Drew. "You ought to make a carrier for that little fellow. Like the Indians used to do. The squaws carried them on their backs so that their hands would be free to do the work."

That seemed like a wonderful idea to me. I wondered why I hadn't thought of it.

"You know, I remember seeing my mother with one. I might set my mind to figuring out how it was configured."

"That would be wonderful. It's hard to hold him and work at the same time. You're not working too hard in this sun, are you?"

"Naw, I'm just takin it easy and enjoyin myself. Thought I'd get what's down stacked. It's going to rain later on this evening."

I looked at the clear sky. I didn't even see a thunder head boiling up over the far mountain.

"How do you know?"

"I heard the raincrows hollering this morning, and that's a sure sign of rain."

I knew what raincrows were. They are shy birds and not aggressive crows. Dad told me they were a Yellowed Billed Cuckoo. I had seen a few but not many. They are a long slender bodied, long tailed bird that's brown in color with a white throat and underbelly. They can produce many sounds, one of which is a long lonesome call they holler before it rains.

"Want some dinner after while?"

"No thank you, Missy. I'll have this up by eleven at the latest. That's when I'll go back home, eat myself a bite and take my daily nap. When you get my age, you'll realize the value of a mid-day nap. It'll add years to your life, naps will.

"As much as Drew gets me up at night, I wish I could take one."

"Why can't you?"

"I can't sleep during the light of day."

"That will change with time," he said. "You get our little man inside out of this sun, and I'll finish up. Thanks again for the cold water." He handed me the empty jar. "I heard Jonas bought some of Steve Banner's land." He added.

"Yeah, I begged him to."

"Why do you want more land than you've got? You're not able to use it all."

"I don't know why I want more. I just love land."

"Better than money?"

"Oh yes."

He chuckled and went back to work, then turned to me as though he had forgotten to mention something.

"Missy?" he said with hesitation.

"What?"

"You know who Abe is sparkin don't you?"

"No." I had no idea and I didn't care.

"It's your sister."

"Susie?"

"Yeap, if the gossip I've heard is true."

This time he grabbed his pitchfork and lit into forking hay around the pole. I walked back to the house letting the information sink in. I had forgotten all about asking Andy what he knew about selling farm produce. I was too busy wondering why Susie and Abe hadn't occurred to me? I had seen the way Abe acted toward Susie when she and Momma were here before Rafe was killed. I suppose I just thought Dad's place was too far away for Abe to travel. I suspect I even thought Momma would never allow Susie to court anybody. Momma clung to Susie too tight to allow anyone else close her.

Drew squirmed and I adjusted him in my arms. I knew for a fact that if Momma allowed Susie to court, she had something in mind.

According to Jonas, Dad's place wasn't too far from here if one went off the mountain and then over to Trade Tennessee and down the river in Ashe County. It was even closer if one could go like the crow flies.

I wondered if Dad's old mule had died, or the rickety wagon finally came apart with no one to patch it. One or both might have happened being that Momma and Susie had not been back.

I am sure they heard Rafe was killed. I suspect that most everybody in several counties knew about it. A boar hog killing a man does get around almost as fast as the story of me running a naked Junie out of the house because I had found her in bed with my husband.

Well, Junie and Rafe were a part of the past and I wasn't going to dwell on them, but this thing with Abe and Susie made me uncomfortable. Had Momma and Susie put Abe up to getting my land? Did they have some kind of devious plan in mind?

Jonas brought home a crib for little Drew to sleep in. Jonas said children shouldn't sleep in bed with their parents. Babies rested better sleeping by themselves and it eliminated the possibility that Drew would get rolled on or tangled in the cover until he couldn't breathe. He topped it off by telling me children became more independent when they slept alone.

"Jonas, have you heard anything about Momma and Susie?" I asked that night as I lay in his arms.

"Like what?"

"Are they still at Dad's place? Are they keeping things up?" I asked.

"Dad said they sold out all the livestock and weren't doing any farming. Dad didn't think they had a garden. He thought about buying the milk cows and perhaps a sow or two but he decided not to have any dealings with your mother."

I could see why that was, being that Pete Jones lived so near Momma, I was surprised she didn't run to him everyday wanting something. I wondered if she knew I had married Jonas. Surely Abe had told Susie and she would have told Momma.

One thing was for certain, they had better not come back here. They had just better not do it!

"Dad said Mert had tried to hire men to work for her, but she wasn't willing to give up cash to pay them. She tried to convince them to work on shares."

"Did you know Abe was courting Susie?"

"Somebody mentioned it. I don't remember exactly when."

"Why didn't you tell me?"

"It must have slipped my mind. How do you know about it?"

"Andy told me today."

"For an old man living by himself on this mountain, he sure knows what's going on."

"Doesn't he ever go into Banners Elk?"

"Come to think of it, he does come to the general store to sit around and play checkers and swap lies once or twice a week."

Jonas snuggled me against him like he was ready for sleep. "Abe might be just the thing for your sister."

"I almost feel sorry for Abe. He sure worked hard around here until I married you."

"Humm, he did change after that didn't he."

"Yeah, and in a hurry."

"Humm," Jonas grunted again.

Andy surprised me the next day with a carrier for Drew. I was hanging diapers on the line when he showed up. I finished and asked him to come into the kitchen.

"Ah, Missy, I don't like being in a house much, especially that one, even if I did help build it."

"Why not this one?"

"Ghosts," he said. "I firmly believe that old man Holloway and Boise's spirits are still in that house, not to mention your departed husband. A person that dies with unfinished business don't tend to leave the earth willingly."

I laughed and didn't tell him there were times when I believed it too. "If they are," I told him. "They will welcome you the same as they have welcomed me." I didn't ask what unfinished business they might have left behind; I thought I might already know.

His sharp eyes judged me and what I said. "You're at peace here?"

"Oh, yes. This place welcomed me from the first moment I saw it." I took my wash tub to the house and he followed. "I've got coffee on the stove. That's one thing Jonas keeps me in good supply of. Jonas likes his coffee," I said as I went in the kitchen door. He hesitated, and then followed me.

"Don't drink coffee much anymore. Keeps me awake at night. Where's our little man?"

"In his crib asleep. I waited to hang out his diapers until his nap time." I sat my wash tub in the spring house and took the carrier out of his hands and looked it over.

It had a wooden back covered with leather and then padded with cotton batting covered with cloth. The seat and straps were also made of leather, batting, and cloth. I could tell that Andy had put a lot of thought and work into making it.

It could be worn on my chest or my back with Drew seated, his back supported and his legs sticking out.

Andy had carefully fashioned buckles and straps like a belt so I could adjust it. I tried it on with delight.

"This is wonderful. I can work now and keep Drew with me. How can I thank you?"

Andy grinned. "Just don't work out in the sun and burn our little fellow. Work before the sun comes up and after it goes down."

"I will," I said and my delight must have been showing for Andy chuckled. "You ought to make these and sell them to women. Why, they're absolute treasures."

"Not many women like work as much as you do," he said, still grinning.

I thought I might as well ask him a question that had been troubling my mind for a few months now. I wasn't familiar enough with the area to know what was available.

"Who has a good bull around here?"

"Now don't you worry about that. I'll take your cow to get serviced for you." He reached up and scratched his head of snowy hair and squinted his eyes until they disappeared beneath his bushy eye brows. "Now, let me see. I reckon Earl Hicks has the best Jersey bull I know of. He lives over the hill there.

"August is a good time. Let her drop her calf in May. Then again, you might want to wait until next summer. That way you'll still have milk for our little fellow until your heifer is old enough to breed."

"You know what I'd like to have?"

"What?"

"I'd like to have a milk goat. I've heard goat milk is the best thing there is for a baby."

"You're right about that. You certainly are, but folks don't seem to like em much. Don't know why."

"I think I'd like them," I said. "You know what else I would like? I'd like to start farming the way Mr. Holloway farmed so I can keep this place up like he wanted."

"He was the best farmer around," Andy said. "He studied those books of his on farming. I have to admit at first I didn't think he was much more than a talker and thinker, but he proved me wrong."

I thought of Dad. He never was much of a farmer. He just managed to do enough to get by on until I got old enough to help out. Oh, how I missed Dad and wished he could have seen his first grandson. I refused to think about Momma.

"You ought to read those books of his," Andy was saying. "You'll learn a lot from them, little Missy. You'll learn a lot most folks don't know exists."

He looked around the kitchen as though he was trying to see something beyond what was there.

"I would have liked to of known him and Boise," I admitted. I seemed to know Boise a little from the diary she left behind.

"If either of them were alive, you wouldn't be here," Andy told me.

I thought of the graves under the shade of the Oak tree. He was right. It seemed that the Holloways had to die in order for me and Drew to live. I shivered as though a cold wind had touched me.

When Andy left, I went in the pretty front room in search of Mr. Holloway's books on farming. I never expected to find the picture album. Finally, I would know what the Holloways looked like, but Drew cried and I rushed to get him before I had a chance to look at it.

I diapered him, and held my little son to my breast. He was such a vigorous little fellow. I looked at his downy brown hair, at his dark slate eyes, at his nose, his mouth, and the shape of his little round face. I looked at his square, chunky hand lying on my breast as he sucked and my heart filled so full of love that tears came to my eyes. A great fear also came. What if I didn't know enough to raise my precious baby the way he should be raised? There was so much I didn't know including how to be a good mother.

Jonas came to my mind. He was educated. He knew a lot. His intelligence would make up for the things I didn't know. He would teach Drew how a man should think, behave, and act.

Drew's mouth grew slack, milk oozed from the corner of his perfect little mouth. I eased him up on my shoulder and patted his back until he burped. I gently placed my baby back in his crib and went back down stairs to look at the picture album.

The first picture filled half of a page. It was of a man wearing a suit and woman in her white wedding dress. Underneath it, in hand writing I recognized as Bosie's, was written: Charles T. Holloway and Francine Brown Holloway on their wedding day. The next picture was of them in plain clothes with Francine showing off their baby daughter. I flipped through the pictures fast, thinking I would go back and have a good look when I had more time.

Finally, I came to what I unknowingly had been looking for, a picture of Boise when she was an adult. At first I felt relieved because she certainly wasn't a pretty woman. She was big and raw boned with a face that was over-long with all angles and sharp points. Her mouth was drawn straight and unsmiling with thin lips turned down at the corners. Her cheekbones were sharp and her jaws sunk inward. I thought her face was the face of an angry, hateful woman, until I looked at her eyes.

Those eyes caught and held me in their grip. It was as though I was seeing into her soul, a soul that refused to ever die. Never had I seen such sweet gentleness and understanding contained in a woman's eyes. There appeared to be a depth of loved that would never reach its ending. I lifted my finger and touched those eyes as though in doing so I might be able to touch the woman.

"I wish I had known you," I said out loud.

"You know me now," she seemed to return.

No, I thought, I don't know you yet.

"You should. You've stepped right into my life."

No. I'm in my own life and you are in your grave. I'm just in what was once your house.

"Maybe so, but we will see, won't we?"

My skin chilled at little, but my mind sunk into those eyes. I hoped she knew how much I ached for her loss, and at the same time, I hoped she knew how thankful I was to be here – a place that was once hers.

I wondered if she and Rafe and their baby were together again. I wondered if dead people could be happy or sad. I wondered if they could be a family in spirit if not in body.

I hoped so.

Don't hate me, I thought, for I never asked to replace you.

"No, but you're certainly enjoying it, aren't you?"

I thought about that and was puzzled and without a definite answer. I was doing as I'd always done – doing the best I could with what I had.

"I'm sorry, sweetie." I almost heard her gruff voice say. *"I shouldn't blame you for what happened to me. I simply need to blame someone other than myself. Besides, you'll get your share of unhappiness, yet."*

I put the album away. I didn't want to be uneasy about anything, especially when it was caused by a dead woman talking to me.

Chapter 7

"Laine."

"What?" I asked as I lay in Jonas' arms. The night was unusually warm for August. A heat wave had reached the mountains and a temperature inversion had occurred making the mountain top hotter than the valley.

"I'm afraid I'll have to stay near the hospital tomorrow night instead of traveling back and forth."

"Why?"

"The hospital is full of sick people. We've actually had to move beds into halls. This heat has brought disease with it."

I was caught between two feelings. I didn't want to spend a night without Jonas, and I didn't want him to bring any disease home to Drew.

"What kind of disease?"

"We're not sure."

"What if you catch it?"

"I try to stay healthy enough not to be subject to disease."

"How?"

"Eating right and not becoming overly exhausted."

I though of him traveling so far twice a day when he was overworked at the hospital. Wasn't that exhaustion? He was just doing it for me, not wanting to leave me alone on the mountain. After all, Jonas did have a house in Banners Elk.

"You are exhausted, aren't you?"

"Yes," he admitted, and was silent as he waited for my response.

"Do what you think is best." I knew my voice sounded with disappointment. I had gotten used to having Jonas with me at night. It was a comfort to know there was someone besides myself that I could rely on.

"Andy still piddling around here?"

I didn't like the term *piddling around* but I suppose it did fit. Andy didn't go at things as though he was working. He did what he enjoyed to the extent of not getting overly tired. After all, Andy was an old man.

"Yeah, every now and again."

"Good. He can keep an eye on things, and you can go to him if something comes up that you can't handle."

I didn't say anything.

"You know how much I'll hate not being here with you, don't you?"

"Yeah," I answered, but I wasn't sure if what he said was totally true.

A person always had choices in what they did or didn't do, but they didn't always have a choice in what happened to them. Even I had choices in the most difficult decisions in my life. I could have refused to marry Rafe and then Jonas. Once I got pregnant, I didn't have a choice in having or not having the baby.

"It's tough on a doctor when he has a family. I never realized how tough until now," Jonas said.

I thought about that. The only difference in Jonas' schedule before and after he married me was the traveling everyday. It wasn't like he actually worked on the farm, took care of Drew, or spent time doing anything but eating and sleeping here.

I washed and ironed his clothes, kept his space clean, cooked his breakfast and supper, and took care of his husbandly needs. Surely that was making up some for his travel time.

"Is the traveling worth it to you?" I asked.

"Of course it is. At least I don't have to be worrying about where you are and what trouble you might be getting yourself into."

Jonas thought I got myself into trouble? That surprised me. I thought I was the one always taking care of other peoples' trouble.

"You understand, don't you?"

"Yeah," I told him. I understood but I didn't like it.

I didn't sleep good during the night. When I dozed off, Drew woke me up to be fed and diapered. I was awake to fix Jonas an extra good breakfast before he left. He ate and kissed me good-by longer than usual.

"Take care of yourself," he said.

I stood there in front of the barn watching the early morning mist conceal Jonas from my sight. My chest tightened and unwanted tears came to my eyes. I felt as though I was being deserted, left alone on this mountain, forgotten and useless as a broken toy.

I don't know how long I stood staring at the spot where Jonas had disappeared. Finally, I turned and went back to the house. There were dozens of things that needed doing.

I fed and bathed Drew and put him in his crib for his morning nap while I rushed to milk and feed all the animals. After I had cleaned up the kitchen, Drew woke up to be fed and diapered, again. This time I put him in the carrier Andy made. I put him on my back and tied a thin sheet over him to shade him from the morning sun. I was going to pick blackberries today. I would need a good supply of cans to feed Jonas and me this winter. Jonas did love berries.

I picked a peck bucket full before Drew woke up. He fussed to be fed, but he didn't cry. I hurried back home, almost in a run because it took a lot of time to get him out of the carrier, feed and diaper him, then put him back in the carrier, and get him and the carrier on my back again.

I was a little breathless when I reached home, but that was to be expected. I was glad when Drew fell asleep and I put him in his crib. I thought about lying down a minute, but I had cans to wash, berries to look and put in the can, enough wood to chop to keep the stove hot for an hour in order to can the fruit. At least I wasn't canning vegetables today, which took three hours cooking in boiling hot water. That kept me busy not only chopping wood, but feeding it into the stove.

When suppertime came, I baked a pone of cornbread and ate a bowl of cornbread and milk. There was no need to cook a meal without Jonas. While Drew slept, I sharpened the ax and chopped an extra supply of wood for canning again tomorrow. During August, I tried to can every day. It was the only way to make sure the howling-wolf-of-hunger stayed away from my door.

Dusk came, the animals quieted down for the night, even the birds were silent as they found a roosting place. Oh, the loneliness of the evening lull. I went out in the yard and couldn't stop myself from looking at the woods where Jonas always showed up. He didn't come. I waited. He still didn't come even when the light faded into darkness. An ache started inside me and filled me to overflowing.

I went back inside wishing I had worked harder. Exhaustion has a way of closing the mind down and making a person sleep. A strange uncomfortable feeling spread over me; a kind of worry mixed with unfounded fear. I got the double barrel shotgun Rafe had given me from where I kept it on the cellar stairs and loaded both barrels. I locked all the doors, closed the windows and put sticks in them so no one could open them, and carried the gun upstairs to a lonely bed. I patted the gun, grinned at myself for my foolishness, and put it under the edge of the bed. I guess the gun was supposed to give me the security that Jonas had been giving me, but what was there to replace the comfort of having arms to hold me?

Sometime during the night, I dreamed that Jeb was back, chasing me around the kitchen, grabbing my breast. I awoke to Drew crying to be fed. I fed and diapered him by the moonlight shining through the window. After he was asleep, I stayed awake for a long time watching the moon cross the sky. When I did sleep, Rafe was on the porch with me. He had the shotgun in his hands.

"Here," he said. "It might be a good idea for you to have this."

I looked at the gun and then at Rafe. He grinned that grin I liked, the one that made him look handsome.

"I've got enough shells here to last you for years, but I expect you to practice shooting while I'm away." He lifted his left eyebrow, still grinning. "If you see Zeb, shoot the bastard and ask questions later. Leaving you here alone don't settle too good with me."

He put the gun in my hands. "Put the butt of the gun tight against your shoulder. Shotguns kick. The tighter you press against your shoulder the less kick you get."

A touch of warmth came to his green eyes as he looked down at me. "You're tougher than the average mountain lion, and I want to keep you that way," Rafe said.

I shot the gun just like Rafe instructed. The kick knocked me backward, but Rafe caught me in his arms.

I woke up with a start and sat up in bed. There was nobody holding me in their arms. It took me a moment to realize that Rafe was dead and it was Jonas I was missing. I looked at the crib where I could see Drew sleeping from the light cast by the moon. Again, I felt bad about denying Rafe's son the right of his daddy's name. There were some good things about Rafe, not many, but a few.

The next evening I was looking forward to having Jonas come home. I was out in the yard listening to the coming of night-sounds as the gloaming settling in when Andy showed up.

"Good evening Missy." He sounded happy, but I heard something like regret in his voice.

"Good evening, Andy. Isn't it a beautiful time of day? Everything is settling down for the night as though the world is ready for sleep."

"Perfect. Nothing gets better than this."

"I love this place," I repeated what I felt.

"I know," he said and looked away from me. "I saw Jonas today."

I waited for him to say more. He didn't.

"And?" I encouraged.

"He said to tell you he had to stay near the hospital again tonight."

I tried not to show my disappointment, but I knew Andy could see right into my soul.

"More sick folks now adays than when I was a boy. Don't raise folks to be as tough as when I was a young'un."

"I guess so."

"Doctors are hard to come by. They stay mighty busy."

"Are many people sick down in Banners Elk?"

"Bout like normal," Andy said.

"I thought you said there were more sick folks now adays."

"I mean as a whole, not just today."

"Oh. So there's no disease or nothing going around."

"Not that I know of."

"I was thinking this spell of hot weather might be making folks get sick."

Andy chuckled. "It hain't that hot. It's seventy degrees on this mountain and seventy-five or so in Banners Elk."

"So, people aren't lining up in the road waiting to see Jonas, nor folks hanging out the hospital windows."

Understanding dawned on Andy's face. "There's enough folks sick, having babies, and banging themselves up to keep two doctors busy. He'd better watch out or he'll be like me, too old to work."

"You're certainly not too old to work. Of course, you do like going to town to play checkers and swap lies."

Andy looked a bit taken back. "Did Jonas tell you that?"

"He said you went to town once or twice a week. I just figured you would be enjoying yourself a little."

"Yeah," Andy said. "I reckon a man has to enjoy himself once in a while. Just so long as it don't become a habit. Well, Missy. I best be getting on."

"Stay and I'll fix you some supper."

"Appreciate the offer, but I got it waiting at home. It would be ashamed to waste good food. How's our boy doing?"

"Growing and healthy."

"That's good."

"I worry about Jonas bringing home something he might catch."

"No need to worry."

"Guess not, when nothing's going around, but you know how mothers are."

"Reckon so. Have a good night."

"You too."

I went back inside and sat down at the kitchen table. I just didn't know what to think.

🕊

Jonas arrived the next night just as it was getting good and dark. I had deliberately not started supper. I acted surprised when I saw him, and I actually might have been a little surprised for I wasn't sure he would come home.

"I'm starved," he said. "Why isn't supper ready?"

"I don't cook a good meal just for myself," I told him as he came to me and took me into his arms. "But I'll put wood in the stove and have something ready in a few minutes," I said as I breathed in his warm and familiar smell.

"Good." He gave me a light kiss on the lips. "I've not had time to cook for myself."

"Still got a lot of sick people in Banners Elk?"

"Yes, but the nurses will have to look after them tonight. Two nights in a row is too long to be away from my wife. Andy gave you my message didn't he?"

"If he hadn't I'd have sent him to find you. I would have been sure you were lying somewhere hurt."

"This place is a long ways from my work. If I ever get rich, I'm going to get me one of those motorized vehicles. Maybe a fancy touring car."

"Is the disease still going around?"

"I'm afraid so."

"What is it?"

"I don't know the answer to that."

"Are you sure you won't bring some disease home to Drew?"

"I wash and change clothes before I come up the mountain."

I looked at what he was wearing. Why hadn't I noticed before that he left and came home wearing different clothes. After all, I did his washing and ironing, but these clothes weren't ironed the way I did them.

"Who does your clothes in Banners Elk?" I asked.

"I hire somebody to come in once a week to clean my house and do the washing."

"I see." I turned from him to fix supper. I wasn't the only person taking care of Jonas. He had another life away from me, another house, a job, and another woman doing his cleaning and ironing. I wondered if she cooked his food too. Rafe had Junie. Did Jonas have someone like that? I'd heard Momma say a man couldn't go long without a woman to ease his manly needs. Wasn't I enough for Jonas?

Chapter 8

Doctors' work doesn't have holidays or week ends. It was Sunday but Jonas was gone when Andy showed up around eight o'clock in the morning.

"Got your work done up?" Andy asked me.

"Yeap," I answered as I opened the chicken house door. I closed the chickens up every night to keep the varmints out. "What are you doing here on a Sunday morning?"

"Thought you might want to go to church."

That stopped me in my tracks. I looked at Andy like I hadn't heard him right, thought I might have got a wrong meaning from his words.

"Do you want me to take you to church? I've got a little buggy you and Drew could ride in. Wouldn't take but a few minutes to hitch it up."

I shook my head. "I don't like church."

"Me either."

"Then why are you asking if I want to go?"

"Thought you'd find it interesting?"

"Why is that?"

"It's the Church of Jesus."

I remembered Hazel and that church. I certainly didn't want to go.

"To Hazel Farrow's church. No way." I told Andy.

"Your mother and sister will be there."

I felt like he had punched me in the belly and knocked the wind clean out of me.

"No!"

"Yeap. I heard Abe's going to marry your sister."

I had to grip the chicken house door. "How do you know that?"

"I was in town yesterday playing checkers and swapping lies. That's where I hear all the gossip. They said Hazel would only agree to her boy marrying your sister if your mother and sister started going to her church. Hazel's real religious, you know."

"In Banners Elk?"

"It's not exactly in Banners Elk. It's out of town a ways."

"I don't want to see them," I said.

"I'd kind of like to go once, especially today," he said rather oddly.

"Why?"

"It's a church of holiness snake handlers."

I opened my mouth but nothing came out.

"Yeap, folks come from all over. Out of Tennessee, South Carolina, and even all the way from Georgia just to cozy up with a bunch of poison snakes."

"Momma's horrified of snakes," I told him. "She'll go into a screaming fit at the sight of one."

A big grin spread all the way across his face and his eyes lit up. "That's why I thought you might want to go."

"I still don't want to go, and I didn't know the Church of Jesus was that kind of church." I had heard talk of such churches, but I had never seen one.

"Word's out that your mother and sister doesn't either. There's a good many folks in Banners Elk that's never been to that church that are planning to go today."

"Not me," I told him firmly. I had images of a big rattler biting Drew. A shiver of dread went all over me. Snakes! Poisonous snakes!

"I'll mosey on down all by myself, then. I take it you'll want me to come back and tell you all about what goes on."

I suppose I really did want to know all about what went on. I certainly wanted to know what Momma and Susie were up to.

"Yeah, come back and tell me."

He left me standing at the chicken house holding onto the rough wooden door. I wondered if any of the people that attended the Church of Jesus took sharp hoes with them. Suddenly I started laughing. If I didn't have Drew to watch out for, I might have gone with Andy just to see Momma and the snakes, but only if I could have hid way in the back near the exit door.

I laughed all the way to the house before I stopped and started shivering, not at the thought of the snakes, but because Momma and Susie would be too close for my comfort. I wondered if they had spent the night at the Farrows'. It was too far for them to travel all the way from Dad's place before church started.

About time for church to start, I began to worry about Andy. He was old and slow. If a snake came at him, he might not be able to get out of its way. Running people might knock him down and step all over him before the snake got him. I didn't want Andy to die, not because he was the only company I had on this mountain, but because he was a good man that didn't deserve to be stomped all over by folk's shoes before he suffered for days and died from snake venom.

I didn't worry about Momma and Susie. Momma would be like a freight train. She'd part the crowd while holding onto Susie, dragging her to safety. What about the people of Banners Elk, the ones that were going just to watch Momma and Susie?

A kind of longing crept over me. I wanted to be there, too. Not at the church, but in Banners Elk where I could know what was happening. I thought about saddling one of Rafe's horses, putting Drew on my back, and riding into Banners Elk. Jonas was there, and Jonas had a house. I had a right to go into town any time I wanted to go.

When Drew woke up, I fed him, bathed him and put on his very best clothes. I figured I could be in Banners Elk just about the time church service ended. Would snake handling people end their service the same time most churches did? Would they take longer if everybody there had to handle a snake before they left? What if somebody got bit? Would they get Jonas? Would he get bit by a snake?

I put Drew back in his crib and hurried outside to the horse pasture. I whistled but the horses didn't pay any attention to me because it was summer time and I didn't feed them at the barn. I had to go into the field and catch the one that was the gentlest. I had never rode with Drew and didn't want to take a chance on getting my baby hurt.

I had the horse in the barn hall and almost had him saddled when I heard the sound of horse's hooves outside. I ran out expecting to see Jonas.

It was Andy on a fine, high stepping horse every bit equal to the ones Jonas rode.

"You're all right? What happened? You're early."

"It didn't last as long as normal." I saw a twinkle in his eyes as he dismounted the horse like a much younger man would do.

"No one was bit?"

"Only one person."

"Who? What happened?"

He dropped the reins to ground tie his horse.

"Nobody I knew. Got a hot fire in the stove?"

"I can stoke it up, why?"

"If I had a nice cup of coffee and a biscuit and jelly to put in my belly, I could tell you all about it."

I put kindling in the firebox, put the coffee pot on to perk, and rushed up stairs for a quick peek at Drew. He was still asleep.

"What happened," I asked anxiously when I got back down stairs.

Andy leaned back in the chair and sniffed at the perking coffee. "I admit I was a bit nervous at first, but a half dozen of the men I know where in the church yard when I got there.

"'Are you going inside?' I asked them.

"'Just waitin on you,' one of em said.

"We took the very back row and set close together, like a bunch of little boys giving each other courage. We were a little early but folks were already there, along with two men I didn't recognize standing with the regular preacher. Harvey leaned close my ear and whispered: 'Them two are preachers from out of town. One came all the way from Virginia. See them boxes? They're full of poison snakes.'

"Well, I stretched my neck until I saw three large boxes sitting near the pulpit. I tried to listen to hear the snakes rattling, but I couldn't hear nothing.

"Folks kept coming in but they didn't pay much attention to us. I recognized some of em. Nodded to the ones I knew. Then through the door came Hazel and a woman I took to be your mother. Abe and a girl were walking behind them, but the girl didn't look a thing like you. She was bigger and lighter in color, drabber, not full of life the way you are. Well, there were enough people already in the pews until neither Abe nor his mother saw us sitting in the back.

"Hazel took them right up to the front pew and sat them down beside her and Abe."

I got up and poured Andy a cup of coffee and placed it on the table in front of him.

"Most all eyes were turned toward that front row, and I could see your momma swelling up with importance. It appeared to me she thought the Farrows were the cream of the crop. Like ringing a school bell, that church filled up suddenly and the preachers looked mighty pleased with themselves at the crowd they were drawing.

"The regular preacher stood up and welcomed everybody, said how proud he was to have so many people attend including regulars and newcomers. He said it was surely because of the two guests preachers that had come to preach the gospel and test the faith of man. I figured it was because of the talk that was going around town about your momma and sister being initiated in the church by Hazel. He grinned at me with twinkling eyes. You realize that folks mean no harm by their curiosity. They have to get entertainment when it's offered."

"He introduced one of the preachers. I can't remember his name now, but he was in his forties with a thick nose that was kind of flat on the end. His eyes were too close set and his hair was thin, long on top and combed back to hide part of his bald spot. Just seeing him on the street, a man wouldn't think he had any peculiar power behind the pulpit or that he handled dangerous snakes on a regular basis. He simply looked ordinary. But folks seemed to think he was a special man by their intake of breath and pleased grunts.

"The congregation took out their hymn books and sung different songs for about fifteen minutes led by the powerful voice of the guest preacher. Finally, he hushed the singing and started preaching. Pretty good sermon – about like any regular preacher would preach. He started by taking out his Bible and laying it on the pulpit. It seemed to fall open of its own accord.

"'Oh, yes,' he said. 'This good-book has opened itself to the second chapter of Acts, and he began to read. *And when the day of Pentecost had fully come, they were all with one accord in one place. Suddenly there came a sound from heaven as of a rushing, mighty wind, and it filled all the house where they were sitting. There appeared unto them cloven tongues like as of fire, and it sat upon each of them. And they were all filled with the Holy Ghost and they all began to speak with other tongues.'*

"He looked up from his reading and slapped his hand down on the Bible with a loud pop. His close-set eyes took in each person in the church house. I don't mind telling you I made sure to be shielded by the man in front of me. I didn't want that snake-eyed man looking at me.

"'That,' he shouted, 'is the word of God. And let me warn you sinners and disbelievers right now. The word of God is all there is a man can live by. God means what he says and says what he means. If you don't have enough faith in God to put your trust in him, why should he put his faith in you? When the Holy Ghost came down with tongues of fire and they started speaking in the unknown tongue. Well, now, believers, God didn't intend for just anybody to do that. He intended it for those that believed in him.'

"The a-mens rose up all over the place. 'A-men,' he shouted. 'Praise God. He has come to look out after those that believe in him. Those that trust enough unto him to put their life in his hand.'

"He grabbed up the bible from the table and shook it in the air like a dog killing a snake, and then he commenced prancing up and down the aisle, shouting a bunch of babble I reckon was that other tongue.

"That's when Hazel came straight up in the air with an ear-splitting squall. Her arms were reaching straight up above her head and her hands were working like she was trying to grab something. Your momma and sister both jumped at the suddenness and loudness of the squall coming from somebody sitting next to them.

"'Praise God," Hazel shouted, and then started running up and down the aisle behind the preacher. She got to the door, turned and passed the preacher up before he reached the pulpit. I could tell the preacher didn't like her stealing his thunder. He shouted, loud. She shouted louder. 'I'm a believer," he yelled. 'Oh, yes, God. I put my life in your hands.'

She swung her arms as she marched and shouted. Spit foamed white at the corners of her mouth. 'I'll drink your strychnine.' I made out her saying though her jumble of unknown language.

"'We all have,' yelled the preacher wanting to upstage her as he hopped and danced and cupped his ears with his hands.

"I looked at your momma when Hazel said she'd drink strychnine. Her mouth hung open and her face looked as blank as a sheet of new paper. Kind of like she heard the right words but they wouldn't sink in.

"'My son, my future daughter-in-law and her mother will drink of poison and take up snakes with me.' Hazel shouted. 'We are willing to prove out faith in God.'

"With that she ran to the front of the church and yanked the lid off a box and dumped three long rattlesnakes in the floor. She kicked them with her foot, scattering them out of their coiled pile. That got my attention. It got your mother's and sister's attention too, for Hazel had kicked the snakes toward them. A loud rumbling noise of approval rose from the crowd.

"'Only those with pure unadulterated faith can take up serpents and drink of poison without being harmed,' shouted the preacher as he went to the snakes. He bent down and grabbed a snake, which was a bad mistake. Those snakes were all excited and letting off their smell. That big rattler turned on the preacher and sunk its fangs in his thumb. He tried not to react, stuck his hand in his britches pocket so the congregation wouldn't see the blood dripping. He dropped that snake back with the others.

"I saw that Hazel was standing back because her kicking had those big rattlers mad as fire. They had quiled up and were singing to beat the band not more than three feet from your momma.

"I think she was paralyzed with fear there for a minute. Then she let out a squall that would top the preacher and Hazel put together. Her hand flew out and clutched your sister by the hair of her head. She didn't stand up from her sitting position on that bench; she leaped on it still clutching your sister's hair. Your sister started squalling as loud as your mother.

"I believe your mother intended to leap over the bench and take your sister with her, but your sister wasn't in a position to leap and your mother wasn't about to turn loose of her hair. The bench flipped over backward flinging your mother, sister, Abe and a couple of others on top of the folks seated behind them. Talk about a fighting, cussing mess."

Andy started laughing, took out his handkerchief and wiped at his eyes.

"Oh Missy," I wish you could have seen what happened next. Inside that church house looked like a nest of hornets boiling mad as they got tangled up over each other. They were all trying to get to the door for nobody knew where those snakes were at by now. Missy, I don't mind admitting that I was the first one through that door, and I didn't stop running until I had forked my horse.

"I looked back from the safety of my saddle and just watched those church goers fighting each other to get out that narrow door.

"Your momma wasn't the first out, but she wasn't far behind me. Last I saw of them, they were running down the road with your mother screaming, and your sister holding her head and crying as she tried to catch up with your momma. Poor Abe didn't know whether to stay behind with his mother or go after his sweetheart. Finally, he lit out down the road.

"I stayed for a few minutes longer, just to set that scene in my mind real good and then headed on back up this mountain where I belong."

He wiped at his eyes a little longer. I didn't know what to do or say, but part of me wanted to laugh with Andy.

"Was anybody hurt or bit?"

"Only the preacher that I know of," he said.

"Did they take him to Jonas?"

"Can't answer that."

"What about the men that sat with you?"

"Oh, they were all swift of foot. Helped push me out the door, they did."

"You enjoyed yourself, hum?" I said as I started to grin.

"Oh, yeah. Hain't enjoyed myself that much in fifty or sixty years."

That day Jonas came home early. The expression on his face was solemn, but his eyes were alive.

"Have a busy day?" I asked, not wanting to give away what Andy had told me. I had no doubt every person in Banners Elk had heard about the fun at the Holiness Church of Jesus.

Jonas put his arm around me and gave me a big kiss. I tried to make myself respond, but Jonas didn't seem to notice my hesitation.

"No, it wasn't busy today. I did have a couple of women with sprains and bruises."

"Did they get in a fight?"

"Not exactly."

"What happened to them?"

"Religion. I believe they got religion."

I waited, but Jonas didn't say anything more.

"Have you eaten your supper?"

"Of course not."

"Your house keeper and laundry woman doesn't cook?"

He looked surprised when I said that.

"Are you jealous?" He sounded as though such a thing would be incredible.

"No."

He lifted his eyebrows and then chuckled. "You already know, don't you."

"Know about you and other women?"

He laughed at that. "Andy has been by hasn't he?"

I didn't answer.

"He told you about Hazel, your folks, and the snake-handling meeting didn't he?"

I still didn't answer.

"According to gossip, your mother and sister went back to Ashe County."

"Why didn't you tell me they were in town?"

"I didn't know a thing about it until today."

"I thought you were a sounding board for all the local gossip."

"I'm too busy to listen to such stuff. That's Andy's job. How did he get the gossip to you so quick?"

"Simple. He came by early this morning and asked me to go to church with him."

"You went?" His voice sounded of total surprise and disbelief.

"Of course not, but he went."

"And he couldn't wait to tell you."

"He got to enjoy it twice by telling me about it. Said he hadn't had such fun in sixty years."

Jonas grinned. "You and that old man think too much alike."

🕊

One of the worse things about being on a mountain is not knowing what is going on someplace else. I had to depend on Andy to keep me up on things, but even Andy didn't know what was going on with Momma and Susie.

I asked Jonas but he claimed he didn't know a thing.

"Don't you ever talk to your dad?" I asked him.

"When would I do that? He lives the same place as your mother, and neither of us go to visit."

"I thought he might come to Banners Elk once in a while."

"He doesn't visit that often, and between being a doctor and your husband, I don't have time to do anything else."

I thought about reminding him the only thing he did toward being a husband was eating two meals that I cooked and sleeping with me at night, but I wasn't complaining. He wasn't like Rafe, making me glad when he was not home. I liked being with Jonas. I liked the way he held me during the night, and I liked what we did together.

Sometimes when I thought about it, I felt embarrassed all over, as though I was doing something bad because I liked it. How was it that doing the same thing with two men could be so different?

Rafe had been forceful, never thinking of anyone but himself and what he wanted. Jonas was gentle, loving and always thinking about me and what I would like or dislike. I looked at Jonas and smiled.

"An interesting man came by the office today. He had a locust thorn stuck deep in the back of his thigh. I had to make a deep cut to get the thorn out and have room to flush the wound. Locust punctures almost always set up infections."

"What did he do, fall on a limb?"

"Stepped on a rotting log and fell on a branch. Do you know what was interesting about him?"

"What?" I asked as I took the plates from the table.

Jonas leaned back in his chair, comfortable after eating supper. "He bought out Sara's Gorge and the land surrounding it."

"Why?" I asked. Andy and Jonas both had told me the far mountains I could see rising near Grandfather Mountain was called Sara's Gorge. Its twin mountains surrounded a deep gorge where water ran fast before it dropped over a great length of rocks and ended in a waterfall. "Andy said Sara's Gorge hasn't got ten acres fit for farming. I hope he didn't give much for it."

"He didn't, but fifteen hundred acres still amounts to a good chunk of cash. He said at least half a dozen other people have tried to sell him their land that joins it."

"What's he going to do with it if he can't farm it?"

"He has big plans."

"What kind, timbering it?" I asked, getting tired of him hesitating. I knew there was a lot of sawmilling going on near by.

He smiled. "Much of the land around here has already been timbered. Laine, I think this might be what this area needs. I think this man might provide some much needed jobs that bring in cash money."

I gave him an impatient look to hurry him long.

"His name is Smith, Rupert Smith, and he is a land developer. He's going to build fancy homes to sell to folks that want a summer place in the mountains."

I thought of Mr. Holloway coming here and building this fancy house. "Fifteen hundred acres. That could be fifteen or twenty houses."

I saw the bewildered look Jonas gave me before he could hide it. "Honey, it will be more like six or eight hundred houses."

"How many?" I was sure I had misheard him.

"Six or eight hundred."

"Oh," I imagined a bunch of tiny houses where folks just had room for a little garden if the brush was cleared. There couldn't be much usable land because of the water fall Andy told me about and all those huge rocks I could see from my pasture land. "Where is he going to find that many people around here with money to buy a house?"

"I know you've not seen any place other than where you grew up and this mountain. You can't be expected to know there are people elsewhere that have money to buy what they want."

I frowned, not liking the way his words made me feel.

"I traveled about a little when I was in college, saw a lot of places, places with fancy houses and people making money. A different life than the dirt road where we grew up."

"How did you afford college?"

"Scholarships, plus I worked. It took me a long slow time to graduate. When my money ran out and the scholarship funds were gone, I'd have to drop out of school and get a job until I had enough to go back. That's why you didn't know I grew up close you. I left home when you were five or six years old."

"Your dad didn't help you any?" Momma had always said Pete Jones was a rich man, and I grew up thinking that was true.

"A little, but I hated to take money from him. I was strong and capable of earning my own way."

"Why did you come back here?"

"Lack of doctors in the area. I thought that people needed me here and that I could make a difference."

"Are you?"

"I'm trying, Laine. That's why I think this development can be a good thing."

I went to him and put my hands on his shoulders and rubbed along his neck. How lucky I was to have such a good man for a husband. I was glad I hadn't gotten another Rafe.

꙳

I was coming back from the barn when I heard it. It was a roaring noise that I couldn't place and it sounded like it was coming up the road. I hurried inside to get Jonas.

"Come outside and listen to this," I told him a bit breathless. "I don't know what it is."

Jonas got up from the table where he was reading a medical book. He seemed a little irritated that I had bothered him.

"What is it now, Laine?"

"I told you, there's a noise outside."

He opened the door and heard it too.

"It's a vehicle. Who would be coming up here in a vehicle?"

He didn't have long to wait. The black, shiny car was in the yard by the time we got back outside. I just stood there and stared at it.

"That's the man I was telling you about, Rupert Smith."

Curiosity flamed in me like a forest fire. I not only wanted to see that car, I wanted to see the man. I instantly imagined him to be a different species of person, one that knew everything, had everything, someone different from me because he was rich.

"Go back inside," Jonas told me.

His words surprised me so much that I did stop for a moment, but my need to see this man and his vehicle was great.

"Mr. Smith, what are you doing here?" I heard Jonas say.

"This is some kind of place," Rupert Smith said.

I moved to the corner of the house and stood behind a lilac bush where I could see what was going on and hoped he nor Jonas could see me.

The first thing I took in was the vehicle. It was a square box shape with wooden spokes, padded seats, and a steering wheel inside the top. Next was the man.

"Yes, it is." There was an edge to Jonas' voice that I couldn't identify. "Why did you drive your nice town car up the rough wagon road?"

"Stitches popped out of my leg. Your office informed me that I could find you here. Do you have two places? I though you lived at your office."

"I have two places." Jonas said. "I should have a look at that leg."

I saw Jonas hesitate, looked toward the house as though he were debating what to do next.

"I hate to intrude on your privacy, but perhaps I could go inside while you place the stitches back in."

"Yes, of course. Do you need help walking?"

"No. I can walk."

He opened the car door and got out. I stood there staring, puzzled that he looked like an ordinary person with unusual blond colored hair beneath a felt hat that set on his head at a cocky angle. Even the clothes he wore were ordinary. His shirt was white, long sleeved, and starched stiff as a board. His pants were pleated, cuffed, and gathered high at his waist with a brown belt. What wasn't ordinary was the needle-sharp creases ironed in his pants and shirt.

He wasn't as tall as Jonas, but broader through the shoulders and thicker through the stomach.

Instead of going toward the kitchen door as I expected, Jonas led him to the fancy round steps that led onto the front porch. So, I thought, Jonas wants to impress this man.

Rupert Smith was walking slow, obviously in pain. I rushed to the kitchen and hurried to the front room to unlock the door by the time they reached it. I opened the door in their face.

Jonas frowned. There was nothing I could do but smile and say, "Hello."

"Good day to you, ma'am," he responded and looked me in the eyes.

I didn't know what else to say as I looked into the bluest eyes I had ever seen on a man. They weren't washed out blue, or sky blue, they were a deep, pure, sparkling dark blue, a different color than Jonas'.

"Sorry to intrude like this." His smile showed perfect white teeth. "I'm afraid I needed to see Doctor Jones."

"Of course, come on inside," I moved from the door.

"Have a seat," Jonas indicated the red sofa.

He sat down and I noticed how gold his hair was as I looked down on him. Jonas kneeled on the pretty rug and touched his knee.

"Put you foot on the table," Jonas said. "Let me have a look at that leg."

"I may have to take my pants off," Rupert Smith said.

Jonas seemed a bit taken back. "Of course. I wasn't thinking. Let's see. Laine, could you leave the room and close the door. Bring a sheet and a couple of towels and knock on the door before you enter."

I went up stairs and got the best towels and sheets that Boise had stored in the linen drawers. I brought them to the door and knocked as Jonas had instructed. Jonas opened the door and took the things from my arms.

"Get my medical bag and bring it to me."

Jonas always kept his medical bag sitting in the kitchen. I got it, brought it back, and knocked on the door again.

"Come in," Jonas said.

I opened the door to see that Rupert Smith was lying belly down on the sofa covered by the sheet, except for one leg. That leg had a towel under it and another towel over it.

"You need to stay off this leg for a day or two," Jonas was saying as I handed him the bag. "I'll have to put some deeper sutures in this time and bandage it up securely. How did you manage to rip the stitches out?"

"Fell while I was walking my land."

"I'll need to give you something to ease the pain before I can put the catgut back in, or I can do like I did before and put drops of opium in your eye. You know how long that takes to wear off."

"Is it really catgut?" Rupert Smith asked.

"Indeed it is. Joseph Lister invented soaking catgut in Phenol to sterilize it before using it in surgery. Of course, other materials are being experimented with."

"You're not going to give me a jug of the area's famous white lightning to drink until I feel no pain?"

"That could be arranged if you insist. That or ether or nitrous oxide or opium drops, or I can put a topical ointment that contains cloves and cinnamon on the skin, but that will only take a small amount of pain away," Jonas said.

"I do need to drive off this mountain unless the lovely lady would allow me to spend the night."

I started to say that he could stay if it was necessary, but Jonas didn't give me the chance.

"It's only a small wound that shouldn't slow down a ten-year-old if he doesn't try to climb over rock cliffs. You've had it done once with opium drops; you might be more careful if it's done without that."

"I see," he chuckled as he turned his head where he could look at me. I smiled back.

"Is this your daughter?" he asked Jonas.

"I'm not that old." Jonas opened his medical bag and took out some things. "Laine is my wife."

"Then you are a lucky man, indeed."

I thought I saw disappointment flicker over his face as his eyes sought mine and he smiled again, but it could have been my imagination.

"Yes, I'm lucky all right. Laine, how about perking a fresh pot of coffee. I'm going to give him a shot of liquor and then use a topical. If he feels the pain of being sewed up, he might not be too eager to rip the stitches out again."

I left the room feeling as if Jonas had dismissed me. Jonas knew I would have to start a fire in the stove, for it had gone out. It would take a while when I wanted to ask this man about the land he bought as well as his plans for it.

By the time the coffee had perked, Jonas had finished his job and Rupert Smith had his pants back on. His face was a bit pale when I brought his coffee and leftover pie from Jonas's supper. He eagerly took the cup in his hands and drank. I noticed that his hands trembled slightly.

"I need coffee only second to needing more liquor," he said.

"You need to stay off that leg." Jonas told him.

"I will."

"You had better."

"This is a magnificent piece of land. Have you ever thought about selling it?" he asked Jonas.

"No," I said firmly before Jonas could speak. "I'll never sell my land. When I die, it will go to my son."

His eyes met mine, again. "I don't blame you one bit."

I heard Drew whimper and left the room. Trouble with having something nice was that everybody wanted it.

When I finished feeding Drew and he drifted back to
sleep, I placed him in his crib and covered him up with a
soft blanket. I went down stairs to find that Jonas and
Rubert Smith were outside on the front porch. Rubert was
leaning against the railing and his face was pale. I went to
the open screen door, but didn't go where they could see
me for I had a feeling that Jonas didn't want me around
Rubert Smith.

"Being a doctor certainly pays well," Rubert was
saying. "This place is worth a fortune. How long have you
owned it?"

"Not long," Jonas said. "I just closed on a track that
joins this one. It's not nearly as nice as this but the tracts
join so I thought it would be a good investment."

"If you ever decide to sell it, let me know."

Jonas didn't answer instead he said: "How many locals
will you hire in developing what land you already have?"

"I want to use as much local help as possible. Working
on a project will give a man pride in what he does, and the
people are a lot less likely to be destructive or steal from
what they work to build."

"You'll find mountain people honest to the core."

"Most, but there are always some that are rogues,
mountain men or otherwise. My wife thinks I have bought
land that is inhabited by Neanderthals and Savages. She is
petrified for me to be here and she refuses to come herself.
If I can ever get her here, which isn't likely, I would like
for her to meet you and your wife, see this place."

"I would like to meet her," Jonas said, but he didn't
sound convincing to me.

"Is your baby a boy or girl?"

"Boy."

"My wife and I have two boys and a girl."

"That's a nice family," Jonas said. "How are you
feeling? Is your head still spinning?"

"The effects are wearing off some. As you can tell, the liquor plus whatever else you gave me has loosened my tongue. I don't usually talk this much. I believe that silence is a blessed thing and a profitable thing as well. The less a man tells about himself and his plans, the better deals he will be able to make."

"Silence is golden," said Jonas.

"According to my beliefs."

"Mine too," Jonas added. "Never let your left hand know what the right hand is doing."

"Is that a Bible quote?"

"Yes, somewhat."

I heard Drew whimper and went up stairs to check on him, wondering about what Jonas had just said. Jonas always seemed so open and honest. Why would he want to be secretive? Why would he need to be?

I went into the bedroom and stopped, horrified at what I saw. Drew was waking up. His face was squinting half way between sleep and awake. His eyes were flickering open and he would start kicking his legs and moving his hands any moment, and his movement would cause the rattlesnake lying on the foot of his crib to strike.

I screamed for Jonas as I grabbed the bedspread off the bed. I crumpled it up in my hands as I leaped to the crib. All I could think about was stopping that snake from striking my baby. The only way to do that was put a block between it and Drew. I hoped the bedspread and my hands would be enough for I couldn't climb in the crib to put myself between my precious son and the deadly snake.

I saw the glimpse of its strike as the bedspread went downward. I felt the huge snake's body beneath the spread and my hands as my fingers tightened on its coils. It moved, fighting to get away from my grip, but I wasn't about to let it go, let it get an inch closer my baby.

Its weight was surprising as I lifted it up over the crib rail. I saw a tail with the rattles come from under the material of the bedspread but I couldn't turn loose to grab that tail.

I was praying with every thing that was in me as I struggled with that snake. I didn't know what I was doing, what I should do. I just knew I couldn't let the snake hurt my baby.

Where was Jonas? What was taking him so long? I saw the tail again.

Get that tail, Dad seemed to say. *Fling it like a whip. Hit its head on the floor.*

But I couldn't turn loose of its body to grab the tail. In desperation I slammed the snake and spread onto the floor and grabbed for the tail. It was firm, ropy, as soft as velvet and as heavy as the largest wrought iron frying pan I had ever lifted. It was as heavy as a sack of cow feed, but I couldn't let its weight stop me.

Crack its head on the dresser, Dad said. *Addle it or break its backbone before it bites you.*

With all the determination and strength that came from overwhelming fear, I swung that snake. The spread remained over the snake not allowing its head to make firm contact with the wood of the dresser. The snake was slipping from my grasp. I dug my fingernails into its scales and gritted my teeth as though that could help me hold on.

This time the spread fell off as I twisted my body in a circle. The snake's head wasn't three inches off the floor, but its head struck the dresser leg on the sharp edge. I dug in my fingers with further determination and continued the momentum of the circle. Its head hit a second time.

Again, Dad was saying. *Again, again, again!*

"Jesus Christ!" Rupert's voice penetrated my mind as Jonas grabbed for me and the snake. His hands were over mine, trying to get the snake from my grip, but I couldn't turn loose.

"Let me have it," Jonas was saying. "Turn loose, Laine, and I'll finish it off."

I was afraid to let go, afraid if I did it would get back to my baby.

Jonas' hand was in front of mine now, gripping the snake as we struggled with it. His other hand shoved me backward, against Rupert. He caught me to keep me from knocking him over. The snake had slipped from my fingers, but Jonas had a firm hold on it. He whipped it just as Dad had been telling me to do. It popped just like a whip a split instant before its ugly V shaped head hit the floor. Jonas whipped it again and dropped it from his hand.

It moved, and I lunged for it, breaking Rupert's hold on me. Jonas grabbed me and stumbled backward.

"It's dead," he assured me, but I wasn't about to believe him. I wanted to pulverize its head until there was no chance of it biting Drew.

"Get the snake out of here," Jonas said to Rubert. "She's hysterical."

Rubert hesitated as he looked at the twitching snake. "You sure it's dead? Is it like a bee's stinger? Can it still poison you if you touch its mouth?"

"Use the broom in the corner," Jonas ordered, still holding onto me. "Get it away from Laine so I can turn her loose and get her calmed down.

"It was in Drew's crib. I thought it was going to bite him."

"In the baby's crib?" Jonas repeated my words with amazement as he looked at the snake then at the crib. "A rattlesnake on this mountain is unusual enough, but in the house and in a baby's crib? That is hard to believe."

"It was lying at the foot of the crib all curled up."

Rupert had the broom and was awkwardly sweeping the dead snake toward the door. "And people told me there were no rattlesnakes on these high mountains."

"I've never seen one," Jonas said again as he turned me loose and went to Drew. He put out his hand to keep me from picking Drew up. "Let me make sure he's not bit."

Drew saw Jonas leaning over him and kicked his legs, moved his little fists and gurgled, his sweet face smiling.

"He would be crying if he was bit," Jonas assured me. "It would feel like fire burning him."

Jonas pulled the thin blanket from Drew and looked him over, then gently stroked his dark hair from his forehead. I thought of my little brother, Joey, being stung to death by honeybees. A rattlesnake would be more deadly, and my precious baby had been within inches of that snake. What if I hadn't come up stairs when I did? What if I hadn't heard him whimper?

"If there's one snake, will there be another?" Rubert asked as he pushed the snake into the hall with the broom and closed the bedroom door to shut out its sight. "I've read they den in pairs."

I knew snakes denned in numbers. I reached for Drew and Jonas allowed me to pick him up. He seemed heavy and I sank down on the bed and held Drew as close to my body as I could get him. I was going to put him in the carrier Andy made and never let him out of my sight again. Rubert was right. There could be another snake hiding in the bedroom.

"I don't know much about snakes," Jonas said, "but I'll check this place from top to bottom."

"In the cellar too," I added, surprised that my voice was shaking. For a moment, I thought I was going to burst into crying, but I bit hard on my lip and buried my face against my baby's sweet head.

"Anything I can do?" Rupert asked but his voice held no conviction, only politeness.

"We've got it under control. You're free to go anytime you feel steady enough."

"I think fear scared me sober. Hearing your wife's screams and then seeing her swinging that snake. . ." He gave his head a shake and didn't say anymore.

☙

Jonas searched every inch of the house, from the inside of the dresser drawers to behind the canning jars down beneath the house in the damp cellar. I followed right behind him with Drew against my chest in Andy's carrier, my heart was still pumping hard and I couldn't ease the fear that was inside me. If that snake had bit Drew, I wouldn't have been able to save my baby any more than I had saved Joey. Drew was so little even Jonas wouldn't have been able to save him from the venom of a four foot rattle snake.

When we came up out of the cellar, the air had cooled with the coming of twilight, and the ground gave off a spicy aroma, a good scent that contented even when something bad had just happened.

"I want a look at that snake again," Jonas said.

I followed him onto the kitchen porch where he had hung it over the railing. Andy was there with the snake stretched out full length on the boards of the porch. He looked me straight in the eyes.

"You and Drew all right?"

"Yeah. We're okay."

"That city fellow stopped in Banners Elk."

"I see," Jonas said. "He was the last person I thought would be spreading gossip. I was wrong."

"Wished he hadn't," Andy said, and Jonas lifted his brows at that. Andy pointed at the pattern on the snake's back. "Never has been a Diamond Back Rattlesnake on this mountain, certainly not one of this size."

"I have heard of rattlesnakes on the mountain before," Jonas said.

"Timber rattlers, but not diamond backs." Andy and Jonas seemed to pass unspoken knowledge between each other.

I looked from the snake back to Andy as realization hit me. At first there was the numbness of pure shock, and then a blinding rage seeped over me.

"I'll kill them," I said.

"Calm down, Missy. Your gettin mad won't do anybody any good."

I didn't want to calm down. "They tried to kill my baby."

"Who's they?" Andy asked logically.

"Momma and Susie," I blurted out, thinking that Momma had blamed me for Joey dying when it wasn't my fault, and now she wanted my baby to die.

Andy shook his head. "Forgetting something aren't you?"

It hit me. Momma was deathly afraid of snakes. She would never get close a snake or let Susie close one.

"Hazel!" I said through clinched teeth.

"We don't know it for a fact," Andy said. "Can't accuse a person of something we don't know for certain. It could be anybody. It could even be an accident. Somebody might have dropped off a snake in the yard just to scare you a little. The snake could have been searching out a warm place to spend the night."

The warmest place was in the sunshine, not in my baby's crib. It was deliberate. I whirled around, headed for the kitchen door. Jonas caught me by the arm.

"Where are you going?"

"For the shotgun," I blurted out in my anger. Rafe had given me that gun for protection and now was the time to use it.

"Laine Jones! Don't show your ignorance." His fingers bit into my arm as he gave it a shake.

I jerked my arm free. "She tried to kill my baby," I hissed at Jonas. "And don't you ever grab me like that. Don't you ever!"

Surprise came to Jonas' face and I saw Andy grin.

"We can't just haul off and shoot somebody, even if they do deserve it," Andy said as though we were having a normal conversation. "No need to end up in jail for killing something lower down than that dead snake. Anybody that would put a poisonous snake near a baby . . ." His teeth clamped, the muscles in his jaws twitched. "Besides, that would be too easy on the vermin. Some folks deserve a long life so they can suffer justly for what they've done."

"She'll pay." I meant what I said.

"Yeap, but you shouldn't have to pay and neither should your baby. Drew don't need his mother in jail. Let me handle this while you take care of your little boy." Andy spat out the side of his mouth as a look of pure malevolence came over his face. "I didn't go through what I did when that baby was born to set back and let either of you be hurt."

He smiled, and that smile was worse than the undertone his voice carried and the malevolent expression on his face, but nothing compared to the look in his eyes.

"My God, Andy! We don't know what happened here. Don't you be as irrational as Laine."

I came in a hair of slapping my husband for saying that.

That night I placed Drew in bed with me and insisted on keeping the light on.

"There's not another snake in the house," Jonas said irritability. "I can't sleep with the light on and goodness knows I need some rest."

"Maybe I should take him into another room," I suggested.

"You're my wife. We'll sleep together," he said firmly.

I didn't bother mentioning to him that we hadn't slept together the two nights he stayed in Banners Elk.

"I want you to rest, Jonas."

"Then turn out the light. I made sure there's no other snake in the house."

"Please understand how afraid I am," I pleaded. Surely he knew I would rather be dead than have something happen to my baby. What if I hadn't checked on Drew the moment I did? If I had waited a minute longer, my baby son would be as dead as my little brother. I shivered as though an icy chill had taken possession of my body.

"Don't start pulling dramatics on me, Laine."

"What?"

"A snake crawled into the house, that's all it was. The snake is dead. There is no other snake. Turn off the light and act like a sane adult instead of a spoiled child."

"Jonas, stop quarreling at me. Just close your eyes and go to sleep," I told him firmly. His cruel words had hurt me to the core of my soul. "The light stays on or Drew and I will go to another room."

"It's useless to argue with a mule," he said and turned his back on the light and me.

I lay still and questioned my decision of marrying him. He had changed. He no longer stood beside me as he once did, backing me up when problems arose. Since our marriage, he had started condemning my ways. Now that I was his wife, he expected me to change into the woman he wanted his wife to be. One of those town-raised girls that filed their nails and rubbed lotion into soft hands; one that wore lace dresses and shaded her face with a hat; one that thought of nothing more than being an asset to their husbands and his career; a stepping stone enabling him to climb higher. I knew it as sure as I knew I was lying beside him. I just didn't know what to do about it. Perhaps there was some validity in the way Jonas was thinking and behaving. After all, I had married him to give my son his name. I owed him something for not marrying him for love alone. I had tried to change some for Rafe. I could do no less for Jonas. I owed him that.

"Jonas," I whispered.

"What now?"

"I'm sorry."

"Go to sleep, Laine."

Chapter 9

My mind would not stop seeing the snake curled up next to my baby. It replayed itself until I was desperate with fear and anger. I had to find out who did this cruel thing and see that it never happened again. There was one thing that kept me from taking immediate action to find and punish whoever tried to kill my baby and that was Drew. I had him with me every moment. I was afraid to take my eyes off him and could not go into a place that required my cunning and silence. Because I was doing nothing right now didn't mean I would continue to do nothing, I assured myself. I would bide my time until the right opportunity presented itself. Instinct told me one thing: retaliation was best when served cold.

Every single day I went through the entire house as though I was obsessed with cleaning, but I was hunting for snakes as though my baby's life depended on it.

I carried Drew in the papoose Andy had made, either on my stomach or on my back. If I put him in his crib, I stayed in the room with him, my eyes searching for a silent movement.

Jonas had adjusted to sleeping with the light on, at least he didn't quarrel at me for leaving it on, but I was getting low on lamp oil and could not bring myself to ask Jonas to buy some in Banners Elk. If I did, it would open up the door for him to tell me how obsessed I was and how I needed to become rational instead of thinking a fine woman like Hazel Farrow was trying to kill my baby. How could Jonas be so blinded by that woman? Why was he taking her part against me?

One morning, when Jonas started to leave, he looked at Drew sleeping on my back, looked me in the eyes and said: "I'll have to be at the hospital late tonight. Don't expect me to come back tonight."

"Is there more sickness going around?" I reminded myself that Jonas had a home in Banners Elk as well as a business. This wasn't his only home, my bed his only bed.

"Always," he answered.

He gave me a light kiss, one without promise or passion. I watched him turn away, get on his horse, and take the short way through the woods. It seemed I was destined to watch my husbands ride away from me. A realization hit me that I must not be a very nice person. Could Momma have been right about me? Was I not nice even as a child? Did I lack something, have too much something?

I remembered the hatred for me shining from Momma's eyes as she watched me doing things for her. It seemed the more I did to help her, the more hatred fill her eyes. But I didn't want to think about Momma. She put a chill up my spine and reminded me of the snake and Hazel. I tried to put Momma from my mind, told myself that part of my life was past and I would never have to deal with it again. The question came to me, just how did one get rid of the plague? Didn't it lay dormant waiting for the right time to come?

I turned my mind from Momma but not from Hazel. I needed lamp oil. What if I left the house? What would stop Hazel from putting more snakes inside? I could put sticks in the windows and lock the doors, but that wouldn't stop her from turning them loose outside. She could put them in the yard where they could find an opening into the warm dry house, or she could put them in barn where they might strike at me and hit Drew while he was on my back.

I needed a good dog. Dogs killed snakes. Dogs barked when someone was slipping around. Dogs don't get on horses and ride away when I needed them near. I felt like crying without much provocation, and that made me mad at myself. "Laine Elder does not cry," I said out loud, *much*, I added silently.

Drew squirmed against my back and began his hungry whimper. I slid him from my back, unbuttoned my dress front, and put him to my breast. His little head turned and his soft mouth nuzzled against me. I marveled at what a perfect little person he was, the smoothness of his cheeks, and the tiny nose and eyes. It was amazing how a body so tiny could contain a whole person.

He sucked as though he would never get full. I was thankful that my breasts were gorged with milk. They ached for Drew to drink more often than he was hungry. My body and Mother Nature were working together to make my baby grow into a strong, healthy man. I wondered if he would be as handsome as Rafe had been, or maybe he would be the spitting image of my Dad. I tried to picture Dad as a young man.

I watched Drew's hand lift and rest on my breast as he sucked. The tiny hand was a miniature of Rafe's, square and blocky. Dad's hand was longer and more slender than Rafe's had been, so was Jonas's. I wished I could stop looking for other people in my little son, but I suppose all mothers looked for something familiar in their child.

I lifted him to my shoulder while he kicked his objection from having his meal interrupted and patted his back until he burped and then put him to my other breast.

What kind of person did it take to put a poisonous snake near such a precious thing as a baby?

Drew was full, diapered, and sleeping on my back when I entered the shade of the woods on my way to Andy Harmon's place. I knew about where Andy lived and the sound of hammering led me along like the ringing of a bell. I felt a little ill at ease toting my jug with coins for lamp oil tied in a rag, but I was desperate for oil and I wasn't about to ask Jonas to get it, even if I had to saddle one of Rafe's horses and ride to town myself.

Andy's house was small and gray with age and its tin roof was deep orange with rust. Neither the house nor roof had ever known paint or fancy care. To me it looked lonely as though it was begging for something it never had and never would have. It went beyond paint. It was the need of family, the sound of laughter inside barren walls.

The shop where the hammering came from was a different matter. It was painted a deep, dark burgundy and had fancy white trim around the windows and large double doors. Lattice work halfway enclosed the narrow porch with roses growing along the lattice. Several coffee cans sat on the porch steps overflowing with red blooming geraniums.

My feet slowed down as I went up the steps. I stood at the open double doors and hesitated to cross the threshold into Andy's private domain. His back was bent, gray head bowed as he hammered on the pine coffin. He appeared old and withered in the shadows, a frazzled gray haired man making the final preparations of life – a final resting place through-out eternity.

He saw my shadow cast across the floor and slowly turned his head.

"Missy?" he said in surprise. "What's wrong?"

"Nothing really," I tried to smile. "I was just hoping you could do me a favor, sometime."

He straightened and laid his hammer down. "Come on in here. Tell me what it is."

I went inside feeling even more embarrassed at my foolishness. I should have asked Jonas to get oil instead of being so stubborn.

Andy looked at the oil jug I carried in my hand and waited. I said nothing.

"You need to borrow some kerosene?"

I nodded. "I was wondering if you'd be going into town any time soon. If you are, I though you might get me a jug full of lamp oil."

"I can do that. Are you in a hurry for it?"

"Kinda."

"Lamp oil," he repeated as he observed my face. "Good ole kerosene. From rheumatism to lighting up the darkness to building a fire, it's good stuff and easy to run out of."

I could tell he wanted to ask me why Jonas wasn't bringing some home. Instead of asking he said, "There's a chair over yonder by the wall. Take a load off your feet. Our little man must get heavy after you've carried him for a while."

"Oh, no. He doesn't ever get heavy, and I don't have time to sit. I want to can turnip greens and squash today." I sat the jar down along with the money tied in the rag. "If there's not enough money, let me know and I will give you more."

"How close are you to being out?"

"I might have enough for tonight if I'm careful."

"You leave the light burning during the night?"

I nodded.

"All night?"

I nodded again, and understanding came to his face.

"You're afraid of another snake, aren't you?"

"Yes," I admitted.

"Jonas fuss at you for leaving the light burning?"

Again I nodded.

"Don't blame you for leaving it on. Let me give you a pint, just in case. I'd give you the whole gallon now, but I've not got that much."

"I'd appreciate it."

"Make yourself at home while I go get some."

I watched him leave the shop, his back still bent as though he had been slumped over too long and it would take a while to come straight. Unlike Jonas, he seemed to understand my fear and not tell me I was being silly.

He wasn't gone long and his back was straighter by the time he returned. He had the jar tied up in a flour sack.

"You can carry it easer in the sack," he told me. "Would you like to come to the house for a spell, have a drink of something cool before you go back?"

"No thanks, like I said, I'm in a hurry."

"Don't like to be away long?"

I didn't answer and he frowned.

"That snake sure enough tore your nerves up, didn't it?"

"It was in the crib with Drew. I could have lost my baby." I felt my chin tremble and bit my teeth together to make it stop.

"Now don't you go getting too upset, Missy. Just keep your eyes peeled and don't let our baby out of your sight." Andy hesitated then added. "A grown man can survive a rattlesnake bite, not a child, and perhaps not a little lady."

"I'll never forgive her," I managed to say.

"Now, we don't know how that snake got there. No use jumping to conclusions. Actually, it would be for the best if someone did put it in the house, that way we know there hain't no more snakes around to multiply."

His words didn't sooth my fear any. Either snakes were breeding near my house or someone was trying to kill my baby.

"What am I going to do?" I asked, trying to keep my voice from shaking.

"Don't you worry over much. Old Andy will take care of things."

"How?"

"First off, I've found you a good dog if you'll have it."

"Yes," I said quickly. A dog was just what I'd been wanting.

"Mars Pytte has a long-haired mixed shepherd he wants to get rid of. He said it dearly loved killin snakes and his wife's cats. Has her down to one old tom cat. His wife told him the dog left or she did. He said he'd rather his wife go, but you know how it is."

"When can I have him?"

"As soon as I go into town next."

"When's that?"

"Soon."

I left Andy's place feeling worse instead of better. Him telling me *soon* reminded me of when Dad would answer "soon" when I asked him questions. Soon never came and I suspected that it never would, but that wasn't why I was feeling bad. There were a lot more reasons than one for that.

Something was bothering Jonas and I thought I knew what it was. Having married Jonas to give my baby a name was wrong of me and I knew it hurt Jonas, but it wasn't the case anymore. I would marry Jonas today just to be his wife and planned on telling him that very thing when he came back home. But then, Jonas was home. He had a home in Banners Elk and he was going to spend another night there. I wondered where Francis Dewhitte would be staying. I refused to let myself think she was Jonas' Junie, but there was a dread gnawing at me and no matter how foolish I told myself I was being, I knew what could happen.

Another thing that bothered me was that I couldn't get enough done in a day's time. Things had piled up on me and I couldn't get them unpiled. The animals needed my care, the land, the garden, the canning. I wanted to earn money like I used to do for Momma, but I just couldn't seem to get it together.

I had never admitted this to anyone, but the darkness of night had started bothering me. I didn't want to go outside after dark. It was as though the panther's eyes were watching me; the big cat ready to leap on me and tear me apart. At times my scars hurt as though they were freshly ripped open.

Having Abe spend the night in the house had helped with my fear. After all, it was him and his dogs that finished killing the panther and kept the barn from burning down. Now he was gone and may have had something to do with putting the snake in my baby's crib, even if I found such a thing hard to believe. Abe had been good to have around until he started getting greedy, or was it that his mother got greedy for him?

Tonight I would have no one to ease my fears.

I had nothing but this stupid fear of mine to keep me company. There wasn't anything I knew to do except to buck-up and get tougher. I had a precious baby, a beautiful home, and a husband I had fallen in love with. Why should I feel depressed?

I was ashamed of myself for feeling down when life was so good to me. I was just a sorry, ungrateful person.

I busied myself with thinking good thoughts in order to lift my spirit. Summer time is wonderful on Beech Mountain, especially when walking through the woods. The earth is aromatic with spicy smells of ginger, galax, ferns, dog bane, and dozens of other herbs. Tree leaves move gentle with the continuous breeze that lifts up from the valley below. It's like walking up a mountain until you reach heaven. I lived in heaven so why couldn't I be singing and joyous? No wonder Jonas wanted to stay away from me.

These were my thoughts as I came out of the woods into my garden near the barn. I stopped before the clearing to watch the house in case someone might be sneaking around. No one was sneaking around. He was walking about as bold as could be.

I would have recognized Rupert Smith even without his shiny car parked near the front door. I wondered if he thought Jonas was here instead of in Banners Elk.

My first reaction was to hide in the woods until he was gone, but he might go back to town and tell Jonas I was nowhere to be seen. Then I would have to admit to begging lamp oil from Andy. Jonas wouldn't like that.

I hid my oil near a tree trunk and walked out of the woods, crossed the road, and met Rupert in the yard. He was near the front porch gazing off in the distance, looking at the points and roll of mountains.

He startled when he saw me.

"Laine," he said. "I didn't hear your approach."

"Jonas is in Banners Elk," I told him.

"I know, but I didn't come to see Jonas."

I either looked puzzled or surprised for he grinned and the grin lit up his face until it was strangely handsome.

"Actually, I came to see you."

"Me?" I felt uneasy, like I needed to return to the woods and hide. I didn't know what to say to a rich man.

"I brought you something."

I wanted nothing from this man. Besides what could he bring me that I would want? He turned his back and strode to the car, opened the back door and a black and tan puppy tumbled out.

"Oh, my," I mumbled as I gazed at the precious puppy. I wanted him instantly, loved the intelligent shine in his eyes as he looked up at me and wagged his tail a bit uncertain.

"A beautiful young woman living far away from civilization requires a good guard dog. This German Shepard will be perfect for you, and it can grow up with your son. A boy should always have ownership of a dog."

He didn't mention the snake and I remember how afraid of it he was, even after it was dead.

"Oh, yes," I mumbled as I squatted down. The pup, seeing my welcome, hurried to me and licked me in the face. I almost cried.

"I always wanted a dog when I was a youth, but a city boy...." He didn't continue.

"Thank you," I said as I buried my face in the pup's neck to keep him from seeing my attempt not to shed tears.

"You're welcome," he said with great warmth in his tone. He turned and gazed toward the mountains again, giving me time to contain myself. I was embarrassed. I never used to be this emotional.

I swallowed hard. "Does he have a name?"

"Not yet. I though you should bestow this regal beast with such. He is a credit to his heritage, worth a king's ransom."

"Ransom," I said. "I'll name him King's Ransom."

Again, Rupert grinned and I thought how that grin improved everything about him. "I took the liberty of acquiring two bags of puppy chow. I've been told that a German Shepard grows so fast that he needs more calcium than some other breeds. I special ordered it. If you don't mind, in a couple of weeks, I'll bring two more bags."

"I'll pay you for them," I said quickly. "And him."

"Please don't suggest such a thing. Being I never had a dog, I would consider it an honor if you allow me to watch him grow. Perhaps I could drive by on occasion."

"Maybe you should keep him," I suggested. That thought tore at my soul. I wanted this pup.

He laughed. "My wife would divorce me. Besides, I travel too much to own a pet of any kind. I could only keep a goldfish if I turned it loose in a pond." His face shadowed. "I envy your husband," he admitted. "I envy your son."

I didn't know what to say as I stood up, the pup leaning against my legs, so I said, "Thank you."

He didn't respond to my thanks. Instead, he looked over my land, outbuildings, and home as though he had never seen such.

"This place looks like a home," he said. "A well loved home. Am I correct in recalling Jonas saying he hasn't owned this place long? He didn't inherit it from his parents or grandparents?"

It must have been his kindness in giving me Ransom that loosened my tongue and made me want to be truthful with him.

"It belongs to me," I said. "I inherited it from my first husband."

His eyes widened in surprise as he gazed at my face. "Your first husband? You're only a child."

"He was killed and I'm not a child." I looked down at the pup, not wanting to make eye contact with Rupert.

"I see," said Rupert.

That night I poured Andy's oil into my lamp and turned the wick down low, but not so low I couldn't see in the corners of the bedroom. I put Drew in bed with me, but refused to let Ransom join us although he wanted to. The pup lay down by the bed, his eyes watching me. Several times during the night he got up and paced the room, his nose sniffing the air.

I hoped he didn't have to relieve himself. I wasn't going to let him outside to do it if he did. Many things could kill a pup, or something could run in an opened door. He always seemed satisfied to come back and lay down beside the bed.

His presence made me feel safer, even though I knew a pup couldn't protect himself much less Drew or me. Rafe's loaded shotgun leaning near my bed did make me feel safer. I wouldn't hesitate to shoot anyone or anything if the need arose. I never intended to stick a pitchfork into a panther again, not when I had Rafe's gun.

I never intended to go into such a deep sleep. I usually slept so light I heard Drew's waking movements before he ever had a chance to cry. This time it was his cry of hunger that woke me. I came awake with a scared trembling shooting through my body as I grabbed for Drew. Relief was quick to hit me when I saw nothing was wrong with my baby. Still, my reaction left me feeling weak as I lifted Drew and unbuttoned the front of my gown.

The pup had risen and was watching me and Drew with bright intelligent eyes. After a moment, he thumped his tail on the floor and then lay back down as though all was well.

It was then I heard it, the scream of the panther just outside my window. I screamed too and the pup came straight up barking with fear and rage, but he didn't go toward the window. Sense came to me and I yanked Drew from my breast and stuck him under the cover, hoping that would protect him, and grabbed the shotgun. I had heard stories about panther coming down chimneys or through windows to eat babies. I took aim at the window expecting to see the panther crash through the glass.

It screamed again and relief flooded me. I laughed out-loud, a sound not of humor but of relief. It was a screech owl. Dad used to claim the sudden scream of a screech owl could raise the dead. It had raised every hair on my body. The light from the window had attracted moths and the bird came to feed on them. It took me a few moments to lower the gun. It was my security, that cold piece of medal making the weak even with the strong; the nonviolent even with the violent.

Slowly, I put the gun back against the wall, my hands shaking as I untangled the whimpering Drew from the covers. I placed him over my shoulder and patted his back with a shaky hand before I finished feeding him. I hoped it was not true, the oldwives tale that milk from an upset mother would colic a baby.

Damn my cowardice! Why did I have to be afraid of everything when I used to be afraid of nothing? What had changed about me?

I finished feeding Drew, looked down on his perfect, sleeping face. I never knew it was possible to love so much. I suddenly had an image of Bosie and her great sadness at losing two babies. I longed to ease her pain.

I awoke the next morning to a beautiful, cool morning. Part of the cool came for the soaked diaper my baby was wearing. I had put an oilcloth under the sheet so the moisture would not soak into the mattress, and I always put two diapers plus an extra thickness of blankets underneath Drew so Jonas would not notice the pee and complain. Last night I had not bothered. Today I would have to wash and air the bedding before Jonas came home.

I changed and fed Drew before I put him in the carrier and took Ransom outside. I had the work to do up, sheets and baby things to wash, and canning beans to get done.

It was evening and I was sitting on the porch snapping green beans when Andy came walking up leading a shaggy looking dog in one hand and carrying a jug of lamp oil in the other.

"Missy," he greeted as he looked at the pup lying by my feet. "What you got there?"

"A puppy." I needlessly answered.

"Humm. Reckon you don't need Bruiser then."

"Yes I do," I said quickly. "It'll be next year before this pup will kill a snake. That dog will kill snakes now won't he?"

"Mars Pytte said so, and I've never known him to tell an outright lie."

"I want him then." I reached out my hand and Bruiser stretched his long nose and sniffed. The pup stood up looking at Bruiser with a mixture of distrust and longing. Bruiser wagged his tail.

"Two dogs?"

"Nothing wrong with two dogs," I told Andy. "They can help each other kill snakes and panthers."

Andy grinned. "Hain't heard nothing about pant'ers hanging around these parts lately. Must know about you and your pitchfork."

I didn't think that was funny. "I never want to see another panther."

"I can see how that is." Andy looked at the house for a moment as though he might be checking for ghosts, and then sat down on the steps. "If I was you, I'd keep Bruiser tied for a few days until he becomes custom to the place. If not, he might take a notion to go back to Mars' place and kill that last tom cat."

"I'll keep him tied." I said. "Want a cold drink of water?"

"Nope. Just came from home."

"Been to town today?"

"Yeah. Started out before good light. Missed traveling during the head of noon."

I knew Andy and his cronies liked to meet early, set around and chaw the fat before they had dinner in Banners Elk. Jonas commented once that they were like a bunch of mischievous boys that had grown into very old mischievous boys.

"Was there enough money to pay for the lamp oil? It might of gone up from what Eula charged."

"It was right down to the last copper." Andy glanced at Drew sleeping contentedly on my back. "He must sleep a lot."

"He wakes up and plays some, but he loves to sleep in this carrier you made him. He's an awful good baby, but he can put up a fuss when he gets mad."

"Soon he'll be too big for the carrier."

"Not for a while, yet."

"You don't mind staying here without Jonas?" he asked suddenly.

"I've stayed here alone a lot." I admitted. "I prefer Jonas was here, especially at night."

"I saw him today."

"Jonas?"

"Yeah. He came by the store in hopes he would catch me. Said he wouldn't get home tonight." His sharp eyes took in my reaction. "Being a doctor takes up most part of a man's life."

"It certainly seems too."

"Takes a special kind of a woman to be married to a doctor. One that's independent and can take care of herself while her husband takes care of others."

"Rafe broke me into that." I said to cover up the hurt I was feeling at Jonas not coming home to me. People had to think something bad was wrong when a man wouldn't travel a little ways in order to sleep with his new bride.

"Rafford Johnson had his ways; ways that were nothing like the Doc's are."

"So I've noticed."

Andy seemed to consider saying something else, then pooched out his lips, nodded and said, "Where did you get that pup? Looks like a pure-bred."

"Rupert Smith brought it by yesterday."

"Charge you for it?"

"Gave it to me."

"Humm. Reckon rich men can afford to be generous ever now and again."

"Do you know him?"

"Nope, can't say as I do."

"Do the men at the store talk about him?"

Andy grinned like I was being a gossip. "On occasion."

"What do they say? What kind of man is he?"

"About like the normal rich man. Likes his own way. Can have anything he wants."

"Have you met his wife?"

"Nope. Don't think she is around."

"He said she was afraid of the place and the people."

"Some folks or ignorant or plain blind," Andy said. "Ought to know nobody in this world is as good as plain old mountain folks."

"What's he doing to that land he bought?" I asked.

Andy shook his head as though he was about to tell me something unpleasant. "Tearing it all to creation, I hear. He's gouged roads out of rock cliffs, cut down trees as old as Adam's dog, trees that took God a mighty long time to grow. He's scaring out big chunks of land so he can build houses touching each other. Folks aren't meant to live on top of each other. No privacy. It causes problems."

My snapping of beans slowed and I looked closer at Andy. "You don't approve of what he's doing, do you?"

"Can't say that I do. Folks from off come to these mountains and change things. They have a way of showing us poor folks just how poor we are. Take that Linville bunch. Came in here and built fancy houses, built themselves a rich community right in the middle of people that was barely getting by. It's one thing when everybody suffers alike, but it tears folks up to see what they don't have."

I thought about Mr. Holloway and this house. "Did the folks like Mr. Holloway?"

"For most part once they got to know him. Naturally, there were some that hated the air he breathed just because he had more than them. That's human nature, Missy. Some folks just got to hate something and somebody. The less they have, the more they can hate."

"Like Hazel Farrow hates me?" I had to ask.

"Could be."

Chapter 10

Jonas had stayed in Banners Elk three nights in a row when Rupert showed up. He brought two more bags of dog food, a collar and leash, a tube of wormer, plus a dog bed.

"Brought you a few things," he said, coming toward me, smiling.

"You shouldn't have." Was all I could think of saying as I looked down on the stuff he had placed on the porch.

"And why shouldn't I when I get so much pleasure in doing so?"

"It costs."

He kind of laughed. "That is the only thing I have in abundance, money."

"That's enough."

The brightness left his smile. "Not always. Believe it or not, but there are things money can't buy."

"Not many things," I said.

"Can money buy your land?" He was fast to ask.

"There are some things money can't buy," I repeated and he laughed as he looked from Ransom to Bruiser tied to the porch post. "Where did *that* come from?"

"Mars Pytte. He gave him up because he killed cats."

"Why did you take him?"

"He kills snakes, too."

"Does he get along with King's Ransom?"

"Like a father and son." I assured him.

"Is that good or bad."

"Good."

"Then I'll have to bring more dog food."

"I can bake extra cornbread."

"Sounds delicious, but dogs need fortified food."

I didn't argue or ask what fortified meant. I'd never known anyone that thought dogs needed special food. I suppose rich men had rich ideas.

"What are you doing right now?"

"Talking to you," I told him and grinned.

"Smarty. Am I stopping something of immense importance from occurring?"

"I was on my way to pick another bushel of beans."

"Beans? A bushel?"

"To can."

"Toucan, like in bird?"

"What?"

"Never mind. The beans can wait. Get in the car."

I stood there looking at him, sure I had heard him wrong.

"I'd like to drive you to Banners Elk, show you around a bit."

At first, I was appalled at the idea. Then the notion began to grow on me. I could see Jonas and his house and office during the light of day. I could check out the store Andy talked about and find a place to sell produce.

"How long will it take to get there in that? How long before we get back?"

"Half an hour or so to drive and you'll be there only until you want to return home."

"Okay," I said feeling daring. "I'll have to put Ransom inside and lock the doors."

"Snap to it, Rapunzel."

"What?"

"Hurry," he smiled at me when he said that.

I thought I heard him say something about my letting down my hair as I ran toward the house, but I didn't want to take time to comb it again as I gathered the things Drew would need. Rupert Smith would have to get used to a person that didn't primp-up when going into town for I wasn't the primping kind.

I took Drew out of the carrier and crammed him extra clothes and several diapers into it. Drew was sure to need diapered and I might want to carry him in the carrier if I had to walk much.

Rupert was standing at the passenger door waiting for me. He opened it, and then closed it after I got in. I concluded that rich city men thought women were helpless. I could open and close a door as good as he could, but I saw no need in telling him.

I felt the vibration of the vehicle as he cranked up the engine before he got inside. A lightness came to my chest as he started the vehicle moving forward. I felt like a child taking a ride on a horse for her very first time. I was excited and a little afraid, although fear wasn't the exact word for what I was feeling. It was the strangeness of something that I had never done before.

"What do you call this thing?" I asked.

"Actually it's a model T Ford, a town car to be exact. Henry Ford started making the town car in 1915. Ford introduced the model T in October of 1908." He glanced at me and then back at the road. "A lot of people refer to it as a Tin Lizzie or a Flivver."

Rupert looked from the rough wagon road at me sitting there clutching Drew. "Don't look so apprehensive."

That was the right word. I was apprehensive and for more reasons than one. I was riding in one of those motorized vehicles, a shining car belonging to an almost stranger – a rich important one at that. I was going to see things I had never seen before, and I was imagining Jonas's surprise when I arrived at his place. If he asked me to spend the night, I would have to tell him no. I had to do up the evening work. I hoped he would insist I stay in Banners Elk with him until he closed and then we could ride his horses back together.

I recalled riding beside him on our wedding night. It was a miserable time for both of us, but he was gentle and considerate. This time would be better. It would be romantic riding in the moonlight, and once we got home … well, I could show him how much I had missed him and make him want to come home every night from now on.

"Cat got your tongue?"

"I'm sorry. I was thinking about the ride."

"Understandable," Rupert said, and started humming a tune. He had a good voice for a rich city man accustomed to having everything.

The closer we got to Banners Elk the better the road was, and the car was definitely faster than riding in a wagon or riding on horse back. I finally figured out that the car was rolling at one constant speed, not as fast as a horse could run full gallop, but longer than a horse could run without killing it. The trip was not as rough and bumpy as riding in a wagon, but it wasn't as gentle as a smooth gaited riding horse.

"On a good road this thing can travel, not as fast as a train mind you, but it can go thirty or forty miles an hour."

"Really," I mumbled. I didn't tell him I had never rode in a train or had any idea what thirty or forty miles an hour meant.

"In my development I want to put in smooth paved roads where riding will be like sitting in an easy chair."

"Paved roads?" I thought of the bumpiness of cobble stones.

"Small gravel and tar compressed together. Similar to what large cities have. If we have time, I would like to show you my development and what I have in mind, but I suppose it would be more beneficial to you to see it when it is nearly finished."

"The men have to work on our roads," I said from lack of anything else to say. "Each man has to spend so much time doing road work. They use a sledge hammer to bust up big rocks to fill chug holes and washed out places with, or shovel ditches so water won't run in the roads and wash them away."

"I know. Good roads are our future. Someday when traveling is made easier and faster, the world will be our backdoor."

"Where did you grow up?" I asked. I didn't care much about the rest of the world being our back door, which I didn't believe. Living was hard enough right here without the world intervening.

"From the mid-west. In the Chicago area. I got my start in building government funded houses for the poor."

"You didn't inherit your money, then."

"Not a dime. I can't claim to be one of the cradle rich blue bloods. I came up poor from an impoverished neighborhood."

I looked him over from his head to the toes of his shoes. He looked clean and pressed, better dressed than most. I couldn't conceive how a person could start from nothing and work their way into a riches.

"How did you do it? Make money I mean?" I finally asked.

"By being lean and mean and determined. I made sure ever thing I did counted for something and toward something. I had a goal in sight and I worked to achieve that goal. I didn't allow anyone to detour me and most important – I repeat – most important I didn't let one person take away from me what I had earned, nor did I take what I didn't earn. I don't give to charity. I expect every individual to earn what they receive."

"You gave me a dog and dog food," I reminded him.

"Yes, but that's not charity, besides, I expect something in return."

I cringed.

"I expect to occasionally visit a big white house that is a home and a piece of land that is a working farm. I expect to get tiny glimpses of a life I never had and always longed for. To me a dog and dog food are a small price when I can reach out and touch my dream, walk on land that is untarnished and watch a determined girl learn and grow into womanhood."

I didn't know what to say, and I didn't entirely believe him for a rich man could have a white house and farm if he wanted, and I wasn't growing into anything. I figured he was trying to butter me up so I would sell him my land. Well, let him have at it for I wasn't one to be buttered up.

"Don't look at me in that way," he said.

"What way?"

"Like you don't believe me."

"You can build any type of place you want," I told him.

"I was down at the country store when one of the men said something I found quite correct. He said, 'You can lead a horse to water but you can't make her drink it.' I can build any house I want but I can't make my wife move herself or my children in it. I can't force her to make it a home."

I was saved from more talk by him driving in front of a big, weathered building with a wide front porch. A couple of horses and wagons were there. The horses laid back their ears and side-stepped until he turned the car off.

"We have arrived at the famous country store," he said. "The place where more knowledge is shared and more deals are made than in a business office in the middle of downtown Chicago. Do you want to go inside?"

"Yes. I want to see if they'll buy my produce."

"What kind of produce?"

"Milk, eggs, butter, molasses, chickens and pigs, and eventually vegetables."

"You have it to sell?"

"I will have."

He kind of grinned and said no more as he got out of the car.

I took his grin to be mockery of my wanting to earn a few coppers at what some called *bread & butter* money. I tried not to feel put-down as I carried Drew into the store with Rupert following behind me.

Several men were sitting around a checker board spread out on top of a pickle barrel. Talk stopped. Checker playing stopped as every face turned toward Rupert and me. Eye brows lifted. Mouths opened or tightened.

"Good afternoon," Rupert greeted them. "I assume you know Mrs. Jones, our good doctor's wife."

Heads nodded.

"Day to you, Mrs. Jones," several of them said in unison.

"Good day," I returned.

"What brings you into town?" One bold man that I didn't know asked, but then I didn't know any of them.

"Want to see about selling produce. Who owns this place?"

"I do," said the bold man.

"Do you buy produce?"

"What kind?"

I told him what I planned to raise.

"I don't have much of a market for that kind of stuff. Folks around here barter with it all the time. Keeps me over supplied."

"What do you buy?" I asked, taking in his stocky, well-fed look. His store was bigger than Eula's but not nearly as clean.

"When I get the time, I'll write you out a list. You can read can't you?"

"When I get the time, I'll bring you samples of my produce," I added in the same tone he spoke to me in. "You do eat, don't you?"

The men around the checker board laughed. "Best not rile her, Hack," one of the men said jokingly.

"You saw that pant'er after she put the pitch fork through it," another one added and they all laughed. "No offence ma'am." The man added. "We've heard a lot about you from Andy Harmon. He says you're one fine woman."

I didn't like those words any better than I did their joking.

"Thank you," I said, turned and went out the door with my head held high.

"They were rather rude," Rupert commented after we got in the car. "I wonder why?"

I thought of Hazel and wondered if she had been spreading some kind of gossip about me, but I said nothing to Rupert.

"Where next?" he asked.

I wanted to see Jonas, to feel his love and assurance. "Take me to Jonas," I told him, and thought I saw disappointment on his face.

"Wouldn't you rather drive around town first? I can show you the hospital Edgar Tufts built. He's the missionary that put together the college and the Grandfather Home for Children. Tufts would convince those with money to invest in helping the poor mountain people less fortunate than them. According to what I've gleaned, a woman named Helen Hartley Jenkins donated him over a thousand dollars, half the money needed to build a hospital that would carry her dead sister's name, Grace Hartley Stokes. And so the hospital your husband works in.

I can also show you the Methodist, Baptist, and Holy
Roller churches. There's a restaurant and a boarding house
here too. Not to mention a similar endeavor in Crossnore
that a woman is trying to get started. I think her name is
Sloup. You happen to live on an isolated mountain top but
you're not in the ice age. Progress is taking place. Have
you ever heard of Linville and Pineola, or the train called
Tweetsie that runs to Johnson City? I also hear rumor that a
new doctor is coming to Avery County. His name is Tate, I
believe.

Tuffs, Tate, why had Jonas not told me about them? I
had read about the train and Johnson City in Boise's diary.
Jonas had mentioned the Children's Home were he had put
the little Munson girl. Those things weren't what triggered
my mind with interest. What I wanted most was to see the
snake handling church and I wanted to see where Hazel
Farrow lived.

"Is the Holy Roller church where they handle snakes?"
I asked.

"According to local rumor it is. I have no personal
experience in such behavior."

"I'd like to see that place," I admitted as I thought of
Momma and Susie running from that church.

"Snake handling curiosity always beats out progress,"
he said.

"What?"

"Twinst heaven and hell, hell is more entertaining."

"What are you talking about?" I asked.

"Human nature. Snakes hold a deadly fascination for
certain types of individuals. I hate the things myself."

"Me too," I agreed and shivered.

The church was a small one-room place with white
siding and a chimney coming through the center of the
roof. I knew what the inside of the building and what the
potbellied stove would look like both in summer and when

it glowed red with fire in the winter. I needed not to go inside. Its outside looked as harmless and familiar as most churches I'd seen.

I recalled Andy's description of the snake handling service he had attended and smiled to myself. I wondered if Momma took to her bed after that, and how long Susie had to wait on her. Were she and Abe still courting, or had Momma refused to allow Susie to see him again?

"What do you think of it?" Rupert asked.

"Looks harmless," I answered.

"So does a live wire with thousands of volts of electricity running through it."

"What?"

"Never mind. Do you want to go inside?"

"No. Do you know where Hazel Farrow lives?"

"Yes. I tried to familiarize myself with this area and its inhabitants."

"You did?"

"Naturally. It's a wise person who knows what lies beneath the surface before he dives into the water."

The way he said that made me uneasy.

The Farrow place reminded me of where Nate and Junie Patrick had lived, except the Farrow's was about twice the size. There was a barn with a milk cow standing in its shade, a garden, and a patch of corn next to a hay meadow that had been recently mowed and the hay stacked. I recalled standing on the Pinnacle with Abe pointing out the shine of the tin roof way down here in the valley. I turned and looked back at the mountain and the protrusion of rocks that I assumed was the Pinnacle.

"Mr. Farrow is dead, so I hear," said Rupert.

I tried to think back to a time when Abe mentioned his father, but I couldn't. He was always talking about his mother.

"Abe was a good employee for a while," I said out loud. "I'd grown rather fond of him."

"He changed?"

I felt Rupert's eyes watching me, as though he wanted to know what was running beneath my surface.

"Yes," I finally said.

"Why did he change?"

I shrugged, but that didn't satisfy him.

"Let me guess. He changed after you married Jonas?"

"He used to work for Jonas at the office until Jonas made him help me."

"I see," he said and I thought he probably did see way too much.

"Take me to Jonas," I told him.

He turned the car around and headed back to Banners Elk. I thought I saw a window curtain move but I couldn't be sure. It didn't matter. They would never guess I was riding in this fancy automobile looking at their place. I suddenly had the strangest longing to have Rupert Smith drive me by Dad's place. I'd like to stand beside Dad's grave, see if the house and land had run-down with only Momma and Susie there. I didn't think neither Momma nor Susie would do much work around the place. They never had.

"Are you in a hurry?" I asked him.

"What do you have in mind?"

"A trip, but it may be too far."

"How far is it?"

"I don't rightly know."

"Where is it?"

"In Ashe County."

"We're in Avery County and Watauga County is between here and Ashe."

"Oh. It's probably too far then."

"It would require most of a day regardless of the final destination. I doubt we could get there and back before dark, besides I have to carry more fuel with me than I have right now. Fuel to power this thing isn't waiting on every corner."

"It's out of the question then."

"Why do you want to go?"

"It's where I was raised."

"You want to visit your folks?"

"No. I don't want to visit anyone. I wanted to see the land where I grew up as a young child."

He laughed. "And your youth was eons in the past."

"What?"

"You spoke of being young as though it was many years ago."

I didn't like him talking as though I were still a child. "I'm old beyond my years," I told him with as much dignity as I could manage.

He looked at my face. "How old are you, in actual years, not in maturity."

I hesitated and considered lying to him, but what was the use. "I'm seventeen."

"At seventeen you have been married twice and have a son. Indeed you are old beyond your years."

"How old are you?" I though it a fair question.

"Thirty-seven."

Twenty years older than me. He was a man before I was even born. He could have been my father. "You don't look that old," I told him truthfully.

"As you pointed out, there are many ways in which to judge a person's age."

Chapter 11

Rupert Smith stopped his vehicle near Jonas's place. The house was neat in appearance almost to the point of bareness. I noticed right away that the wooden boards of the house had been freshly painted as I sat in the seat silent and staring.

"Want me to go in with you?" Rupert asked me.

His words brought me back to Rupert and away from my awe of seeing my husband's house turned office in the light of day. What must Rupert be thinking of my actions?

"It has a new coat of paint," I said.

"A day or so ago it was painted." His voice sounded a bit impatient. "Want me to go in with you?" he repeated.

"Oh, no," I answered too quickly. "I'll just run in and wait around until he closes up the place."

"I'll wait on you," he said.

"There's no need."

"Doctors are in great demand around here. There is no way of knowing when he can stop seeing patients. Besides, I took you away from your gardening and food preservation. It is only right I return you back home to them."

"No, really…"

"Don't argue with a hard-headed developer that's used to getting his own way. Go in, talk to your husband, and come back out and tell me if you want to stay or return to your beautiful mountain paradise."

"But…"

"Go, scat – scat – as they say in the mountains."

He got out with the intent of opening the door on my side, I think, but I beat him to it. Drew was beginning to wake up now that the car had stopped and walking might lull him back to sleep. I hoped so for I didn't want to breast feed him until I got into the privacy of my husband's house.

Jonas's living room had been turned into a waiting room. Nineteen chairs were lined up against the walls, I counted them. Seven people were seated, two old men, three old women and two young women with a child each.

A section of a hall had been enclosed with a door and open window to make a small reception room. A woman I had never seen before sat behind a desk. She was young, but older than me. Thin built with hair so yellow I suspected she was doing something to it. She was attractive in an unstable sort of way – as though a hard wind would blow her make-believe self away and reveal the real her. Her face looked like she was afraid of not getting what she wanted and hated others because of it. She appeared high-strung, jittery, sitting there is her snow-white, highly pressed uniform and little white nurse's hat perched on her head.

I looked for Jonas or another door that would lead to his living quarters. The only door was the one beside the open windowed office where she sat. I went to the door to open it, but it was locked.

"You'll have to wait your turn," said the woman in a bossy voice as she looked me over with distaste.

I moved from the door to her window, not liking how she was looking down her nose at me. "Is Jonas here?" I asked.

"*Doctor Jones* is in. Take a seat and wait your turn." She put special emphasis on Doctor Jones as though she was telling me I had no right to use the name Jonas.

"I'm not a patient," I told her firmly.

"Then leave. *Doctor Jones* is a busy man."

"*Leave*," I repeated as fire shot through me. I had no intention of being talked to in such a way, but all the people were looking at me and I didn't want to make a fool of myself. I leaned my head in the open window causing Drew to be held forward more than normal. "I'm Laine Jones. Jonas is my husband and you can unlock the door now."

She looked me up and down and her mouth puckered as though I had put a bad taste in her mouth. Her arm lifted and she slammed the window shut. I jerked my head to safety but the window frame hit Drew's head before I could move backward. He woke with a cry of pain. I didn't know I had moved or that I had picked up a heavy metal waste basket and smashed it through the window glass. Nor did I realize that I had the cow-bell, once sitting on the window shelf, in my hand until I threw it like I was aiming to kill a gray squirrel.

She screamed as it struck her in the face, a line of blood appeared from the corner of her eye to the corner of mouth before she clamped both hands over her face and continued screaming.

Jonas was there. "What is going on out here?" he demanded as he hurried to her, seeing blood seep through her fingers and jerking her hands away so he could see the wound. She was crying hysterically now and not talking.

"Unlock this door and see how bad my baby is hurt," I said as I cradled Drew against my chest. "She hit his head with the window."

Jonas looked from her to me, his face a picture of confusion and surprise. He hesitated a moment before hurrying to the door.

"Where did you come from? How is the baby hurt? What happened to Francis? What's going on here?" he asked all at one time.

"That trashy woman burst the window out and attacked me," the woman found her voice suddenly as she pointed a bloody hand at me. "My face is mangled for life."

"She hit Drew on the head. The soft spot. It could kill him!" My voice was filled with fear for my baby.

Jonas had closed the door behind me, but people had crowded to the window, all silently watching. Jonas seemed to comprehend everything suddenly. He grabbed my arm and hurried me and Drew into a room.

"Where was he hit?"

I touched a puffy red spot on the top side of his head.

"Close, but not on the fontanels." His hand rubbed over Drew's head, his eyes taking in his reaction as Drew's fist bobbed at his mouth. He lifted Drew's eyelids and shined a light into them. "I don't think he's hurt."

"He's crying," I told Jonas.

"See if he's hungry."

Angry at Jonas's calmness, I yanked my dress buttons loose. Drew stopped his crying in lieu of his hunger.

"Sit in that chair and don't move, Laine, and I'll be back in a minute."

I knew he was going to her. I could still hear her hysterical crying.

"She did this! That crazy woman did this to me! I'll have her committed to an insane asylum." The woman shrieked as Jonas obviously went to her.

"Hush, let me look at your face," came Jonas's soothing voice through the wall.

"Who is that horrible being? Such as that can't be your wife."

"You're not hurt much. Your jaw has a fairly deep scratch with some bruising starting to show, but only requiring a bandage."

I heard a door open and close. I thought Jonas was returning to me as the door to the room I was in opened. I looked away from Drew, grateful for Jonas's quick return, but it was Rupert.

"I heard the screaming from my car and ran inside. A woman told me what happened. Is your son hurt?"

"Jonas said not." I managed to say as I sat there looking at Rupert – a stranger that had brought me to town.

"Where is Jonas?"

"With her."

Rupert listened. We both heard their voices.

"Calm down, Francis. You're perfectly fine. I'll take care of you," Jonas's words were clear.

I don't know what kind of expression I wore on my face, but Rupert was gazing at me hard.

"Do you want to leave?" Rupert asked me.

"Yes." I admitted, caught between tears and anger.

He nodded. "I know there is a back door to this place. What do you say we use it?"

For a moment, I hesitated as I looked down at Drew. He appeared content as he sucked. Yes, I did want to leave here, leave the crying woman behind, the people, and Jonas.

"Let's hurry," I told him taking Drew from my breast.

I don't know if anyone saw us leave. I didn't care. Moisture was sliding down my cheeks as Rupert held the door open for me. I quickly rubbed at my face as I got in and he closed the door fast, almost running around the front of the vehicle. It came to life and we were soon gone.

The ride back up the mountain was a silent one. Neither of us spoke for a long time.

"You okay?" Rupert finally asked.

"Yeah."

"Anything I can do?"

"No."

There was more silence along with more bumps in the road. Drew was lulled back to sleep by the motion.

"Want to talk about it?"

"No."

We continued our silence until he stopped in front of the barn where Rafe used to park the horse and wagon. Strange how things and people could change is such a short time. You could have someone one moment and the next moment they were gone – forever. Joey was dead, Dad was dead, Rafe was dead, and it seemed to me my baby could be next.

"I only know what the woman told me," Rupert said without getting out to open my door. "I gather there was a problem when you told the nurse you were Jonas's wife."

"I need to go inside now. Ransom will be waiting on me. Thanks for taking me into town. It was … was educational." I didn't want to show sadness in my voice, didn't want him to know what I was feeling, but I think he did.

He looked at me longer than necessary and then held out his hand to shake mine. Reluctantly I placed my hand in his. He closed his hand over mine, held it a moment.

"I'll bring dog food in a couple of weeks. In the meantime, take care of yourself. Treasures such as yourself are rare."

I pulled my hand free and hurriedly got out.

"Don't forget your carrier."

I wasn't about to forget that or anything else that had happened this day.

Chapter 12

I didn't think Jonas would come home that night. He wasn't the kind to like having his business routine interrupted, especially by his wife. He was the kind to let me boil in my own juice. That's why I didn't think he would come home to me.

I finished the outside work and only ate a chunk of cornbread crumbled in a glass of milk for my supper. Usually, I tried to eat good so I would have plenty of milk for Drew, but one meal would not slow things much. When I finished eating, I washed out my glass and went up stairs with Drew still sleeping on my back.

I felt the familiar softness of the carpeted stairs, the silken feel of the stair rail, the hall that lead to the upper porch. I went onto it and just stood there watching the grayness of dusk settle over my land like a dark blanket thickening itself. A strange kind of calmness came over me, one that didn't lessen the hurt inside me, but one that kept me from breaking apart.

I felt alone when I needed to feel my husband's nearness, his support, but I would get over it.

From the porch I could see the small pasture lot near the barn where the mean boar hog used to be. The mean sow was still in there with her litter of pigs. She was dangerous especially with her babies by her side, but she was not like the boar had been. She was contrary and protective, but she wasn't the killer such as the boar had been. Still, a person could be hurt bad or be killed by a contrary, protective animal.

My mind's eye recalled Junie running naked from Rafe's room. I saw her cross the yard in an attempt to escape me and hide her nakedness from her husband. Nate had been standing in the road holding their baby girl. She had taken a short cut to the barn through the hog lot, the one where the boar hog and sow stayed. She hadn't closed the gate. From the upper porch I saw myself chasing Junie with Rafe right behind me yelling to the top of his lungs. I thought the boar hog was attracted to the pot I was carrying, but it could have been the angry sound of Rafe's voice.

I could still feel Abe's thin arms go around me, carrying me to safety, still feel the painful force of his body landing of top of mine.

"Don't move," he had demanded in a whisper, "Don't move an inch. Don't make one sound."

I wondered if his actions had really saved my life, if we could have done anything different that would have saved Rafe's. If Rafe hadn't been mad and yelling at me, the boar hog might not have attacked him. That was a lot of ifs to wonder about but none of them mattered now.

What mattered was the way Jonas had cared for me back then. He loved me even back then and I wondered if his love for me could disappear. If not, why didn't he come to me like he used to?

I pulled my mind away from my vision of the past. I didn't want to think about the past. I had my land; I had my baby; I just didn't know if I still had Jonas.

"*Laine Elder,*" Dad's voice seemed to whisper through the rustling leaves. "*Love doesn't die a fast death. It has to be beat to death in a slow painful agony.*"

I tried to make my mind reach out and get hold of Dad, bring him in close where he could surround me with his love, but it didn't work. He was gone as fast as he had come, but his words stayed with me.

A stillness came over the gloaming of night, a silence so deep and penetrating that I knew it would shatter. And shatter it did. Bruiser went wild with angry barking, mimicked by Ransom. I had untied Bruiser for a while and hadn't let Ransom in the house and now they were after something in the woods. I ran to the bedroom, grabbed the loaded shotgun, and ran outside ready to help my dogs fight off whatever was there. By the time I got into the yard, I heard Jonas cursing – Jonas actually using bad words – really bad words.

"Off, Bruiser," I yelled as I ran through the trees. "Off Bruiser, off, back off!" I think the dogs thought I was egging them on for the sound of their barking became vicious. I had to rush in, dodging the hoofs of the rearing horse as Jonas fought to keep it from running away or throwing him, and grab Bruiser's collar to keep him from biting the horse's legs in his attempt to get at Jonas. Ransom was still wanting to attack, but he didn't know what to do without Bruiser showing him. "Stop!" I demanded and kicked at Ransom. He looked at me, puzzled that I wasn't praising him. "Stop!" I repeated and this time both dogs settled.

The horse was turning in circles, his head held high, foam dripping from his mouth, his sides lathered.

"Easy, easy, easy." Jonas was saying, still fighting the frightened horse for control.

The horse was easing up even though his eyes were rolling their whites at the dogs.

"I'll try riding him to the barn, and don't you dare let go of those damned dogs," Jonas said, still excited as much as the horse. "I don't want to end up back in Banners Elk again tonight."

I nearly laughed at that but knew I had better not. I had seen Jonas upset but never this mad. I didn't look forward to what was coming next. I stayed put and held onto both dogs. Drew wiggled on my back awaken by the noise but not crying. Bruiser nosed me in the face and Ransom wiggled and licked any place of me he could reach as though he was pleased with himself and glad that I had joined their pack.

I didn't go to Jonas. He put the horse in a stall, slammed the barn door shut and came back to the woods to find me. His eyes were blazing as he looked down at me and the dogs.

"Who's dogs?" he demanded.

I stood, turned them loose. "Mine." I answered.

"Where the hell... "

Bruiser crouched. I grabbed at his collar, caught him just as he lunged at Jonas.

"Don't use that tone of voice. He thinks you're threatening me." I didn't know if that was true or not, but it sounded good.

Jonas shook his head in disbelief and took a couple of backward steps. "I should have known," his voice was almost a whisper, "I should have known the moment I met you that I'd never live in peace again."

I giggled and Bruiser calmed down. Jonas held his hand out toward Bruiser but the dog growled.

"He's vicious."

"He's been as gentle as a kitten," I said and remembered Dad's words for the red bull.

"Mountain lion kittens," Jonas said. "Can you tie him up or better yet use that shotgun on him."

"He's only protecting me."

"Don't know about that. Can we go to the house now? Today has been a long one. Don't turn that dog loose," he added. "I dread to see what Drew will grow up to be with a mother like you."

I didn't know if that was a compliment or not.

"I'm just about hungry enough to fight that dog and eat him raw."

"You've not had supper?"

"Nor lunch. After your unexpected visit, I had a run on patients. One man swore his horse had kicked his knee cap when there wasn't even a red spot. Everybody in town wanted first-hand news about you and Francis Dewhitte. I can hardly wait to hear the stories Andy Harmon is sure tell you."

His voice was tired, but not as mad as it sounded at first.

"Laine, if I didn't love you so much, I'd regret not shooting that boar hog the day Rafford Johnson brought him home."

I looked up at him and through the last fading light before darkness was complete, I saw love still shining in his eyes – along with a degree of amusement. I was glad I hadn't beaten his love to death in a slow painful agony.

Jonas pushed his plate back, a signal that he had finished eating, downed his head as though in deep thought.

"Laine, we need to talk."

I picked up his plate and put it in the dish pan of hot water that sat on the back of the stove. I had hoped things could go back to normal without this coming talk, but I wasn't that lucky. I sat down at the table across from Jonas ready to listen to whatever he had to say.

He took my hand in his. "I am becoming concerned about you obsession with Drew."

"What?" This was not what I expected.

"You're becoming too protective."

I didn't believe what I was hearing. "Mother's are supposed to be protective."

"Not to the point of violence."

I pulled my hand from his as images of mother animals protecting their young flashed through my mind. It was natural for a mother, even a human one, to protect their baby. Jonas should know that. He was a doctor.

"I am not too protective, nor am I violent."

"Only when compared to a water buffalo."

"Talk straight, Jonas," I said, anger building in me.

"If you insist, Laine, I can't have my wife making a spectacle of herself the way you did today. It is embarrassing and it hurts my business."

"According to what you said earlier, business increased, besides you claim to be overworked so much you don't come home for three days in a row."

"Don't get smart."

"Smart?" I gritted my teeth but I could not stop my words. "It was that damned hussy in your office that got smart and violent and all the other words you are applying to me. You don't care if she did hurt Drew, do you?"

"You're being silly."

"Violent, smart, silly. Surely you can find a few better words than those to describe your wife."

"Unfortunately, I can, but now isn't the time to use them."

I hated the calm way he said that, as though he was so much better than me. "Perhaps you're the silly one for hiring someone like Francis Dewhitte."

"She has proved to be a hard worker."

"But not a nice one."

"She is a professional, one that is educated."

"Listen at you jumping on me and defending her."

"You're my wife, Laine. I expect more from you than I do others."

"Shouldn't I expect something out of you, like siding with your wife when someone hurts her baby?"

Jonas gave a long drawn-out sigh. "There's no reasoning with you so let's drop it. I'm getting nowhere."

"The least you can do is be reasonable and tell the whole truth. You're embarrassed by me aren't you?"

"Yes, deeply embarrassed."

"Then get a divorce."

Shock showed on his face. "You're talking crazy. People don't get divorces and I certainly don't want one. I just want you to act respectful, like a lady."

"You married me, Jonas, *me,* and you can take me or leave me." I turned my back and went up the stairs. He was beating on my love for him.

🕊

I lay there with the light on, Ransom sleeping by my bed, his ears pricked, listening to Jonas snore. He had wanted to leave Ransom outside with Bruiser, but I refused. He had wanted to put Drew in his crib and turn out the lamp, but I refused.

"Then let's go into another room for a while. I don't want to make love to my wife with an audience."

I eased out of bed, careful not to wake Drew. I didn't want to be fighting with Jonas, and I needed him to hold me, needed to feel okay again.

Jonas wasn't as gentle and attentive as he normally was. Instead, I could feel his anger and disappointment mingled with his need. He sought his own release with little consideration for me. He didn't hold me against him afterwards, dropping small kisses over my face as he usually did. He didn't rub his smooth hands over my body and make contented sounds. He simply rolled over and began to snore. I got up and went back to our bedroom. He woke and followed.

"I'm exhausted," he mumbled and was snoring the next breath.

I couldn't help wondering what Rafe would do in this situation. I imagined he would have tossed Drew in the crib, kicked the dog, and broke the lamp. Perhaps I shouldn't be complaining to myself about Jonas. Rafe's death had put me out of the frying pan, but Jonas hadn't put me into the fire – yet.

Chapter 13

Several days passed before Andy showed up. He came to the porch where I was breaking beans to can. Bruiser and Ransom both wagged their tails without barking at Andy; both dogs gave him their trust.

"Have you heard the news?" he asked, his eyes twinkling as though he couldn't wait to tell me as he leaned his weight against a porch post.

"What news," I asked, thinking he was getting ready to depart the local gossip about my spat with Francis Dewhitte.

"There's a new doctor in town."

"Tate?" I remembered what Rupert had told me.

"So Jonas told you about him."

"Rupert did."

Andy shook his head as he took a quick peep at my face. "Don't trust rich developers as far as I can throw 'em. He's been about a right smart lately, hain't he?"

"Not in a few days."

"That's good. Don't hold for him messing around these parts. He don't belong. No developer does." He grunted then changed the subject. "Tate's another saddlebag doctor. Goes to folk's houses."

"So does Jonas."

"Your Jonas likes to be in his office more that Doc Tate does. Tate used to work for a logging camp until old soft-talking preacher Tufts hired him away from 'em. That man can talk money right out of a pocket, especially a woman's pocket."

"Jonas hasn't mentioned either one of them," I said, but he continued on as though I hadn't said a word.

"Yeap, Tuft's a smooth talker alright, knows how to get what he wants. Have to admit he can do good for poor folks. Course some folks don't like him. Claim he's sticking his nose where it doesn't belong. They claim mountain folks could and should take care of their own just like we've been doing all our lives without the help of outsiders."

"What do you think of this doctor Tate?" I wanted to know where Andy stood on things that affected Jonas.

"I'm not too bright on such things as charity and handouts. I just know there's always some good in the bad and some bad in the good. Seems like another doctor falls under good." He grunted as though he hurt as he turned loose of the porch post and sat down on one of the steps. His bibbed overalls spread out about him and I thought he had lost weight. "Francis Dewhitte is working for the new doctor since Jonas fired her."

"He fired her?"

"Yeap, fired her the day you straightened her out. He never told you?" Andy was grinning, but I just couldn't admit out loud that Jonas had not told me anything about Francis Dewhitte.

"I've been wondering what the gossip was."

"Most folks sided with you. Seems she's made a lot of sick folks mad. Heard she started the fight by hitting our little Drew."

"With the window."

"Heard you put a hurtin on her with her very own prized cow bell. Folks claim she had that cow bell sitting there for folks to ring when they wanted to talk to her, like she was a queen or something."

"Jonas thinks I'm too protective of Drew," I admitted, needing to talk about it.

"You're not. It's a mother's duty to protect her baby. I'm proud of you and so is most everybody in Banners Elk."

"Really? You're not just saying that to make me feel better?"

"Nope, I'm not. When you stopped by the store with that fancy developer, seems a couple of men put money on how long it would take you to straighten out Francis Dewhitte."

That shocked me, made me right mad.

"Those men put odds on everything just for the fun of it. Let one win against another and it's on. 'Bout all the fun those old men have anymore."

"Who did you bet on?"

"You, if I'd a been there. Seems it took you less than five minutes. Reckon Francis had forgotten about the Doc sewing up Jeb's head or she would not have messed with you."

I had almost forgotten about splitting Jeb's head and thinking I'd killed him nor did I want to be reminded of it. It left me feeling uneasy. "You really don't think I'm too protective?"

"Nope and Jonas won't either when he becomes a daddy."

I looked hard at Andy.

"Now don't go getting me wrong. I'm not saying Jonas doesn't care for Drew, I'm saying he's not formed an attachment to him. Sometimes it takes a man a while to do that even with his own blood."

There was no need for Andy to try and talk around me. I knew exactly what he was saying. He was saying Jonas couldn't forget that Drew had been fathered by another man. Every time he climbed the mountain, looked at this big white house, or laid down in bed beside me, Jonas was reminded it all once belonged to Rafe.

"Reckon you hain't heard the big news."

I dreaded what else he was going to tell me so I said, "Rupert Smith bought out the entire town of Banner's Elk?"

"He's trying and so is another developer according to gossip, but that hain't the news I'm talking about."

"What is?"

"Want to guess a couple more times?"

"Nope."

"Kill-sport," he grinned. "Reckon I might as well go ahead and tell you straight out. Abe Farrow married your sister."

I dropped a handful of beans."

"They slipped off and done it. Hazel and your momma are fit to be tied. Seems they developed a dislike for each after the snake handling."

"Poor Abe," I said, for he surely didn't know what he was getting himself into. And Susie, how in the word did Abe pry her away from Momma long enough to marry her? "Where are they living?" I hoped it wasn't with Hazel. If it was, they were too close to me for my comfort.

"They're with your momma. Susie refused to leave her behind and she refused to be anywhere close Hazel. Your momma said, 'Snakes and crazy women were part of the devil's liar and her daughter would never be a part of that as long as she was alive."

This was a first for me - I agreed with Momma, at least on the snakes and crazy women.

"Hazel said her son had ruined his life good and proper because a girl always ends up just like her mother."

"I hope not." I couldn't help thinking that Hazel had wanted Abe to marry me, obviously not because of the person I was or would become, but because of the land and house I would bring into the marriage. All the things that would benefit her. I could just see Momma and Hazel both trying to get every ounce of benefit they could from the union. In my opinion Momma would win hands down.

He grunted and moved his legs to a more comfortable position. "You don't need to worry none. You're not like any woman I've ever set eyes on."

I started to thank him, but I wasn't sure he was complimenting me.

"When have you met my mother?"

"Saw her at the church house, remember?"

Of course I remembered. "Seeing isn't knowing."

"You don't have to take a second look at hell to know you don't want to join folks in the fiery flames." He cleared his throat and spat off to the side and then added, "You can do a lot of cookin with fire, but too much heat burns the bread."

"Great words of wisdom?" I threw a hand full of beans in the bowl.

"Truth. It's the plain honest truth." Andy said as he maneuvered himself to his feet.

"What's wrong? You're not moving like your normal self."

"Ahh, I got horse-kicked. Seems like I don't move out of the way as fast as I once did."

"Did you see Jonas?"

"Naw, no need for that. I've been kicked afore. I'll mosey on now that I've departed my news."

I watched him walk through the yard limping like a much older man. So that was why I hadn't seen him in several days, he'd been horse kicked. I wondered how he'd heard the news of Abe and Susie. I suppose he'd managed to limp to the store and joined in with that gossiping bunch of old men. Of course men didn't call their sessions gossiping, with them it was philosophizing.

🕊

"Tell me about Susie and Abe," I said to Jonas as soon as he reached the kitchen that night.

Jonas turned his cold blue eyes on me and shook his head. "It amazes me how isolated you are on this mountain and yet how you manage to know everything that goes on in a fifty mile radius. Was it Andy or the interloping land acquisitioner that conveyed this information?"

I didn't like the way he referred to Rupert. Rupert had done nothing out of line, but now wasn't the time to point that out. It was Susie that lay heavy on my mind and Momma that worried my entire existence. If somehow, someway Abe did manage to get Susie away from Momma, I knew where Momma would head – straight for me - like an arrow aimed for my jugular.

"Andy came by for a few minutes," I told my husband. "I think you ought to check on him. He was kicked by a horse."

"I know. It was Hack Pennel's horse."

"If you know, why didn't you examine him?"

Jonas fixed his eyes on me again. "Because Andy Harmon has his pride."

I didn't have an answer for that even though the words *male dominance* did run through my mind.

"Men aren't like women and children," Jonas continued. "They like to take their suffering in silence."

Again, I thought of male arrogance and I knew that Jonas had his share of it, just as Andy did. Perhaps all men did. Didn't Dad suffer Momma and her ways in silence until the day he died?

"When did Abe and Susie get married?" I asked, trying to hide that Jonas' words and his attitude toward me hurt.

"A day or two ago, according to the man that delivered salt blocks for cattle to Hack's store. He was making a trip from Wilkesboro to Elk Park unless his salt blocks sold out. It seems he stopped at Eula's store and she said that Abe was from Banners Elk and he should let the people there know of the wedding."

"What else did he say?"

"It seemed Eula had exaggerated things into a feud. A modern Shakespearian tale of star-crossed lovers."

"A what?"

"Never mind, Laine. I was just saying that Eula was doing what she does best, spreading gossip after giving it her special twist."

"You don't think Momma and Hazel are mad?"

"Oh, yes. I think they are mad, and in more ways than one, especially Hazel. She lost that all-important male of her family, the one she counted on to make her life easier." Jonas kind of grinned. "While your mother has most likely seen the bright and shining light of her good fortune. She now has a man to do all the work your dad and you used to do."

"She's lost control over Susie," I told Jonas.

"Do you really believe that, Laine?"

His words made me stop putting supper on the table for a moment. Jonas was right. Susie couldn't break away from Momma that easily. What made me think that she could? Was my mind growing dull? Had I been so occupied lately that I no longer had the ability to think straight? I had to admit I was feeling unusually tired. I marked it up to lack of peaceful sleep.

I continued putting food on the table, trying to hide the delight that had just struck me. If Momma had someone doing her bidding, she would leave me alone.

"Hazel, now, is a different matter. I've got a feeling she won't let this rest. She's not the kind of woman to sit back and let your mother, or anyone, pull a coup on her," Jonas said in his most logical manner.

I didn't care if Momma and Hazel locked horns and never got loose of each other. It would serve both of them right. It was like Andy had said, I didn't need a second look not to jump into those fiery-flames.

"Has the new doctor helped with your work load?" I wanted to get away from talk of Momma now that my worry had been lifted; still, there was a discomfort in me, a sixth sense that came to the forefront. I heard Dad say as plain as if were standing beside me, *'A wise daughter never lets down her guard, especially Mertie's daughter.'*

"Yes," admitted Jonas. "I think I can now manage to get home every night."

"It's where you belong." I rubbed my fingers along the back of Jonas' neck and felt a tingle run through me. How could I be happier than I was at this moment? At last I had the husband I always dreamed of having – one ready and willing to give me his undivided love, one that wouldn't stay away at night anymore.

That night I turned out the light and Jonas didn't complain about making love in the same room with Drew and Ransom. I had been wrong, I could be happier than I had been at supper.

Chapter 14

Bruiser and Ransom were pitching a fit. They were either going to eat someone or something up. Their sound reminded me of Abe's dogs when they went after the panther, but panthers seldom came out during broad day light. More likely they were after somebody, maybe Jonas again. Jonas hadn't been gone long and he might have doubled back for something, but I wasn't going to take a chance on it being him and not a vicious animal. I grabbed the loaded shotgun and ran to my dogs with Drew on my back.

What I saw made my blood run cold with fear. I cocked one of the barrels and took aim without calling the dogs off.

In the fork of a tree, just out of the snapping reach of the dogs, was Hazel. Her eyes were huge in her pale face.

"Call them off," she whispered as though her full voice would egg the dogs to jump higher.

"Why should I?" I asked while my fingers stroked the gun as though it was my salvation.

"They aim to tear me to pieces."

"Yeah," I agreed. "They will too, just as soon as you come down or fall out of that tree fork."

"Why?" she whispered.

"You're trespassing," I said. "Just like you trespassed when you left the rattlesnake in Drew's crib."

She frowned, her huge eyes confused. "Why are you talking craziness at a time like this?" Her voice was a little louder than before.

"A woman that puts a poison snake in a baby's crib deserves to be eat up by dogs."

"I didn't put no snake in no crib."

"And I'm to believe you? What are you doing here? Releasing more snakes? It won't do you any good. As soon as these dogs finish you off, they'll kill any snakes you've turned loose."

"I'm not coming out of this tree," she said defiantly as her chin raised.

I couldn't stop the malicious smile that came to my face. "I think you will, one way or the other."

"Are you threatening to shoot me?"

"Yes, and then I'm going to let these dogs eat every scrap of flesh off your body, then I'm going to burn your clothes in the cook stove and feed your bones to the hogs."

Her eyes sought mine trying to determine if I was trying to frighten her or if I intended to do exactly what I was saying. I don't think she found an answer as I wasn't sure if my words were a threat or a promise.

"I didn't try to hurt your baby," she said too fast. "I swear on everything that is holy. I didn't know anything about that snake until the gossip reached me."

I didn't believe her and she read it in my face. "Go ahead, kill me, pull the trigger."

I looked her in the eyes. "Such a death would be too easy on someone that tried to kill my baby. I'm going to knock you out of the tree and let the dogs have at you. I want you to suffer like my baby would have suffered."

She climbed higher in the tree much like a snake slithering upward. I laughed, a sound that wasn't from amusement, and she knew it. I turned; leaving the dogs holding her treed, and went to the chopping block for the ax. I had no fear she would get away because the dogs were still vicious in their barking. I came back and started chopping the tree down.

After two chunks of wood flew out, I paused and looked up at her. "Start talking," I said.

"I didn't bring no snakes here. I didn't come to harm nobody. I put aside my pride and come to ask for your help."

"Help? My help?" Now why did that sound so weak and totally silly? Surely she knew it did.

"You've got to get my son back. You've got to make him see what's right."

"You tried to kill my son. Why should I care about yours?" I took another chop, then another. The tree wasn't large. A dozen more chops and the tree would topple.

"No! Stop that chopping! How can I convince you I did no such thing?"

I chopped twice more. "Tell me who did."

"I can't. I don't know."

Three more chops and she felt the tree give a little. She gathered her dignity, her snake charming mode, and tried to dominate me.

"Go ahead, chop it down. Kill me if that's what you want. I have no fear. I put my faith in God."

"I put mine in these two dogs, and in that shotgun I know how to use in case you think you can out run the dogs." I chopped another two times and the tree shivered. "Who put the snakes in the crib?"

"I didn't."

I chopped again. "Who did?"

"I don't know."

"Two more chops and then she'll go down."

I watched Hazel look into the snarling face of Bruiser, seeing his waiting teeth and the drool of anticipated slobber that ran from his mouth. He was quivering with excitement as he waited for her to hit the ground. I gave the tree one light chop and drew back for the second chop. Hazel was beginning to believe I would do as I threatened.

"Wait!" she screeched. "Don't do it and I'll tell you what I know."

I stopped the second chop in mid swing, but she was silent, obviously trying to think of something to satisfy me besides the truth.

"Time's up," I said.

"No. Give me a moment."

"Nope, time's up."

"I had the snakes in their boxes, all of them. When I checked, one of them was gone. I thought it had escaped until that developer's story got back to me."

"I'm to believe that?" I said as I lifted the ax.

"It's the truth, I swear it."

I laughed and struck the tree again. This time it swayed away from me without falling. "You were lucky with that one. You won't be with the next one for it'll fall for certain."

Something passed over her face, true terror I'd call it.

"Abe," she screamed out his name. I looked around expecting him to show up, and then I realized he would have shown up sooner than now if he was around. "I think Abe took my precious snake and you killed it."

"Abe tried to kill my baby?" I couldn't believe he would do such a thing, not after all the concern he showed for me and my unborn child.

"No! You misunderstand me. He didn't want to hurt him. He just wanted to scare you a little."

"Scare me?" I didn't believe her.

"You wouldn't help him! You wouldn't even give him a calf after all he had done for you! What do you expect an honorable man to do? Let you get away with all your selfishness?"

I gave the tree another chop, a hard one, and watched the tree slowly fall. I laid down the ax and picked up the shotgun, not knowing if I would shoot her, let Bruiser have her, or hoped the force of the falling tree would shove her all the way to hell. I never found out for Andy stepped from behind a larger tree trunk, walked up to Bruiser and took hold of his collar.

"Down," he ordered. "Hush up!" He held onto Bruiser as the tree reached the ground. She wasn't shoved to hell; she hit the ground running. I'm not even sure she realized Andy was there holding onto Bruiser's collar. I lifted the shotgun and took aim. A shot at this close range would splatter her. I saw her head explode; her brains and blood coat the trees. I saw her headless body jerking in the throws of death. I lowered the shotgun.

"I knew you couldn't do it," Andy said as he grabbed for Ransom and caught his tail.

"You weren't going to stop me," I said in a shaky voice.

"I wasn't going to stop you," he repeated.

"Why not?"

"I needed to see what you'd do when time ran out."

"You knew I couldn't kill her."

"I didn't think you would."

"And if I had?"

"I would have helped you dig a deep hole."

I looked at him – speechless.

"You had the right to do it and I wouldn't have blamed you."

"You would have helped ….."

"Yeah, I would have."

I looked at the woods where she had disappeared. "Now what?" Not knowing what to think of Andy, not exactly believing him. From the corner of my eyes, I thought he might have grinned, but I could have been wrong.

"I don't think you'll ever be troubled by Hazel Farrow again."

"She'll have it all over Banners Elk that I went crazy and tried to kill her."

"Don't think so," said Andy. "She'll be too afraid you'll set the law on Abe for trying to kill your baby."

"You heard her?"

"Yeap. I've been here for sometime and I noticed right off that you weren't swinging that ax hard."

This time I did see the humor in his eyes and knew he never believed I'd kill Hazel or let her be killed by my dogs. He was welcome to his belief for I thought I'd do it until that very last moment.

"With a mother like you and a father like Rafford Johnson, that boy you're carrying on your back ought to turn out to be some kind of hell raiser," Andy added as he looked toward Drew, still sleeping peacefully.

I didn't tell Jonas what happened. Andy suggested that neither he nor I mention what had come about unless Hazel made something of it. I wanted to tell Jonas, but I agreed with Andy because Jonas wouldn't understand my actions. He wasn't a mother or a father.

That's one of the reasons why I was nervous as a dog-chased cat by the time Jonas got home.

"What's wrong with you?" Jonas asked.

"Nothing," I said. "Why?"

"You're pale as a sheet. Are you sick?"

I shook my head, fighting tears. I wanted to burst out the truth about Hazel and me not knowing if I'd kill her or not. Suddenly Jonas became alert. He jumped up from the table and grabbed me by the arms.

"Of course! I should have known sooner. After all, I am a doctor."

I opened my mouth to say something, but I didn't know what to say.

"You're pregnant," he said. "You haven't had your period since we've been married. Why didn't you tell me?"

"Women don't have their monthlies when they're suckling. They can't get with a baby."

He laughed. "Laine, that's an old-wives-tale. You're pregnant," he repeated. "You're going to have my baby this time."

He pulled me to him and kissed me hard and then released me. "You'll have to take it easier, not work so hard. I'll hire Andy to help you, cut your firewood and such."

"I cut wood before Drew was born," I managed to say through my stupor of shock at the thought of another baby this soon. Surely I was protected from such. Drew took a lot of milk. He was growing fast; besides, I didn't want another baby right now. Maybe a few years down the road I'd want one, but not now. I could barely get my work done with carrying around one baby. How could I grow and sell my produce if I had two babies in a year's time? "I can still work," I added mostly for myself.

"That was when you were Rafford Johnson's wife. He wasn't the kind of man to take care of his wife and baby, I am."

I shook my head at Jonas, not knowing what to say or do.

"You're happy aren't you? You do want my baby?"

"Of course I do." I told the truth but didn't add not yet. "I'm, I just didn't know, can't believe it's possible."

Jonas laughed again and took me in his arms. "My naive little wife," he said as he kissed me. When he turned me loose there was a puzzled look on his face. "Why isn't Drew on your back?"

"I don't think there's anymore snakes around here. I'm trusting Bruiser and Ransom to keep evil things run off."

"Good. It's about time you started thinking right. I don't want your emotions to affect our baby before it's even born."

"I don't believe I'm having a baby."

"And I believe you are; after all, I am a doctor."

"But…"

He put his finger over my lips. "Come up stairs. I want to examine you to make sure. I can guess how far along you are by the size of your uterus. It wouldn't surprise me if you got pregnant that very first night. You are a healthy and fertile country girl."

I silently followed him upstairs to our room where Drew was awake and gurgling as he played in the crib. Ransom was lying in his spot as though he knew it was his job to watch over Drew. Jonas had my hand in his and led me past the open bedroom door.

"We don't need an audience for this."

"Jonas…" I tried to object.

"We'll know in a few minutes, Laine. We'll know for certain."

He was right. I was pregnant according to Jonas and very much so. I have never seen him so happy. I suspected it was because he had now done as much as Rafe, and maybe a little more. He now had everything Rafe had before his death, including a wife in the family way. I instantly felt guilty for my thoughts. Jonas was a wonderful man, and hadn't he loved me before I met Rafe, at least a day before.

I tried to smile, tried to appear happy. I feared Jonas would sense that I wasn't, but he didn't. He just took my lack of words as surprise at such a joyful event.

"Your sweet face is flushed," he finally said.

"Being examined is embarrassing, even when it's done by your husband."

"I examined you in such a way even before I was your husband."

"I know."

"And I'll be doing similar for the rest of our lives."

His smile was contagious and I smiled too. I reminded myself how lucky I was to be married to Jonas and not Rafe. At least I had a husband that came home instead of one that stayed gone for weeks leaving me stranded and alone.

Chapter 15

The timber had changed color by the time Rupert Smith came back with more dog food. I heard the roaring sound of his strange looking vehicle long before he reached the barn. I picked up Drew from where he was rolling about on the kitchen floor and went outside to meet Rupert. Andy had told me I shouldn't carry Drew around so much. Boys needed to kick about enough to develop strong muscles, besides a baby that was carried never learned to walk. I remember how fast my little brother Joey could run and promised myself I'd never let Drew out of my sight, nor would I ever have honey bees.

Rupert smiled at me as though he was meeting an old friend. "Mrs. Johnson, you're looking fit."

"I am fit." I wondered if he knew about the baby. I suspected he did, for Andy said that Jonas had told, and within minutes the entire town would know.

"Hope you haven't run out of dog food. I had to go out of town."

"Did your family come back with you?"

"No," he answered and was quick to change the subject as he pulled a bag of dog food from the vehicle. "Autumn comes early on this cold mountain. Leaves are still green elsewhere."

"The higher you go the colder it gets. Heaven is surely frozen solid," I said.

He chuckled. "I've also heard it gets hotter closer hell."

I stepped out of his way and watched him carry a fifty pound bag of dog food on each shoulder until he had two hundred pounds sitting on the porch.

"Where do you want to store this? We don't want wild animals or the dogs to get into it."

"In the spring house," I suggested.

"It needs to be stored in a dry place."

I thought of the woodshed built onto the side of the house. I had been picking up deadfall and storing it for winter but Andy had not cut any wood even though Jonas had asked him too. He hadn't come around much lately. When he did, he just didn't look himself.

Rupert thought the woodshed being part of the house was a good thing. I told him the history of the house, about the Holloways, but nothing about Rafe.

"Your first husband was married to Holloway's daughter, right?"

"Yes, he was. Bosie died during childbirth."

"Tragic, but life changes things, time changes things, and so do people."

"The land doesn't change," I added for I needed something I could count on to stay the same.

"Oh, but it does. It must change if there is to be progress."

"It doesn't change here," I insisted.

He looked at me and his face gentled as though he were hearing something I had not said. "If you ever sell this mountain, your land will change and change drastically."

"Even if you bought it?" I couldn't resist asking.

"Especially if I buy it or another person that fancy themselves a real estate developer. We specialize in coming into an area, stripping away nature and replace it with houses." He smiled. "It's not all bad, Lainey, my dear. This thing developers like to call progress brings in jobs and money. Money provides an easier way of living, but nothing comes without its own special price tag. Remember that everything in life has some kind of price tag."

"I won't sell my land no matter how much you pander to me."

He laughed - a good, honest laugh. "That's what I like about you, Lainey, girl. You don't practice tact or female wiles. You say exactly what you think."

"Doesn't everybody?"

He reached out and touched Drew's dark hair. "No. Very few people ever say what they really think. He's a fine boy. You're obviously a good mother. By the way, I brought something for you, too."

Gifts from an outsider? I must have looked less than pleased.

"Don't get jumpy. It's nothing that will compromise either of us. It's prenatal vitamins. When my wife was pregnant, the doctor insisted she take vitamins during her pregnancy to make sure the unborn child had everything it needed to grow up strong and healthy."

"Jonas is a doctor," I reminded him.

"Did he give you vitamins?"

"No."

"I didn't think so. People in this area are so independent they actually believe they have been selected by God to receive all the good in the world, including good food containing all the necessary elements of life."

"I grow my own food, and it is good."

He put the brown bottle in my hand and folded my fingers over it and held on for a moment before he turned loose.

"Take one each day. You don't weigh much more than a hundred pounds. Two babies can compromise even a large woman's health making her feel tired and unable to put one foot before the other. Take the vitamins with or without your husband's approval."

He patted my hand and glanced at the two dogs lying on the porch. They weren't barking at him, but their eyes were watchful.

"Four bags should do them several months but I'll try to get back before the snow flies. That wagon road isn't really suitable for traveling. During bad weather, it will be impassable. By the way, I almost forgot to tell you there is another land developer in the area, besides myself, that's trying to buy land. His name is James Travin. If he shows up here, take your shotgun to him."

He turned and walked away with that. I didn't follow him to his vehicle. I stood where I was, watching him get the vehicle started. Why hadn't he told me more about this new man? Why had he said to take my shotgun to him? Did he not want competition or had he heard about Hazel? Would Andy tell about that; would Hazel?

I watched as he drove away, bumping and rattling, but my mind was on Hazel. I had been puzzling over her for days; how could Hazel have been foolish enough to come to me? I couldn't get her Abe back for he was with Susie and Momma. I was convinced she had something else on her mind, something she thought I could do about Abe and Susie, but I hadn't figured out what.

I went inside, put Drew in his carrier and then headed toward Andy's even though I had wanted to dig my potatoes today. I walked slow, kicking the few leaves that had fallen on the ground. I didn't much like fall of the year. It seemed to me like the end of things instead of just a resting spell. It made me restless and a little afraid of the hard times ahead. I had already put up enough food to eat, enough food for us and the animals until spring time finally came. I knew that lazy folks could come in a hair of starving to death. Their animals often did.

I heard scraping coming from Andy's shop. I didn't holler from the woods like you do to neighbors when you want to be polite. Andy was like family, the only family I had. He was my substitute for Dad and even somewhat of a mother by telling me things he'd heard his own wife or mother say. Most important, Andy was my friend, one that I could count on.

My dogs laid down in the grass as I stood in the doorway, my shadow cast across the floor. He was sanding on a coffin, stopped and looked at the shadow and then me.

"Something wrong?" he asked.

"No."

"Get lonely?"

"Yeah." I didn't want to tell him I was worried about him. "Hadn't seen you in a while."

He took a deep breath, let out something more than a sigh, and laid his piece of sandpaper down. "Leg's been bothering me where I was horse kicked," he admitted. "Thought I had best stay off it a while so it can heal."

"You need to see Jonas."

"What could Jonas do? He's a doctor not God, and it would take God to roll some of these years from me and make my old bones strong again. Ah, Laine, how good it is to be young. Relish every minute of it for your youth will be gone before you know it."

"Time flies." I came into the room and sat down on a block of wood. He grinned as though I had said something funny.

"Now, Missy," his voice grew tender. "Tell me what's bothering you."

"Hazel."

"I had an idea that might be part of what's on your mind."

"I don't believe she came to ask me to help her get Abe back."

"I do." Andy surprised me by saying. "Hazel is the kind to concoct all kind of ideas in her head. She wants her son back and she came up with some scheme that involved you."

"I had forbid her to come on my place."

"Shows how easily the mind will forget when it wants something bad enough."

I shifted the carrier to a more comfortable position. Drew was sound asleep. Riding on my back was sure to make him sleep.

"Hazel had a plan, didn't she?"

"And you threw a monkey wrench in its gears."

"What do you think it was?"

"That we may never know, thank goodness."

"Is there gossip at the store?"

"There's always gossip."

"I mean about Hazel."

"Nope, not a word. Goes to show that three people can keep a secret. You haven't told Jonas have you?"

"No."

He nodded. "Gossip is there's a new land developer in town." His eyes watched my face.

"James Travin."

"Jonas told you?"

"Rupert Smith did."

"You've seen him again?"

"He brought dog food this morning."

"Don't trust him too much."

"He wants my land."

"He wants everybody's land," Andy said. "Developers! They ought to be called destroyers. So, he brought you more dog food as a bribe."

"And vitamins."

"Vitamins?"

"He said two babies could pull a woman down."

"So I've heard. Maw said she lost a tooth and a thousand strands of hair for every baby she bore." He frowned. "Take the vitamins. They can't hurt you. Have you been feeling poorly with this 'un?"

"A little draggy. Rupert said if James Travin showed up I should take my shotgun to him."

Andy chuckled and then said, "Good advice. Use it on Rupert Smith. He's got his eyes on your land and you."

"My land, not me," I corrected Andy. "But you and I both know I'll never sell that land. Rafe would have wanted it for Drew."

Andy just looked at me and didn't say anything more about land or developers. "If Abe shows up, use it on him, too. Good intentions can turn into bad when a person don't get what they're after."

"Jonas, go by Andy's place and have a look at his leg, " I told Jonas the minute he rode into the yard.

"What happened?"

"Where he was horse kicked. It's still bothering him until he can't get about."

"Did he come by today?" He slid off his horse and led it in the barn to unsaddle before he turned it into the pasture.

"I went to check on him."

"And?"

"And he said his leg was still bothering him."

"I'll ride by in the morning."

"What's wrong with now?"

"I'm dead on my feet. I need supper and some sleep."

"Busy day? Lot of sick folks?"

"Busy day indeed. Doctor Tate and I both were called to the hospital."

He hesitated and I started to ask why, but he continued.

"Six poisonous snake bites, six!"

I instantly thought of Hazel and Jonas nodded as though he read my mind.

"Hazel Farrow's doing. She took it upon herself to call a group of her snake-handling friends together. Six of those women got bit."

"Serves them right," I said as I followed Jonas toward the house.

"Don't be cruel, Laine. Poisonous bites are not only painful but deadly. Imagine thousands of bee stings in one spot."

I didn't have to imagine bee stings; I had seen it happen to my baby brother.

"Did they die?" I asked, feeling guilty.

"Not yet, but it was touch and go for a while. We may still lose one woman."

I hoped it was Hazel, but I didn't say so. Jonas would lay into me if I did.

"What about the preacher?" I assumed they were at the church when this happened.

"No preacher. This was a private gathering."

I shivered knowing it had something to do with me.

"One of the women said Hazel called them together in order to build a strong enough force to get her son back."

"Hazel's crazy."

"Fanatical, is the correct word, Laine. Calling someone crazy is immature and you've shown enough of that lately."

That hurt my feelings and I didn't know what he was referring to. I did think Hazel and her kind were crazy, but there was no use in me getting into an argument with Jonas. I longed to tell him Abe put the snake in Drew's crib, but Jonas would ask me how I knew. I didn't want to tell him about Hazel and how badly I wanted to shoot her. He would not only call me immature but he would surely say I was dangerous as well.

"Is Abe still living at Dad's place?"

"According to the gossiping tongues, he is."

"Have you talked to your Dad?"

"No, and can you just hush up for a while? Can't you simply allow your husband to eat supper and rest for a few minutes without questioning him to death?"

I asked no more questions, not even about the new developer, as I hurried to get supper ready for I didn't have it cooked. I had thought he would go see about Andy before he ate.

Jonas had finished his supper when he noticed the vitamin bottle sitting near the cook stove. He picked it up and read the label.

"Where did you get this?"

"Rupert Smith brought it this morning along with dog food."

Jonas' face flushed red. "Why?"

"He said his wife took them when she was expecting. He called them prenatal vitamins. Do you ever give them to women?"

"No," he said firmly. "Women who eat right don't need them."

"Andy said they couldn't hurt."

"I don't care what Andy or that developer says. I'm the doctor and your husband. I'm capable of taking care of my own wife and her needs." He sat the bottle down with a bang. "I don't like the idea of him hanging around you."

"He's only interested in my land."

"Of course he's only interested in your land. A rich man such as him could have his choice of any high-class woman in the world. He wouldn't be interested in a dumb country-hick like you."

I felt as though Jonas had slapped me. His words cut so deep that I picked up the bottle, dropped it into the empty slop bucket, turned my back to him and went up stairs to check on Drew. No need for Jonas to see me fighting tears.

The next morning, there was frost on the ground. Leaves fell from trees along with acorns pecking the ground like rain. I got up before daylight and fixed Jonas an early breakfast. I wanted him to check on Andy before he went to work. Uneasy feelings were gnawing inside me, warning that something bad was about to happen. I yearned to get Drew from his sleep and put him on my back, but that was being silly. He was sleeping soundly and breathing normal. Maybe it was the stress of two babies making me feel nervous and afraid, not to mention I was still hurt by Jonas' harsh words.

"It's plain cold," Jonas said as he came downstairs. "I'm afraid it will be a bad winter."

"Maybe not." I put eggs with biscuits and sausage gravy on his plate. "Jonas, I'm going to need some help butchering the hogs."

Jonas lifted his brows and shrugged. "It's not time yet. When it is, Andy can help you."

"What if he's not able?"

"You can always sell the hogs."

I said no more, wondering who Rafe had sold hogs to. This time a year ago, I was soon to be Rafe's wife instead of Jonas'. Life changed so fast I didn't want to think on it.

If worse came to worse, I could butcher hogs by myself. Hadn't I always helped Dad? Thing was, I'd have to be the one to shoot them and slit their throats so they could bleed-out. Then I'd have to boil water in a large barrel, insert the hog to loosen the course hair, scrape the hair off, then lift the hog into the air by its hind legs, fasten it there and gut it. After that, I'd have no problems.

I had finished the milking and done-up the outside work when I heard the vehicle chugging up the road. I wondered what could be bringing Rupert back up the mountain this soon. I looked into the slop bucket, grabbed the vitamins and stuck them behind the sack of flour where Jonas would never see them. I had taken one yesterday, if Rupert should ask.

I picked Drew up and went outside to meet him. The vehicle looked the same, but the man wasn't Rupert that got out. He was rail-slender with black curly hair and a narrow pinched face. He had the look of a hungry dog, one that could use a good worming. He made me think of a weasel that had not quite had enough food growing up and was now ready for amends .

It dawned on me that this was James Travin. Real estate developers drove around in vehicles. I wanted to turn around and run back inside for my shotgun. I distrusted this man more than I distrusted preachers, but it was too late. He had seen me and was fast closing the ground between us.

"Good morning Mrs. Jones," a bright smile widened his mouth and showed every tooth in his head. He looked me over as though I was a piece of candy.

The sound of the car had fooled the dogs just as it had fooled me, but the sound of his voice brought them up off the porch in full rage.

Reluctantly, I called them off. They both sat down with their fur touching my feet, their lips snarled as they eyed him. I think I was snarling too, for I hoped he'd jump back in his vehicle and leave, but he didn't.

"Do they bite?" he asked pleasantly.

"Yes."

"They mind you good?"

"No."

"Could you clip a chain on them?"

"No. Not when a strange man is standing before me."

"I'm not strange and I assure you I'm harmless."

I didn't answer.

"My name is Travin, James Travin, but you can call me Jim. My friends do."

"What do you want, James Travin?" His big smile dulled just a bit.

"Just cruising about and ended up here. Your husband certainly set you up nice."

I looked from him to my dogs and itched to yell, sic. He took one step back.

"I hope I'm not interrupting you from something important."

"You are."

I saw anger shoot through his eyes before he got it somewhat under control.

"I buy land," he said arrogantly, as though he was the most important person in the world.

I bristled. "Not from me."

"You haven't heard me out."

"Nor do I intend to. Leave and don't come back. My land is not and never will be for sale"

"Surely…."

"My dogs are restless," I warned.

"Surely you're courteous enough to talk…"

"Bruiser," I said softly and the dog rose to his feet, his hackles raised. Ransom mimicked him.

Travin backed up and started his vehicle. I saw his lips move but couldn't hear what he said for the noise of the engine, but I thought it was "You'll regret this."

I watched him turn the vehicle around and drive away. I knew I had just confronted someone far more dangerous than Hazel Farrow. This man was not only greedy, he was intelligent.

Chapter 16

October brought snow flurries and unusual cold weather. The air was so crisp and tingly it made my skin prickle. I started dragging in deadfall and chopping it for wood just as I had done last year. I had told Jonas we'd need more firewood this winter because a baby needed a warm house.

"You'll have to stay at my place this winter," he told me impatiently.

"No, I won't."

"There you go again, with your typical four-year-old selfishness. Can't you ever think of somebody other than yourself?"

I said no more to Jonas about firewood or the hogs. I didn't know what had gotten into him, but I didn't like it. I had to admit he treated me better when I was Rafe's wife.

I stopped to rest and adjust Drew's carrier straps when the idea hit me. *"Use my horse,"* Rafe seemed to say as though it wasn't my idea at all. I could take one of Rafe's horses, hook up the single tree and use a rope to drag downed trees home.

Things were going just perfect and I had two small trees lying in the back yard when Andy showed up, still limping and looking thinner than ever.

"What in this world are you doing?" he asked.

"What does it look like? I'm hauling firewood."

He shook his head. "Does Jonas know you're doing this?"

"Jonas is a busy man. His patients take all his time."

"Am I hearing resentment?"

I looked Andy in the eyes. "It's truth you're hearing."

"I see."

"I asked Jonas about firewood. He told me I could spend the winter in Banners Elk."

"That's such a bad idea?"

"It's ridiculous. Animals have to be fed."

"Yes, they do."

"I'm getting my own firewood."

"I'll help as much as I can. Wish I knew a man or boy that wasn't tied up with his own work. Right now Rupert Smith and that James Travin are fighting over ever able-bodied man and boy in three counties. They've even tried to hire old men that sit at the store and jaw."

"Who hauls coal?" I tried not to think of Zeb when I asked.

"Don't rightly know, but I can find out for you."

"Tell them I'll need a big load, maybe two. How's your leg doin?"

"Better."

I thought he was fibbing. "You look tired."

"So do you."

I laughed a little.

"Are you taking those vitamins Rupert Smith left you?"

"Yeah, but don't tell Jonas. I think they help a little. I'm not as tired when I wake up."

"I should take 'em," he said with a slight grin.

"Might not hurt."

"Exactly when is this baby due?"

"I'll probably be needin you to deliver it the end of March or the first of April."

"Be out of town then," he said quickly. "You'll have to count on Jonas or the good doctor Tate."

I grinned and Andy did too. "You can name this baby Andrea if it's a girl. Won't hurt to have two babies named after me. Give me a little clout down at the store."

I imagined how those men could go on about nothing at all. "Jonas wants a boy,"

"I want a girl. You need a girl," Andy added.

"I need a houseful of strong young men that know how to run a profitable farming operation."

"It's danged near too cold to do much farming on top of this mountain. Don't hardly give abody a long enough growin season."

"We make do, don't we."

"Hand me the ax," Andy said with determination. "If you can drag in trees with that horse and a baby on your back, I can chop."

"You don't have to."

"I want to."

I got one more tree dragged in by late evening, and Andy had chopped until he looked exhausted.

"I'm quitting for the day," I told Andy. "I have to have supper ready when Jonas gets home or he'll fuss."

"I'll turn the horse loose."

Drew was awake. I took him off my back and handed him to Andy. "You get him out of his carrier and I'll take care the horse." Andy didn't object.

When I got back, Andy was sitting on the step with Drew in his lap. "He's talking," Andy said.

"Jonas says he only makes noises, but I think he's talking too."

"He said dog and Andy."

I agreed. Drew came as close to saying those words as a four and a half month old baby could.

"James Travin came to see me," Andy said. "Wanted to buy my land. Asked how many acres I owned. I said it wasn't enough for him to want. He said he would buy ten square feet if it was priced right."

"He came here too."

"I know. He said you were rude, without proper manners. Pulled your shotgun on him, did you?"

"Nope. I was just carrying my gun when I talked to him. I told him to leave and not come back."

"Sure got his bloomers in a twist? Used to getting his own way, I'd say. Prime cradle-rich."

"He's not getting my land."

"He bought Hazel Farrow out. Slick talked her out of everything she owned."

"You're kidding."

"No kidding about it. He joined that holy-rolling-snake-handling church and has those people eating out of his hands. Heard he even has his own snakes. Shipped in a big load and is selling them to the church members."

I was speechless.

"It wasn't only Hazel. He's bought several people out. Convinced them to leave the mountains. Convinced them there's easy living down in the flatland."

"You're kidding."

"Wish I was Missy, but I'm not. He's not only buying em out, he's clearing em out. He's doin it with a vengeance."

"Vengeance?"

"He's not only taking their land and homes for almost nothing, he's sending em off without a snowball's chance in hell of surviving."

"What are folks saying about him?"

"Those folks that aren't sucking up to him are thinking vigilantes. I suggested they turn him loose on top of

Grandfather Mountain one night. Chances are he'd fall off a rock cliff before he found his way back."

That sounded like a fine idea to me. "What's the talk at the store?" I asked And.

"He's trying to buy Hack Pennel out. Said he'd pay Hack cold, hard cash for the store while he allowed Hack to stay there and run it for a fair cash-wage until the day he died. I pointed out to Hack, that he was older than I am."

"Hope Hack gave him a piece of his mind."

"Hack called me a liar," Andy said solemnly. "But he's thinking it over right hard. Travin offered him more money than Hack's seen in the past twenty years. Then what would a man as old as Hack or me do with a pile of money? Can you answer me that?"

I looked into Andy's troubled eyes until he looked away and downed his head, but he continued to talk.

"Time was when this hardscrabble mountain of rock wasn't wanted by anybody other than us that was too poor to live anywhere else or those running from the law. Mountains have always been a good place to hide but it hain't that way no more."

Who's running from the law?"

"I'm talking way back in time, Missy, when this land was first getting settled."

"There were Indians back then." I took Drew from his arms and he didn't object.

"During the summer there was. Winters were too cold to live through, even for Indians."

He looked across the yard and pastures to the blue haze of the mountains beyond. I watched memory show on his face, a kind of longing for things that once was.

"Look what our mountains have come to now. It's summer homes. The cradle-rich must have fashionable vacation homes where they can escape the heat down below. To my way of thinking, it's like getting outta hell when the temperature rises. Here is prime cool air with a view. Flatlanders don't have none of that where they come from. Right now land is cheap, labor is cheap, and the market can only get better."

"I won't sell my land," I said.

"We never know what we'll have to do. In the end, we never know."

"You won't sell your land," I said with confidence.

His eyes came from the distant mountain to rest on my baby. He reached out and touched Drew's little fist.

"I can't live forever. Nobody can."

"We can live to the bitter end," I said thinking of Rafe. I wondered if Rafe thought he would live forever.

"I have no children. I've outlived all the relatives I liked. Don't know what will happen to my place after I'm dead."

"I'll buy it," I said.

"You've got more than you can handle right here, regardless of the feisty little thing that you are." His lips twitched, but he stopped the grin before it reached his mouth.

I knew he thought I was silly. He thought I was a wife that belonged in the house not working a farm. Undoubtedly, he was wondering where I could get that much money. I knew Rafe had left me money, but I didn't know how much for it was in a bank somewhere. I would have to check on it.

"How much do you want for your land?"

He reached out and patted my hand. "I'm like you, Missy. I couldn't bear to sell it. Besides, I think I've got me some time left."

"I didn't mean to sound like you were dying and all."

"I know." This time he did grin.

It was dark and the weather was bitter by the time Jonas arrived. Wind was blowing the downed leaves in circles as though a storm was brewing. I watched out the kitchen window as he unsaddled his horse and released it in the field, leaving the side door to the barn open in case it wanted to take shelter from the rising wind. He looked nearly dead on his feet and none to happy as he entered the kitchen. I had put Drew to bed and had our food on the table.

"This is stupid," he said as he washed his hands in the wash pan of warm water I had waiting on the stove.

I didn't need to ask him what he was talking about. I knew he didn't like the ride up the mountain. I sat a steaming cup of coffee in front of him and gave him a kiss right on the mouth.

"I hope it'll be worth your while." I gave him my inviting look, but he didn't respond. "Grumpy."

He looked me in the eyes.

"What is it?"

"I'm losing hours a day, Laine. Time when I could be working."

I knew what was coming and I didn't want to hear it. I wasn't moving to Banners Elk. I'd better change the direction of his thoughts.

"Andy said Hazel Farrow sold out." I sat down across from him and began to eat.

He lifted his cup to his lips, drank, set it down. "Her and others."

"How could they do such a stupid thing?"

"You can't see other people's problems. Life is all about you and what you want."

His voice sounded harsh, as though he was mad at me. I didn't like it but I wasn't going to start an argument. I was tired and so was Jonas.

"Andy said Hazel was moving in with her daughter." I wanted to know for certain that Hazel, with her snakes, would be far away.

"That's not the gossip I heard."

"Really?"

"She's trying to buy a place near your momma's. She's not giving up her son without a fight."

That might be far enough away. I could imagine her and Momma living next to each other. Talk about a clashing of hell-fire and brimstone.

"You think that's funny don't you?"

I realized I was smiling and stopped. "If they're fighting with each other, maybe they'll forget about me."

Jonas started to say something, stopped, and shoved food in his mouth. Was he going to say he wished he could? Surely not. Jonas loves me. I know he does.

"Gossip is that you made an enemy of James Travin."

"He came here uninvited. I told him to leave."

"After sicing the dogs on him."

"I didn't sic my dogs on him."

"According to him, you did."

"He's lying."

Jonas gave me that unbelieving look. "He's giving more for land than your buddy is offering."

"My buddy?"

"Rupert Smith. Your buddy."

"He's not my buddy. He came here to see you."

"I'm not here when he comes now, am I?"

"Are you jealous?" I questioned in disbelief.

"No." He answered. "But that doesn't mean I want the likes of him hanging around my wife. People are starting to talk."

I laughed. I couldn't help it. Rupert Smith was the last person to hang around me. "That's silly," I told Jonas. It was beyond silly. It was stupid.

"Naturally. A man with his money could have any woman in the world that he wants. He certainly wouldn't be after my wife."

I dang near threw my plate at him. Instead, I got up, raked my food into the slop bucket, and put the plate in the dishpan of water on the stove. I went outside into the cold air. Bruiser got up off the porch and rubbed against my legs. In that cold night air I could feel the force of the storm that was coming.

Chapter 17

Andy didn't show up the next day to help me with the firewood. I half expected that he would. Finally, when the evening shadows got long, I stopped to rest. I couldn't keep my mind from thinking about Andy. He didn't look good yesterday. What if he was sick?

It didn't take long for me to decide what to do. I diapered Drew and headed through the woods with my dogs at my heels.

Andy wasn't home. I looked in his shop, in his house, and around the farm. His saddle was missing from the barn along with his riding horse. It must be his day at the store. I had satisfied myself that he wasn't laid-up sick and headed back home.

I heard the sound of a vehicle chugging up the mountain before I ever came out of the woods. I had to hurry to beat the vehicle to my place. I didn't beat it by much.

Both dogs bristled then lowered their scruff when Rupert got out. What Jonas had said last night ran though my mind. I wasn't as friendly toward him as I could have been.

"Evening, pretty lady."

That didn't endear me to him. It aggravated me. He must have sensed my feelings for he looked away, quick. He bent over and petted both dogs.

"I brought all the dog food I could haul. Saw Andy at the store this morning. He said by the end of the week only a horse and wagon could get up the mountain."

"Winter comes early." I looked away from him. "You ought not to bring anymore dog food. They're my dogs. I can feed them."

"If I don't bring dog food, I'll have no excuse to come here."

His words brought unease all the way to the tips of my toes. "You're not coming just for dog food?."

"I come to bring dog food, and like I said, I admit I come to look over the farm and see what you're up too." He looked uncomfortable. "Why do you think I come?"

"Simple. You're after my land."

His face appeared to droop. "I thought we'd settled that." He let out a long breath as though something had saddened him. "If you ever want to sell this place, I'll buy it, but I had rather you have it and live here for the rest of your life. I'd like to think, regardless of where I travel, there's a piece of land owned by little mountain girl that will never change."

I said nothing. He turned from me and got a bag of dog food and headed for the wood shed. I stood where I was, watching. After he had the four bags stacked, he came to the porch and sat down in a chair.

"Come here," he said.

I went to the porch.

He looked at me for a moment as though he was trying to see something. "I've not got much time. I've have business to take care of in Banners Elk so I'll not beat around the bush. I will buy your land any time you want to sell it, but I have no intention of taking it from you. That's the second time I've told you that today and I want you to imprint it in your mind permanently. You can believe in me and trust what I tell you."

"You're buttering me up."

"I admire you. Hell, I like you too much to butter-up. I'm here…."

He seemed at a loss for words. I watched the expression on his face as he started again, searching for the right words.

"I'm here for the reason I told you before. I want to see what you do on this farm. The old men at the store talk about you. Your determination; your grit, and I want to see just what a little ole girl can accomplish when she goes against the grain."

I frowned but he continued.

"There's a friendly wager going on. Some say Jonas will make you come to Banners Elk, others bet you won't budge."

"They're betting on me?" I was surprised, not to mention irritated. I wasn't something to be gambled on like. . . like I don't know what.

"They would bet on the sun rising if someone was foolish enough to take them up on it. It's the old men's harmless way of having fun. It's not an insult toward you."

"Are you betting?"

"Yes," he grinned just a little.

"How much?"

"I am betting Hack Pennel two hundred dollars cash if you winter in town against a signed, notarized first refusal on his store if you stay on the mountain."

"It is about land."

"In a way. As you know by now, James Travin is taking great pleasure in buying land out from under me. Naturally, he and I have a mutual dislike for each other. We have had several misunderstandings in the past."

"I don't like him either," I admitted.

"Between you and me, and that means don't tell Jonas or anyone, I'll do everything in my power to keep him from buying anymore land here." He gave a short chuckle that was not from humor. "As though he and everyone else doesn't already know it."

"Why?" I needed more than what he had said so far before I could believe him.

"James Travin was once married to my sister."

I hadn't expected those words. "Once?"

His lips grew thin. His jaw muscles twitched. "She died and I blame him."

I wanted to know more, wanted to ask him questions, but he held up his hands.

"Someday, perhaps I'll tell you about her, but not now. Just believe that I'm on your side and you can call on me if you need me."

I must of shown what I was thinking. How would I be able to call on him for anything when I was isolated on top of a mountain?

"Tell Andy if you need me." He stood up from the chair.

"Wait. I want to know more."

He hesitated then sat back down. "I'll tell you a little more, but it's not for gossip, understand? What I tell you is between you and me and no one else."

I nodded.

"I was doing pretty well in real estate when James Travin married my younger sister. He believed money was in our family and he would get Amy's share. As I told you before, my family had no money. I haven't a dime that I haven't earned."

His face reddened. He stopped talking for a minute before he continued. "I don't know how James Travin got the money to buy an insurance policy on himself and Amy but he did. He became a wealthy man when Amy died."

"He killed her?"

"If I could find one shred of proof…"

I looked into his eyes and knew he was telling me the truth. There was anger and sorrow and uncertainty all mixed together. I knew what he didn't say was that he would kill James Travin if he had proof, and I believe he would do just that. Something inside me reached out and connected with Rupert Smith.

"I shouldn't have told you any of that. I beg you not to repeat my lapse into weakness. It's just…"

"I remind you of Amy," I took a guess.

He nodded and I was a little disappointed. I had wanted him to like me for being myself.

"In a way," he amended. "She was young and trusting, a natural born innocent that never changed. You're young but not trusting of anyone. You were born with natural intelligence that changes as the need arises." He let out a strange kind of laugh. "Here I am giving you a sob story much like in one of those movies where the bad guy ties the young, innocent girl to the train tracks and expects the audience to believe the story is real."

"Your story is real?"

He nodded, stood up, and walked through the yard. I caught up with him and took hold of his arm. "I'm not your sister."

He hesitated, looked at me for a lingering moment. "Thank God," he said, then hurried away.

I watched him start the vehicle and drive out of sight. I listened to the fading sound, telling myself his story was too far fetched for me to believe. Some men will tell a woman anything to get her land.

Something else was telling me Rupert Smith wasn't lying or telling me the whole truth.

The next day I heard a sound that brought goose bumps to my flesh. I heard the sound of a horse-drawn wagon rattling toward the barn.

"Hello?" A man's voice called out.

"Hello," I hollered back and hurried from the corn field where I was chopping off corn stalks to shock. I recognized the black dust of a coal wagon.

"You Mrs. Jones? Where do you want this?" The young man that didn't look anything like Zeb asked.

I pointed to the coal shed. "Jonas send you?"

"Nope. Andy Harmon."

"How much do I owe you?" I wondered if I had enough left in the jar hidden in the cellar to pay him.

"He done paid me."

"Andy did?"

"Yeap."

He clicked his tongue, snapped the lines, and drove to the coal shed.

I went back to the corn field with Drew sleeping on my back. A tear or two slid down my jaws just thinking of how Andy reminded me of Dad. Regardless of how hard I tried, I couldn't hold them back. They slid even after it dawned on me that Andy was betting I'd winter right here and making sure I could.

I felt weak all over by the time the boy had shoveled all the coal from the wagon and left. I kept feeling Zeb's hand squeezing my breast, and the clang and bounce of the frying pan hitting his head. I remembered my fear at seeing his head wound gap open and the blood running on my kitchen floor; the fear of thinking I had killed him and would be hung for it. I listened to the sound of the wagon leaving, remembering Zeb riding away as fast as the horse could go.

It was my attempted laughter that allowed me to go back to the house for a drink of cold water instead of hiding

in the corn field a while longer. Still I jumped when Andy
came out of the woods. I waited for him to catch up to me.

"Heard the wagon leaving. Was it the first load or the
second?"

"He's bringing another?"

Andy nodded.

"Thanks for sending him. How much do I owe you?"

"Nothing."

"What? He said you paid him."

"Not with my money." Andy reached down and slapped
at his leg. "Danged if my knee hain't locking up again."

"Where you were horse kicked?"

"Nope. Where I've got old."

"Jonas gave you the money for coal?"

"Don't think I'd be spending my money on the likes of
you, do you?" He slapped his knee a couple more times and
then shook his leg before he continued toward the kitchen
porch.

"You'd spend your money betting on the likes of me." I
watched his reaction to my words. His mouth twitched.
"Want to fess-up?" I asked when he tried to ignore me.

"To what?"

"Betting I'll winter on the mountain."

"No betting about it. I know you won't leave this
mountain upright. Jonas would have to hog-tie you across
the saddle."

"He won't do that."

"Reckon not."

"Want a glass of water?"

"Yeap." He sat down in the porch chair and slapped his
knee again. "Old age hain't for the timid."

When I brought him the water he was a little pale. "You
should get Jonas to look at that knee."

"Nope."

"Why not?"

"Hain't no need. Not even your Jonas can make an old man young again."

"But…"

"Hush up about me, Missy. There's not a part of my body that don't hurt at one time or another. The Higher Power intended it to be that way. If old folks stayed frisky, they'd never agree to pass on over."

"You may be right."

"Know I am. Say, how did you know about the bets?"

"Rupert."

"Figures."

I took Drew from my back and he woke up. Andy didn't reach for him like he sometimes did. I knew he was hurting bad.

"What was Rupert doing here?"

"Brought more dog food."

"For a real estate man, he hain't all bad."

"You like him?"

"Wouldn't go that far."

"Do you trust him?"

Andy hesitated. "Wouldn't go that far."

I looked him in the eyes.

"Yeah, I trust him as much as I can trust a developer."

"What about James Travin?"

Andy shook his head. "He's a snake in the grass, a poison snake shaking his rattles to beat the band."

I didn't much like Andy reminding me about snakes. "Do you know anything about Travin?" I couldn't come right out and ask if he knew Travin had married Rupert's sister.

"Just know I don't like him."

"What does Rupert say about him?"

Andy looked at me real close. "He's not said nothing to me about him."

"He told me to shoot him." I repeated what I had told Andy before.

"No love to lose between those two."

"Why not?"

"Don't know. It does seem like Travin is trying to upstage Rupert. He comes in behind Rupert and pays folks more than Rupert offered. Has one of those fancy lawyers riding around with him so folks can mark their X on the deed right on the spot. He pays cash money on the barrelhead."

"Before Rupert can up the price?"

"Seems so."

"Has this happened other places?" I asked.

"So I've heard. Why are you so interested?"

"Cause I don't like snakes in the grass."

"That's what I thought you'd say." Andy slapped his knee again. "I see you're shocking corn."

"Ought to be shucking it, but I thought I could haul the shocks into barn stalls and shuck it later."

"If my body would cooperate, I'd help you more."

"I'm fine, now that the coal has arrived. By the way, who's betting I'll winter here?"

His eyes twinkled. "Me and Rupert against about six of 'em that say Jonas will haul you off this mountain before Groundhog Day."

"How much will you win?"

"More than the coal costs."

Chapter 18

The weather turned cold on Halloween day. The temperature dropped to twenty degrees. Jonas had told me he wouldn't be coming home tonight. He was going to stay in Banners Elk to keep trick or treaters from messing his place up.

Every time Jonas didn't come home, I got similar feelings that I had when I was married to Rafe. Feelings of being alone and afraid. Just like back then, I wouldn't let them get the best of me. If anything, I went out of my way to show Jonas I could manage even if he didn't ever come home.

I dressed Drew in the warm clothes I had made him, strapped him on my back, slung a wool blanket around both of us, and went to the barn. After the work was done up, I stood studying the hog lot. I had too many hogs and no way of selling them. I had Rafe's team, wagon, and crates, but I didn't know where to take live hogs to sell. I wasn't even sure I could sell cured hams and shoulders unless I did like Rafe and drove all the way to Eula's store. I was sure I couldn't feed all these hogs during the winter.

I had no choice. It was hog-killin time.

I found a fifty-five gallon barrel and rolled it from the shed to the tree nearest to the barn. I carried rocks and built walls to hold the barrel off the ground high enough to feed wood into a fire below it. I maneuvered the barrel on the walls with it leaning at an angle where I could pour in and dip out water. The water had to be scalding hot to loosen hog bristles.

As I carried water from the creek, I couldn't stop myself from remembering stories told about people falling into the barrels of scalding water. Tomorrow Drew would have to stay inside the house with Ransom watching him. I wouldn't take a chance with my baby.

I gathered large pieces of dead-fall the rest of the day, thankful they didn't have to be chopped up. I hoped I had enough. If I didn't, I could add a couple buckets of my precious coal. I had five hogs to butcher including the ones Dad had given me and the mean old sow Rafe had brought home. The sow would be old and tough, not fit for much more than sausage. Still, I thought it best to kill her instead of raising another litter of pigs. By spring Drew would be learning to walk and I didn't want him near a mean sow. Rafe's son wouldn't be killed the same way he was – by a mean hog.

This job would take me all week long.

That evening, just as dark was settling, I tucked Drew in his crib and went out onto the upper porch. Needles of cold shot through my dress and chilled me to the bone. It was sure enough hog-killin weather and everything was ready – everything but the hardest part. Tomorrow morning before the hogs were fed, I'd have to shoot one between the eyes and then slit its throat before it died.

Morning came too soon. I woke up early just as I planned, dressed warm, left Drew sleeping, and got Rafe's gun and the sharpened butcher knife.

It was bitter cold outside, nearing zero, I figured, which was fitting. My insides seemed frozen solid with what I was about to do. I hurt as though ice was inside my chest squeezing my heart. The metal of the gun seemed to have frozen my fingers to it. I knew I would turn loose if it were physically possible.

"How did you manage doing this, Dad?" I silently asked into the darkness. "How can I take the life from something I have cared for?"

I listened for his voice but he didn't answer. He didn't need to tell me things had to die so others could live. Even a blade of grass was alive before a cow bit it off. Every vegetable in my garden was alive before I plucked it off the vine to can.

But animals weren't vegetables. They breathed, they grunted, they looked at me with big sad eyes. They trusted me to keep them from harm.

The mean sow came up to the rail fence. She was a dark shadow moving about. I couldn't see her eyes looking at me or her snout twitching as she tried to smell slop I wasn't carrying.

"Steady the gun barrel on the rail," Dad's voice said as plain as the daylight that was soon to come.

I lifted the gun and rested the barrel on the top rail. The sow's snout touched the barrel smelling of it.

"Lift it between her eyes."

I lifted it.

"Squeeze the trigger."

Suddenly I could feel the hard muscled strength of Rafe behind me. His arms were around my shoulders. His hands were helping me hold the gun. I looked up at Rafe. He grinned, and I thought I saw a touch of warmth come into his green eyes.

"Don't look uncertain, my little wife. You're tougher than the average mountain lion." He was smiling. *"Hold it tight against your shoulder. Squeeze, don't jerk the trigger."* Rafe instructed.

Rafe's finger pressed on top of mine and the gun fired. It kicked but I didn't fall. Rafe's body kept me standing.

I know I opened the gate and went inside the lot, but I don't remember it. I only remember that a hog's neck is tougher than I thought it would be. I remember having to stab the knife tip hard.

Drew was crying. I didn't know how much time had passed. I didn't know how long I had been huddled behind the cook stove. I just knew I had to get up off the kitchen floor and wash my hands before I went upstairs to him. I didn't want to get blood on my baby.

The water in the wash-pan was warm on my cold hands. The heat from the cook stove filled the kitchen and went up the stairs to the bedrooms but I was chilled to the bone.

A pale, heatless sun shown in the window as Drew sucked his breakfast. It shined on Drew's face, into his eyes. I saw that the slate blue of babyhood was almost gone and the color of grass green was taking its place. Just as I already knew, the blood of Rafford Johnson carried strong.

My mind reached out for Rafe, thankful that he had been there standing behind me, but the room was empty except for me and my baby. *Tough.* No, I wasn't as tough as a spring butterfly, but I could pretend to be tough for my baby, for me.

When Drew had his fill, I left him in his crib, put on a coat, and went to the hog lot. The mean sow was laying there, cold and stiff. Thankfully, I no longer was looking at something alive. There was no longer a heart-beat sending the warm blood of life through the veins. It was a piece of meat waiting to be butchered. I could do that. I had helped Dad many times before.

"Folks do what has to be done to stay alive," Dad told me often. I could do no less.

I left the hog and started the fire beneath the barrel of water. I should have started the fire first thing. It would have been hot by now if I had been thinking right.

I hurried back to the house to check on Drew. I could put him on my back, if he was crying, while I harnessed the horse and dragged the hog near the barrel. Ransom was lying next to the warm kitchen stove and Drew was sleeping peacefully upstairs. He wasn't crying for his momma, he wasn't even missing being on my back. I tiptoed from the room.

The smell of fresh blood made the horse nervous. He lifted his muzzle, snorted, and pawed the ground as I tied a rope to the hog's legs and fastened it to the single-tree. He became skittish and side-stepped as I tried to make him pull the hog from the lot. I finally had to turn loose of the reins and grab hold near his head to stop him from rearing up. I patted his face, sweet talked, and soothed him until he moved forward pulling the weight. He was well acquainted with pulling a sled and wagon and paid no attention to Rafe's drunken singing and total lack of driving. He just didn't like the blood-smell, but he was a smart horse. He would settle down.

He didn't like the smell of fire either. He must be remembering the barn catching on fire when the panther attacked me. His eyes were rolling in his head and his ears were laid back as we neared the fire. I finally took off my coat, placed it over his face, grabbed his halter and led him blind.

He was as relieved as I was when I took him to the barn hall. Unfortunately, I wasn't through with him yet. Once the hog was scalded and scraped clean of hair, I had to hang it by the hind legs to a stout tree limb in order to gut it.

I covered the hog with several layers of sacks to hold the heat of the scalding water close to its skin and took the bucket to the water. It was difficult work dipping out bucket after bucket of the scalding water without getting myself burned. I thought about making a pine-knot torch and trying to singe the hair from the hog. There had to be an easier way than this.

I wasn't comfortable being away from Drew this long. I hurried inside to find Drew awake. His feet were in the air and his little hands were grabbing at his toes. He looked at me and smiled. I fed him again, even though he wasn't much hungry. I couldn't leave my baby alone too long. What if something happened to him?

By the time I had one side scraped clean, I was wondering what was so bad about hairy hog skin. I decided it wasn't bad at all when I tried to roll the hog over to get the other side. How had Dad done it?

I searched until I found a fence post, tied the ends of a rope to each bottom foot and then to the top of the post. I braced the bottom against the ground and hog's back. Grabbing the top of the post, and putting all my weight into the pull, gave me enough leverage to roll the heavy hog.

Trouble was I fell and the sow rolled onto me. By the time I had wiggled, pushed, and scraped myself free, I concluded for a fact a pine-knot torch to singe the hair off was the way to go. I shuddered as I tried not to think of what else had to be done before I could rest. Once I finished scraping, I had to drag the hog to a tree and hang it to a limb, and then came cutting the head off, tying off the gut so manure didn't get on the meat, and then the gutting. After that came the butchering.

When Jonas got home, I was so tired I could barely put his supper before him. I sat down in a chair but only stared at my plate.

"Why aren't you eating?"

"I'm not hungry. "

"You need to eat nutritious meals in order for my baby to develop healthy and strong."

I forced a few bites down.

"What did you do today?" he asked as though he was in a good humor.

"Butchered the mean sow," I told him without thinking.

His fork of food stopped halfway to his mouth. He glared as though I had said something awful. "You did what?"

"It's below freezing so I butchered the first of the hogs."

"You're crazy!"

I didn't know what to say to that. I just knew I didn't like it.

"You could have lost my baby. You still might. Come into the front room. Let me examine you."

"You know good and well I won't lose our baby. If a mountain lion attack didn't cause me to, nothing will."

"Each pregnancy is different." He dropped his fork and jumped to his feet.

"Sit down and eat. I know when I've okay and when I'm not."

"Don't argue with me."

"Jonas, if you don't sit down and eat, I'm going to walk right out that door and go to the barn just to get away from you."

His eyebrows lifted before he sat back down. "What's gotten into you to be so careless? Don't you care as much about this baby as you did for Rafford Johnson's?"

How dare he say that to me. If I had twenty babies, I'd still care for them all alike. "You say something like that to me ever again, Jonas Jones, and I'll take the frying pan to you and then sic Bruiser on your bones."

"That's your solution to all your problems, threats of violence."

"I do not threaten with violence."

"No, you just hit people over the head with cow bells and sic your dogs on developers."

So, Jonas had heard about James Travin, but it wasn't Travin that irritated me. It was his mentioning Francis Dewhitte as though I had been the one in the wrong.

"I'm tired, Jonas, and I don't intend to argue with you or anyone else tonight. When you've finished, put your plate in the dishpan." I got up and went upstairs to bed.

I slept like a dead person. Jonas woke me up to feed Drew when he cried. Every bone in my body ached. Even my hair seemed to hurt. I didn't tell Jonas, but I was concerned that I had worked too hard and it would hurt my baby. I thought about the new baby as Drew sucked. I did want this baby, but how on God' green earth could I love it as much as I loved Drew?

I thought about Rafe. He wasn't much of a man in my opinion. He was lazy when it came to work, but his mind seemed to be planning all the time. He drank a lot and he chased women like Junie, but when he lay dying, he told me that he loved me.

Memory brought tears to my eyes. I had wanted to love Rafe, wanted to make him a good wife. Perhaps I failed Rafe, but I didn't want to fail Jonas. Jonas was my second chance at being a good wife, and I did love Jonas. I loved the way he held me against him; the way his lips touched mine; the way his body gave me pleasure when Rafe's never had.

I stepped over Ransom and eased the sleeping Drew back into his crib and went to the bedside. Jonas had fallen back to sleep. I saw the way his dark hair fell over his forehead and the way his face looked while he slept. I saw the shadows the lamp cast on him and the growth of beard. He seldom shaved here. He must do that once he reached Banners Elk.

I turned out the lamp and eased back in bed, feeling the warmth of Jonas's body. "Please, God," I prayed. "Help me be a good wife, and don't let me do anything to hurt either of my babies."

Jonas left early and I was both regretful and pleased. I would have liked to linger over breakfast, listen to him talk about things like his work, or what was going on with people off this mountain. Jonas wasn't much for gossip. He wasn't much for talking to me, either. He carried his thoughts as though they were private and didn't belong to me. I had to rely on Andy for my need for human conversation, or as Jonas would say, local gossip.

I was glad Jonas left early because I still had half the hog to butcher and make into sausage. Besides, I hadn't rendered the lard from where I stripped the fat off the guts. Good lard was a necessity.

What I hadn't expected was for Andy to show up with two men I had never seen before. I offered them a cup of coffee and they all refused. I just looked at them standing there in the yard and waited for Andy to tell me why they were there. It didn't take long.

"We came to help with the hog killin," Andy said.

"How did you know I was killin hogs?"

"Jonas stopped by my place."

"And he sent the others from town?"

"Seems so."

For one brief moment, I considered telling them I didn't need help. The moment passed. I couldn't shoot and cut the throat of another hog. I still heard the squeal of pain as the bullet struck, still smelled the first stench of hot blood let by my own hands.

"Thank you," I said as I fought tears, which I hated. I must be more tired than I thought, more affected by my condition.

"Show us which ones." Andy said. "Could I use your gun? I didn't bring mine."

I gave him Rafe's gun and went to the hog lot. I pointed at two more hogs, and then hurried away. Surely it was being in the family way that caused me to react like this. I wasn't this weak when I lived with Dad, hadn't been this squeamish ever before.

Or perhaps I was still reacting to seeing the boar hog rip Rafe apart.

By the time to do up the evening's work, the men had finished and had the meat salted down in the smoke house. I was thankful that Mr. Holloway had several bags of salt stored there for this purpose. I was astounded at how much work three men could get done in a day's time. A man could make a fortune if he had two sons. Maybe this baby would be a boy, too, and they could make this farm produce in the way it should.

"How do I pay you and the men, or has Jonas paid?" I asked Andy.

"Jonas said you'd give them each a pig."

Jonas had seen a way to get rid of my livestock, which was okay for I had more on the way from the sows I got from Dad. The two pigs I told Andy to give them belonged to the mean sow and the boar that killed Rafe. They were already showing their parents temperament and were becoming vicious. They were fit for butchering not breeding.

"You want a pig, too?

"Nope. Don't want nothing else to care for."

"How about a ham?"

"That I can handle." He strode off to tie the pigs in sacks for the men to take home. After they had left, he came back inside where I was putting chunks of meat into the sausage grinder.

"There's news."

I stopped cranking. "What?"

"It's about your sister."

A lump of ice began to form in my chest as I waited for him to continue.

"Word has it she miscarried."

It seemed impossible that Susie could be in the family way, but then she was married to Abe.

"Folks said she wasn't far enough along to know if it was a boy, but she made Abe build a little coffin, put in the remains, and bury it next to your brother and dad."

For a moment, I felt as though I was back in the graveyard watching Momma try to dig up my little brother from his grave.

"She named the baby Wesley Elder Farrow."

Dad's name.

Chapter 19

There's always something about watching large snow flakes fall, the way they silently cover everything even when they are such delicate things, that touches me on the inside. It's like watching a part of God's creation without being part of it, and certainly not able to control it.

It didn't seem right that this quiet evening beauty would keep Jonas from coming home tonight. Sometimes I thought he stayed away more than necessary, as though he was trying to make me move to his place. Other times Francis Dewhitte slipped into my mind like cold wind.

I built a fire in the cook stove, the heating stove, and the fireplace. I didn't care if I was wasting coal and wood. I needed to be warm, and I missed Jonas.

I also noticed that I wasn't giving much milk. Drew became fussy and wanted to suck every hour or so. I made mashed potatoes without adding any lard for seasoning and thinned it slightly with cow's milk. He slurped it up like a little old man.

It wasn't good and dark outside but I needed to go to bed and rest. I was shivering when I crawled beneath the covers and sweating when I woke up a few hours later. I don't remember much about getting up to feed Drew, but I remember the wall opening up and me watching white horses grazing in a green pasture. Next came Susie burying her dead baby, a dead baby that had become my dad.

"You're sick," said Boise's voice. *"You're sick and you're going to lose your baby before you die, just like I did."*

I sat bolt-upright. Pale morning light was coming through the bedroom window, doing nothing about warming the room. I looked at the empty side of the bed and then at the crib. Drew was asleep. My feet hit the cold floor and I padded to him, checking to see if he was cold. The blankets and the warm pajamas I had made protected him during the night. I got him out of bed, still asleep, and tucked him under the cover beside me. There was no reason for either of us to get up this early. It was freezing outside.

I was sick when I woke up. My head and throat ached. The thought of breakfast made me grab the pot from under the bed. Everything left in my stomach came up until bile burned my throat. I thought about a drink of water and gagged.

Feeling Drew beside me was a comfort and I was thankful that he liked to sleep as much as he did. I hoped the baby I carried would be as easy to care for as Drew. I drifted back to sleep, but it wasn't restful. Crazy dreams kept coming at me, scaring me, warning me that bad things were about to happen.

"See what you get for taking my place," Boise said. *"See what you get for bringing another man into my house."*

Ransom had his front feet on the bed licking me in the face as he whined to be let out. I made my eyes open. The room was full of daylight, the sun way up in the morning sky. I was shivering until my teeth chattered and knew I had to get up and build a fire. Drew was awake and beginning to fuss for food.

I wrapped myself in one of the quilts, slipped cold shoes on my feet, and went down the stairs. Ransom rushed out into a foot of snow, scattering it like goose down. He

bounced and whirled and jumped over Bruiser's back just
like it wasn't below zero. I closed the door and rushed to
the cook stove. If I could get the fire started, the room
would be warm in no time. My hands shook as I put
kindling in the firebox. They continued to shake as I struck
the match. My teeth chattered until I feared I'd never be
warm again. A spasm hit me and I grabbed the slop bucket.
I gagged but only burning bile came up. Finally, when the
spell eased off, I stuffed the fire box full of split wood,
closed the kitchen door off from the rest of the house and
went up stairs to bring Drew down. I needed to feed and
diaper him in a warm place.

He was heavier than normal. I stopped at the top of the
stairs to catch my breath. The steps were such a long ways
down I had to be careful placing my feet. I didn't want to
fall or drop my son.

Rafe was standing at the bottom of the steps looking
from me to Drew. *"So, this is my boy, the fruit of my loin."*

I didn't know what to say to Rafe. He already knew
Drew was his son.

*"Don't stand there gawking. The kitchen is warm. If
you had a quilt you could sleep on the floor."*

I turned around and made my way back to the bedroom
and got a quilt. I didn't think I was going to be able to carry
Drew and the quilt, but I did. The kitchen was warm, but
Rafe wasn't there. I wondered where he had gone, but
wondering never did do me any good. He always came and
went as he pleased and I never knew when either would
happen.

I put the blanket on the floor near the stove and lay
down on it with Drew. Things seemed so strange, like I was
looking through a thick glassed bottle. I fed Drew; I put
wood in the cook stove; I drank water, vomited, and slept.

Sometime during the day I remembered I had not fed the animals or milked the cow. "I'll do it later I told myself and fell back to a restless sleep.

I awoke again. This time from hearing Momma's voice telling me I was a lazy no-account for allowing my brother, Joey, to die. For a moment, I thought Joey was in the room with me, pulling at my hair. When he began to cry, I realized it was my baby, my little Drew, and he was hungry. I took him to my breasts but they were empty.

Potatoes were too difficult to peel, cook and mash. I had to make gravy. I moved Drew to the center of the quilt and got up, holding onto the wall. I took wood from the wood box and fed it into the stove. I needed to bring in more wood; I needed to do up the work; I needed to make gravy and feed Drew.

I made gravy through a stupor and fed Drew as though from memory and not a conscious effort. I was relieved when he fell asleep on the warm quilt. If only I could lie down and sleep along side him, but I couldn't. A lazy no-account would not leave the warm room, feed and milk. I was not lazy or no-account. I would show her, show them all, that Laine Elder could do anything she set her mind to. "Just watch me," I told them. "Just watch me."

There was no one to watch me as I put on my coat, got the milk bucket, opened the kitchen door, and went out into the cold. It was late evening and the wind had settled a little. No more snow was falling to add to the foot already on the ground. Bruiser and Ransom ran in front of me, helping make a path. It never occurred to me before how much a path broken through the snow helped. My feet did not want to step high, sink into the snow and then pull themselves back out.

Doing up an hour's worth of work took days, weeks, almost a life time, but I managed. I managed it.

Sometime during the night, my fever broke. I woke with my head clearer. I was relieved to find that Drew was in bed with me and Ransom was next to my bed. I heard him lift his head when I felt to see if Drew needed a dry diaper. But Jonas wasn't beside me. I wondered if he was in bed sleeping warm and comfortable. I wondered if he was alone.

Morning came and the weather on top of Beech Mountain had settled. No cold winds were blowing and a pale sun was shining down making the snow sparkle. How thankful I was to be better. I was better enough to be miserable.

I built a fire and made biscuits and gravy. I had to eat something. The baby in my belly needed nutrition. I put my hand on my stomach and felt the bulge. I guessed that I was nearing my fourth month. I hoped my baby would start kicking soon. I had a need to know it was alive. I needed to know that my being sick hadn't killed it. How did a mother being sick affect a baby? Did it get sick like its mother? Did it have to suffer and feel everything the mother felt?

I was at the chicken house carrying them water when Jonas rode into the yard as silent as a falling flake of snow. The only sound I heard was the squeak of leather. It was early for him. He was warmly dressed and freshly shaved. He wore a winter cap instead of a hat. Ear warmers were pulled down with the strings tied under his chin. He had appeared to ride the horse slow for it wasn't lathered much.

He smiled when he saw me, slid off the horse and took him into the barn to unsaddle and brush down. I didn't go to the barn. I went to the house. There wasn't enough energy left in me to run and greet him, even if I had wanted to.

I was putting supper on to cook when he came in the door. "There's more snow on this mountain than in town," he said.

Naturally, I thought. "How much is in Banners Elk," I asked.

"About six inches." He bent and kissed me on the cheek. His nose was cold.

So, six inches of snow had kept him away for two days. "Many folks sick?"

"Stomach complaint is going around."

Surely what I'd had. "Serious?"

"Only for the old and weak."

"Did the complaint or the snow keep you away for two days?" I couldn't stop myself from asking.

"Both, plus I had important matters to take care of."

Things more important than a sick wife, I thought, and then felt instantly guilty. Jonas was a busy doctor and he did have a long distance to travel up and down the mountain.

"What important matters?"

"For one, James Travin wants me to start working for him."

I stopped peeling potatoes. Hatred of the man flooded me. "Doing what?"

"Don't take that tone of voice. I know how you dislike the man and it is for no reason. Actually, James is a nice person. He happens to have made a lot of money and he's willing to distribute some of it by buying up no-account mountain land."

Nice like a rusty nail in the foot. "Doing what?" I repeated.

"James has a large number of people working for his company and he would like to have one doctor that can keep records of every employee's health. Also, he wants to make sure their families get proper medical care."

And he wants you in his pocket so he can get my land.
Surely Jonas was smart enough to know that. A doctor had
to be intelligent in more ways than one or he would never
make a licensed doctor.

"How would you be working for him by doctoring his
workers?"

"James would be paying their bills."

"Doesn't he pay them enough to afford a doctor?"

"He wants to give them extra benefits."

"You have so many patients you can't come home now.
Why would you want to add on more? Do you plan to give
up sleeping and your family?"

Jonas seemed a bit uncomfortable as he pulled out a
chair and sat down. "There's Doctor Tate and the new
hospital." He stopped talking as though considering his
next words.

"What about 'em?"

"All the patients that can afford to pay are going to him.
I'm getting the ones that are half starved."

"Couldn't they work for Travin or Rupert? Andy said
they were fighting over workers."

"Some people live too far away to travel the distance
twice a day. You know there's not many roads and a lot of
rough hilly ground. They don't own horses like I do.
Besides, there are old people that can't work and need more
medical care than average. Most of the time they send word
that I'm needed and I have to go to them. When that
happens, I can only see two or three patients a day."

"Doesn't seem any different than always."

He was irritated at me. "It is different. I'm not earning
any money."

I turned and looked at him. I saw worry in his eyes that
I hadn't seen before. "What are you in need of money for?"

"Medical supplies are not cheap. Keeping up two
houses is not cheap either."

"You're not keeping up this place," I reminded him and he didn't comment.

"Sometimes I feel like I'm keeping the world alive. Right now, working no more than five or six days a week would be a blessing."

"Then work five or six days a week."

"I knew you wouldn't understand. James is offering me . . . us, a chance at a normal family life."

"You can always stop being a doctor and be a farmer. This land is rich and ready to grow things again. Mr. Holloway made good money and he was old."

"I'm a doctor, Laine. I don't know how to farm."

Now that was plain silly talk. "Everybody knows how to farm. If you want to know more, Mr. Holloway has a wall full of books, most of 'em on farming. You can read up on it."

Jonas rubbed his fingers through his hair. "When will supper be ready?"

❧

I didn't tell Jonas I was sick for I knew he would fuss at me for not being more careful than to catch something that might hurt his baby. He wasn't home long enough to notice how I was feeling, anyway. When he did manage to get up the mountain, he came home late and left early without telling me anything about James Travin or what was going on in Banners Elk.

It was three days later before I felt good enough to visit Andy. I needed someone to get information from. I needed to know more about James Travin even though I already knew enough. I didn't like him and furthermore, I didn't trust him. I couldn't understand why Jonas did.

There was no smoke rising from his shop and a thin stream of heat coming for his house. I knocked on the door.

"Get on in here, Missy," he called out.

I found Andy sitting in the living room next to the heating stove. It was the first time I had been inside his house, and I knew he wasn't feeling good or he would have been in his shop. The living room was tiny and made even smaller by the bed taking up half the room. I had almost forgotten how folks used to sleep in the living room.

"What're you doing with that baby out in this cold? What's wrong?"

"Nothing." I closed the door behind me.

"Now I know there is, so out with it."

His face was lined and sagged. For the first time, he looked older than his years.

"Jonas is talking about selling his land to James Travin," I burst out without intending to do so. My distress had built up more than I realized for I was about to cry.

"You don't say?"

I nodded as I took Drew from my back. He was wide awake and ready to play. He looked at Andy and smiled, but Andy didn't seem to notice. All his wrinkles had drawn together in the center of his face.

"Why would he do a thing like that?"

"Jonas said folks that pay are going to Dr. Tate and he's left with the ones that can't. He said medical supplies and stuff costs more than he's got."

"I've heard some talk on that line."

"He can't sell to Travin."

"Humph, didn't he just buy that tract of land?"

"You know he did."

"After you were his wife?"

"Yeah."

"Then you have to sign the deed before he can sell it."

I felt a spark of hope. "Are you sure?"

"It's the law. What a married man and wife obtain during their marriage is considered to belong to both parties."

"What about the land Rafe owned?"

"Not certain. Could be Rafford left it to his son with you as his trustee, or it could belong to you jointly, or it might be yours straight out."

"How can I find out?"

"Rupert should know, but he's out of town until after the New Year."

"If that's the case I won't sign. Travin can't have it."

"Why don't you buy it?"

"What with?"

"Missy, Rafford Johnson had money in the bank. He was as slick a trader as melting lard, and you know good and well he never missed an opportunity to grab hold of something."

Andy was right, but I wasn't sure how much money Rafe left behind. "How can I find out?"

"I need to go into town directly. I'll check around."

"I'd appreciate that. What about Travin? Have you found out anything about him?"

Andy stretched his leg and moved it closer the fire as though the cold was hurting it. To me, the small room was way to hot and I took off Drew's little cap and unbuttoned his sweater. I could feel sweat starting to ooze from my body.

"Travin is buying up land like it was candy while Rupert is away. Folks always have been and always will in a bad way come winter. By spring they'd be willing to sell their soul to the devil."

I felt like James Travin was the devil. I couldn't put my finger on exact reasons, but he scared me.

"Jonas likes him," I repeated in astonishment.

"The man can be a charmer. He talks a good tale and you know how charmers work. They study people and find their weak spot and then drive the blade home."

"Jonas is intelligent," I continued.

"I know he is, Missy. Intelligent folks can be conned as easily as others. Sometimes more so because they know they're smart. Dumb folks thinks on things long and hard because they know they're dumb and don't want to be taken advantage of."

Suddenly, a strange fear hit me. What if something happened to Andy? Would Travin manage to get his land? "Would you sell your land?"

"Missy, I wouldn't willing sell one square foot of my land."

"Good."

"But I can't live forever," he added. "Nor can I take land with me." He grinned as he watched me. "Now, don't you go getting that expression on you sweet face. I'm one of the dumb ones but I'm not a complete fool. I know who I want to get my land after I'm dead and gone."

"Who?" I couldn't keep from asking.

"Now, Missy. I'm not going to tell you my life story right here and now. Just because my wife and I didn't have children doesn't mean I didn't get around in my time."

I must have shown my surprise at his words for he chuckled. "You leave my affairs to me," he added.

"Just so you don't go crazy and sell out to Travin," I said for good measure, wondering if Rafe left enough cash behind for me to buy out Jonas and Andy. For some good reason, I didn't think so.

"There's one thing a body should always take heed by: You should never corner anything that's meaner than you, and I'm meaner and older than Travin."

The weather was mild and Jonas came home that night. He seemed happy and it wasn't long until he told me why.

"James is willing to double what I paid for the land. I can afford to add onto my house, make a real nice office."

I started to remind him that he was complaining about too few patients and traveling to them. What did he need with a better office? Instead, I said, "I want to keep that land."

"It's not yours to keep. That is one piece of land that belongs to me."

"You bought it after we were married. It's half mine."

I didn't expect his reaction. His face turned as red as a turkey's waddle and his lips tightened against his teeth. I could tell he was barely stopping the words he wanted to say to me, and I wanted to erase his anger if I could.

"Rafe left me some money. You can use it if you want."

This time he glared at me with angry eyes. "You'd not only strip a man of his dignity, you'd cut off his balls."

I was shocked. "What are you talking about? What have I done?"

"Nothing," Jonas snapped. "Sweet little Laine never does anything does she?"

"I think you'd better explain yourself." My anger was rising faster than I could force it down.

"I've spend every day since I met you trying to explain myself, but what good has it done me? Life is all about Laine and what Laine wants. It has no consideration for a poor man that's spent his entire life trying to help others."

I wanted to use the frying pan on him. Instead I controlled myself and said, "My goodness. Being an expectant father sure makes some men contrary."

Jonas and I didn't talk much after that. At least he didn't sleep in a different bed. He even put his arm around me during the night. Still, I slept fitfully. I hadn't expected to dream what I did. I dreamed Momma had slipped Susie tansy and other herbs to make her abort her baby.

Why? I had asked the dream, thinking Momma should love having a baby to cuddle and pamper. I recalled that Momma had never really cuddled and pampered Joey. She had seemed to worship Joey as long as someone else did the work. It was Susie she cuddled and pampered. Susie meant everything to her and she never wanted to lose one moment of Susie's undivided attention.

I woke up in a wringing sweat long before Drew wanted to be fed. I tried to tell myself I just had a nightmare and there was no truth in it, but I couldn't convince myself.

"Jonas," I said at breakfast. "I had a dream."

He looked at me, his eyes no longer glaring but a long way from loving. "What is it now?"

"I dreamed that Momma slipped Susie herbs to make her lose the baby."

"Good Lord in Heaven, Laine. Can't you stop coming up with stupid things? I don't have time to listen to more of your foolishness."

I put his plate in front of him. It was going to be a long hard winter.

Andy showed up at the house even though the snow hadn't melted. At least he wasn't walking. He rode a big-footed horse. I was coming out of the barn as he came through the woods from the direction of his place and stopped to wait on him.

"'Day Missy. Care if I put my hoss in your barn hall while you give me a hot cup of coffee?"

"Not at all. I'll put a fresh pot on while you're doing that." There was something about the look on his face that made me uneasy. I figured Rafe hadn't left me any money to speak of. James Travin would get Jonas' land regardless of how hard I fought.

Andy's breath was coming fast as he sat down at the table. "Storm's a comin," he said. "Storm clouds are broodin fast."

"I smelled it in the air when I first got up." I didn't tell him how much I dreaded winter. Staying here by myself last winter left a bad memory. I put fresh biscuits and apple butter on the table along with coffee, cream, and sugar.

"For the past few years, I've wondered if I'll see spring. It's a toss-up if I'll be walking this earth or laying in it. I've got my coffin ready. It's a plain pine box settin over in a corner. See that's the one they use for me. I don't want fancy like most folks."

"Don't talk like that."

"Hain't nothing wrong in talking about death. It's as common as life. Nobody gets outta this world alive, or hadn't you noticed."

"Are you trying to be funny?"

"Nope."

"Good. Have I got any money?"

"Oh, yeah. You got plenty of money. Most is in the bank in Johnson City, but you have some in Banners Elk, too. "

"Good."

"I got em to print it out right here on this paper." He pulled out two sheets of paper from the bib of his overalls and handed them to me. "Won't do you much good."

"What?"

"Jonas hain't gonna sell you his land."

My back stiffened; my teeth was grinding.

"I bought it, but you'll have to sign by the X."

"You bought my land?"

"Bought Jonas' half and I'm now trying to buy your half."

"I don't want to sell."

Andy rubbed a chin that hadn't been shaved in a few days. "Don't blame you there, but you're not selling a thing."

I opened my mouth, but he held up his hand. "How long would you think I've got to live?"

"Another ten years," I said.

"Don't think so."

"We never know."

"Sometimes we do, but it's no big deal. To everything there is a season. I've taken a longing here lately to see my old woman. Reckon a man can reach out touch his wife if they're both dead? I'd like to do that. I truly would. Supposin she's still young while I look like this."

I didn't know what to say.

"Life goes on regardless of death, Missy."

Still, I said nothing.

"Jonas won't sell you his half of the land, nor will he take your money."

"How do you know?"

"I asked him."

"So you bought it."

"Seemed like a good idea."

"Why?"

"Reckon advanced age makes me go a little crazy at time." He grinned just a little. "I bought it for you, Missy. I got myself a lawyer and had him write up the deed, and make out a will for you. When you sign the deed, I sign the will."

"You are a little crazy."

"Tell me, what does an old man need with more land or money? Can't buy me back my youth and can't buy me one more day longer than God will give me."

"Does Jonas know?"

"Nope, and he best not."

I agreed with that.

☙

The next morning Jonas put me and Drew on one of Rafe's horses and we rode into town to meet Andy, leaving Bruiser tied and Ransom in the house.

"You sure you'll sign the deed and not change your mind?"

"I told you I would, didn't I?"

"You've been known to change your mind."

"I won't."

"Why Andy and not James?"

"Andy's one of us."

Jonas grunted as though I was funny.

"Mountain land belongs to mountain people," I added.

Jonas laughed.

We rode on in silence and Jonas asked no more questions, but there was something like a smirk on his lips. I was puzzled. What had happened to him to make him act this way toward me? Didn't he love me anymore? I was about to ask him just that when he turned toward me.

"Laine, I don't know what to do with you this winter. I don't want to freeze my hind end off traveling this mountain twice a day and you won't stay at my place."

"I can winter on the mountain just fine."

"You're pregnant."

"I was last winter, too."

"You weren't as far along as you are now."

"Winter will be over by the time I have it in March."

"April. You're due the middle of April."

"The middle of March."

"I'm the doctor, Laine. I've examined enough women to come within a few day of their due date."

"You're a doctor that's wrong about me."

"You just have to make an argument about everything, don't you?"

"Have it your way." I was thinking the doctor always knows best, doesn't he, but I was wise enough to stay silent.

Signing the deed reminded me a lot of getting married. I guess signing legal documents were signing legal documents regardless of what was coming about. Andy's attorney looked important as he handed Jonas cash money and Andy the signed deed.

"Thought you were going to put this on record at the courthouse," Andy said.

"The original, yes. I always make copies for each party."

I was a party, but he didn't give me a copy. Didn't wives count?

"Good. I want all this legal stuff right. Don't want to be hanging around here for the next twenty years correcting your mistakes."

He sounded ill tempered but I saw the twinkle in both Andy's and the lawyer's eyes.

"An old coot like you will be hassling somebody for the next thirty years if somebody doesn't do the good deed of killing you." The lawyer returned.

"Not worth the effort now. I'm as broke as a convict."

"You're a liar, too."

"If you two can tear yourself apart, I need to leave. Patients are waiting."

We got up and went outside.

"Are you staying in town and riding home with me this evening?"

"I need to get back, Jonas. I've not milked or done up the work yet."

His jaw muscles twitched, but he didn't argue with me.

"I gotta get back, too. She can ride back with me."

"Thanks, Andy. I would appreciate that. A pregnant woman with a baby on her back riding through the snow toward a mountain top isn't an ideal situation."

"I'll look after her."

"I'm counting on that, Andy, and believe me, I am grateful for what you've done for my wife."

"Keeps me from being lonely," Andy told him.

My eyes met Jonas' and he nodded slightly, turned and headed to his beloved office and patients.

"Well, Missy, do you need anything while we're in town?"

"I don't need a thing."

"Let's hit it then."

We were barely out of sight from town when Andy fumbled in the pocket of his bib overalls and pulled out an envelope. "My will," he said. "You now own more land."

I took it with shaky hands. "I don't know what to say. Thank you doesn't seem like enough. Let me pay you for it."

A bit of a sigh slipped from his lips. "I'm afeard you'll pay for it all right, but not in the way you think. A woman that owns a lot of land will be hassled by James Travin and everybody else. When a woman has more than they need, she draws the resentment of others. If I was you, I wouldn't go telling a soul what I owned, not even my spouse."

I put the envelope deep in my pocket. I wasn't about to tell anybody. "Does my land belong to me?"

Andy nodded. "I asked the lawyer about that. Seems Rafford Johnson was smarter than I thought. While he was in the hospital with his injured foot, he did make out a will and had it put on record. The land is yours until your death and then it goes to your first-born child."

"The money?"

"That's yours, free and clear. Between Rafford, the Holloways, and now me, you are a woman of means."

I was relieved, but I didn't feel one bit different than the day I married Rafe – at least not much.

Chapter 20

My baby kicked. It felt just like a tiny butterfly fluttering in my stomach. I laughed right out loud. Being sick hadn't killed my baby. It was alive just as Drew had been, but how was I going to manage two babies and a farm?

I don't know why I thought of Susie. I didn't want to, didn't want to know that she never got a chance to feel her baby kick. Besides, Susie, Momma, Abe, and Hazel were out of my life for good and I was glad of it.

I went out onto the upper porch and looked out over my land. I felt like I was on top of the world looking out over nothing but white snow. Everything appeared pure and innocent, but it wouldn't last long. Nothing did. This time last year I was alone and waiting for Rafe to return. Today I wasn't alone, I had Drew, but I was waiting on Jonas. The difference was that I waited on Jonas with love not dread.

I saw him coming through the woods from a different direction than normal. Something was on the saddle behind him. I laughed and ran downstairs when I realized what it was. Jonas was bringing home a Christmas tree.

I laughed but almost cried. Last year I didn't know what day Christmas came on.

Jonas had a small white pine cut out of the woods without many branches, but it was the prettiest tree I've ever set my eyes on. It made me feel like we were a real family, the kind of a family I always dreamed of having. I was so happy I didn't trust it. Something bad was surely going to happen. No one got as much good as I'd gotten lately.

I ran out through the snow to meet Jonas at the barn. I didn't take time to put my coat on. I didn't care if it was cold outside. My insides were bubbling over with warmth.

"A Christmas tree, a Christmas tree," I said as Jonas handed me down the tree. I wanted to grab him and hug him until he was flooded with my love. He was the most wonderful man I'd ever met in my life.

"Here's your Christmas present," he said with great ado, and handed me a brand-new double bitted Ax. "Hack Pennel sharpened it for you personally." His mouth puckered just a little and his brows furrowed slightly as though he didn't know if he should be aggravated. "The men at the store took up a donation to buy you this. They were undecided whether or not to buy a pitchfork instead. Hack said you could trade if you wanted."

"Those men bought me a present?" I couldn't believe it. "Are you picking at me?"

"Nope. They bought the ax and Hack brought it to my office with a bow on it. The bow blew off on the way home and I didn't know it."

"Why would they buy me a gift?"

"That was my question."

"What did Hack say?"

"I didn't ask. I only questioned it." He led the horse into the barn.

I picked up the ax and the Christmas tree and headed back to the house. I leaned them on the porch and rushed inside to the heat, but a warm glow was already surrounding me. I was given a present by a bunch of men. The glow faded when reality hit. They had to be up to something, some strange kind of humor or another bet.

When Jonas came inside I asked him, "Did Hack sell his store?"

"Not yet." He took off his winter cap and coat and hung them on nails.

"Why not?"

"Hack's a wily old fox. He's playing James against Rupert, seeing who will give him the most money. He better watch. Neither one might buy it."

I put my arms around him and kissed his cold cheek and then his lips. "I love you," I whispered in his ear.

He grinned. "What brought this on?"

"You," I said. "And our first Christmas tree."

He patted my bottom. "By next year Drew and our baby will be big enough to enjoy it." He patted again. "You won't be doing any early planting next spring."

"Why not?" I nibbled at his ear and he pulled away. He was like a horse, didn't like to have his ears messed with.

"You'll have this baby in April. You won't be able to plant until the last of May."

"Wrong. I'm having it in March."

"That would mean you conceived in a month or month and a half after Drew was born. That doesn't happen, Laine. It takes a mother several months for her body to go back to normal and start producing eggs. Especially, when she's breast feeding."

"I'm not normal," I bragged. "And you think you know it all, but you don't."

He pinched instead of patted. "Want to bet a new pitchfork on it?"

"Against what?"

"Spending one night at my house."

I thought about it. He would lose. "You're on."

He looked like he didn't believe I'd said that.

"Jonas."

"Humm?"

"Will you go by and look at Andy?"

"What's wrong with him?"

"He's gone down hill. He don't look or act himself."

"Now?"

"Not right now. You can stop by in the morning."

"You like that old man, don't you?"

"I guess so."

He smiled as though it was okay. "He's taken the place of your dad."

No one could take the place of my dad, but I didn't need to say it. I thought about Susie and the baby she never felt kick.

"Have you heard any gossip about Susie or Abe?"

"So that's why you're worried about Andy. He's not able to get out in this weather to bring you all the gossip."

"I go to him."

"Not when the ground is slick, you'd better not."

I ignored that. "Have you heard anything?"

"Only that Hazel is building a house near them and your mom is mad. Mert says the whole hollow will be full of poisonous snakes before anybody realizes what happened, and then folks will be sorry they let such trash move among them."

How good it was to know Momma had someone to hate instead of me.

Jonas said Andy was just old and his parts were wearing out. His knee and his hip joints were shot.

"Do something," I told Jonas.

He shook his head. "I can't make an old man young."

"But you're a doctor."

"Not a witch doctor. I only do human things within my personal limitations."

"What about the new hospital or Dr. Tate?"

I knew I said the wrong thing by his reaction. "You don't like Dr. Tate?"

"I like him fine. He's a good man and a good doctor."

"What is it then?"

Jonas dipped warm water into the wash pan from the reservoir in the cook stove. He splashed his face and dried on a towel. I thought he wasn't going to say anything.

"It doesn't seem fair." He carried the water onto the porch and tossed it in the yard.

I wanted to tell him he just made a spot of pure ice, but now wasn't the time. "What doesn't?" I ask him.

"I spent years working here, helping folks even when I wasn't getting a dime or a potato for it. I didn't even get a long-over due thank you for some people. Now, there's a new doctor with support and money pouring in for him. Why, Laine, that man is treated like he could walk on water."

"And he doesn't deserve it?"

"Now, I didn't say that. I'm sure he does, but what about yours truly? What about old fateful? What about one of their own that has been thrown over for an outsider? It makes me feel like I'm no good just because I'm a mountain man, their mountain man."

I put my arms around him and hugged him tight. "That's why I don't want one inch of our land going to an outsider. They look down on us."

He opened his mouth and I knew he started to tell me I didn't know what I was talking about, but he closed it.

"I guess it's normal." I rubbed my hand along the hard muscles of Jonas's back, glad that he was strong and young. He had his life in front of him and so did I. "Folk's never seem to know what they've got among'st them. What's theirs' is no account. It's the new fangled, store bought stuff that's valuable to them."

"People and things are different, Lane."

"Think so? How about helping me string some popcorn after supper to go on the tree? I set it up in the living room today."

"I'm exhausted."

I grinned. He just didn't want to string popcorn.

Why did I keep dreaming about Susie's dead baby? Really, it wasn't much of a baby when she lost it. She couldn't have been eight or ten weeks along, at least no more than three months. Jonas said that was the riskiest time, those first three months. When I insisted on a reason, he told me some women just carried different than others. I reminded him that Susie was my sister and look how easy I carried.

Andy had made Drew a high chair for Christmas and I had him sitting in it eating fruit, or applesauce as Jonas called it, that I had sweetened with honey.

"Why the sad face?" Jonas asked.

"I was thinking about Susie."

"Not again."

"Jonas . . ."

"I don't want to hear it."

"I'm worried."

"You're pregnant. Pregnant women always worry."

"She's my sister. She shouldn't have lost that baby."

Jonas rolled his eyes at me. "How many times do I have to tell you women are different, even sisters. Look how different you and Susie are in other ways."

"She's bigger than me and she's stronger."

"She has never done the hard physical work you have done. Muscles hold a baby in and muscles push the baby out. Muscles are the fabric of life."

"Something isn't right and I know it."

"If a fetus isn't developing right, mother nature has a way of knowing and taking care of the matter. The heart will stop beating. The mother's body signals there is no longer a need to protect and feed the dead fetus and mother nature allows the dead fetus and it's no longer needed placenta to leave the body in order for the body to grow healthy and ready for a live fetus."

"Thanks for the lesson in doctoring," I said a little cynical. "All that is well and good, but I know Momma gave Susie something. I know it!"

"When the snow melts, why don't you go visit your Sister? You could hire Andy to drive you home. You could even spend the night."

I saw the humor shining in his eyes. He was just trying to shut me up permanently.

"I might do that." But Jonas and I both knew I never would. Momma seeing me would open up a box of trouble. Me seeing Hazel, knowing she tried to kill my little Drew, along with me almost shooting her, would be disastrous. Besides, I never wanted to go where Dad used to be and no longer was.

I was restless and it was ground hog's day. The sun was out and I knew we would have six more weeks of bad weather. There was no way the ground hog wouldn't see its shadow. I fitted Drew on my back for nothing would fit on my stomach now that I was big again. I headed through the woods toward Andy's.

When I got there, I saw something I didn't like, or someone. My dogs bristled and growled, but I hushed them before they barked. They didn't like James Travin any more than I did. I thought he looked like a weasel; I wondered if my dogs thought he smelled like one.

Travin wasn't in his fancy motor car, but there was no way I wouldn't recognize him. He leaving on a fancy high-stepping horse. A nicer piece of horse flesh than even Jonas owned.

Andy was in his shop this time. Heat vapors were rising stronger from that chimney than from the house. I didn't bother to knock on the door, I just walked in.

He looked around and there was a certain kind of look on his face, one of determination and yet one of – of a deranged old man. Both expressions changed when he saw it was me.

"Laine, come on in here. I hadn't expected to see you. Not today anyhow. I'm keeping in until the sun goes down."

"Too late. That ground hog already saw his shadow. What was he doing here?" I asked as though I had a right.

"Same as always. He's after land."

"Your land?"

"My land and everybody else's."

"I hope you told him where to go." I took Drew from my back and took off my coat.

"An old codger like me knows how to handle somebody like him."

I hoped so, but I wasn't so sure. Old folk's minds had a way of fooling them, telling them the wrong things.

"Why are you out gallivanting when you're nearing the size of a wash tub? You could fall down in this kind of weather."

"I was restless and I wanted to see you."

"It's too soon for spring fever."

"On this mountain it's never too soon for spring fever. Know what I've been cravin? A bait of ripe black cherries. I'd give a whole ham for a cup of cherries."

"Open you a can of blackberries and eat them with cream."

"I said cherries not blackberries."

"When you hain't got something you have to make do with something else. Now, what did you come for? Beside from being restless."

"I got to thinking that come March you might come stay at my house."

He looked surprised, shocked even.

"Day and night?"

"Well, during the day anyhow. Jonas will be there during the night."

"Why during March?"

"That's when I'm going to have my baby."

"Jonas says it due in April."

"March," I said firmly.

"I'll come around often when your time is nearing, but I hope to never deliver another baby, even if it is yourn. I'll let you know right here and now, I hain't got over such as that to this day. Seeing such as that does something to a man. Makes him wonder how there's a human being livin."

"Jonas has promised to be there this time – before hand."

"Then why do you need me?"

"I don't know. I just want you close. You make me feel – safe."

He chuckled. "I'm making Drew another carrier. One that's bigger. You're going to have you a time gettin about, Missy. Drew won't be a year old when this little'un gets here. Course havin one that hain't walkin might be better than when he does."

"I know that."

"You'll have to slow things up a little. Not run yourself into the bone yard."

"Or speed up one."

Andy nodded and looked sheepish. He grunted and twisted and looked at the sun shining through the window onto the floor. I wondered what he was thinking about saying that he thought he shouldn't.

"Spit it out," I said.

This time his chuckle was strained. "What makes you think I have something to say."

"You tongue's foaming."

"Smart, hain't you."

I just looked at him and he got up and put more wood in the stove.

"Men are their own kind of creatures." He spat in the stove and then closed the door. "God made 'um the way they are, and I've heard they can't help themselves, and I'd say that's about the truth most of the time."

"What way?" I asked, puzzled at what he had jumped into so fast, and why?

"The needin way. You know, breedin and such." His face reddened beneath all those wrinkles and drooped flesh. "Sometime it don't mean nothing. It's just like . . . like scratching an itch."

I was caught near speechless and trying to figure out where he was going with this. Was he saying I should limit Jonas, not have another baby in less than a year from now?

"Oh hell," he mumbled. "I'll tell you a tale I never told a soul in my life and I'm not proud of it. I'm down right ashamed of myself when I think back on it."

He picked up a stick of wood and started whittling. I reckon he didn't want me looking him in the eyes.

"Back when I was a younger man, and my dearly beloved Lilly Bell was at her worst, I done something I've spent years trying to get forgiveness from."

Was this a confession? If so, I didn't want to hear it. "Andy . . ." I began, but he held up his hand. "I need to tell somebody this, Missy, and looks like it aims to be you."

"But . . ." He held up his hand again.

"They 'uz this place a ways from here called Hot Hollar. Two sisters lived there, pretty gals but they weren't like most women if you know what I mean."

I frowned and he noticed.

"They didn't hanker after a husband and religion. They hankered for men, all men, any man. There must have been something amiss with em, or perhaps something extra added. Anyhow, that's why they called it Hot Hollar, because of them.

He squirmed. "I had kinda hook up with one of em for a while ever now and again."

A strange look came to his face as he slowed his whittling. I reckon a memory of some kind hit him. His expression went back to normal, but his voice had softened some, taken on a different tone.

"I thought I was something special and I thought she was something special, but I was wrong on both counts. She only wanted the quarter-dollar I brung her. I only wanted the relief my sweet Lilly Bell couldn't give me any longer."

I swallowed hard wondering why he was telling me such a thing as this. Was he fixing to die and needed somebody to unburden his soul to? If so, I wasn't the one. Maybe his mind was going soft like old men's mind had a tendency to do. Maybe he was bragging in a strange sort of way. Or maybe . . .

"Now I'm telling you this Missy, cause it's a thing all women ought to know and don't seem to. Men love like I loved my Lilly Bell. It's a good true kind of love between a man and a woman. On the other hand there's the other thing, and I don't reckon it's called love. Reckon it's a condition similar to a case of poison ivy. Men think God give them an itch to scratch, therefore, He give them the right to scratch it."

I wasn't liking what he was saying for I was beginning to wonder about Jonas and Francis Dewhitte when Andy looked me right in the eyes and then dropped his gaze.

"So, don't you think hard thoughts about that little boy's daddy. Junie was nothing more to Rafford Johnson than that Hot Hollar woman was to me. Less I'd say. Junie was after that man from the day she set eyes on him."

I think I gave Andy a look that must have said he was plum crazy. There was no reason to dig up dead bones that should be left to rot.

"That's my story," he added fast. "It does have a moral, maybe two. Men scratch their itch without thinking and it don't mean a thing to them. On the other hand, a woman needs to know that a woman can tickle a man's itch until he has to scratch it or pert near die from wantin to."

I looked Andy Harman right in the eyes and held his gaze. "Did James Travin poke some strange kind of liquor down you gullet? Did he cram a handful of funny pills down your throat or wave vapors under your nose? If not, you need to go to bed and sleep off your story telling spell."

"You may be right, Missy. I reckon you are."

I wasn't a happy woman as I walked back home. Andy wanted tell me something without telling me something. And I would lay money that it was about Jonas instead of Rafe. Dead was dead and over with was over with. What was happening now might be needing a little salve rubbed on.

Was Andy thinking a woman in the family way couldn't carry on with her husband. If so, he was wrong. Or was he saying Jonas had an itch that some woman, like Francis Dewhitte, was helping him scratch? Which ever way, Andy didn't rub no balming salve on me. He lit a raging fire.

The January thaw was late in coming. Actually, it didn't make it to the top of Beech Mountain all during the month of February, but the temperature did rise to near freezing during the day. Each morning the ground was frozen solid, but by late evening it was mudding-up on top and made traveling slippery. Jonas came home complaining every evening.

"Stay in Banners Elk," I said a little too sharp.

"Really?" Jonas shot back. "And have all those old mustached gossips at the store saying I'm no better than your first husband."

"Are you?" I asked none too sweetly.

His brows lifted. "Am I what?"

"Better than my first husband? He fooled around on me and it cost him his life. I'd hate to lose another husband in a similar sort of way."

Jonas' eyes widened; his mouth cracked open but nothing came out.

"I'm not a dumb child any longer, and I won't take nothing off nobody."

"As if you ever did, and what are you talking about if I may ask?"

"I'm talkin about the Francis Dewhittes of this world. If my second husband has an itch to scratch, he'd best do his scratching at home and not with some Hot Hollar slut."

Jonas shook his head and changed the subject. "There's more gossip about your sister, and I know I'm crazy for telling you, but you'll hear it from Andy anyway."

He waited for me to say something, but I didn't.

"She miscarried again. She was hardly six weeks along when she lost this one. She caught the blood and tissue with a baby blanket, made Abe build a casket, and buried it along side her other miscarriage."

"Poor Susie."

"Poor Susie is right. She named this baby Angie because she knew it was a girl. Your sister has mental problems. She needs help."

"She has a problem with Momma, Jonas, and she has always needed help. She's Momma flesh and blood."

"You're not?" he questioned in a gentle voice.

"Nope. I'm one hundred percent Dad. And you can make fun of me all you want, but I think Momma is feeding something to Susie."

"What are you going to do about your thoughts, Laine? Send over the sheriff and have him tell your mother to cut it out?"

"That's not a bad idea. It might shake Momma up enough to make her stop."

"Lord help us."

I ignored that. "Jonas, you could have your father talk to Susie. Ask if Momma is giving her some sort of tea, or if her food tastes strange."

"Laine . . ."

"If I'm right, I'll remind you of it."

"No doubt."

The morning broke cold and spitting blue frost. When I went outside it was like breathing needles of ice. As much as I loved this mountain, I equally hated this bitter cold. But a body can't expect all good without a little bad.

The animals stood on the sheltered side of the barn and ate the hay I'd thrown out for them. I didn't milk but once a day. I was turning the cow dry to have her calf. I wished my little heifer was old enough to give milk but she wasn't. I would have to find another cow that was fresh. I'd weaned Drew a few months back because of the new baby, and he was drinking over a quart of milk a day besides all the soft foods I fed him. He was growing big and chunky just like Rafe.

I heard the rumble and knew what it was instantly even though I hadn't heard the sound all winter. The sound was unmistakable for the sound of a vehicle was the sound of a vehicle. I figured it belonged to James Travin. He was coming to hassle me about my land again.

I wasn't my normal sweet self today. I was tired. My back ached and my feet hurt. Drew had woke up early and wanted me to entertain him instead of going back to sleep so I could do up the morning work.

A weasel had gotten into the chicken house during the night and killed my best hen and I was mad at Bruiser for letting it happen. I sure wasn't in the mood for another weasel showing up after me.

I considered going to the house and welcoming the vermin with my shotgun, but I just took a stand right there in front of the barn and waited in the bone chilling cold.

Oh what relief to see that it was Rupert. I went to the car door knowing I was smiling. He smiled back.

"Good morning Mrs. Jones," he said brightly. "What a fine day to travel. The ground is frozen and the snow has gone from the wagon road. I was able to travel rather fast and easy this morning."

He couldn't keep his eyes from looking at my huge belly even as he pretended to look at the dogs.

"Ransom has tripled in size and they both look healthy."

"Morning," I said. "They are, and it's cold as ice this morning," I hoped I wasn't blushing because of my big belly poking out Mr. Holloway's overalls. Folks thought women my size should stay out of the sight from of men. "Come on inside and have a cup of coffee while you warm up." I invited, thankful that Jonas had remembered to bring coffee home last night. With all these men around, it took a lot.

"The thought of warmth is so tempting I'll do it even before I carry in the dog food. I know you've run out by now."

"Just about. I mixed table scraps with the food to make it last longer."

"Sorry I haven't been here sooner, but my return was delayed."

"James Travin was here all winter," I told him as I opened the kitchen door. "He tried to buy Jonas' land but Andy got it instead."

"So I've heard." He shed his gloves, heavy coat, wool neck scarf, funny fur lined hat with ear flaps and laid them in another chair before he sat down and calmly said, "Right now, James is busy working on Andy, trying to buy him out."

Andy hadn't told me that nor had Jonas.

"You look surprised," Rupert said.

"I am." But I shouldn't have been. I'd seen him at Andy's and Jonas once said Andy had more land than I did. So naturally, Travin would be after it.

"Andy won't sell out." I told him with conviction.

"Andy Harmon is no longer a young man. His time is limited and he knows it."

I didn't like him talking that way. Andy might not have felt too good this winter, but he could live to be a hundred, a lot of folks had. "He could outlive us all," I told him firmly.

"He could, but Mother Nature has her way almost every time."

"Andy won't sell," I repeated with more conviction than I felt.

"If he does, I'd prefer he sold to me."

"Or me," I threw in.

Rupert grinned. "Yes, you definitely need more land than you've got right now." There was humor shining from his eyes as they met mine.

"Don't mock me."

"Sorry, but I wasn't intending to mock you."

"Yes you were."

"Not intentionally. You'll have to admit you have more acreage than you can utilize or care for. If you insist on farming it, I might be able to help you out. I have a rather disgruntled man working for me that prefers farming to carpentry work. He might be willing to help you."

I didn't like that idea. I wanted to take care of my land myself. I wasn't up to another Abe, somebody I would trust when I shouldn't. "Mother Nature cares for it while I can't. Besides," I put my hands on my belly. "Someday soon I'll have sons to help run this farm."

"Or a little girl as pretty as its feisty mother."

I ignored that and put our conversation back on proper ground. "How is your family? Did your wife come with you this time?"

"My family is fine, and no, my wife didn't come with me. I doubt she ever will regardless of how long I plead with her."

"Why not?"

"She is used to city life."

"She doesn't know what she's missing."

"So I tell her."

I poured him coffee and sat cream and sugar on the table.

"Has everything gone well with you?" he asked as his eyes studied my face.

"Yeah."

"And Jonas?"

"I reckon Jonas is doing good, too."

"He shouldn't be as busy now that Dr. Tate is here." He seemed to be watching me extra close when he said this.

I shrugged. "I can't tell the new doctor makes much difference in that. Jonas is gone most all the time, regardless."

"Do I hear a note of anger in those words?" His smile softened his words until he seemed to be teasing me.

"I'd like to have a husband that's home for longer than two meals and a night's sleep."

"Why? Most women love for their husbands to be gone – out of their hair, so to speak."

"Does yours?" I couldn't resist asking and his smile faded.

"I fear she might at that."

"Well I don't." Suddenly, my words seemed strange even to me. How did I know I didn't? Rafe had been pure misery when he was home on rare occasions, and Jonas had always been gone during the day. But it seemed good when Abe was here. It was good knowing if a problem came up, someone was there to give me a hand.

He lifted his cup and took a drink. "Are you out of vitamins yet?"

"Almost."

"I brought some more."

"I probably won't need them. I'm going to have my baby soon."

"You should continue taking them until you stop breast feeding."

Blood rushed to my face. Men didn't talk about such things unless they were a doctor like Jonas.

"When is soon?"

"Within two weeks, I think, but Jonas says it won't be until next month."

"Why do you think it will be sooner?"

I felt my face turn red again. I wasn't going to tell him I was sure this baby got started the first time Jonas and I . . . "I got a feeling."

He frowned. "Are you staying by yourself? You don't want to be alone when the time comes."

"Andy promised to be around during the day, and of course Jonas will be here at night."

"You're not going to stay in town?" A mischievous grin lit his face when he said that.

"No. You got your first refusal yet?"

"I got it."

"I guess Andy won his money, too."

"I think so; at least he is in the process of getting it. Those men don't like to give up cash."

"I thought Travin was working on Hack."

"He is but Hack is hemming and hawing."

"He gave you a first refusal."

"Means nothing if he doesn't want to sell. But it is a good way to assure myself Travin can't cut my throat while my back is turned. It helps the people hang onto their property by giving them a little cash money."

"Don't you have enough money to buy it out right?" I was instantly worried that Rupert was running out of money.

"They don't often want to sell it out right, but they will take a little cash in return for a promise to let me buy it before anybody else."

"It's legal?"

His eyes took on an extra shine and all his white teeth showed like a grinning possum. "Want to join in? Do you need a little cash?"

I couldn't stop the aggravation that flooded over me. Was that why he was here? Was he still after my land?

His grin faded fast as he held up his hands. "Whoa, there, let your hackles go back down. That was meant for humor, only humor. I know you won't sell your land, and I would never make any attempt to buy it unless you asked me. Believe me on that, Laine, believe me."

How could he not want it? It was the most wonderful piece of ground in the world.

"I don't like your humor in regard to my land."

"I will remember that forever, I promise, if you'll forgive me. Will you? I'll give you dog food if you do. I'll bring you another puppy."

Something in his voice made me want to laugh for I believed him.

Chapter 21

The robins came. They settled in the yard, around the barn, in the bare limbs of the trees. I heard their voices calling and hurried outside with Drew. "Bird" I said as I pointed with delight. "Birdie."

"Ba – ba," Drew tried to mimic me. He could say several words now, but his favorite was dog – eeee. He could crawl like a streak and was standing up and trying to walk with me holding his hands. His little face lit up when he saw Jonas, and I had taught him to say Da Da, but Jonas was always in a hurry or so tired he didn't have time to play with Drew.

Andy adored Drew and often referred to him as his 'little name sake'. Drew eyed Andy's wrinkled, aged face with a strange kind of curiosity. It was as though Drew didn't like to see an old sagging face that could never be described as pretty, and Drew did like pretty things. He liked the pretties Andy made him like carved horses, dogs, and birds. He even made Drew a sling shot and a large wagon. Andy said the wagon was Drew's but I claimed it. It was perfect to put Drew in and pull him around. I was pleased for there would be room for two boys in there.

When Andy discovered I had turned my cow, Pet, dry, he brought me a gift I hadn't expected.

"Got something for you," he said as he came into the kitchen.

"For me or Drew?" I poured him coffee from habit. Andy no longer told me he didn't drink much coffee. I poured and he drank. Habit.

"Kinda both."

He sipped his coffee and I noticed the hand he held the cup with was shaking more than normal.

"Sit down. You look tired this morning."

"I am."

"Any particular reason?"

"Yeap. It's what I brung you and Drew."

I lifted my brows.

"It's in the barn." He let out a breath of exhaustion as he pushed his hat back from his forehead.

What had Andy brought that needed putting in the barn? "What?"

"Take that frown off your face, Missy. You're gonna like this."

I wasn't so sure. His eyes were twinkling too bright. "What?" I repeated.

"It's a milk goat. A nice Nubian goat, big floppy ears, Roman nose and intelligent eyes. She's big in size, too, gives over a quart at a time. I milked her last night. You'll have to do it this morning, though. You'll have to tie her up. She won't stand. And you'll have to milk from behind. Don't kick backward as good."

I was tickled to have milk for Drew, but a goat? I had mentioned wanting a goat some time ago, but I never expected to get one.

"I've heard goat's milk is the best milk there is. Much better than cow's milk for babies and animals. Easy on the stomach," Andy said.

"Where did you get a goat?" I hadn't seen one anywhere around, not even back at Dad's.

"A man brought it in to Hack's wantin to trade on a pound of coffee. I gave him the price of coffee plus a quarter extra. I think he bought snuff with the quarter."

"I'll pay you for her."

"Knowing some about goats, I'll say you'll pay for her, all right, but I don't want nothing. Like I said, she's a gift for you and Drew."

A warm feeling came over me. "You do too much for us, you know that."

"I know, but being I'm too old to seduce you. I'll just resort to spoiling you along with my little name sake. After all, I have started telling those old scoundrels at the store that Drew's really my son."

I nearly dropped the coffee pot.

"They wanted to place money on me being a liar. Can you imagine that?"

"I can." I could imagine anything coming from that bunch. "That was a good ax they sent me as a Christmas present."

"I know, I picked it out."

"They were picking at Jonas weren't they?"

"Yeap. Some said he wouldn't bring it to you."

"You wagered he would?"

"Yeap."

Nothing but a bunch of old men reverting back to being mean boys. I wondered why women didn't do that.

"How are you feeling today, Missy?"

"Fine, why?"

"Rupert has a bunch of scrap lumber he said I could have if I'll bring my horse and wagon to pick it up."

"Coffin lumber?"

"Maybe, some. Thought I'd try my hand at a milking stockade for that goat. I seen one once."

"You don't have to."

"You hain't tried milkin her yet."

"Am I going to regret my gift?" I was becoming down-right leery.

"Naw. She's a good 'un. I just want to make sure you'll be all right tomorrow if I'm not here. I want forewarned enough to get Jonas back here this time. Like I done told you, I'm not going to be the man delivering this one."

"I think I've got another week."

"What does Jonas think."

"Same as always. He says I'm in a hurry, a month off." I looked at him hard. "Why don't you want to deliver this one? Every one at the store *knows* you're this one's daddy?"

It only took a few minutes to realize why the man had wanted to trade the goat for coffee. Being milked was not what she had in mind. I gave her grain to eat, tied a rope around her neck and then hobbled her hind legs. I got a quart of milk pumped out, one squirt at a time. When I untied her, she came to me and rubbed her head against me just like a cat. I scratched between her six-inch-growth of horns. From what I could tell, she was young. Perhaps this was the first time she had been fresh and only needed to get used to being milked. *Perhaps I could sprout wings and fly.*

As I petted her, I remembered the danged old red bull Dad brought home. He was more aggravation than he was worth. I hoped this little brown nanny goat didn't turn out to be the same.

I shut her up in a stall, not wanting to turn her out until she got used to the place. She promptly turned to the door and started scraping her bottom teeth on the wood. I had heard goats would eat anything, even a tin can. Guess I'd find out if such things were true.

I strained the white milk and tasted it. It was smooth and creamy, by far the richest milk I ever drank. No wonder folks said it would grow anything. I hoped it would grow my Drew into a big, strong man. I took one more swallow as good measurement on growing the baby in my belly.

Jonas laughed when I told him what Andy had brought for Drew. "I thought the old man was your buddy," Jonas said, his blue eyes twinkling as though he had a secret about goats.

"You have a problem with a goat?" I asked, just a bit peeved.

"Not me, but you might."

"How's that?" I couldn't keep the snap out of my voice.

"Goats are browsers. There's no fence they can't get out of, and no garden they won't get into."

"I'll keep her in a stall."

"I repeat, they're browsers, Laine. They need to browse to keep healthy and give milk."

"I'll tie her to a rope, move her about."

"You'll probably have to. Before long, you'll be the one that feels tied."

"Drew needs milk, Jonas. That goat does give milk – rich milk."

"Milk is over rated. Children don't need to drink milk forever. Their bodies need to utilize nutrients from solid food."

I didn't agree, neither did I feel like arguing with Jonas. Just because he was an educated doctor, he thought he knew it all. Because I was a girl that never finished high school, he thought I was stupid and should take everything he said as fact. Well, I had drunk nearly a half-gallon of milk every day of my life, and I am healthy. But this evening, I was as tired as Andy after he wrestled with the goat.

"Torment," Jonas said suddenly. "You'll have to name her Torment."

"Pessimist."

His brows shot up and I couldn't tell if his expression was one of surprise or mischief. "You know what a pessimist is?"

"It's you, from the p to the t."

🕊

During the night I couldn't rest. When I lay in bed, I couldn't breath good. When I stood up, the baby pressed on my bladder until I had to go outside to the toilet. Finally, I found the pot, took it into another room and used it.

It had turned off cold during the night, much colder than I expected it to be in March, even on this mountain top. *If March comes in like a lamb, she'll go out like a lion,* and vice versa. It was nearing the end of March and she was roaring like the lion. According to the ground hog, six weeks of winter weather wasn't going to be enough. I hated the last month of bad weather before spring started teasing the world. I hated smelling for spring in the air when all I got was blue frost. I hated finding cold when I needed warmth.

I also hated the last month of my condition when I didn't have room in my belly for the baby, a bite of food, and my bladder. I hated the unnatural pull on my back and the natural inability to get about nimbly. Tonight, I was just one big pile of hating.

I stepped over Ransom and crawled back in bed beside Jonas. I didn't want him to have a restless night just because I was uncomfortable. He had spent the winter reminding me that his small house in Banners Elk had a coal furnace plus inside plumbing. It stayed warm and comfortable all the time, if a person had enough sense to live there.

I had a warm fire going in the cook stove plus two heating stoves by the time Jonas woke up.

He yawned as he came into the kitchen. "Not much cold this morning," he mumbled. "Reckon we're getting a March break."

I didn't tell him the house was warmed by the fires I had built. He'd find out soon enough when he went outside.

"I didn't sleep too soundly. You were up during the night, weren't you?"

"Yeah, I just couldn't get comfortable."

"Were you in pain? Women often have false labor."

"I wasn't exactly in pain. Mostly I was plain uncomfortable. Do you suppose it could be my time? I think it is."

Jonas let out a bewildered breath as he sat down at the table and waited for me to pour him hot coffee. "Will you please let up on that? You claimed you were having this baby by the middle of March, even when I told you it was due the middle of April. Time proved me right, so why can't you accept that as a doctor, I might know what I'm talking about?"

"I have a feeling . . ."

"Women go on feelings and men go on facts. Accept it, Laine. You have two more weeks before that baby is due. Knowing women and babies, both of you always run late."

"Maybe you could examine me before you leave." I didn't believe I suggested that. Jonas might be both my husband and a doctor, but that didn't stop me for hating being examined. It came close to feeling of being stripped naked publicly.

"I don't need to examine you. Have you forgotten last night already?"

To me, that wasn't an examination. That was a natural course of action for Jonas. He didn't come home just for supper and a warm bed.

"If you had been anywhere near labor, I would have know."

"The baby has moved down. See how low its head is." I put my hand low on my pelvis to show him what I was talking about. "It's much lower than Drew was when he was born. I had to relieve myself a half-dozen times during the night."

"So that's why I didn't sleep good."

I didn't comment. ,

"Laine, naturally this baby is lower than Drew. You insist on perching Drew on your stomach most of the day. His weight pushes our baby downward, makes you carry it lower."

"My back hurts." I made one last stab at convincing Jonas that the baby could come early.

"Much, or are you just uncomfortable?"

"Not awful much."

"False labor pains. Expect them from now until the real labor sets in."

"I had Drew fast."

"You didn't recognize what labor pains were with Drew. You'll know with this one."

I thought of the way I felt as I sat his food in front of him. I suppose he could be right.

"What if I need you?"

"You won't. I repeat - you're not in labor. You've got several weeks yet."

"If I don't?"

"Send Andy after me. Send him in time to get me here."

"Andy won't be here today. Rupert gave him a bunch of scrap lumber and he wants to get all of it he can before others get it."

"I'll stop by his place and ask him to check on you before he leaves and again before he unloads his lumber. Will that satisfy you? Will that stop your complaining."

"Don't bother Andy," I said, getting mad.

"Get Drew and ride into town with me."

"I have the work to do."

"Leave it if you're afraid you're going into labor. The baby is more important than doing the work."

"Could you just come home early?" I suggested in a meek tone.

"I'll come home early."

"Promise?"

"Anything, if it will satisfy you."

I didn't say anything more. I grabbed his coat sleeve and kissed him before he went out the door. He returned a little peck hurriedly, not wanting to be kept from his precious work any longer.

I watched him leave by the short way, not going toward Andy's. A sinking feeling came over me. I wanted to cry. Either he had forgotten about Andy or he didn't believe I was unusually uncomfortable.

I washed Drew while the kitchen was good and warm. Jonas said babies should be bathed every day, but I didn't believe that was necessary. Babies didn't get much dirty during the day. Jonas told me he bathed before he left Banners Elk. I liked that idea, not because he got dirty, because he was washing off germs he could bring home to Drew.

I carried the pan of water to the end of the porch and pitched it out, knowing it would freeze, but I wouldn't walk on that spot. I filled up the dog bowls with Rupert's feed and watched them eat for a moment.

When I got back inside, Drew had pulled every pot and pan from the bottom cabinet. I sat down in a chair and watched him. How could I possibly love another baby as much as Drew? Yet, I knew I would.

He wasn't as tired as I was. I longed for his nap time to come. I longed to take a nap with him, but I couldn't. I did up the work while he slept. That's when the idea hit me. I could take Drew to the barn now; let him play in the wagon or in a pile of hay while I did the work. Afterwards, he and I both could take a nap. The animals certainly wouldn't mind being fed a little sooner than normal. And the goat? Well, I could take a nap after tackling her.

She surprised me. She didn't give me much of a problem. I tied her head and hind legs. She ate, and I milked from behind. I didn't get a full quart. Like Jonas said, she needed to browse. I'd stake her out near the woods after my much needed nap, but I would have to carry her water now.

I balanced Drew on my stomach with one arm and dipped a bucket of water from the spring branch with the other. It wasn't easy for the edge of the water was frozen and tricky standing on, but I didn't want to take the time to get an ax and break the ice. But I did after I had taken the water to the goat. Dad always said no decent farmer would take a chance on the livestock slipping and breaking a leg trying to get water.

It was balancing Drew and swinging the ax that pulled a muscle. Sharp pain ran from my stomach all around my back.

"Shit," I said out loud. Just what I needed right now. a pulled muscle to add to false labor. Jonas would really like me complaining about this, too.

By the time I got back to the house, the pulled muscle wasn't hurting. I strained the goat's milk and let him drink it still a little warm. I longed to drink a few sips, but there wasn't enough for Drew. My big-eyed goat needed a little

greenery, but she would have to wait. I was one tired
woman that ached all over.

My sleep wasn't restful. I knew I was tossing and
turning. I knew I wasn't exactly asleep, but I couldn't make
myself wake up. Dreams came and fluttered through my
head. They were bad dreams that I couldn't remember, but
I couldn't wake from them, nor could I stop them from
coming.

Once I though I heard Drew wake up, and then I
thought I had watched him go back to sleep. Boise came
and sat down on my bed, the young Boise I had seen in the
picture. *"You'd better wake up,"* she said. *"if you don't
want to bleed to death. I bled to death. My baby came
early, too."*

I tried to tell her my baby wasn't early. It was due
today.

That's not what the doctor said."

I'm its mother, I know.

*"Girl, you don't know a thing. You're a baby yourself,
one that's all brag and no brain."*

You're as insulting as Jonas, I told her.

*"Have you ever considered that he is right? If you were
intelligent, you'd wake up and save yourself."*

Rafe came. *"Go away,"* he said to Boise. *"I don't want
you here, and neither does she."*

Boise looked at him, looked through him. *"I made a
mistake with that one, a bigger mistake than I made with
my dear Henry."*

Who's Henry? I asked before I realized he was the man
she wrote about in her diary. The first man she got pregnant
by before he was killed. The reason she and her father left
their hometown for Beech Mountain.

"Get out of here," Rafe said in his most cruel voice.
"You're already dead and rotten, but she's not."

"She will be if she don't wake up."

"What's it to you? She'll be mine again, after she dies."

"That's why she has to wake up. She belongs to the doctor now. You can't have her back. We're together again. We belong to gather, you and I."

"Like hell we do!" He laughed. It was that drunken laugh of his that I feared.

I woke up shaking with fear. Drew was sitting up in his crib, silently playing with toys. Ransom was not there. He was outside with Bruiser. Why was I afraid? Why was I shaking all over? I'd dreamed of Boise before. Heard her voice talking to me, felt her presence. I'd had nightmares often, nightmares about Rafe, and I had never felt the same panic I was feeling now. Something was wrong, bad wrong.

I swung my legs out of bed and knew what it was. I was bleeding! I tried to stand and the room spun around. I sank back onto the bed. Strange, what ran through my mind. I didn't want to mess up my clean bed linens. Blood was hard to wash out. I came to my senses and tried to think straight.

What had happened? What was going on?

Simple. I had torn something when I swung the ax. Something that was now bleeding. My baby wasn't being born. I was simply hurt. I needed to go down stairs, get warm water and wash myself. Maybe I'd knocked up a sliver of ice and it had cut my upper leg without me knowing it. Yes, that was it. It wasn't my baby coming. Jonas said I had two more weeks and he was a doctor. What did I know? I was still a baby myself; one without a brain.

Drew whimpered to be taken from his crib as I left the room, but I couldn't tend to him right now. "Watch after your son," I said to Rafe as though he could hear me.

Silly. Oh, I was being silly talking to the dead. I should be praying to God to keep me alive so I could take care of

Drew as well as the baby I was carrying. I put my hand on my stomach and felt my baby kick hard. I realized I was praying, silently praying with every fiber of my being, mind and soul.

How do I save myself? How do I save this baby?

"It's a cut," I said out loud as I made my way down the stairs by holding onto the banister. My legs felt like rubber, too shaky to hold up my weight. I watched them move what seemed an inch at a time. No wonder they were so slow. Blood covered things moved slow. They had a right to move so.

I got to the kitchen. The fire had almost gone out. Why was the lifter this heavy? Why did kindling wood feel like an oak log? Would the fire coals catch the kindling? Could I get the kitchen warm enough to keep me from shaking with this cold? They caught, and I put in larger wood. Such heavy wood.

I opened the reservoir and dipped heavy water into the wash pan. I must get this bleeding to stop. Blood loss would hurt my baby. Wasn't Jonas and the – that white haired doctor concerned about my blood loss? Why was I losing blood? Oh, yes, how foolish of me. Why did I think it was because of ice? I had been attacked by a mountain lion. My entire side was ripped from its claws. I was bleeding bad, but Jonas said my baby was alive. I wouldn't lose my baby.

I took off Mr. Holloway's bibbed overalls I was so found of wearing and lifted my shirt. There were welts on my side, but not the raw gashes I had expected to see.

I forced my mind to come back from the time Drew was born. This was a different time, a different baby.

I dropped my bloomers and grabbed a wash rag. I ran it over my bloody thighs. There was no gash, no cut from ice, no laid open flesh by razor sharp claws. I was bleeding because of a baby.

Was this normal? Did I bleed when Drew was born? No, not a first. My water broke first and then I started to bleed. Andy was there when it happened. He helped me to bed after Abe ran off to get Jonas.

Who was going to get Jonas this time?

I could take Drew and we could ride the horse to Andy's.

Andy wouldn't be home. He was getting lumber from Rupert.

I was alone, and I was having this baby all by myself. I would die. My baby would die. Who would take care of Drew? He wasn't Jonas' son. Jonas wouldn't want him. He'd take up too much of Jonas' time. Jonas wanted his patients. Jonas had Francis Dewhitte.

She wanted me dead. She wanted Jonas.

Abe said so, and Abe had married Susie. Susie lost two babies. She'd take Drew. Momma would take Drew so she could get this house and land.

Momma would be mean to Drew. She'd let the honeybees kill him like she did Joey.

The kitchen spun around and I grabbed for the wall. I was hot, burning hot. Suddenly blood was washed from my legs. It ran across the kitchen floor. My water had broken. Where was my pain? Shouldn't I be hurting? Birthing was a painful process. It was ripping the insides out.

I was hurting.

I was exploding with pain. It had been so great, I hadn't acknowledged it. Now that I did, everything about me hurt. My hair roots were hurting. My fingernails were hurting. I was digging into the wall. Trying to keep myself standing upright. Why was I afraid to sit down?

I could lie down if I wanted. I squatted.

Time was flying. I heard one tick of the living room clock. Time was almost standing still. Everything had stopped. It was waiting on me. Waiting on me to die.

But I wouldn't die.

Boise could have Rafe.

Francis couldn't have Jonas.

Susie couldn't have Drew.

Momma couldn't have my land.

I would have this baby all by myself.

I decided that for certain. As I did, the pain hit. I went to my knees and screamed.

Bruiser and Ransom went wild. They dug at the door trying to get inside. I feared they would be smart enough to leap through a window. I didn't want them to break a window. Dogs had been known to eat afterbirth. Would they eat a baby, too?

The dogs settled down. I mustn't scream anymore.

Pain hit again and I sat flat on the floor with my back against the wall. The next pain had me gritting my teeth, scraping my fingernails into the linoleum floor.

"H-e-l-p m-e." I was talking to Boise, to Dad, to Andy, to Jonas. Somebody had to help me for I wasn't strong enough to do this alone.

I had done it with Drew.

But I wasn't alone.

Andy was there to catch the baby as it came out. He hadn't done the work. I did the work. I did – I did – I did.

I didn't scream. I whimpered. I took a gasp, clinched my teeth, balled up my fists, and I pushed. I pushed with every fiber inside me. I pushed beyond me. I pushed for Drew. I pushed for this baby. I pushed and pushed until I felt my flesh tearing. From my bent head, I saw the bulge coming from me. It was a protrusion of bloody multi-colored flesh. The protrusion had black hair. Hair darker than Jonas'.

Where was Jonas when I needed him?

The protrusion hung up. I reached down and touched the hair. I wanted to pull it the rest of the way out, but my hands were shaking. They had no strength. I balled them into fists again. I was angry, angry at my weakness, angry at Jonas, angry because I wanted to get this baby out while it was alive.

A wave of sickness hit me. I thought I was going to throw up. Instead, my entire body convulsed and I pushed. The shoulders came through and the protrusion seemed to plop out.

I closed my eyes, leaned my head against the wall and said a prayer of thanks. It was out. Finally, it was out, but it wasn't over. I had to get enough strength to open my hands and lift my baby up. I needed to clean its airway. I needed to hold him by the heels and thump him on the bottom like Jonas had done to Drew.

My baby needed to cry. He needed to scream.

I raked at the film and the mucus. I reached the wash rag lying on the floor and wiped its little face.

What a pretty face.

I raked fluid from its mouth. Pulled membrane from its body. Looked at the strange rippled cord. The cord was pulsing, throbbing like a heart beat.

I took him by the legs and tried to lift him. He was still connected to me, and he wasn't a boy. My baby was a little girl.

Love flowed over me like a spring wind, soft and gentle. I had a little girl, and I wasn't going to let her die. I wasn't going to die. I was going to grip the cord and pull. I had to get the afterbirth out. Once the cord stopped pulsing, I had to rip strips from my shirt and tie the cord off.

I could do that. No big thing. First I had to get my baby to breathe. I pulled her onto my knees, let her head hang down and patted her back. Nothing. I thumped her hard right on the butt. Fluid came from her mouth; her body twitched. I thumped her again. This time she sucked in air.

She started to cry.

I cried, too.

The dogs whined and scratched on the door. Bruiser let out a nervous howl, and Ransom mimicked him.

I stroked my little girl's wet body with a trembling hand. "We're not alone," I told her. "Your brother is upstairs, and our dogs are worried about us. We're not alone."

I pulled at her cord, but nothing happened. I remembered Jonas rubbing my stomach. I rubbed and pressed – rubbed and pressed. Her crying slacked off. She squirmed on my legs like she wanted off, but we were still connected.

A pain hit me and I pressed hard. It eased the pain and I felt something move inside me. More pain. Almost as bad as pushing the baby out. I pushed. I breathed. I sweated and I pushed again.

It came out. Ripping, tearing hurt. My mind flashed up Drew's birth. Ripping, hurting pain, but Jonas had been there. I was safe with Jonas.

Jonas wasn't here, but we weren't alone. Drew was upstairs and the dogs were at the door.

Rub the womb, I recalled. Rub it into a hard not so the bleeding will slow down. I rubbed with one hand and held the other against my little girl. I heard the clock tick. I leaned my head against the wall. It ticked again. My baby whimpered. I rubbed. Drew cried, but I couldn't go to him right now. He was safe where he was at. I wasn't finished with my baby girl. I had to tie and cut the cord.

Oh, what a strong shirt I was wearing. I worked at it before it tore. I had to focus on tying the cord off. My fingers weren't working right and they were sticky – sticky with my blood.

I did it, but I couldn't get up to reach the knife. It was in a drawer. Why did I put the knife in a drawer? So Drew couldn't get to it easy. Neither could I.

I would rip the cord in two. I tried. Nothing was ever this tough. It was like leather. I raked at it with a broken finger nail. It gave a sliver. I raked again and again. The clock ticked, I raked away cord tissue, and my baby squirmed.

The wood had burned down by the time my baby was loose. I lifted her onto my chest, reached the overalls and wrapped them around her. I clutched her to my chest as I rested my head against the wall. When I opened my eyes, I saw the mess. It was worse than hog killin time.

I wanted to get up, wanted to go to my crying son, but I couldn't do it just yet. I had to rub my womb a while longer. I had to stop bleeding so badly. I had to take care of my little girl.

I don't know how long I lay there. It had to be hours before I could get up. When I did, I wasn't steady on my feet. I tried to hold onto a chair back while I hugged my baby close. I managed to lift the stove lid and fill the fire box with wood. I was still bleeding, but not as much, and Drew was still crying.

I stuffed the kitchen towel between my legs, wrapped the hand towel around my baby and lay her on the table while I washed my hands. I got a biscuit from the stove warmer and the rest of the goat's milk in a cup, picked my baby up and slowly made my way up the stairs.

I wasn't going to clean anything right now even if I had been able to do it. I needed to feed Drew, lie down and let my new born baby suck.

Poor little Drew's nose was running and he sobbed like he had nearly cried himself out. His face brightened when he saw me. "Ma, ma, ma," he said and lifted his arms, but I couldn't take him. I didn't have the energy to lift him. Even my tiny baby was more than I wanted to carry.

I carefully placed my baby in the blood stained bed where she could stay warm. She wiggled and cried a little as her fists bobbed at her mouth. I held the cup of milk to Drew's lips. "Here sweetie, drink this for Mommie." I said soothingly. Drew drank and I handed him the biscuit. "Eat that and be a good boy for mommie, okay. Mommie has to rest now. I'm going to be in bed near you. Mommie will be right here."

He stopped sniffling and gummed the biscuit as I slowly made my way to the bed. I still had the towel between my legs and wished I could put clothes on, but that wasn't possible right now. I was too tired.

I managed to lift my shirt and let the baby nudge at my breast. I think she latched on enough to drink a little for she seemed to grow content and we both went to sleep.

I have never heard such a racket in my life. I didn't know if the dogs were mad or happy. They were somewhere between growling, barking and howling – and then they were silent. I wanted go back to sleep, but I couldn't.

A voice was yelling my name. Something turned over down stairs. Heavy, running steps sounded on the stairs. Someone flew into my room. I opened my eyes as Andy grabbed me. He danged near lifted me right out of bed.

"Missy, Missy! Are you alive? Is the baby alive? My God! Oh my God in heaven. He can't let you be dead. You can't die. What about your baby? Have I lost you both?"

"Put me back down," I managed to whisper.

"Thank God! Thank the good Lord in heaven." He heaved as though he had lost his breath and was just getting it back..

"Put more wood in the stove. It's cold." I managed to say. I felt like the snows of winter had covered my body. Even my teeth were chattering.

He reached down and touched my face with his rough hand. "It's not cold in here, and you don't have a fever and you feel warm enough. The baby?"

"She's still alive," I whispered. "Where's Jonas?"

I felt Andy pull the cover back to look at me and the baby. "No wonder you're cold. You don't have much on and you and the bed both are soaked. I've got to take care of you both. I should never have left this morning. This is all my fault. My fault," he mumbled as he rushed from my bedroom.

When he returned, he held a warm bitter brew to my lips even though it was extra sweet with sugar. "Drink this. I have to warm you up a little before I get clothes on you and change your bed things. The best thing to do for farm animals when they give birth is to keep them warm."

"My baby?"

"She's fine. I've got her in a warm blanket with a couple jars of warm water. Don't kick. I've got a hot frying pan wrapped in a towel near your feet."

"Drew?"

"He's still eating on the bread. Don't worry about him right now. He's fine. I'm going to take your shirt off. I need to get a warm dry gown on you. Can you sit up? Ah, Missy," he added. "I can't believe you had the baby all alone."

"I wasn't alone," I said. "Drew and the dogs were here."

Andy said nothing as he lifted me up and slipped the gown over my head.

"I made a mess in my bed and down stairs." I thought of the kitchen and how it looked.

"Don't worry about it. You and the baby are alive and that's all that matters. I should have been here, though. I should never have said I'd not deliver this one. I should have been here," he repeated. "When you needed me, I wasn't here."

"You're here now. I still need you, and so do my babies. Drew was crying for me and I couldn't go to him," I told Andy. "Jonas, didn't believe me. He didn't go by your place."

"Don't worry about Drew, he's just fine. Right now I'm going to take the bed things off. I've got things in here from the other bed. Can you roll to the edge?"

"Where's my baby?"

"In the crib. I put Drew in the floor."

"He'll get cold."

"He'll be fine for a few minutes. As soon as I'm done here, I'll put him back in the crib and bring the baby to you."

"She's okay?"

"She's okay."

Andy sat by my bedside with Drew in his lap. He had made thin potato soup and spooned bites into his mouth as he talked to him. I was so tired that the lulling of his voice put me to sleep.

I dreamed Jonas was sitting beside me instead of Andy. I wanted Jonas to be here, but I was thankful for Andy.

He woke me up grumbling about never diapering a baby before. I opened my eyes and watched him trying to fold a cloth diaper at odd angles and then trying to hold Drew down long enough to pin it in place.

"Glad I never had em," he mumbled right low. "If I'd a-had to diaper em."

I glanced at the window. It was getting dark. I wondered where Jonas was. I didn't ask Andy. I closed my eyes and was drifting back to sleep when I realized I hadn't done up the evening work.

"The work." I tried to raise up and halfway succeeded.

"You lay yourself back down. You'll not be doin any work for a couple or three days."

"But . . ."

"You snuggle that baby girl up good and warm. I'll do up the work once Jonas gets here."

I eased back in bed, my eyes staring at my baby. Oh how pretty she was. Her face was so small and delicate. Her nose perfect. Her lips oh so sweet.

"Andy?"

"Humm?"

"I like you better than Hazel."

"Not for long you won't."

I heard the kitchen door open. Ransom and Bruiser both sounded on the stairs. They came bounding into my room. Bruiser ran to me and Ransom made a fast inspection of Drew before he came to me.

"What tha hell! No! Oh no."

Jonas was running.

"I'll get the dogs back out." Andy said as Jonas entered.

"What in the hell happened downstairs? Are you all right?"

Jonas came to the bed and looked down on me. I pushed the cover back a little. "Your daughter."

He stared, speechless. He reached for her and carefully unfolded the blanket Andy had her wrapped in. Something came over his face and it wasn't the look of a doctor.

"My baby girl. My daughter."

I said nothing, just watched while the look of a doctor returned and he examined her. "What did he use to cut the cord with? It's shredded. She's okay, but little."

"Little?"

"I'll weigh her in a few minutes, but I'd say she won't reach seven pounds. What did you do, Laine, to put you into labor early? You weren't in labor when I left this morning." He eased my baby beside me.

"Yes, I was. She was born not long after you left."

"Andy was in town then."

"I know."

"Who delivered the baby?"

"Nobody."

His face turned pale. "The kitchen?"

"I've not worked up strength to clean it yet."

He tossed the cover back, lifted the gown and felt of my stomach. He pressed and rubbed my womb until it hurt.

"I bled a lot."

"So I saw. Why didn't Andy clean the kitchen for you?"

"He was taking care of us and Drew."

"How long was she born before he got here?"

"A long time." I answered.

He shook his head and looked like he wanted to say something, but didn't.

"What are you thinking about?" I figured he was going to tell me he was sorry he wasn't here, sorry he didn't believe me when I said I was in labor. And I wanted to hear it.

"It'll be all over town tomorrow that my wife didn't even need me to deliver her baby."

Chapter 22

He was wrong. Andy spent the next three days at the house except for nights and early mornings when he hurried home to do up his own work. He had turned his cow dry during the winter and he expected her to calf any time. Other than that and feeding his horse and a few chickens, he had nothing to do.

It was on the third day when James Travin showed up. Andy had informed me I was to lay in bed for ten days. He said getting up on the ninth day was bad luck. I ignored that.

Andy was on the back porch playing with Drew. He insisted his little boy needed some sunshine and fresh air. "He's a bit peaked," Andy insisted. I had noticed it was Andy that looked peaked. While he was staying here, he did almost nothing and that little bit exhausted him.

I eased out of bed and looked out the window. I thought the sound I heard might be Rupert, and I needed to put on a dress if it was.

It was James Travin.

I tiptoed down stairs where I could listen to what he wanted. I didn't trust him.

"I heard you might be here," Travin said. "I went by your house."

"Animals told you where I was, did they?"

Travin ignored that. "Have you thought over my offer?"

"Not had time."

"You don't look busy."

"I am," Andy said.

"That her boy?"

"A man might gather that, now, mighten he?"

"Mind if I sit down?"

"She'd probably mind."

I heard his steps on the porch and the scrape of a chair. He didn't care what I minded. For a little, I'd go out there and run him off, but I wanted to hear this.

"It's not every day you get an offer for land in the amount I gave you."

"That price was per acre, wasn't it?"

"Don't be funny. You know it wasn't. That was the price for all the land you own."

"I'd rather sell it by the acre. That way neither of us gets cheated."

"I don't cheat."

"I've heard different."

"Rupert Smith tells lies about me."

"Does he, now?"

"He does."

"He offered me more for my land than you have, and he's willing to pay by the acre."

"How many acres do you own?"

"Can't rightly say. It's never been surveyed."

"Rupert Smith doesn't have the available cash that I have. He's trying to arrange bank loans."

"You're not?"

"I have cash."

"I'd have to have the entire amount of cash in hand." Andy coughed. "I'm too old to give credit to a sharp swindler." He cleared his throat, spat, and blew his nose.

I peeped around the door and saw that Andy was humped up and hunched over like a dying old man.

"I have the cash."

"It'd have to be more'n twice what you've offered afore I'd worry my brain with thinking on the offer. Then I might not take it. I've not got long left to me and I'd like to enjoy some thing afore I go."

"That's ridiculous."

"Yeah, your offer was at that, ridiculous."

Travin's voice rose in irritation. "You know what I meant."

"I know all right. I may be an old, dying man, but I'm not plum stupid."

I wondered at that. He'd have to be stupid to be talking about selling his land to Travin. I had a good mind to run Travin off right now, but something made me stay still. Maybe it was my exhaustion and still feeble condition. Maybe it was hiding behind a door in my night gown. Maybe it was because I wanted to hear more of this conversation.

"I am offering you an enormous amount of cash for that land of yours. If you use good intelligence, you take me up on it."

"Now you listen here, Mr. Travin, Mrs. Jones is upstairs asleep and I don't want her disturbed. As you already know, she's just had a baby and she needs her rest. So, I'm tellin you right off, don't come around here talking about buying land, and don't come to me again unless you're willing to meet my price. If you do, I'll double my price again and I'll only sell by the acre."

I saw James Travin's head snap up as though he was insulted. He stood, tall, straight backed, and sleek as a weasel. Oh, how I longed to sic my dogs on him.

"I'll take my leave," he said curtly.

"Good day to you."

He stalked through the yard, started his vehicle, got in and drove off.

Andy chuckled. "Come on out here," he said. "Being you're already on your feet."

I came outside, amazed at how Andy's appearance had changed once Travin had gone. He looked ten years younger.

"You ought to be in bed, you know. You have to get well soon for I hain't hangin around here long. I got things to do."

I sank down in the chair, irritated that Travin had also sat in it. "You can't be talking to that man about selling you land."

"Why can't I?"

"He's a crook."

"I know that."

"But . . ."

"Talkin don't cost a man a thing. Besides, there comes a time when it's best to keep your hand near your enemy's throat, especially when he's trying to cut yours."

"Then you're not thinking about selling to him? If you want to sell, I'll buy it. You said I had money in the bank."

"Not that much money."

"How much would it take?"

"There's only one piece of land I don't want that belongs to me and that's the graveyard down in Banners Elk. I don't want that, but a body can't rightly sell a graveyard even if he owns it. Folks might come back and haunt a man for doing that. It's been known to happen, you know."

"Then why are you wasting your time with James Travin?"

"Don't you worry your head, Missy. I'm just havin a little fun with him, that's all."

"You're not really thinking about selling it, then?"

"Naw. What I'm thinkin about is how to take it with me."

That night I told Jonas about Andy and Travin.

"Andy Harmon has the right to sell his land if he wants to sell it, so don't you interfere."

"I'm not interfering."

"You'd never do that, would you?"

"Jonas!"

"Don't get excited. James is talking to every one about buying their land."

"Does he have that much money?"

Jonas shrugged. "Probably not. It makes him feel powerful to make people think he does."

That made sense. "Andy said he was just having fun with him."

"Laine, you need to realize that those old men at the store do nothing but sit around and think up things to do, unless you count their gossiping, trying to get the best of each other, and down-right jumping in the middle of everybody's business. Right now they are in the middle of James' business and they are having a ball."

"You don't think Andy is serious?"

"No, I don't. He hordes that land almost as much as you do. If he sold James that land, he would be rolling over in his grave a hundred years from now."

Jonas could not imagine how his words relieved me. Andy owned more land than I did. Why, Andy's land almost surrounded mine. It would be pure torment to watch it being torn apart to make houses for a bunch of folks from off.

"You know what I've been wondering about?" Jonas said in a different tone of voice.

"What?"

"You?"

"What have I done now that you don't like?"

"There you go jumping to conclusions again."

I didn't say anything. I was too tired to argue, so he continued.

"I have been wondering why you don't feel more pain when you're in labor."

"I felt pain." How could Jonas think I didn't?

"Most women are in severe pain hours and hours before they give birth. Screaming, earth shattering pain, but you never are."

I screamed, but I wasn't going to tell him. My pain was somewhere near to shattering, too, but I wasn't going to admit that, either.

"It might be possible that the panther severed some of your nerve endings, causing you not to hurt like most women do."

If that was so, then I was one lucky woman. The panther attack wasn't nearly as painful as birth.

"Maybe some women don't carry-on like others do," I told him sweetly. "Then again, maybe you've never been around to hear my screams or see me doubled over in earth shattering pain."

Jonas opened his mouth and then snapped it shut. He looked a bit odd right then.

I gained my strength back fast. At least Jonas said it was fast. But it wasn't fast enough for me. It was April and Beech Mountain was starting to warm up. Not only were the Robins there, other birds were too. They woke me up each morning singing and night birds sang me to sleep.

Two babies were in my room and Jonas fussed.

"Drew is a big boy now. He needs to sleep in his own room." Jonas insisted.

"He's only ten months old." Drew was born on June the 15th and Darcy Elaine was born on March 26th. Just about as close together as two babies could get. Of course, Jonas claimed Darcy wasn't due until the last of April and that she was premature, but I knew better. She weighed six pounds and eight ounces. That wasn't premature.

"He needs his own room, Laine." Jonas said firmly.

"I'll move him just as soon as the weather warms up."

"What does that have to do with anything?"

"In here I can check on him during the night to make sure he's not uncovered and getting cold."

"He'll cry if he's cold."

"Now, Jonas, a few more weeks aren't going to hurt a thing. Besides, once you're asleep nothing wakes you up."

"I wake up easier than you think."

I reached out and put my arm around him without disturbing Darcy. "Go to sleep, now, honey. I'll talk to Andy when he comes around again. Maybe he can use some of that scrap lumber to make Drew a little bed, one he won't roll out of."

"You shouldn't have Andy doing so much work for you." Jonas sounded a little troubled.

"Why not?"

"He's not been looking well lately. Surely you've noticed."

"Has he been to you? Is something wrong with him?" The thought scared me.

"No, but he has lost a lot of weight and he's started looking old."

"He is old, and you know that old people lose weight."

"He's slowed down, Laine. Slowed down a lot lately."

"I think that's because of his leg. I have an idea that horse broke a small bone and it never healed right."

"I see. You're a doctor now."

"Don't pick at me."

"How about a nurse. I'll let you be that."

"Okay, I'll be a nurse. Jonas?"

"Humm?"

"You don't know of another boy that I could hire to help me on the farm, do you? It's time to plow and neither Andy nor I need to be doing it."

"I'll ask around."

He didn't sound like he meant it.

☙

Rupert Smith showed up a few days later with a smile on his face and an arm full of gifts. He brought two boxes containing tin can of baby formula, three dozen diapers, blankets and little sleepers with feet in them.

"What's all this?" I asked.

"For the little girl."

"There's so much, and baby formula?"

"Just in case you need it. I brought some bottles too. This is some of the stuff my wife insisted all mothers needed. Except she had about fifty times more. How are you doing?"

"Good, and thank you for this. I have to admit I can use it." I was thinking about giving the formula to Drew and using the goat's milk for cooking.

"I heard you had the baby alone."

The old men were at it again, and doing a fine job it seemed.

"Who told you that?"

He grinned. "The local store."

"Are they giving Jonas a rough time?"

"They're trying. They're all trying to buy you from Jonas."

I had to grin. "Who is offering the most?"

"I am."

"You're joking?"

"I suppose I am, but those old men are enjoying it."

"Is Andy providing fuel for their gossip?"

"Naturally. He has the second highest offer in for you, but I keep topping his offer."

"You better watch yourself. Jonas just might take you up on it. He doesn't like traveling, you know."

"He ought to buy him one of these new vehicles. It makes traveling pleasant, well, sometimes it does."

"That's a thought. Suppose I could attach a wagon behind it?"

"They come in trucks. Lots of farmers are getting them to haul produce in."

Now that got my attention.

"I'll bring you a picture of them the next time I come by."

"Do that. Are they expensive?"

"Yes, but I'm considering one myself."

He brought dog food to the porch and sat down.

"What's Travin up too?" I asked him outright.

"In what respect?"

"Everything."

"We don't have that much time. It would take me a month to tell everything that man is trying to do."

"He wants to buy Andy's land."

"I know he does."

"Why aren't you trying to buy it?"

"I've got an offer in, but Andy doesn't want to sell."

"I don't have enough money to buy it," I told him. "Travin said you didn't either."

"James Travin is a liar and a crook."

"Does that mean you do have enough to buy it?"

"I could come up with the money if Andy was willing to sell."

Relief hit me and distress was hot on its tail. Andy couldn't live forever. Somebody else would have to own his land. Unless I could grow enough crops to buy it.

"I need help on this farm," I said to Rupert.

"I thought you wanted mother nature to take care of it."

"Mother nature isn't making me money and I can't do it myself yet. I don't want to break myself down and be no good. It'll be several months before I can plow."

Rupert gave me a disbelieving look. "You plowing?"

"How else can I farm? Land has to be plowed and seeds have to be planted. I need a lot of corn and molasses. Molasses sells good and everybody needs corn to eat and feed their animals with."

"Abe Farrow did it last year, didn't he?"

"Yeah, he did. He was a good worker, strong and young."

"I heard he and your sister weren't getting along too well."

"Really?"

"Gossip has it that their mothers are trying to break them up."

I could believe that.

"Hazel is rumored as saying your sister isn't fit stock to have children. She says Abe should divorce her and find a strong woman."

"You're kidding?"

"Nope. There is also gossip on your mother's part. She claims Abe is abusive and the law should lock him up in jail until his limbs rot off. She also claims Hazel practices witch craft, is a fruitcake, and should be locked up in an insane asylum for the safety of the general public."

"What about Susie and Abe? Is there any gossip on them?"

"Abe wants to take Susie and move to another state."

"They need to do it during the night so Momma and Hazel can't follow them."

"True," Rupert said. "Was Abe a good worker for you? Do you think he is the kind to beat on his wife?"

"He was a good worker, and I never did see any mean streak in him." I remembered him putting the snake in my baby's room. "Hazel said he was the one that put the snake in Drew's crib."

His face grew intense. "Was she telling the truth?"

"I don't know."

"Is there any way you can find out?"

"I'm certainly not going to hunt him up and ask him."

"Why not?"

"For one thing, I'd have to go back to Dad's place and I don't want to get within ten miles of Momma or Susie. For another thing, if Abe did it, I'd want to shoot him dead on the spot. I'm not going to tell you what I'd like to do to Hazel. It's not Christian."

"Fine reasons for you to stay away."

I saw the twinkle in his eyes.

"Well, now, my lady of historical value, do I get to see this new baby or will I have to come back after Jonas sells you to me?"

"You can see her, but don't count on Jonas selling me just yet. He's grown really found of little Darcy and he knows where I go she goes."

Rupert stood up and looked out over the farm. "I'll check with one of my workers. Like I said before, he's a farmer at heart and might be just what you're looking for."

"Really?"

"Really."

He showed up the next morning ridding a huge, raw boned horse as boney and ugly as a mud fence. If I didn't know better, I'd of thought he and the horse were brothers. I went out in the yard to meet him. He sat on the horse bareback and with an ease that said he'd been seated there often.

"Day, miss. I'm come to see ye maw. Tell 'er Mr. Smith done sent me."

"He sent you to see me. I'm Laine Jones."

"You're a mite young," he said.

"So are you," I returned. "I was expecting a grown man instead of a puny boy."

The look on his face showed that he didn't contain any humor in that huge body of his.

"I be almost grown. I turned eighteen some time back."

"You must be little for your age."

"Could be. Maw were kinda on the short side, but she were broad aplenty. Could be I took back atter her. What air ye paying?"

"What was Rupert paying you?"

He told me and I must have frowned. It wasn't as much as we had paid Abe.

"I could tally-up a mite less iffin room and board were added fur me and my mount."

I thought of this over-grown boy sleeping in my house. More than likely he'd break down the bed and all the chairs.

"An out building'd suit, but I'd admire the barn."

"The barn will be fine."

He slipped from the horse in a fluid motion. He was even bigger and taller on foot, even with his shoulder blades sticking out his shirt and his feet looking like sled runners in his rough worn boots. I would go broke feeding him.

"What you gotten in mind fur me to do?"

"Everything."

This time he frowned. "You might ought to spell that out a lit'le plainer."

"I want to turn this place into the most productive farm that ever was. I want to raise acres of corn, potatoes, beans, cabbage and any other crop that will grow. I want to raise hogs, chickens, cattle plus the feed to feed them all with some left over to sell. I'd like to have several acres of sogram cane and a molasses mill to go with it. And that's not all I want; I want to earn enough money from it to buy all the land that joins me. Think you can do that for me this summer?"

"By fall, but narry a bit sooner."

"Do you have a big brother that could pitch in?"

"I got brothers. They hain't here abouts."

"Then you'll have to do."

He nodded, spit in the palm of his hand, rubbed his hand over his overalls and then held it out for me to shake.

"We'll shake on a trial basis. Give it a couple of weeks and see if we both like our arrangement."

"Fair enough."

We shook hands. It felt like I had put my hand into a large roughed up vise, but he turned loose fast without squeezing.

"Where you want I should start plowin?"

"The garden," I pointed. "The corn patch, the land from the corn patch to the edge of the woods, and then the land that runs on top and over that little rise."

He nodded and led his horse toward the barn.

"I'll have dinner ready at twelve."

He nodded again.

I watched him go into the barn and wondered where he came from. His face was tanned dark or he had Indian or something in his blood line. His hatless head was growing a thick crop of brown hair and his eyes were as black as a lump of coal. One of his spread out hands would have covered the top half of my body. Mercy, I hoped this giant was gentle.

I couldn't keep myself from looking at him from the window every so often. I wasn't sure I wanted him helping me. He was gentle with the horse and knew how to plow. He was using his own horse, and I wondered why when Rafe's horses were grazing in the field.

He never snapped the reins or raised his voice although I could occasionally hear a gentle sound coming from him and assumed he was talking to his horse. It seemed to take no time for him to finish the garden. He didn't bother to ask me which field was next. He took the closest one.

I hurried to peel a large pot of potatoes and opened cans of beans, apples, and corn. I chose to bake cornbread instead of biscuits. Still, I wasn't sure I had enough to fill him up.

I didn't think I could carry enough to the field to fill him up. So, at twelve sharp I went onto the porch to holler at him. He was coming through the yard with his hair dripping wet and hugging his head.

"Been sweating?"

"Warshed up. I turned my mount into the field to graze. Hope it's pleasing."

"Of course. Dinner's ready."

"I'm a mite hungry," he admitted sheepishly.

He looked out of place when he sat down at the table, and I was surprised when he downed his head and his lips moved in grace.

"Dig in," I said, and he did.

I was right. This boy could eat.

"I didn't ask you name," I said after a while.

"Barnabus," he said. "Barnabus Jackson."

"Where're you from?" I expected him to tell me some where in the high mountains.

"Flat lands. Down nigh Charlotte."

"Flat lands?"

"Yeap. Lots of farm land down younder. No mountains."

"What are you doing up here?"

"Mr. Smith brung me with 'im."

"You don't like working for him?"

"Yeah, but I favor farming."

"Why?"

"Miss Jones." He looked a little bewildered. "Iffin you don't mind, I'm pleased to eat afore talkin."

Andy showed up during the evening. He was now trying to come by once a day just to check on me and the babies. He spat out his whole wad of jaw tobacco when he saw Barnabus. He watched him for a long time before he came to the house.

"What is that? Where did it come from?"

"That's what's going to buy me your land."

He frowned.

"He's my new farm hand."

"Never seen nothing like him or his horse. What do you reckon they were fed while they was growing up? And what do you mean, buy you my land?"

"I'm goin to earn enough money by farming this land to buy your land so you won't sell it to James Travin or anybody else."

"That would take years."

"I got years."

"You might but I don't."

"In that case, Barnabus has got brothers. I can speed things up."

Andy shook his head. "Where did he come from?"

"You don't know?"

"How would I know?"

"I thought Rupert might have told you."

"So, Rupert sent him to help you."

I nodded. "Thank goodness."

"You needed somebody, if he's safe."

"I think he's a fine young boy."

Andy lifted his brows.

"He told me he just turned eighteen some time back. I don't think he's through growing yet."

"In that case, you don't need his brothers. What does Jonas say about him?"

"I'm not sure Jonas will even notice him."

"I think he might."

"He eats a lot."

"I don't know about this, Missy. I really don't. I'm thinking if Rupert sent him, he can't be a threat to you. It's just . . ."

"He's big and ugly?"

"I reckon that's it."

"He's gentle with the horse and he seems polite. We're giving it a try for a couple of weeks just to see if things will work out."

Andy stayed all evening playing with Drew and watching Barnabus. There were times when it appeared he wanted to tell me something, but he never did. I figured he was concerned about Barnabus and it made me nervous toward him, even if I knew Rupert wouldn't send me a dangerous worker. When he left, I heard him mumble something about a mountain gorilla. It brightened my mood up a little.

I fed him before Jonas got home and kept the left-overs warm. He had settled in the barn by then. I was waiting for the right time to tell Jonas about Barnabus

"Well?" Jonas finally said. "How do you like your new farm worker?"

"You know about him?"

"Rupert came by my office."

"And ask your permission?"

"To tell me he was safe. It seems he isn't a beauty contestant."

"That's true."

"Good. I won't be jealous."

"Probably not."

After supper, I asked Jonas if he wanted to go to the barn to meet our new farm worker. I always milked Torment while Jonas looked after the babies, and I didn't expect Barnabus would be able to do the milking. His thumb and forefinger were larger than her entire sack.

"No. I'm not interested."

I didn't argue. Jonas had plenty of time not to be jealous.

When I got to the barn, Barnabus had all the animals fed and had pulled early spring weeds and was feeding them to Torment.

"I'm partial to goats," he said.

"She's a good 'un."

"You milkin her?"

"Yeap. She gives a quart at a time."

"She'll need dryin up soon."

"Why?"

"She's totin two lit'le 'uns."

I looked at her fat sides. "How soon?"

"Six weeks."

"How can you tell?"

He placed his hands on both sides of her stomach. "They's here. Take around five weeks to travel here." His hands moved backward. "Once here, they's must drop to here. Six weeks, yeap, that's it."

This was April and my cow would calf the first week of May. I could milk Torment for two more weeks before I turned her dry.

"Fixed me a place in the loft," he said. "Nothin parable to sweet-smellin hay."

"Do you need a quilt, pillows or something?"

"Quilt sounds mighty comforting."

"I'll bring it out when I finish here."

"Obliged," he said and headed for the loft.

Chapter 23

Andy was right. I didn't need Barnabus' brother. There wasn't enough work on the whole of Beech Mountain to keep two Barnabuses busy. I couldn't imagine why Rupert would ever let him go if he could carpenter as good as he could farm. He was my blessing but I almost regretted having him. He made me feel useless. He could do more in an hour than I could have done in half a day and he never seemed to hurry. He didn't talk, ask questions, complain, or stop. He began early and continued at a steady pace that appeared slow until I walked beside him. His slow pace was my run.

He did ask me for one thing. The second day of plowing he asked if he could use the two horses I had. He said he didn't want to over-work one horse. He worked his horse from almost daylight until noon, the second horse until supper, and the third horse until it was too dark to see.

It took no time to have the ground plowed, disked, and harrowed. Next came planting. Barnabus had rigged a log with V shaped planks fastened to it, and then pulled by the horse. He was laying out rows to drop the corn in. Drew and Darcy were taking their afternoon naps, and I was in the barn choosing the best ears of corn to shell and plant when I heard the noise. At first I thought it was crows chasing a hawk. I listened harder and realized it as the sound of human voices screeching.

Oddly enough, Indians on a raiding party came to my mind. The dogs were lying near me and came to their feet in a rage. We ran to the door and went outside to see what was going on.

Two big footed horses were coming out of the woods. On their backs were two yelling, cussing women that were striking out at each other with tree-limb switches. I didn't believe my eyes, didn't believe I could possibly be seeing what I was seeing. It was worse than a nightmare.

The dogs headed straight for them as though they shared my horror. They must have recognized the smell of Hazel, but they couldn't have recognized Momma's.

I took out at a dead run for the house and my shotgun. I couldn't have been more fearful if it had been a wild Indian raid.

Barnabus had reached the edge of the woods by the time I got back outside. He was calling the dogs off.

"No," I shouted. "No! Turn em loose. Turn em loose!"

Momma's and Hazel's switching at each other had stopped. They sat stock-still as they both stared at Barnabus. I think they were more afraid of him than they were the dogs.

I was running, stumbled, fell down with the loaded gun, got to my feet and ran on with the gun alternately pointing at one and then the other. I would have preferred to come face to face with another panther than these too women. At least I could kill the panther outright.

Barnabus looked toward me, but they were still staring at him, speechless. His appearance must have been mighty overwhelming as he stood there with his britches held up by a long rag running through the belt loops. His shirt was off. His bony arms, back, and chest had more hair than Bruiser. His long horse-face had several days' worth of beard. All of him was covered in dust.

He looked at the gun, looked at them, and then stepped out of the line of fire.

Both dogs came to me, bristles raised, fangs showing, waiting for me to sic them on.

"I'll kill you both," I yelled at them.

"It's me, Elaine Elder. Your mother," Momma said as though that fact was the most important thing in the world.

"That's why I'll shoot you first."

Momma sucked in an indignant breath and Hazel snorted with pleasure. I turned the gun on her. "The second barrel is yours."

Hazel's thin lips drew away from her teeth. "Where is he? Where is my son? I know he came here."

"I won't leave without my Susie," Momma shouted at me. "Give her back to me."

I looked from one to the other, transfixed on what they had just said. They were hunting for Abe and Susie and they thought they were here? Amazement and repulsion ran over my skin, prickling up goose bumps. Surely those two wouldn't come crawling out of the woods, too.

Barnabus calmly looked from them to me, his expression one of calm waiting as though he witnessed such a scene every day of his life. I wanted to yell at him to get the ax, get the shovel, get something that would make these women disappear and Abe and Susie never show up on my land.

There was a rumbling in my head, a confusion of sound. It couldn't be thundering on this sunny day. A moment later I recognized the sound of a vehicle straining for speed on the rough road. But there were thudding sounds too.

Jonas came out of the woods behind them. His horse was lathered, its sides heaving. His hat had blown off somewhere showing hair lying straight back from the blowing of wind. His eyes were the size of silver dollars.

No color was left in his face. He appeared as winded as the horse.

He took in the scene, took in me standing there trembling, a gun pointing at the two women, at Barnabus calmly watching it all. He knew I was going crazy with wanting to make them disappear, to make them never have set foot on my land.

"Where are the babies, Laine? Think of the babies," he added urgently as he slid off his exhausted horse and came toward me.

The dogs were between us, their fangs still showing, their chests still rumbling from the tension they were sensing.

"Don't come any closer," I said to Jonas. "I don't want to hit you instead of them."

"They're leaving," he said, holding up his hands in a ridiculous way. "They're not going to bother you. They're going to turn those horses around and leave. They won't ever come back."

"Not without my Susie." Momma was still braver than Hazel.

"They're not here. Laine would never allow them to be here."

"I don't believe you," Hazel shouted. She couldn't allow Momma the last words.

The vehicle was traveling wide open when it reached the curve to the house. Rupert hit the brakes and skidded way further than the barn and end of the road. It was the grass that stopped him. His feet hit the sod before the vehicle came to a complete stop. He came toward me at an angle and then stopped when he saw I was holding the gun.

"Stay out of this, Rupert," Jonas said. "I'll handle my wife." He turned toward those two crazy women. "Turn those horses around and get back where you belong. I'm not about to take that gun away from her."

"I want my baby girl," Momma whined.

"Get your baby girl and take her straight to hell. It's my son that's important."

"Shut up," Rupert said. "And get off this mountain. Neither your daughter nor you son are here."

The way he said that turned all eyes on him.

"You got them?" Momma screeched.

"Abe came to me in desperation. He was willing to sell his soul in order to get away from the two of you. He said he'd work for free if I'd send him away, far away."

"You didn't," Jonas said.

"I didn't hire him," Rupert said. "But I did loan him enough money to get him and his wife a long ways from here. They're going to start a new life in a different state. They're long gone on a fast moving train."

The gentle spring wind brought another sound, the sound of a team and wagon. Two old men sat on the seat, four sat in the back on sacks of feed. They were popping up and down as the wagon hit chug holes. Andy was bringing up the rear riding his horse.

"This has turned into a three-ring circus," Jonas said scornfully as he eyed the seven men and then turned back to the women. "Leave before I take Laine's gun and shoot you myself."

I raised the gun into the air and pulled the trigger. Momma nor Hazel hesitated. They sawed on the reins and dug their heels into the horses' sides, each switching their horse and cussing at each, and then cussing at me.

"What the hell do you think you're doing?" Jonas yelled as he reached for my gun.

I sidestepped and moved the gun from his reach. "Ending the three-ring circus," I said, clicked to my dogs, and went toward the house. I needed to check on my babies.

Jonas and Rupert followed at my heels. I slammed the door, but they opened it and came into the kitchen. I went up stairs to check on Drew and Darcy, still clutching the shotgun as though it was a life line.

They were sound asleep regardless of all the commotion going on outside. They didn't know their mother was falling to pieces, wanted to scream and yell and run and hide. I gently closed the bedroom door and went down stairs where Rupert was building up the fire and Jonas was putting on a pot of coffee. Andy and his group of gossiping men had almost reached the porch.

"Are you all right?" Rupert asked me.

"I'm just wonderful."

"For goodness sake, Laine, put that shotgun up. You make me nervous. Stop playing at being Annie Oakley. Surely, you're mature enough to handle an unpleasant situation without resorting to a gun."

I cocked the second trigger and held it cocked for a moment, the barrel pointing at the floor between Jonas' feet. He didn't move. I eased the trigger down and took the gun into the other room and leaned it behind the door. I'd reload later. Two loaded barrels were better than one.

There was a twinkle in Rupert's eyes when I came back into the kitchen and took over making coffee.

Jonas sat down at the table along with Rupert. Relief showing all over him.

"Are you going to invite them in?" Rupert nodded toward the porch and the men that had gathered there. I recognized Hack Pennel and several of the men at his store. Both excitement and disappointment hovered around them.

"I'll give them a cup of coffee before they leave," I tried to sound calm, undisturbed by the events that had just happened.

"Perhaps this isn't the best time to tell you this," Rupert said. "But Abe wasn't the one that put the snake in the baby's room."

I looked at him, waited. "How do you know?" I finally asked.

"Truth was one of the conditions of the loan."

"Who did it then, Hazel?"

"He wasn't sure."

"And you believed him?"

He nodded.

"What if it had been him?" I asked.

"I would have bought them both a one-way ticket to Alaska."

"Was it Hazel?" I demanded this time.

"Abe wasn't sure and neither am I."

"I should have shot her."

"No," said Jonas. "You shouldn't have. Hazel and your mother deserve each other. They will focus their revenge on each other instead of you."

Revenge, I thought. Sweet revenge.

When I gathered all the cups I had and went out onto the porch to give the men coffee, they were watching Barnabus laying off the rows.

"Indian," Hack Pennel was saying.

"Half Indian," another man said.

"Half Indian, a quarter German and a quarter . . . something else."

"Gorilla," said Andy. "Mountain gorilla."

"Elephant man," said another. "I saw one at a circus once. They called him the elephant man."

"He don't look like no elephant," Hack said.

"He's as big as one, but he don't look like no man I've ever seen."

"You old gossips stop talking about my hired man." I told them firmly.

"What is he?"

"One fine person," I told them. "I plan on keeping him, too."

Right then and there they started betting on how long I would keep him.

They all left, but Andy came back. "Just wanted to make sure you're all right, Missy."

"I'm all right," I said as I put Drew on the porch to play and covered my bodice with a blanket so I could let Darcy suck without being exposed.

"That was some commotion," Andy said as he looked toward Barnabus.

"Yeah, it was. Why did they all show up here?"

"Those two lunatics went to Hazel's old place first, then to Jonas' office in search of their kids. They were fighting each other like two sow cats with their tails tied together, both of them bound and determined to find their child first.

"They figured they might be hiding out at your place, and headed up the mountain."

"And everybody followed?"

"You got the picture."

"Even all those gossiping old men?"

"Didn't have nothin better to do with their time."

"What were they betting on?"

"If you'd shoot them or not."

"How'd you bet?"

"Oh, I knew you wouldn't kill them. I said you'd fire one warning shot and they'd turn tail and run. We all miss-figured one thing. We never considered that Rupert Smith had helped them get away. Now why would he do a thing like that?"

"The same reason he sent me Barnabus."

Andy was thoughtful for a few moments. "And that is?"

"Because he could."

"Maybe, maybe not. Men usually have mighty good reasons for what they do or don't do. Say, does this Barnabus ever slow down or stop to talk? He can talk can't he?"

"He never slows down nor speeds up. He does talk while he helps me do up the work. Animals bring out the best in him."

"I don't wonder. I take it you like him?"

"Yes, I like him."

"What about Drew?"

"Drew's not afraid of him, but he doesn't want anything to do with him."

"Does he like children?"

"His eyes and face softens when he looks at them."

"The dogs . . ."

"They've never growled at him once, not even the day he showed up. Do you know something about him that I don't?"

Andy shook his head. "That's just it. Nobody knows anything about him."

"He told me he was from the flatlands down near Charlotte."

"He doesn't look like a city person."

"I like him."

"That's what counts."

"Strange isn't it," I said and then stopped.

"What's strange?"

"If he'd been good lookin, folks would still be questioning me for hiring him. Those old men would be gossiping about me hiring myself a pretty-boy, and they'd be taking on bets about Jonas being jealous. Now, they're saying I'm a little crazy and they know Jonas will never be jealous of him, so they're betting on how long I'll keep the likes of him around."

"How long will you?" Andy didn't hesitate to ask.

"Like I told you earlier, long enough to help me earn enough to buy your land, if he doesn't eat me out of land and home," I added.

Andy became serious. "Missy, you don't need no more land."

"It's not a matter of need. It's a matter of want. I told you that before."

"Owning too much is as bad as owning too little."

"There's no such thing as owning too much land."

Andy shook his head and looked toward Barnabus. "If he turns out to be a good 'un, more land might not be so bad on you. Besides, knowing you, you might end up with fifteen or twenty sons and they'll need a piece of ground. Drew will get Rafe's land after you're gone, and that piece Jonas sold to me hain't fit for farming. Yeah, you might could use my land come time."

"That's why I plan on buying it." I told him firmly.

"Missy . . ."

He seem to want to tell me something, but something stopped him. "What?"

"Nothing. Absolutely nothing. I'll look after you when the time comes, don't you worry."

I was worrying. I didn't like the way he said that, or what he didn't say.

"Rafe made money selling things, and I can too."

"As long as you've got two mean dogs, a double barrel shot gun, and a mountain gorilla, you might at that."

"Not to mention a town full of old men that laugh at me."

"Naw, they don't laugh – much."

After Andy left, I sat there and let the sun warm my cold bones. I wasn't sure I would ever feel warm again, or would feel safe from Momma and Hazel, safe from poisonous snakes, safe from those that wanted to come in on me and take away my land, take away my peace and contentment.

I turned Torment dry and Barnabus moved her to a different place to browse every morning, noon, and night. He ate three meals a day, worked at a continuous pace, and never complained about anything.

I noticed that each Saturday night, he took off his work clothes, put on slightly better clothes, and washed his dirty clothes in the creek and hung them on tree limbs to dry. I never offered to wash them for him. I knew he would not appreciate my offering.

Barnabus was a complete person, needing nothing nor no one.

His odd looks was even growing on me – a little.

He surprised me when he stopped working an hour early and headed to the barn. A few minutes later he came to the kitchen door.

"She's got it Mrs. Jones."

I opened the screen door and looked at him.

"She done brung her calf out. Want to see the little hef'er?"

I picked up Drew and followed him to the barn. He had left the back door open and Pet was standing in the hall licking her little calf. She was such a brown Jersey color she was almost pink with a very pink nose and huge eyes. She was as delicate as a little fawn.

"Ever see anything so sweet, did ye ever?"

"Twice," I answered. "When my babies were born."

"I'd reckon," he said as though he wasn't convinced.

"Wait until you have babies of your own."

"Won't."

"Sure you will."

He downed his head and moved a sprig of hay with the toe of his boot. "Have ye not looked at me?"

"Of course I have."

"I wouldn't do this here to a body." He said. "I best get at it. Thought you might not ought to miss such a sight as this here."

He was gone.

When I left the barn, he was dropping field corn and covering up the seeds with his feet.

I wished I knew of some woman that would fall in love with Barnabus, but I feared there never would be one.

That evening when Jonas got home, I approached him with my question.

"What do you think about Barnabus' looks?"

"What are you talking about?"

"Do you think he's so ugly no woman will ever want him?"

He grinned and shook his head in a bewildered manner. "What a woman won't think up."

"Well, do you?"

"Laine, I can't answer something like that?"

"Why not?"

"Because I wouldn't know how?"

"Are there any single women in Banners Elk or close by?"

"Plenty."

"One that would like Barnabus?"

Jonas took Darcy from the carrier on my back and snuggled her against his chest.

"Da da," Drew said and lifted he arms from where he played in the floor, but Jonas ignored him as he turned to me.

"Laine, if you somehow did manage to hook him up with someone, he'd probably leave with her. Or most likely, some old widow woman might marry him for the work he's able to do and you'd neither see hide nor hair of him again."

Jonas was right. I wouldn't be match-making, at least for a long while to come.

"Have you heard anything from Momma or Hazel?" I asked as I took up food for Jonas, Drew, and myself. Barnabus had already eaten as he normally did and gone to the barn to feed.

"Andy hasn't been around lately?"

"Not in a couple of days."

"He started trusting Barnabus to look after his favorite little lady?"

I didn't like the way Jonas said that. "Have you heard anything about Momma or Hazel?" I asked more pointedly.

"I suppose they're back in Ashe County. Say, there's an idea, Laine. Your mother could marry Barnabus. He might be the only man living that could control her." Jonas laughed as he cuddled Darcy in the crook of his arm. "Who knows, he might make you a better daddy than Andy has."

Drew crawled to my legs and pulled up. I put him in his high chair and sat a plate of food and spoon in front of him. He ate looking from me to Jonas.

"What's wrong, Laine? Cat got your tongue?"

"Why are you being mean?"

"It's the truth isn't it? Here, take daddy's little girl so daddy can eat. I'm starved. It's been a long day."

Chapter 23

When Andy didn't show up the next day, I decided to go to his place. I had Drew in the large carrier on my back and Darcy in the little soft carrying pouch Andy had fashioned out of leather and cloth.

When I got near the house, I didn't like what I saw. James Travin's vehicle was parked outside. If I'd been alone, without the growling dogs and both babies, I'd have slipped up to a window and listened to what was going on it Andy's shop.

As it was, Andy must have heard the dogs and came out onto the porch. I stepped behind a large tree trunk and told the dogs to be silent.

"Have a good day," Andy said to Travin.

"My attorney will be here next week," Travin said.

"Fine." Andy turned his back on Travin and went inside and closed the door.

Travin went rigid; his chin shot upward as though Andy's actions had highly insulted him. I saw his mouth move but he didn't say anything loud enough for me to hear. But I didn't need to hear him to know it wasn't complementary and it made me dislike the weasel even more, if that was possible. He came right in line behind Momma and Hazel.

Why Andy talked to such a man was beyond me.

When his vehicle was chugging down the rutted road, I went to the shop, opened the door and walked inside. Andy was sanding on a coffin as though he didn't know I was outside, but I was sure he did.

"Why do you let him anywhere near here?" I demanded.

"Laine Jones, you're beginning to sound like my wife."

I laughed and so did Andy.

"I don't mean to sound like a wife, but I'm serious. I don't like that man."

"You think I do?"

"You seem to. He's been hangin around you lately, tryin to steal your land no doubt. Why is his lawyer showing up?"

"James Travin is trying to whoo-doo folks around here. He thinks he's smarter than every body else being he's rich and educated. The way I figure it, its an old man's job to wise him up a bit."

"He'll nail you to the wall." I said harshly, not wanting Andy anywhere hear him. "He's after land."

I turned my back so Andy could get Drew out of the carrier. He put him in the floor to play in the shavings.

"You shore are hung up on land, hain't you, Missy?"

"I'm not hung up on land."

"Yeah, you are. You do realize you won't die if you don't own all you see."

I tried to smile at Andy, but it was difficult. Didn't he realize what a sneaky weasel James Travin was? Didn't he realize he was no match for that man? But I wouldn't insult Andy by saying such to him. Still, uneasy feelings troubled me more than I could understand.

"Don't you start pickin at me, Andy Harmon. You like land just as good as I do. Beside you understand me perfectly."

"What makes you so smart."

"Must be those vitamins Rupert has been giving me."

"No doubt. Maybe I should take some."

"Why? Aren't you feeling okay?" It hadn't gone unnoticed to me that Andy was looking older with every day that passed, but that was the way with old folks.

"I'm fine, Missy. I just can't pretend to be a young buck any longer."

"That's what you get for hanging around with those old men at the store."

He ignored that. "Why did you drag those babies all the way here?"

"My babies needed an airing."

"What did their momma need?"

"To see how you're doing."

"And catch up on local gossip?"

"I missed you."

"Flattery. How pleasant to an old man's ears."

"I'm serious."

He didn't seem to believe me.

"How is your mountain gorilla doing?"

"I wish you wouldn't call him that. He's such a nice boy."

"That nice boy is older than you, Missy."

"Well, I feel older." And I did. I was a mother of two and I'd been married twice. Both of those things made a woman age fast.

"Want to know about your relatives, don't you?"

I couldn't deny that. "I asked Jonas about them, but he didn't know anything."

"Rupert hasn't been by lately?"

"Not since the three ring circus."

"He's not telling where he sent your sister and Abe. Talk has it he picked them up in his car and took them to catch the train, and bought their tickets himself. Your momma and Hazel threatened, begged, and screamed at everybody they came into contact with, but nobody seems to know what direction they went."

"Did they have a go at Rupert?"

"Oh yeah, but Rupert called in the sheriff and threatened to have them jailed."

"It worked?"

"Seems so."

"Where are they now?"

"According to Jonas' dad, they're home fighting with each other tooth and claw. You know, Missy, those two old cats need each other. They can fight until the cows come home and it won't matter to a soul, and it will keep them happy."

Andy was right about that. Momma and Hazel could spend their days fighting with each other, planning, tricking, and belittling. What kind of life was that when they could be working and making something of importance?

"Andy, does Hazel have those snakes?"

"Once a snake lover, always a snake lover."

"Rupert said Hazel lied to me. He said Abe wasn't the one to put the snakes in the baby's crib."

"I'm glad. I never did think Abe was a bad sort. He let his momma's greed get the best of him. Don't you repeat that with your young'uns."

I walked back through the woods carrying my babies. The trees were putting out their leaves and the rich earth gave off a sweet, dank smell. I looked around me at the life of my beloved mountain. Gray squirrels were clambering and birds were busy building their nests in the tree branches. A few nests were already hatched out and the parents hurried about finding food for their young. There was no place on earth that I'd rather be than right here. No place else I wanted to raise my children. Andy was right. I didn't want to repeat Hazel's or my own mother's mistakes with my babies. I wanted them to be raised perfect. I wasn't sure how to do that, but I was going to try.

I was glad Rupert helped Abe and Susie leave and I figured he knew where they were. He had several other places that he was developing and Abe could be working at one of them. A man needed his work to feel good about himself; so did a woman, but she needed more than work. She needed her family, her husband and children. I hoped Susie wouldn't lose anymore babies. I wanted Susie and Abe both to know what loving them was, and how it would hurt to have one harmed or killed by a snake.

What puzzled me to desperation was Andy. He had no business messing with James Travin. Allowing him to come to his house and talk about buying land. A man like Travin would set an old man like Andy up, whoo-doo his land right out from under him. Then where would Andy be? Where would I be? I couldn't buy Andy's land if it was already sold to Travin. But surely, Andy had enough sense not to do that. Andy didn't need money. He wasn't so old yet that he was becoming incompetent.

I dawned on me right then what I was going to do. I was going to buy a first refusal from Andy.

I turned around and headed back to Andy's. I went into the shop but he wasn't there. I went to the house and opened the door and walked in. Andy was in bed. He sat up when I entered.

"What's wrong?"

"Nothing. What are you doin in bed?"

"Takin my daily nap. Don't you know folks live longer and think better if they take a nap during the day?"

I had heard that. "Andy, can I do something?"

"Probably."

"Will you sell me a first refusal on you land?"

He swung his legs out of bed and rubbed his fingers over his face and through his shock of white hair.

"I don't see why not. If you'll go on back home and let me rest in peace, I'll talk to my lawyer buddy about it the next time I'm in town."

"You can't just write me out a piece of paper saying I have first refusal?"

"Land deals need to be nice and legal. You can't just swindle people out of their land. You have to go through the correct steps."

"You mean there's a right way to swindle people?"

"Yeah, Missy. That's how it appears to me. There's a lawful way to swindle."

"I guess that's how James Travin manages to swindle people all the time. He knows the right way. He even swindles insurance companies and they're supposed to be smart. Does he get by with it because he has his lawyer around? Do lawyers know the right way?"

He lifted his hand and rubbed his scratchy chin as though my words had thrown him into deep thought. "Humm," he grunted. "I reckon it takes a dumb man to outsmart a smart man. And it just might take a country lawyer to outsmart a citified attorney that knows it all."

"What are you getting at, Andy Harmon?"

"Missy, have you ever heard of the common laws of England? They were written up for a way poor folks could solve their differences. It was based on common sense and it still hold true today."

I frowned.

"Missy, dumb folks have dumb way of leaving a city man without a leg to stand on. You run on back home and don't you worry about land and land developers. I'll see that you get my land when the time is right."

This time I didn't walk back home, I floated.

I didn't want things, including land, given to me. I wanted to earn it myself. I wanted to show those old men at the store, along with everyone else, that Elaine Elder Johnson Jones could do anything I set my mind to do. I wanted to top Mr. Holloway in farming. I remembered Boise's diary and her saying that he had books on farming that he studied. I could do that too. Once I learned, I'd share my knowledge with Barnabus.

I hurriedly fed my babies, put Darcy in the crib to sleep and put Drew on the fancy living room carpet to play while I searched through Mr. Holloway's shelves of books. One titled "Mountain Soils" caught my attention. In Bosie's diary she had mentioned how mountain soils had all their good drawn out by over farming one crop. She wrote about how he out produced every farmer in the area. I opened the book and settled down to read.

I took Drew and the book into the kitchen and read while I was fixing dinner for Barnabus and myself.

He came in as usual, his shirt back on, his hands, face, and head wet with wash water. He believed in washing up before a meal. I dished up his food, rounding the plate with all it would hold. He always had a second helping and sometimes a third.

He hadn't taken many bites when he noticed the book lying on the counter. "Mountain Soils," he said. "You've got pert nigh every kind of dirt there is on this here land, except a lot of sandy ground. There's even a mite of that near the creek."

"How do you know?"

"I've plowed it."

That he had.

"Certain crops grow best in certain kinds of dirt. I've studied up on it a mite." He downed his head and began to eat. I was ashamed of myself for thinking he wouldn't be able to read or write.

"Most mountain dirt lacks one thing," he added. "It lacks lime. Iffin a body could fetch lime-stone up here . . ." he hesitated and his bushy brows drew together. "Exceptin this here mountain be mighty cold. Temperature's three weeks behind the flatland near Charlotte."

"The man that farmed this place before me did good, better than everybody else."

"How's that?"

"He read a lot of books. He has a wall full of them."

His eyes brightened. "Don't reckon I'd be allowed to read em?"

"Sure," I told him and then wondered about it. If he worked before daylight to after dark, when would he read?

He took a book, stuck it in the bib pocket of his overalls and headed back to work laying out rows to plant potatoes in. It was late in the season for planting potatoes. They needed to be planted before the corn, but they'd make enough at least for seed potatoes. I hadn't had many bushels left over for planting and had to cut them into sections so they would go further.

I watched him out the window and was surprised to see him with the book in his hand, reading while he laid out the rows straight and true. He never wavered and he never slowed his steady pace.

The next day he returned the book and asked for another one. I wasn't a third through mine.

"Cabbage, broccoli, cauliflower, head lettuce," he said a few days later. "That's what needs planted on this here mountain top. Weather's too hot to plant sech in the flatlands. Yeap, a bounty of cabbage and tators. Tators don't blight as soon in cool."

"Broccoli, cauliflower, head lettuce? Where will I get them?"

"Seeds. You'll order em."

"Isn't it already too late?"

He scratched at his bush of hair. "Might'n be for broccoli and cauliflower. Late cabbage, what don't sell you can bury em in a wintering pit and sell em all winter."

We talked about all kinds of things and all kinds of ways to market or winter the things we could grow. It was kind of like being a lonely child and then suddenly having somebody to play with.

How good it was having someone who shared my eagerness in farming. How good it was to think I could pay for Andy's land.

Chapter 24

We had planted nearly all my potatoes, corn, and beans. I'd had Jonas bring home cabbage seed from the store in Banners Elk. Still, I wasn't satisfied. I'd visit Andy to see if he had left-over potatoes that were shriveled too much for eating. Maybe he could ask all those old men if I could buy what they didn't need.

Like always, I loaded up my babies and headed out the door. Barnabus was coming through the yard, his beardy jaws stretched in a grin.

"Come here." He headed for the barn and I followed.

There in a stall, bedded thick with hay, was Torment. Near her hind legs were two of the cutiest things I'd seen in a while. Her babies were both nudging her sack, trying to suck.

"They's little nannies," Barnabus announced proudly. "Come fall, you'll have to find ye a little billy."

I had planned on raising animals, but goats had not been a part of the plan. On the other hand colicky babies could drink goat's milk, and there was such a thing as goat cheese. I would try anything if it brought in land-buying money.

I left for Andy's and Barnabus went back to the field. Plans ran through my head as my feet found the path both Andy and I had worn. Jonas was right. I had tried to replace my dad with Andy, and I was thankful. My babies needed a grandpa. They needed someone that would tell them stories of a time past, give them some spoiling, love then unconditionally, as my dad had done me. I now realized even when Dad gave me to Rafe, he was doing it out of love for me.

It was the sight of James Travin's vehicle that stopped my good feelings. A cold fear came over me. Something wasn't right. Something was going on in that house that I wasn't going to like. I knew it as sure as I knew I was carrying my babies; as sure as I knew I would draw another breath.

I took out at a run as though every second was important. I had to get to Andy, had to get there before it was too late. My feet wouldn't go fast enough regardless of how hard I tried to make them move. The distance from the woods to his door was too far for me to ever close it. I couldn't get there in time; I wouldn't get there in time to stop what was going on.

I flung the door open. There sat Andy at his little table along with Travin and a man in a suit - Travin's attorney, no doubt. Andy was signing a piece of paper.

They looked up as I rushed in. Andy was shocked, clearly concerned as he looked at me and then looked away. The attorney's expression was hardly curious. It was the look on James Travin's face that tore at my soul and pitched me into the dark depth of desperation. Travin was the epitome of triumphant. His eyes glowed and his lips spread in pure joy. Got ya! His expression seemed to say.

"What's going on here?" I demanded before I realized I was the one speaking. "Andy? What have they done?"

The man in the suit glanced at Travin as though he was asking if I was of importance. Travin shook his head.

"My affairs are not your concern," Travin told me. "But I take pleasure in being the first to tell you that I have just bought myself a piece of land."

Andy reached out and scooped up several stacks of cash-money and pocketed it. He looked sheepish as well as a bit demented. Something was not right with him.

Travin snatched up the paper Andy had just signed and handed it to his attorney, who placed it in his inner coat pocket. A cold unbelieving fear seized me. I longed to rush across the room, grab the paper and rip it to shreds. Something had been done that could never be undone and there seemed nothing I could do about it.

""Good day," Travin said in his most joyous manner and all but pushed me aside as he went out the door, his attorney right behind him.

I looked from their despicable backs to Andy. He was humped up like a badly beaten dog. Once the door closed, his appearance changed. His head lifted. His shoulders straightened. He grinned, but a pallor was still cast over his face.

"What have you done?" I demanded. "Surely you didn't sell *him* your land!"

"I sold him every inch of land I own."

"What?" I screamed. "You did what?"

"Calm down, Missy," he said with a chuckle. "I know exactly what you're thinking and exactly what I've done. I just regret you showed up at this most unfortunate time."

"How can I calm down? You sold Travin your land after you promised me . . . after I . . ." I couldn't go on. I felt tears sliding down my face. I imagined the trees being torn down, the land ripped up, houses and outsiders every where, folks like me helplessly looking on, wondering what was going to happen to their homes, the land they loved.

"Pull up a chair and sit yourself down, Missy. We've got a little while to wait before Rupert gets here in his vehicle. I thought it best not to ride my horse into town. I've just not been up to my normal self lately."

I sank down in the chair the attorney had been sitting in and closed my eyes to keep from looking at Andy, to keep him from seeing my horror. "What have you done?" I moaned. "Oh, Andy do you realize what you've done?"

"I've taught a crook a good lesson."

His words jarred me. Who did he teach a lesson? Who was a crook? Travin was for certain, but how did he teach him a lesson? Travin had given Andy money. Andy had given Travin a signed paper. Andy said he had sold him every inch of land he owned. I no longer had time to buy it from him, and he had promised.

"Don't get your bloomers in a twist," Andy said with too much delight.

My eyes shot open and I just glared at him, glared at the happy expression on his face.

"I've got to get into town, get this money deposited in the bank in a hurry. Travin is gonna be wantin it back pretty soon." Andy chuckled. "But he hain't getting a dime back. It was all nice and legal, all in accordance to the law of North Carolina. Missy, do you know that North Carolina is a race state? According to law what ever is put on record at the court house in Newland first holds steady and fast."

What was he talking about? I didn't understand. "He really bought your land?" I whispered as I tried to get beyond the impossibility of it.

"Rupert is waiting in a turnout down the road where Travin can't see him. As soon as he passes, Rupert will be here."

"What good will that do? He'll be too late?"

"The only person that will be to late is Travin. I've never been the kind to cotton to a man that takes advantage of folks, especially if *folks* is an old person or a young'un. Yeap, Travin needed bringing down a notch and I figured I was still man enough to do it."

I heard the sound of Rupert's vehicle stop outside. Rupert was beeping on his horn as Andy got up.

"You might best go on back home, Missy. The least you know the better."

"I'm sticking to you like lice until I know what you've done."

Rupert honked on horn again.

"Run on back. Rupert and I know what we're doin."

"No!" I told him firmly. "You're not getting rid of me."

"Law, Missy, we don't have time to waste. So you might as well come along. You're up to your eyeballs in this, even if you don't know it."

It was hard for me to fit in a seat with a baby on my back and one on my chest, but I was trying.

"Hand Drew here," Andy said. "We'll sit in the back." He took Drew off my back.

"I didn't think Laine was to be involved in this." There was displeasure in Rupert's tone. "Secrets can be kept by one, occasionally by two, and never by three."

I turned on Rupert, but Andy spoke before I could get words and thoughts together.

"Naturally, she showed up just as Travin was leaving. Bad timing, but she is involved, after all."

"I bet that went over well."

"Travin couldn't have been more pleased than when she showed up. It was obvious she knew nothing about what was going on," Andy told him. "Course, I though she might up and kill me and Travin both right on the spot."

"What are you talkin about? I don't think I can take much more right now."

Rupert chuckled. "Andy, you've not told her?"

"She thinks I've sold my land to Travin."

"You told me you did!" I said loud enough to disturb Darcy's sleep. "You said you sold him every inch of land you owned."

"That's true. I did."

My world sank even deeper, but I didn't want to cry again in front of Rupert.

"Don't torture her," Rupert said firmly. "Tell her the truth, Andy, or I will. She'll find out soon enough as it is."

"Ah, Missy, I didn't want you to know nothin about this, not until the time it became necessary. If some kind of problem arises, I wanted you to be in the dark. As you already know, Travin has been after my land. He knew I owned a large tract, more than anybody in the area. It was Rupert here that first had the idea."

"It was you that wanted to teach him a lesson," Rupert added.

"Well now, it don't set kindly with me when a man out and out wants to cheat me." Andy said. "Travin thought I had gotten old and senile, taken on that old folk's disease. He was counting on me being a dumb hill-billy that don't know how much land he owns. I know every inch of land I own, down to a fraction of an acre."

I remembered overhearing Andy and Travin talking right after Darcy was born. Andy told Travin his land needed surveying, that it was only fair to sell it by the acre.

"Travin didn't know that," Andy continued. "He came up with the idea that he could buy out my land by the entirety and pay only about half its value. Naturally, this dumb mountain man that's old and senile played along."

But what did that matter? Andy had signed a deed and taken Travin's money. I saw it happen. Travin's attorney was there. "But . . ." I injected.

Andy held up a hand. "Let me finish, Missy. I did sell him every inch of land I own. I sold him the graveyard in Banners Elk."

"You own more land than I do."

"Not anymore, I don't. The only land left in my name when Travin bought it was that graveyard." Andy smiled like he had accomplished the biggest feat in the world. "The rest of my land belongs to you free and clear. I had you a deed made a few days before I gave you the land I bought from Jonas."

Rupert could stay silent no longer. "Being that North Carolina is a race state, the deed was not put on record at the court house. Travin had his attorney check the records before they left Newland to know how many acres actually belonged to Andy and to see that it was titled free and clear in Andy's name, and had no liens against it. As soon as they left the court house, Andy's attorney put the deed, made in your name, on record. I know. I watched him do it. Then I headed out. If things had gone wrong, I'd have shown up in time to stop Andy from signing that deed."

I looked over my shoulder at Andy. I couldn't believe what I had heard. The land was not Travin's. He would not rip everything apart, bring strangers in. The land was mine. It really was?

I shook my head.

"Yes," said Andy. "By law, you own the land. By law Travin owns the graveyard and I have his money right here in my pocket. He patted his overalls.

"Something will go wrong," I said. "Things can't work out that easy."

"Seems it has," Rupert said. "I saw the deed in your name. It was put on record several hours before Travin's will arrived at the court house."

"Then what will happen? Won't Travin come back on Andy?"

"Chances are Travin nor his attorney will know what happened for some time to come. Being his attorney checked the records a few hours ago, he won't check them again." Rupert said. "Sometime soon, Travin will have men come in and start clearing the land. That's when you and

Andy will stop them. You can hold you shotgun on them while Andy goes for the sheriff." He was smiling.

"That's when we prove Travin doesn't own the land." Andy added.

"I don't like that." I was upset at their plan, and not understanding it completely. "I don't want him to think for one minute that he owns our land."

"He has to think it long enough for me to get this money in the bank. Don't you see, Missy, Travin is going to get a dose of his own medicine. He's not only going to be without the land he thought he bought, he's going to be without his money, too."

"Isn't that same as stealing?"

"Nope, not when it's Travin. He just paid a high price for a graveyard." Andy patted Drew on his little head. "We'll call it a little attitude adjustment complements of a mountains and her people."

We weren't far behind Travin's vehicle and about a half mile from Banners Elk when we heard shouting. We came around the bend in the road and there in front of us were several men standing around Travin's overturned vehicle.

Both Travin and his attorney lay against the bank, blood stains were on their clothing, but they were both conscious, or there about.

"Holy hell," said Andy as Rupert jumped out. Andy and I were a little slower because we both carried babies.

"Their vehicle got too close the bank," a man was saying to Rupert. "The bank gave way and the vehicle turned over. Grover Clark happened to come along. Once he saw they were alive, he hurried into town, yelled what had happened to Hack sitting on the porch, and then went on to get Jonas."

The man didn't much more than get the words out until Jonas showed up. He jumped from his horse and rushed to Travin.

"How are you James?" Jonas asked.

"Broke my leg," Travin moaned. "Probably have a concussion.

"Legs can mend, and your pupils are equal, but we'll get you to the hospital. Can you hang on while I check your friend."

"No," said Travin, but Jonas ignored him.

I had reached Jonas' side by the time he bent down to examine the attorney.

"His coat and shirt's all bloody," Jonas said. "Here, some of you men raise him up and take his coat and shirt off so I can see the extent of his injury."

They did and tossed his clothes aside. They fell down the bank a ways. I picked them up and carefully laid them near the attorney and then got out of the way by going back to Andy and Drew.

"Missy, it might be best if you and your babies waited in the vehicle," Andy said.

I figured he was right.

Jonas had a man bring a wagon and take both injured men to the hospital while the rest of the men hooked horses to the vehicle and pulled it up the bank and upright on its tires. No one tried to start it. They just pulled it out of the way enough for a team and wagon to get by.

Rupert looked at Travin's wrecked T model and shook his head. "Now that wreck was a shame," Rupert said to Andy. "Henry Ford would not be pleased to see one of his vehicles rolled over. Did you know that in 1908 the price of a T model was six hundred dollars, now it's down to three hundred. Do you know why? Because Ford is one smart man. He believes in waste not want not. He has even designed ways to use the wood from his packing crates.

What small amount of wood that's left over, Henry makes into Kingsford Charcoal and sells it. Yes, in my book, he's a smart man."

Andy got in as Rupert started his vehicle. I noticed that the attorney's suit coat and shirt were still lying on the bank. I didn't bother to say a thing about it as we drove into town..

"Reckon those two won't be puttin nothin on record today," Andy said.

"To our good luck," Rupert added.

"What does it mean if they can't register the deed?" I asked.

"The longer they wait, the stronger your claim," Rupert said.

I looked at Rupert. "Why have you gone to all this trouble for Andy and me?"

He frowned and seemed to think long and hard. "The most truthful answer I can give you is revenge," he finally said. "But it's not tasting as good as I had imagined it would."

🕊

By the time Andy was finished at the bank, Jonas had arrived there too. "Doctor Tate has both men in the hospital," Jonas told us. "James is sedated but ranting and raving about a deed to Andy's land. Do either of you know anything about it?"

"Don't know a thing," Andy said with a mischievous grin. "Don't know why we would." He looked at Rupert and then at me. Neither of us had a comment.

Suddenly Jonas looked puzzled and then unduly concerned. "What are the three of you doing in town together?"

"Goin to the bank," Andy answered. "Rupert promised to bring me in today. Laine happened to show up and I thought she needed to get off the mountain, spend a little time in town."

"Good idea," Jonas said. "She can stay at the house and ride home with me this evening."

"Wish I'd know I was comin in earlier. I'd have left food out for Barnabus." I reached out and lightly touched Jonas. "If Rupert's takin Andy back any time soon, I reckon I'd better get back too."

Jonas looked at me hard. "Suit yourself," he said and walked away.

"Why didn't you tell Jonas about the deed?" I asked when Jonas was out of hearing.

"Time, Missy. I'd like to have all the time I can on my side."

We got back into the vehicle and headed back up the mountain without stopping anywhere. I could tell that both Andy and Rupert were thinking about something.

When we reached the other vehicle, Rupert stopped. I noticed that the jacket and shirt were gone. Some of the men must have picked it up and taken it to the hospital.

"That right there just might have been a turn of luck," Andy said.

I saw a large limb lying by the side of the road that I hadn't noticed before. Travin must have been in a hurry to get to the court house, was driving fast, dodged the limb and got onto the soft bank causing him to turn over.

Rupert tapped his fingers a time or two on the steering wheel. "If neither James nor his attorney can find that signed deed, they can't prove Andy signed a thing unless one of us speaks up."

"Why would we speak up? I don't have a burning desire to make life easy on those two crooks. I do have a desire to make mine as pleasant as I can. So what do you say we all three just stay quiet and claim we don't know what they're talking about." Andy added.

"The deed's bound to show up," Rupert said.

"Yeah, but the longer it takes, the prettier we're sittin."

I looked from Andy to Rupert and was silent.

"Let's make a pact," Andy continued. "You and Laine don't know nothing about any deed, and Travin can't claim you do. When it does show up, I'll take the heat if there should be any."

"Yes," said Rupert. "I think that is prudent thinking."

"And if it doesn't show up?" I asked.

"Then Lady Luck has turned a favorable eye toward us." Rupert answered.

Rupert took Andy home first and then insisted that he drive me home too. I tried to convince him that I enjoyed walking, besides, my dogs were still waiting for me at Andy's.

"Send them home," Rupert said.

I pointed at the woods and repeated home a few time. They just looked at me and whined. I figured once I got home, I'd have to walk part way back and call them, but I was wrong. They were on the porch wagging their tails by the time Rupert and I arrived.

"See," Rupert said. "They're smarter than you thought. How's Barnabus Jackson working out for you?"

"Wonderful," I told him.

Rupert looked at all the plowed and planted land. "He's been busy," Rupert said.

"I'm plan on selling enough crops to buy Andy's land."

"You don't have to do that any longer. It is yours free and clear."

"No it's not. I'll pay him just like I planned. I owe him for more than land."

"Laine," Rupert said my name and then hesitated.

"What?"

"Remember what Andy said about the deed. You and I know nothing about it. We weren't there when it was signed. Do you think you can stick to that?"

"Without a doubt."

"Good. Do you need anything before I go? Can I help you carry Drew?"

"No. I'm used to carrying them both."

When I got to the house, I built a fire and put on a large pot of potatoes to cook for dinner. Perhaps now that the land was mine, I didn't have to plant as many potatoes this year. I took the potato peelings to the chickens and saw Barnabus hoeing weeds from the early corn rows. He hadn't been there while Rupert was here.

He came for dinner at the correct time, but it wasn't quite done. I was just taking the corn bread out of the oven.

"Why you be with him?" Barnabus asked.

"He took Andy into town and I went along for the ride."

"He can't fetch me back," Barnabus said. "I works for you."

"You're happy here?" I took the opportunity to ask.

"Yeah, I'm happy here. It be peaceful, most of the time."

It wasn't too peaceful when Jonas got home. "Now then, Laine," Jonas said firmly. "What is James Travin talking about?"

I gave Jonas my most innocent look. "What are you talking about?"

"You know what I'm talking about."

"I don't know if you don't tell me."

"Why is James claiming he bought Andy's land?"

"I don't know."

"You were with Andy today."

His look told me that he wasn't believing me. "I know that and so do you. I arrived at Andy's just as Travin and that other man were leaving."

"So, he did buy Andy's land."

"No!" I told Jonas firmly. "I know he didn't. Andy has told me over and over again that he would never sell his land to anybody but me."

"Then why is James claiming he did?"

"Maybe he hit his head too hard. What does the other man say?"

"The other man is James' attorney. He's backing up James' story. They both claim the deed was in the suit jacket."

"And?"

"And the jacket isn't to be found."

"We didn't get it."

"I know. I vaguely remember it lying on the ground when we left."

"Maybe some of the men picked it up."

"I'm sure they did."

"Then why are you harping at me about a deed when you know Andy wouldn't sell him his land?"

"Because I want to know what you know."

"You already do." I knew better than to tell Jonas what was going on. Jonas would think it his obligation to inform the proper authorities. That was the problem with too moral a man. You could never teach anybody a lesson

"Perhaps. However, I have no doubt James will have the sheriff and no telling who else show up here to talk to you."

"Well," I said rather snappishly. "I'll talk to the sheriff, but if Travin shows up here, I just might play at being Annie Oakley again."

Jonas reached around and gave me a playful slap on the rump. It felt good to be able to giggle again.

It wasn't long, just nearing dark when the sheriff showed up.

"I want to talk to her alone," he told Jonas.

"Nope," said Jonas. "Laine is my wife and she can talk to you in front of me."

"I rather talk to her alone."

Jonas looked at him, his chin firm his mouth set rigid.

"Fine," the sheriff said, and began asking questions.

I told him exactly what I had told Jonas. I had arrived at Andy's when Travin was leaving.

"Did Travin tell you he had bought Andy Harmon's land?"

"I knew that Travin had been aggravating Andy, so I asked what was going on. Travin told me that his affairs were none of my business."

"You and Travin don't get along, do you?"

"I don't like him."

"Why not?"

"I think he's a liar and a crook. I believe he wanted to swindle Andy out of his land, but as you should know by now, Andy couldn't nor wouldn't sell his land to Travin."

"You think Travin is lying, then?"

"Didn't I just call him a liar and crook? Didn't I make myself plain enough?"

"How can you be sure he is lying?"

I thought about my answer for a while. "Ask Andy. He can tell you if he wants to."

"I've already asked Andy. I want to hear what you say."

I looked him straight in the eyes. "I own a lot of land."

"So it appears." The sheriff added. "Andy Harmon must be really fond of you."

Chapter 25

I was a nervous wreck. I couldn't sleep for worrying what was going to happen. I knew Travin wouldn't let it go without putting up some kind of fight. I wouldn't if I was him.

Andy didn't seem too worried when he came by the house a few days later. I was in the garden finishing my late planting. I had brought a blanket and chair from the kitchen porch and a sheet from up stairs. I draped the sheet over the chair and place Darcy in its shade. Drew had started out on the blanket, but the dirt was more interesting to him. I placed him near the fence so he could pull up and walk about by holding to the fence rail. He was so proud of his feat that he acted like he had suddenly sprung into manhood. "Me, me," he would holler to get me to watch him and tell what a good little man he was.

Andy came into the garden but he didn't pick up Drew like he usually did. "You look tired," I told him.

"Restless and old. It's such a nice day I had to get out and walk about a little."

"What about Travin," I asked out right. I couldn't wait any longer to know something.

"Is he fit to be tied. He's done everything in his power to take a case against me, but he can't prove a thing. Where land is concerned, there has to be some kind of proof, a signed contract, exchange of money, some sort of paper trail that can show evidence."

"He won't give up will he?"

"No, he'll never give up. He's not the kind. His kind likes the fight better than the kill."

I didn't like the way Andy put that.

"I'm not worried about that, Missy. I am worried about you. That's why I wish you'd not shown up at my place, while Travin was there. Then again, it might not make any difference. He'll hound you the rest of his life over your land. Him, along with a lot of others."

"I'll take the land and my chances." I tried to make it sound humorous but Andy ignored my attempt.

"At least you have a strong husband. He'll stand beside you."

I knew Jonas better than that. "If Jonas finds out what really happened, he won't stand beside either of us. He'll go straight to the sheriff."

"You think he'd turn us in?"

"I know he would."

"He'd go against you?"

"In a second."

"Hummm."

"Jonas goes on what he thinks is right, not on what anyone else does."

"He'd go against his own wife?" Andy said rather thoughtfully.

"That he would." I didn't want Andy to have any misunderstanding about that.

"Without a doubt?"

"Without a doubt," I said.

Andy rubbed the tip of his boot in the soft dirt of my garden. "Then we best not let him know."

That, I agreed with.

"What about Rupert?" I asked.

"What about him?"

"What's happening with him? Does Travin think he's involved?"

"There's no doubt in Travin's mind that Rupert is involved. That's one of the reasons Travin hasn't turned his goons loose to beat a deed out of me or at least all the cold cash I own."

His words scared me. I'd never considered Travin might actually hurt Andy.

"He'd be in trouble with the law and all the folks around here if an old man like me came up hurt. Besides, he wants me to stay healthy. He can't get blood out of a dead man."

That scared me even worse.

"What I expect Travin to do is have somebody come to my place and pilfer through everything I own trying to find my money. That's why I'm here. You have Barnabus here all the time plus those two guard dogs of yours. Not to mention you and that shotgun you like to tote around. I want to take all the cash I have and hide it on your place. What do you say?"

"Of course, but what if something happened to it?"

"I just gave you reason it will be safer here, what do you say?"

I remembered the root cellar under the house. It was hard to find and I could make it even harder by stacking stuff in from of the moveable wall. I remembered Boise's can of money. It would take a while to search through a thousand cans of vegetables.

"Yeah, I think there are several hiding places around here."

Andy looked at my babies and then at me. "Missy, I've got to speak my mine. I'm determined that you realize I haven't done you a favor by what I've given you."

"Oh yes, you have."

"Now, listen. You've now got more land and more money than anybody in the county. And folks will think you didn't earn it, therefore you don't deserve it. They'll take every opportunity to filch it away from you. Expect it, Missy, expect it!

"And the folks around here won't be the worse. There will be outsiders, men like Travin, women like your own mother and Hazel. They'll try their damnedest to get something from you, even if nothing more than a piece of your hide.

"Don't ever let your guard down. Don't let sweet talk, threats, sneakiness, laziness, religion, or love come into play.

"And there's one other thing I have to mention, Missy. Your husband won't have an easy time of it. He'll be cast in your shadow. This land is in your name, not his and that can put a squeeze on a good man's balls if you know what I mean."

I looked Andy straight in the eyes. "You thought I could handle all that or you wouldn't have put what belonged to you in my name."

"I think you'll have to become one hell-of-a woman, but keep in mind, I've not done you a favor."

James Travin didn't take his loss like a man. He took it like a lunatic. He brought a law suit against Andy, me, and Rupert.

Rupert brought in his big guns. Two attorneys joined in with Andy's. One was a skinny little man with a face like a bird. The other one was over weight and jowly. I wouldn't have given a plug nickel for both of them until I heard them speak.

Rupert Smith knew what he was doing and he knew what Travin would do. He also knew the law.

"Travin needs written confirmation where land is concerned, and he doesn't have it," Rupert told me.

"Then how can he law us?"

"It's more of a complaint against Andy than a law suit. He can't take a civil suit against Andy without any proof."

"It's a good thing the deed got gone?"

"It is a good thing."

"What Travin is doing is taking Andy before the Magistrate. If Andy or his attorney should not show up then Andy would automatically lose the case."

That concerned me.

"However," Rupert continued. "If the Magistrate were to rule against Andy, which he won't, Andy would then take it to a higher court. Like we've been telling you, land deals have to be in writing, so this is no big deal."

"If it's no big deal, why did you bring in your lawyers?" I asked Rupert as he sat on my porch beside a couple of new bags of dog food.

"Laine, learn to always expect the unexpected and be prepared."

"Then something could go wrong."

"No. Nothing will go wrong, but if it does, I'll be prepared to handle it."

Andy showed up at the Magistrate's office in Newland, along with his and Rupert's lawyers, Rupert, me, Jonas, Hack Pennel and the entire gossip bench gang, and half the town of Banners Elk and Newland.

James Travin had his legal squad there trying to give off power and authority.

I sat behind Andy Harmon in the courthouse with Jonas by my side and my two babies in my lap.

When Travin came in he looked at me. "You haven't beaten me," he said under his breath. His new attorney poked him with his elbow regardless of the leg cast Travin was dragging.

"Silence," his attorney advised under his breath, but Judge Huckelbee from Newland, was looking their way.

I felt Jonas tense beside me and saw the look he was giving Travin. I knew James Travin would never be able to fool Jonas again, unless Jonas found out the truth.

When the Judge allowed Travin and his injured attorney to state their case, they ranted and raved so much and so loud that no one appeared to believed them, even the Magistrate appeared unconvinced.

Travin accused every person that was present at the accident of setting it up. He said the entire town of Banners Elk was against him. He claimed Rupert was paying them money undercover.

"Mr. Travin," the magistrate said. "Those are rather large charges you're bringing before me. Are you claiming an entire town cheated you?"

"Yes, Your Honor. I am."

"You're accusing the entire town of planning your ill-fated accident?" The magistrate added in disbelief.

The crowd sniggered and the magistrate banged his gavel.

One of Travin's attorneys chose to speak up. "Your Honor, we are here today to ask for an investigation. Mr. Travin and his Attorney, Mr. Vance, both swear that Mr. Travin paid cash to Mr. Andy Harmon for his land. After which time an accident occurred and the deed disappeared. All we are asking here is that justice be served."

"Do you have any proof of your claim?" the magistrate asked.

"Your Honor, Mr. James Travin is a busy, important man. He would not waste his time on trivia or lying to obtain land."

The magistrate banged his gavel. "And neither shall I. I have already taken the liberty to talk with many parties involved including Mr. James Travin. I have not found one shred of evidence backing up Mr. Travin's accusations. Actually, I have found the opposite. Mr. Harmon never deposited a dime in his account. Actually, on the day of contention, Mr. Harmon withdrew ten dollars. Also, Mr. Harmon had no land to sell, other than a small graveyard tract, and I can't see a shrewd developer wanting that. Andy Harmon had sold his land to Mrs. Elaine Jones some time before this incident occurred and the records clearly show that. Considering all the evidence brought before me, I see no just reason to waste anyone's time, emotions, and assets. I dismiss this case."

I thought Travin was going to blow a heart gasket. His face turned blood red, his body trembled.

"This isn't a court of law!" he yelled at the magistrate. "You're a mockery! A mountain hick!"

"Remove your client," the magistrate said calmly, "before I have him arrested for contempt."

Andy looked over his shoulder and winked at me. He appeared pleased, but there was something else also. Something that I didn't like. His face had turned an odd color, neither pale, blue, nor transparent, but a mixture of both.

"Jonas," I said, but he had already jumped to his feet and was moving a chair to get to Andy.

"Stop it," Andy said firmly.

"Not this time," Jonas told him.

"It's nothing."

"It's something and we both know it."

"Give me a minute and it'll pass. No need to scare Missy."

I was already scared. "Take him to the hospital," I told Jonas. "Please take him. Something is bad wrong with him."

And it had been wrong for some time. I'd seen it in his face, his actions, his weight loss. He was no longer the stocky reminder of strength. He was thin and frail.

Jonas offered to help him stand.

"Not yet," Andy said. "Let me catch my breath. I just got a little excited is all."

But it wasn't all. Andy's jaws clenched, his eyes rolled back, and he tumbled from his chair before Jonas could catch him. Rupert plus several men crowded around him.

"Let's get him to the hospital as fast as we can." Jonas said. "Appears to be his heart."

Rupert helped Jonas lift Andy. Rupert looked down into Andy's face and shook his head. "Old buddy," he said softly. "I believe this one is it."

I know Andy heard him; know he tried to open his eyes and speak, but he didn't.

Andy never made it to the hospital. He didn't even make it out of the courthouse. Jonas told the men to take him to his office out of respect or perhaps desperation.

I had gone a little crazy. Just like with Joey, I wanted to make Andy live, insisted that Jonas could do it. I wasn't ready to give him up yet. I needed him too much.

I was even screaming at Travin, and he and his attorneys were already gone from the courthouse. I need someone to blame Andy's death on. Needed someone . . . oh how I needed someone.

When I calmed a little, Jonas was holding me in his arms, rocking me back and forth much like I often did my babies. Rupert and Hack Pennel had my babies across the room, trying to keep them quiet.

I looked into Jonas' eyes and realized I wasn't alone. I'd never be alone as long as I had Jonas. My husband was the solid thing in my life; my husband, my babies, and my land.

"He's not gone," I said to Jonas. "Andy will never be gone from me." I started to cry and tried to stop but didn't seem able to do it.

"Be strong, Laine. People are watching you."

"Are they placing bets?"

Jonas shook his head.

"They should be." I managed to say through my tears. "Andy never loses on a bet."

If you enjoyed this book: visit peggypoestern.tripod.com to check on the status of Peggy's latest books or to leave feedback.

Books may be purchased regionally at selected stores in Northwestern North Carolina, Southwestern Virginia, and Eastern Tennessee.

To purchase online, visit amazon.com.

To purchase autographed copies, order special print editions, or to contact author; e-mail, call, fax, or write:

Peggy Poe Stern
Moody Valley Farm
475 Church Hollow Road
Boone, NC 28607
828-963-5331 Tel
828-963-4101 Fax
moodyvalley@skybest.com

Heaven High and Hell Deep

and

Laine's Beech Mountain Story

Peggy Poe Stern

Book 1, ISBN # 1-59513-055-1 $16.95

A mountain girl in the early 1900's copes with a marriage arranged by her dad. Her story is titled from an old saying "I own my land, heaven-high and hell-deep."

"Your pa gave his consent for us to marry," he said the words as though it was a simple matter. It wasn't a romantic proposal of love and devotion. It wasn't a proposal at all. I opened my mouth but nothing came out. I tried again.

"I don't know your name," I managed to say … .

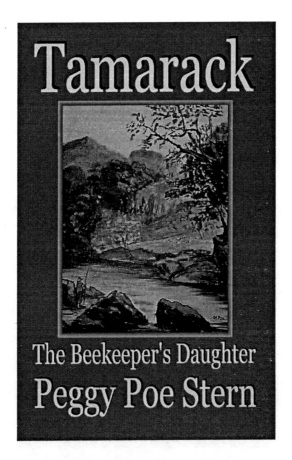

Tamarack

The Beekeeper's Daughter
Peggy Poe Stern

ISBN # 1-59513-054-3 $14.95

A gripping story about the dark side of a mountain family: a legacy of abuse that leads to murder. Told from an authentic mountain perspective, the reader experiences the family's desperation as well as their strength and determination to keep on going. The author's simple unabashed voice completely absorbs the reader. So many emotions are evoked that the story echoes long after the last page is read.

When Robins Weep

The Christmas Tree Lady

Peggy Poe Stern

ISBN # 1-59513-053-5 $17.95

A happenstance encounter between an Appalachian mountain girl and a Florida developer embarks them on a romantic relationship. Existing family ties coupled with completely diverse lifestyles complicate their love.

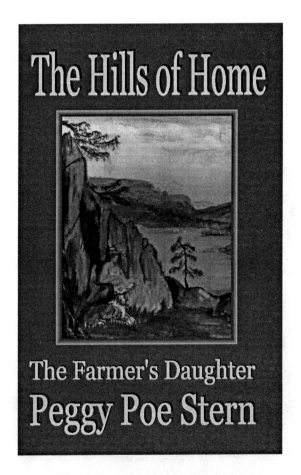

The Hills of Home

The Farmer's Daughter
Peggy Poe Stern

ISBN # 1-59513-052-7 $16.95

Theo Walden learns of love and understanding in her hills of home, plus a whole lot more. Granny teaches her that life isn't always fair or good. Greta fills her young head with ghost stories scary enough to keep her awake at night. Popaw and Daddy show her what its like to be mountain men: fair, tough, and yet gentle. Most important, Theo learns that wealth doesn't make a person happy. Love does.

Stud from Horney Hollow

The Collier Mistress

Peggy Poe Stern

ISBN # 1-59513-051-9 $16.95

Willi Smith, a hard-nosed Florida real estate broker, had determined to get above her roots by obtaining wealth for the security it should bring. Having set her career before relationships, she realizes that her biological clock is ticking. She wants a child, but doesn't have a man.

Burl Horney, a widowed mountain Christmas tree grower, travels to Florida to sell his trees. Little does he know how he is being caught up in her quest.

Mountain Splendor

Long Hope Mountain Gal

Peggy Poe Stern

ISBN # 1-59513-050-0 $16.95

Needing to make the farm payment, Ramona pretends to be a man and takes on her recently departed husband's next job assignment; guiding a group of Yankees through the mountains.

"You Barlow?" I had a naturally deep voice for a woman. Husky some called it, but I tried to make it sound manly. He nodded, looked at my horse and then at my clothes, all a trademark of Jake Triplet.
"Where's Jake?"
"Dead," I answered, and saw a faint flicker of surprise ….

Blood Moon Rising

Restless Revenge

Peggy Poe Stern

EAN # 978-1-59513-049-5 $16.95

The fires of hell would burn me in time for what I was about to do, but right now, that didn't matter. I was on my way to kill him. Someone should have killed Buck Walsh a long time ago for the things he did, but people were scared of him. I'm scared of him, but that no longer mattered either. He had raped me.

Wild Thing

Aggie's Legacy

Peggy Poe Stern

EAN #978-1-59513-048-8 $17.95

Cadence Williams settled beneath the quilt willing to go into a deep sleep. He hadn't slept much for the past two nights. Fear mixed with self-anger kept him awake. He hated fear. It was a sign of weakness, especially when it was his own. It angered him to fear when he wasn't sure if the cause of it was real or imagined. Yet, his gut told him *that thing* was near his house, moving in the woods like a dark shadow, stalking him when he went outside to do up the work, and even coming to his window during the night to watch him.

Above-all
a sequel to
Heaven-high and Hell-deep

Laine's Beech Mountain Story, Book 2
Peggy Poe Stern

EAN #978-1-59513-047-1 $17.00

His hat was pulled low over his black hair and his shirt sleeves were rolled up almost to his elbows. His hands appeared strong and in control as he held the reins of his high stepping horse. He looked a little thinner than he used to be and a lot more tired.

"What's wrong?" he asked me fast.

"You've got to go back to Banners Elk," I told him, forgetting about supper.

His eyes widened with concern. "Should you ride? I can deliver the baby here."

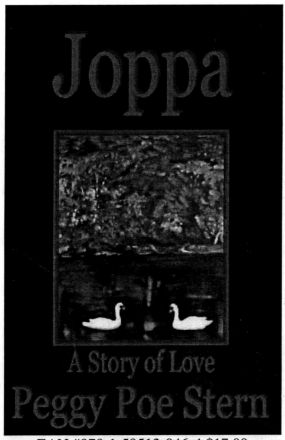

Joppa

A Story of Love

Peggy Poe Stern

EAN #978-1-59513-046-4 $17.00

"Leona," he sipped his hot coffee. "I know I'm going to regret asking this, but tell me the story of Joppa and Harry Barnard from the beginning to the end.

"It's a seventeen year stretch of time," I warned.

"This place isn't overrun with customers."

"If I tell you, will you use it against me. Claim I'm crazy; refuse to help me?"

"Attorney-client information is privileged. I don't tell anything you say not to tell."

"You'll think I'm a fruitcake."

"You're not?"

Thunder Hole

The Blackberry Summer
Peggy Poe Stern

EAN #978-1-59513-045-7 $17.00

He started to say more then hesitated before he added, "Do you know what I want, Billie, really want?"

"Besides me being five years older?"

Her ignored that. "I want you to go to college."

She laughed.

"I'm serious."

Her laughter stopped too sudden and she looked at Malone with eyes beyond those of childhood. "It won't happen."

"Why not?"

An Honorable Man

Surviving Daniel

Peggy Poe Stern

EAN #978-1-59513-045-7 $17.00

After twenty-four years of marriage to Daniel, Carrie Jane can take it no longer. Leaving everything behind, she slips off one evening to start anew.

"Tell me, Dad, why does this woman interest you?"
He scratched at his gray hair again before he spoke.
"Something wasn't exactly right about her. A teenage girl might run away for any number of reasons, but a woman her age doesn't. She was . . . well, I kinda pitied her. There has to be a mighty powerful reason when a woman hides in a moving van."

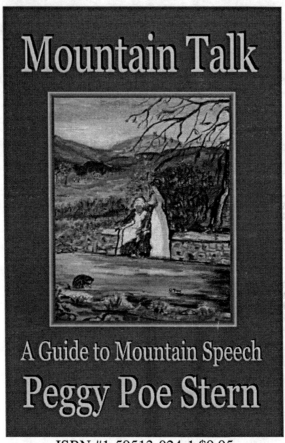

Mountain Talk

A Guide to Mountain Speech
Peggy Poe Stern

ISBN #1-59513-024-1 $9.95

The isolation of the Appalachian Mountains preserved some of the old sayings and speech of the earliest American settlers. This guide is a dictionary of commonly used mountain words and phrases.

To Everything
There is a Season

A Guide to Growing Things in
Harmony with the Moon Signs
Peggy Poe Stern

ISBN #1-59513-025-X

The pull of the moon affects all living things just as it influences the ebb and flow of the tides. Old timers have learned and past down the wisdom of gardening and living in tune with the signs, phases, cycles, and seasons effected on the earth by the moon, sun, stars, and planets. This guide assists in determining the best times and methods to take advantage of these time honored traditions. In addition to Peggy's own comments and excerpts on country life, this guide contains generous useful information for living close with the earth.